The PANCHA TANTRA
of Vishnusharma

For Uday,

Who will be my partner in crime.

This is a bribe, my friends.

Mrinal Nayak
4/26/23

Also by Meena Arora Nayak

Adbhut: Marvellous Creatures of Indian Myth and Folklore
The Kathasaritsagara of Somadeva: A Retelling
The Blue Lotus: Myths and Folktales of India
A Dust Storm in Delhi
Evil in the Mahabharata
Endless Rain
About Daddy
In the Aftermath
The Puffin Book of Legendary Lives

The PANCHA TANTRA
of Vishnusharma

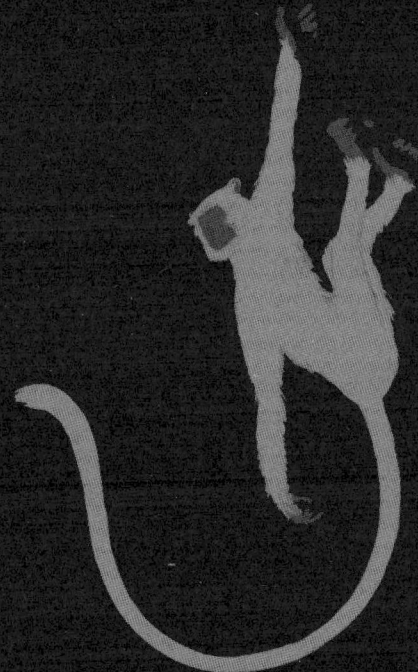

A Retelling by
meena arora nayak

ALEPH

ALEPH BOOK COMPANY
An independent publishing firm
promoted by *Rupa Publications India*

First published in India in 2023
by Aleph Book Company
7/16 Ansari Road, Daryaganj
New Delhi 110 002

Copyright © Meena Arora Nayak 2023

The author has asserted her moral rights.

All rights reserved.

No part of this publication may be reproduced, transmitted, or stored in a retrieval system, in any form or by any means, without permission in writing from Aleph Book Company.

ISBN: 978-93-93852-19-9

1 3 5 7 9 10 8 6 4 2

Printed in India.

This book is sold subject to the condition that it shall not, by way of trade or otherwise, be lent, resold, hired out, or otherwise circulated without the publisher's prior consent in any form of binding or cover other than that in which it is published.

For Babu

Om
Glory to Saraswati, the Goddess of wisdom and learning

May we all be protected by
Brahma, Rudra, Kumara, Vishnu, Varuna, Yama,
Indra, Kubera, Chandra, Surya, Vayu, Ashwinikumaras
Saraswati, Prithvi, Mahalakshmi, Diti, Aditi and Adityas,
Brahmi, Maheshwari, Kaumari, Vaishnavi, Varahi, Indrani,
Chamunda, Chandika, Durga, Gauri, and other mothers,
Vahini, Vedas, Tirthas, Yajnas, Ganesha and his Ganas,
four Seas, Mountains, four Yugas, Serpents, Siddhas,
eight Vasus, Munis and Rishis, and the Navagrahas!

Namaskar to the composers of Nitishastras:
Manu, Brihaspati, Shukracharya,
Parashara, and Parashara's son, Vyasa,
as well as the other scholars of niti.

CONTENTS

Introduction	xiii
Author's Note	xxxi
Kathapitha	1
First Tantra: Mitra Bheda (Breach of Friendship)	5

Frame Story: A Devious Wolf Ruins the Friendship
Between a Lion and a Bull
1. The Tale of the Curious Monkey Who Did Not Mind
   His Own Business — 10
2. The Tale of the Jackal Who Faced His Fear — 22
3. The Tale of How Dantika the Merchant Lost His Reputation — 29
4. The Tale of How the Sanyasi, Jackal, and Emissary Caused
   Their Own Suffering — 36
5. The Tale of the Weaver Who Became Vishnu to Win the Princess — 50
6. The Tale of the Crow's Scheme to Kill the Wicked Snake — 60
7. The Tale of How the Greedy Crane Was Killed by the Clever Crab — 62
8. The Tale of the Dimwit Lion and the Wise Hare — 66
9. The Tale of How the Bedbug's Selfishness Cost the Louse Her Life — 75
10. The Tale of How the Blue Jackal Was Really Just a Jackal — 78
11. The Tale of the How the Camel Was Deceived into
    Sacrificing Himself — 85
12. The Tale of How the Titihari Bird Defeated the Mighty Ocean — 92
13. The Tale of the Tortoise Who Did Not Heed the Advice of
    Well-Wishers — 94
14. The Tale of the Fish Who Learned That It Is Better to Act Than to
    Depend on Fate — 96
15. The Tale of How the Sparrow, Woodpecker, Bee, and Frog Teamed
    Up to Kill the Elephant — 100
16. The Tale of the Clever Jackal Who Schemed to Eliminate
    the Competition — 110
17. The Tale of How the Nagging Needle-Beaked Bird Lost Her Life — 118
18. The Tale of the Chataka Bird's Unwanted Advice — 120
19. The Tale of How Paapabudhi's Cleverness Killed His Father — 123

20. The Tale of the Crane Who Did Not Consider the Harm
    with the Benefit   128
21. The Tale of the Iron-Eating Mice and the Boy-Devouring Falcon   130
22. The Tale of the Senseless Monkey and the Intelligent Thief   134

Second Tantra: Mitra Samprapti (Acquisition of Friends)   141

Frame Story: The Great Friendship Between a Crow, Mouse,
Tortoise, and Deer
23. The Tale of How Hiranyaka the Mouse Was Ousted from His Home 159
24. The Tale of Shandili and Her Hulled Sesame Seeds   162
25. The Tale of the Jackal Who Desired Too Much   164
26. The Tale of the Man Who Received What He Was Meant to   173
27. The Tale of Somilaka and the Vanishing Gold   181
28. The Tale of Tikshana Vishana and His Loose-Hanging Balls   185
29. The Tale of the Mice That Freed the Elephants   194

Third Tantra: Kakolukiyam (Of Crows and Owls)   204

Frame Story: The Enmity Between Crows and Owls
30. The Tale of How the Crows and Owls Became Enemies   219
31. The Tale of How the Rabbit in the Moon Saved His Relatives   222
32. The Tale of How the Clever Cat Ate the Gullible Hare and Bird 227
33. The Tale of How the Brahmin Lost His Donkey to Thugs   234
34. The Tale of How the Ants Killed the Snake   237
35. The Tale of the Gold-Giving Serpent and Why He Killed
    the Farmer's Son   242
36. The Tale of Why the Gold Hamsas Left Padmavana   244
37. The Tale of the Chataka Bird Who Roasted His Own Flesh
    for a Fowler   246
38. The Tale of the Old Man Who Thanked the Thief in His House   251
39. The Tale of How the Brahmin Got Rid of the Thief and
    the Rakshasa   253
40. The Tale of the Two Snakes and Their Secrets   256
41. The Tale of the Man Who Was Grateful to be Cuckolded   259
42. The Tale of Chuhiya's Selection of a Worthy Husband   264
43. The Tale of the Nexus of Fools   268
44. The Tale of the Speaking Cave   270
45. The Tale of Why the Serpent Became the Vehicle of Frogs   277
46. The Tale of the Ghee-Blinded Brahmin   280

Fourth Tantra: Labdha Pranasha (Loss of Acquired Gains)   289

Frame Story: The Monkey Escapes the Crocodile Who Wants His Heart
47. The Tale of How the Snake Lost All Sense of Morality   297
48. The Tale of Why the Donkey Returned to the Lion to be Killed   303
49. The Tale of the Potter Who Ruined His Own Chances   307
50. The Tale of the Jackal Who Thought He Was a Lion   309
51. The Tale of the Brahmin Who Loved His Wife Who Loved a Cripple   312
52. The Tale of How Far Men Will Go to Please Women   316
53. The Tale of How the Donkey Gave Himself Away   318
54. The Tale of the Naked Woman and How She Lost Both Her Husband and Lover   321
55. The Tale of the Clever Wolf Who Knew Chanakya Niti   325
56. The Tale of the Dog in a Foreign Land   329

Fifth Tantra: Aparikshita Karakam (Impetuous Actions)   331

Frame Story: The Barber's Reckless Actions
57. The Tale of the Woman Who Killed Her Mongoose Son   337
58. The Tale of the Wheel of Greed   339
59. The Tale of the Intelligent Young Men Who Revived a Lion   344
60. The Tale of How the Overconfident Fish Brought About Their Own Demise   346
61. The Tale of the Donkey Who Loved to Sing   349
62. The Tale of the Weaver Who Wished for Two Heads and Four Hands   352
63. The Tale of Somanatha Sharma's Daydreaming Father   355
64. The Tale of How the King's Rash Decision Led to the Monkey's Revenge   356
65. The Tale of the Fearful Rakshasa Vikala   362
66. The Tale of the Blind Man, Hunchback, and the Three-breasted Woman   365
67. The Tale of How the Brahmin Escaped the Rakshasa by Asking a Question   366
68. The Tale of the Two-headed Bherunda Bird   370
69. The Tale of How a Crab Saved the Brahmin   372

Notes and References   374
Bibliography   381

INTRODUCTION

THE ELIXIR

In the sixth century, the Sasanian king of Persia, Khusru Anushirvan, heard about an elixir in India that revived the dead. Rumour had it that it was extracted from medicinal herbs that grew in the country's high mountains. The king sent his physician, Burzoe, to India to find the elixir, sparing no expense, and bring it back to Persia. Burzoe searched high and low in India's mountains and forests and markets and streets, but nowhere could he find any such life-restoring potion, or even herb. In despair, wondering how he would report his failure to the king, he doubled his search. Then he met a sage who informed him that the elixir of life he was searching was not an herbal drink at all, but a book. The mountains he had heard about were a metaphor for great men of learning, and their writings were the herbs from which the book's wisdom was extracted, like an elixir. Hence, the dead were not people who perished, but the ignorant, who were figuratively dead, and the knowledge from this book dispelled their state of lifelessness. The sage also told Burzoe that this book was kept in the royal library and could not be removed; however, having access to the library, the wise man was able to smuggle it out for a brief period of time, just so the Persian physician and scholar could see it. Burzoe memorized the book, line by line, and then, later, translated it into Pahlavi. When Anushirvan received this tome of wisdom, he was so awed by it and by the idea of the knowledge that could be contained within a book that he created a whole library, and, in it, he gave Burzoe's acquisition the pride of place. As for Burzoe, the only reward he asked from the king was to have an account of his journey to India included in the book. Anushirvan then had his minister, Buzurjmihr, write Burzoe's biography and insert it at the beginning of the book. And that is how Burzoe's story and the secret of the elixir was revealed to the world.

    This invaluable treasure of a book that Burzoe translated into Pahlavi and brought back to Persia was the *Panchatantra*, and Burzoe's legend (in its various versions) is commonly related to demonstrate why this ancient text was considered panacean wisdom literature across the globe. In its Kathamukha (preamble), the *Panchatantra* calls itself a Nitishastra—a treatise of customary and social laws that teach people right conduct and guide kings to govern for the well-being of their subjects. Underpinning these laws are the ethical principles of purushartha—dharma, artha, and kama, which are the key goals of a person seeking happiness and plenteousness in life. This is why the *Panchatantra* not only counts itself among other Nitishastras, such as the dharmashstras, kamashastras, and arthashastras, but it also surpasses these, because 'extracting the summary of all popular Nitishastras of statecraft and polity', it is the quintessence of their wisdom and knowledge.

THE AUTHOR

Many Indian scholars believe that Vishnusharma, the author of the *Panchatantra,* is the same Vishnusharma (known as Chanakya), who authored the *Arthashastra*. For evidence to support this claim, they cite the detailed niti-related passages of the former and state that only a strategist as highly experienced and well-versed in statecraft and polity as Chanakya could have composed them with such accuracy. Hence, they date the *Panchatantra* to about 345–300 BCE, (as opposed to 250–300 BCE, which is the dating in Western scholarship). This would align the work to the rule of Chandragupta Maurya in whose court Chanakya served as an adviser. This period of time also validates the age of the *Panchatantra*'s Vishnusharma as eighty years, a declaration he himself makes in the Kathamukha. This assumption about the text's authorship does not seem far-fetched, especially if one also takes into account the manner in which the octogenarian accepts the challenging task of educating the princes with a 'lion-roar'—a characteristic that is quite reminiscent of the Chanakya of legend and history.

However, this inference is not quite supported in Western scholarship, which questions if there really was a Vishnusharma who composed the five tantras, as described in the preamble of the work. After the first English translation titled *The Fables of Bidpai: Morall Philosophie of Doni* was published, the author of the *Panchatantra* came to be known in Europe as 'Bidpai'. Bidpai or Pilpay (of the French version) was, most likely, a reference to the sageness of the author, and it may have been a corruption of the word, 'Vidyapati'—master of knowledge—or of 'Vijaypai', which was a common appellation for brahmins. Hence, it is quite possible that 'Bidpai' was simply an attribution to an anonymous author, or even multiple authors, who compiled the work under the umbrella term, Vishnusharma, in the same manner that the term 'Vyasa' was used for the composers of the Mahabharata. However, all this is mostly conjecture; there is no indisputable evidence to prove the authorship of the *Panchatantra*.

HOW THE *PANCHATANTRA* CAME TO BE
The Kathamukha of the *Panchatantra* also relates the tale of how this book came to be composed. King Amarashakti of Mahilaropya was renowned for his wisdom and glory. He had three sons, but all three were unschooled ignoramuses and an embarrassment to him; therefore, he urgently sought a teacher to educate them. His ministers advised him that because a conventional education would require no less than twelve years, what was needed to expedite the princes' learning was an innovative way of instruction. One of Amarashakti's ministers then proposed the name of Vishnusharma, who was an octogenarian scholar, known for his inventive teaching. Vishnusharma not only accepted the task of educating the princes but also promised with a 'lion-roar' that he would accomplish it in six months. The Nitishastra he used to teach the princes was one he himself composed specifically for the purpose. It had five sections or tantras: Mitra Bheda (breach of friendship), Mitra Samprapti (acquisition of friends), Kakolukiyam (of crows and owls), Labdha Pranasham (loss of acquired gains), and Aparikshita Karakam (impetuous actions). Each of these encapsulated lessons about living: social conduct, interpersonal relationships, the role of wealth and desires in a person's life, human weaknesses and strengths, treachery and deception and how to deal with them, fate versus action guided by free will, and other such aspects of the human experience. In addition, the lessons included instruction about the science of governance: treatment of ministers, strategies to deal with enemies, border security, ruler–subject relationships, selection and placement of officials, etc. Tutored with this multidisciplinary text, the princes became accomplished administrators and worthy human beings. Hence the 'delightful, edifying Panchatantra began to be hailed for its 'beneficence [to] humanity'.

LITERARY FORM, GENRE, AND STYLE
The above prefacing tale also serves as an introduction to the schema for the whole text, unifying the five tantras like a five-section syllabus. Each tantra is presented by an invisible narrator (supposedly Vishnusharma) as a lesson. It begins and ends with a stanza related to the frame story, which establishes a thematic framework for the section. Within this structure, numerous tales are 'emboxed', most of them relating to the theme of the frame story. However,

often, these 'boxed' tales, too, contain other stories about topics that need further elucidation.

This story-within-a-story technique is a common literary device in classical Indian texts, such as the Mahabharata, from which the *Panchatantra* borrows a few stories, and Somadeva's *Kathasaritsagara*, which borrows from the *Panchatantra*, although in the latter, the tales are not emboxed. In the *Panchatantra*, the emboxing of tales is like a weave that is demonstrated through the word, 'tantra'. Tantra has been variously defined as book, chapter, framework, etc. The German Indologist Johannes Hertel, an early scholar and first editor of a key critical edition of the *Panchatantra's Purnabhadra* recension, even translates this word as klugheitsfall—case of cleverness. However, its most significant meaning is 'warp', as in a loom. The warp are the vertical threads tied to the beams of the loom from top to bottom, in perfect tension, so that the weft threads can be woven over and under them to make the desired pattern. Thus, it can be said that the tantras of the *Panchatantra* are like five thematic warps through which the weft of stories, aphorisms, wisdom verses, etc., are woven. In other words, the *Panchatantra* can be seen as five tautly and intricately woven fabrics of niti.

These tantras are presented in an innovative genre of storytelling called champu, which is a combination of prose and verse. This Sanskrit genre, evidenced as far back as the Vedas and popular between the second and tenth centuries CE, was devised as a creative bridge between prose and verse, to make complex narrative prose more fluid and to give verse a narrative progression.

Dandin, the seventh century proponent of Sanskrit poetics, mentions this genre in his *Kavyadarsha* as simply a mixture (mishrit) of gadya and padya (prose and verse). Later scholars added more meaning to Dandin's simple definition by describing champu style as the seamless flow from prose to verse and back to prose, in order for each to enhance the other. Monier-Williams adds more clarity by defining champu as an 'elaborate composition in which the same subject is continued through alterations in prose and verse'.

In the *Panchatantra*, the prose component includes the story and the dialogue, and the verse comprises short, pithy stanzas full of advice, maxims, aphorisms, and assertions of common sense. Additionally, the emotions of the characters are, mostly, expressed in verse. Each of these forms flows into the other, fluidly, the movement as seamless as a person's thought process. For instance, here is an example of how dialogue organically leads to versified advice.

'You're not wrong, my friend,' Damanaka said. 'One must behave with people in a way that is most suited to their disposition. To engage with a king, one must know his state of mind. With such insight, even a rakshasa can be controlled.

> Laud an irate king.
> Love those he loves.
> Hate those he hates.
> Praise his charity.
> Tactics, not mantras
> control a monarch.'
> (From Tantra 1: Framing story)

Similarly, here is an example of an aphoristic stanza about deception from the same story.

> Milkweed blooms pretty,
> and it never fails to fruit.
> But none pick the flowers,
> and none eat the fruit.
> Everyone knows its poison.

What is especially noteworthy is that this genre is considered most suited for scholasticism. When the writer's key purpose is elucidation rather than beauty and elegance, then his use of champu makes learning easier. Hence, the efficacy of this technique for a wisdom text like the *Panchatantra* is abundantly clear. While its stories provide easily remembered context, the rhythmic stanzas, which contain most of the lessons, can be readily memorized. Moreover, to suit the purpose of education, the language used in both the prose and verse is simple, comprehensive, and accessible, filled with commonly known proverbs and idioms, and also humour, which makes learning more fun and engaging.

Another delightful element of humour in the *Panchatantra*, which further aids the learning process, is the use of evocative names that define the traits of the characters. Often these also draw attention to a foible; for instance, the lion who is so consumed with his loftiness that he jumps into the well to attack his contender is called Mandamati (of low intelligence); or the bird who nags a monkey so much that he kills her just to shut her up is called Suchimukha (needle-mouthed); or the fish called Shatabudhi and Sahastrabudhi—of a hundred intelligences and a thousand intelligences—get caught in a fisherman's net because of their oversmartness; whereas, the frog, Ekabudhi, of single intelligence, is able to escape.

FIRST TANTRA

The first tantra, 'Mitra Bheda,' (breach of friendship) is the longest of the sections, comprising almost half of the entire work. Aside from its frame story, it has twenty-two emboxed tales. Its framing story is about a deep friendship between a lion named Pingalaka and a bull, called Sanjivaka, and how, manipulated by a devious jackal, Damanaka, they turn against each other. This theme of friendship and its subsequent rupture runs throughout the book, but especially thought-provoking is the question that is superimposed on it: can a bull and a lion really be friends? They are not only of different species, but they are also natural enemies—one a grass-eater and the other a meat-eater, who preys on grass-eaters. Moreover, they belong to two different environments—one is from the wilderness, and the other lives in domesticated milieus. Thus, friendship between the two is an anomaly. By depicting it, the question that the *Panchatantra* seems to ask is—can friendships between humans from different sections of society, different castes, different backgrounds, etc., work? And the narrative itself generates an answer: when the lion, the king of the forest, accepts the grass-eater as a friend and then begins to adopt his friend's beliefs, to the extent of giving up hunting prey, he not only throws the natural balance awry, but he also creates an imbalance in the power structure, which weakens the system. Hence, even though the jackal's orchestration and his lack of remorse at the pain and suffering he causes leave the reader feeling discomfited, as well as suspicious of the learning that Vishnusharma is imparting to the princes, she can see the justification of why this breach had to happen.

The jackal, Damanaka, is the protagonist of the first tantra, but he is an anti-hero and a trickster. A trickster character, as a Jungian archetype, is a 'distillate of the human experience'. He is a character who defies conventions and flouts accepted rules and behaviour. He is clever, yet slippery and unpredictable, and he likes to bring about havoc and disorderliness in people's lives. Damanaka is the perfect exemplar. He is highly intelligent and able to manipulate the bull as well as the lion. He is filled with ambition and feels no remorse at upending the world in which the lion and bull live in peace. In fact, he rubs his hands in glee at the prospect of it. Thus, it is he who brings about the breach of friendship. And it is also he who persistently questions the nature of this friendship, leaving the reader grappling with her own answers to what is right and what is wrong.

The character diametric to Damanaka is another jackal, Karataka, who is Damanaka's alter ego. Throughout the story, he admonishes Damanaka for his treachery and condemns him for his heartlessness. These two have a 'dialogical form, which can be seen as a dialogue within one personality, i.e., at a certain stage one single mediator is splitting, and we get two characters—Karataka and Damanaka [...] They represent opposing views and wisely defend their positions.' They are 'the bifurcation of one single synthetic character—the manifestation of a bipolar worldview that combines the opposing principles of life'.

The *Panchatantra* does not hold Damanaka accountable for the suffering that the bull and lion experience at the break-up. In fact, none of the various recensions in India attach much significance to this outcome. In the Southern recension, which is one of the key iterations of the text, Damanaka applauds the lion for killing his enemy, and the lion, quickly recovering from the grief of losing his friend, continues to enjoy his kingly life, with Damanaka as his minister. In the Northern recension, on which this retelling is based, the scrupulous Karataka makes some mundane statements about how important it is for kings to be discriminatory in selecting ministers and advisers, and these, somewhat, counter Damanaka's iniquity. However, this weak and ambivalent ending is hardly a catharsis for the reader, who is heartbroken at the tragedy of it all.

Unlike the Indian recensions, other international versions of the *Panchatantra* are not so forgiving of Damanaka. For instance, in the Arabic version, *Kalila wa Dimna*, the leopard, who is highly trusted by the lion, overhears Kalila (Karataka) berating Dimna (Damanaka) and tells the lion's mother about Dimna's role in the slaying of Shanzabeh (Sanjivaka), the bull. Dimna is then captured and put on trial, which lasts for ten days. At the end of it, he is imprisoned in a dungeon without food and water and dies of starvation. Kalila, too, although innocent, dies of heart failure in fear of being implicated by Dimna. Similarly, in the first English version, *The Fables of Bidpai: The Morall Philosophie of Doni*, Damanaka (a mule in this version) is found guilty and punished. He is skinned alive, his carcass is left for the ravens, and his bones are offered in a sacrifice to the bull in honour of his innocence.

SECOND TANTRA

The second tantra, 'Mitra Samprapti' (acquisition of friends), is about acquiring friends and the benefits of friendship. The frame story relates how a crow, mouse, tortoise, and deer become friends. Although, all four of the characters are different species, unlike in the first tantra, this particular friendship is not questioned or disapproved of; in fact, it is encouraged, because these creatures are the weakest among the species. Therefore, the underlying theme of this book is that friendship between the small and powerless is beneficial to all involved, because not only does it make each one's talent shine, but also the sodality in the alliance empowers everyone.

This is the shortest among the five books, with only six emboxed tales; the rest are extended stories about some of the key characters of the frame story. However, in its brevity, this tantra has a focus that gives it the most currency. It includes stories that, through a multiplicity of life experiences, highlight learning skills that are highly desired in today's world, such as analytical and critical thinking. These are depicted through a number of parallel sub themes; for instance, the dialectic of fate versus action and free will and the role these play in a person's life. This theme is demonstrated in a tale of a weaver who encounters the god of destiny in conversation with the god who oversees action and is given the opportunity to experience both, a life ruled by destiny and a life determined by action, before deciding what kind of life he wants to live. Juxtaposed with this theme of choices is the story of a young man who absolutely believes that a person will receive what he is meant to, no matter what. And, without engaging in a single act of free will, he circumstantially acquires three wives and an heirdom to a throne. Another apposed theme, that is extensively explored in this tantra, is of wealth—the importance of having it versus the benefit of lacking it.

By depicting an unbiased view of both sides of these important aspects of life, and by having the characters question their own choices, the *Panchatantra* clearly demonstrates how pedagogically different it is from the conventional rote learning of didactic material that used to be and still is imparted by oracular teachers. The approach it advocates is one that facilitates learning through enquiry—a methodology that is greatly encouraged in today's education. In other words, by considering the pros and cons of both perspectives in these paired stories, a learner would have to use critical thinking and problem-solving skills to draw conclusions. These are 'soft skills' that are a required part of any curriculum today.

THIRD TANTRA

'Kakolukiyam' (of crows and owls), the third tantra, draws from Kautilya's six-fold state policy that is derived from his Mandala theory of dealing with neighbouring rulers. The methods Kautilya prescribes are 'peace (sandhi), war (vigraha), observance of neutrality (āsana), marching (yāna), alliance (samsraya), and making peace with one and waging war with another'. This policy is woven into the tantra's frame story that describes a vendetta between crows and owls. To deal with the enemy, each of the kings—the owl king and the crow king—asks his ministers for advice, and the counsel that the advisers give is based on the political thought of the *Arthashastra*. Hence, this tantra is an epitome of a lesson in the administration of securing borders and destroying the enemy. One of the methods it delineates is deception. In fact, the use of deception as a means to destroy the enemy is the tantra's key theme, and it runs through most of its seventeen sub-stories.

This unapologetic, equivocal attitude of state-level treachery and violence, to the point of carrying out systematic pogroms to destroy the enemy, makes it appear that the *Panchatantra* supports the Kautilyan notion of ends justifying means in governance. This may be so, but the use of an insinuating simile at the end of this tale of crows and owls shifts the narrative from state to individual accountability and, with that, to the consequentialism of dharma. This is how the simile is embedded in the tale: the crows' secret agent, a most respected elder and minister of the king, infiltrates the owl camp by deceit and is able to set fire to the owl fortress that has no escape route; hence, all the owls are burned alive. Prior to carrying out his plan, when this minister informs the king of his intention, the simile he uses to describe the end result of his operation is, 'They will all be incinerated inside the cave, as though suffering the tortures of Kumbhipaka.' According to Hindu tradition, as described in a number of Puranas, such as *Bhagavata* and *Garuda*, Kumbhipaka is one of twenty-eight hells. The word literally means 'cooked in a pot'; thus, a person condemned to this hell is cooked in a pot of boiling oil, and the evil deed that condemns a person to this hell is the cooking or burning alive of animals or birds. What a masterful stroke of irony! This is clearly a jibe at the honoured minister who wins an absolute victory for his king and state with actions that make him a candidate for the hell he himself perpetrates. Subtle, tongue-in-cheek word play, such as this, transforms the *Panchatantra* from a simple schoolbook of lessons to a satire exposing the ills of state and social institutions.

FOURTH TANTRA

The frame story of the short fourth tantra, 'Labdha Pranasham' (loss of acquired gains), is based on the '*Susumara*' Jataka tale about a crocodile's treasured friendship with a monkey and how he loses it when his wife develops a hankering for the money's heart. The crocodile's ploys to lure the monkey to his home across the ocean is the warp into which the ten side-stories are woven. One of these, 'The tale of the brahmin who loved his wife who loved a cripple', is another Jataka, the *Culla-Padma*, which is about the treachery of women. Hence a key theme in this book is advice to men about women's insidious allurement and how not to fall prey to it.

In this tantra (and in others, as well), some of the most cutting comments and castigation are directed towards women and their duplicitous behaviour and heartless betrayals. Here, for instance, are two stanzas from this tantra, describing the character of women:

> They who are by nature dry and cruel,
> how can one seek in them the dew of love?
> They who are by nature of harsh hearts,
> how can one seek in them soft warmth?
> They who are by nature arid and sparse,
> only fools and fledglings seek in them nectar.
> The wise and intelligent never trust women.
> (From 'The tale of how the donkey gave himself away')

> A whirlpool of suspicion,
> an abode of rebellion,
> a city of audacity,
> a treasure chest of faults,
> a palace of a thousand treacheries,
> a box of trickeries,
> poison topped with amrita,
> untamed by the best of men—
> this device called woman was created
> to destroy all dharma in the world.
> (From 'The tale of how the sanyasi, jackal, and emissary caused their own suffering')

Descriptions such as this give the impression that the *Panchatantra*'s attitude towards women is misogynistic. Admittedly, derogation of women is quite evident in it. However, the text's stance is actually ambivalent, and sometimes, it seems to even be supportive of women. For instance, in some of these tales, the women are portrayed not only as highly intelligent but also prideful about their ability to outwit their husbands. On the contrary, the gullibility of the men is laughable. Hence, what appears to be overt prejudice against women comes across more as the caricature of men. Added to this is the clever wordplay that surprises the reader; for example, the name of city in which the *Panchatantra* originates, which is also the setting of the first three tantras, Mahilaropya, literally meaning 'adorned with the attributes of women'. The word is clearly a pun, suggesting both praise for women and condemnation of them; i.e., cities that are congenial for wise discourses (such as those in the *Panchatantra*) are as though adorned with the attributes of women; or, conversely, cities where friendships are breached and deception is a state policy are as though they have assumed the characteristics of women. Hence, it is up to the reader to decide whether the text's portrayal of women is downright derogatory or more of a comment on society's attitude towards them.

FIFTH TANTRA

The last Tantra, 'Aparikshita Karakam' (impetuous actions), is unique, because out of its thirteen stories, nine feature only human characters. The framing tale is about a barber, who, under a misconception, assaults monks, rashly assuming that it will bring him gold. Hence, the main theme of the tantra is simple: reckless actions, especially when they are triggered by greed, end in failure and grief. And, the most hard-hitting of the stories is about how greed lodges in one's head, like an ever-whirling wheel, making one forget everything else in life. This is the last tale in the book, and it is structured as a second framing story with its own emboxed tales. Although this tale about greed is a fitting end story, the conclusion of the *Panchatantra* is rather abrupt. It is just one sentence in which a third person narrator declares how this great work by Vishnusharma will enlighten the world.

It is hard to say if this is how the original *Panchatantra* also concluded. Quite possibly, since this work was designed to be an instructional book of lessons, a more elaborate conclusion would have been incongruous with its objective. However, the nineteenth-century Sanskrit scholar, M. R. Kale, referencing H. H. Wilson, a renowned orientalist and first professor of Sanskrit at Oxford University, thinks that the text may have had a different ending. He states that in many of the prevalent versions that Wilson found, the ending was a passage in which Vishnusharma asks the princes if there is anything else he can teach them, and they respond by saying that they have learnt all that is essential about a king's duties. Thereafter, Raja Amarashakti, delighted at the metamorphosis that Vishnusharma has brought about in his sons in just six months, lavishes the sage with wealth and riches. And Vishnusharma himself, satisfied at having accomplished what he set out to do, hopes that the *Panchatantra* will serve to enlighten other people, as well.

M. R. Kale's own version does not include this passage, but what it does include are two more stories at the ends of the fifth tantra—the second to last is about a bherunda bird with two heads that work against each other, and the last is about the wisdom of travelling with a companion. In addition, there is a concluding stanza containing advice for all humanity, which nicely wraps up the text's overall purpose:

> Mantra, pilgrimage, or brahmin,
> god, astrologer, cure, or guru—
> whatever faith one puts in them
> is the amount of reward one reaps.

Clearly, the retellers and readers of the *Panchatantra* sought a more satisfying end to this 'edifying' work that was composed 'for the beneficence of humanity'. Therefore, in many reputable Sanskrit, Hindi, and vernacular versions that came later, these two stories and the verse were included, as they are in this retelling.

THE TRADITION OF ANIMAL STORIES

In his *Phaedo* (fourth century BCE), Plato talks about how Socrates, while awaiting his death sentence, gave verse to Aesop's fables, (which he probably knew by memory). Plato also describes how he joked about pain and pleasure, suggesting that if Aesop were to create a fable about these opposing sensations, they would have a joined head, which would explain why one immediately follows the other. How interesting it is that the great philosopher who gave to the world the Socratic method of argumentation would, in his last hours, gain a sense of peace from the simplicity of animal stories. The fact is that animal tales are neither simple nor just a teaching device for children; they are multi-layered, complex tales that hold value for people of all ages and convey meaning through a variety of genres—myth, folklore, wisdom literature, etc.

Tales depicting anthropomorphic animals can be traced back to the earliest literatures from around the world. For instance, in Mesopotamian myths, there is evidence of embedded animal fables dating to the old Babylonian period (seventh century BCE). In Indian traditions, animals have been a part of literary culture since the Vedas. For example, in the tenth Mandala of the Rig Veda, the dog, Sarama, serves as Indra's messenger to Panis, who stole his cattle, and discusses the situation as any human emissary. The epics, Mahabharata and Ramayana, also abound with animal characters that speak in human tongue and behave in human ways. Two good examples are the famous birds, Jatayu and Garuda; the former helps Rama in his search for Sita and the latter is Vishnu's bird vahana who is featured in almost every Smriti text. Aside from these demigods, there are also allegorical fables in these texts, such as the tale in the Mahabharata of the tortoise and the elephant who constantly fight in sibling rivalry. Additionally, animal and bird characters often serve as metaphors depicting metaphysical truths. The Upanishadic parable of the two birds in *Mundaka Upanishad* is a good example:

> Ever united, named alike,
> Two birds clasp the self-same tree.
> Of these two, eats one the fruit sweet,
> The other looks on, eating not.

(The bird who eats is the individual self, and the one who doesn't is the Supreme Self, untouched by human experience. This fable is also the basis of the tale of the bherunda birds—the second to last tale of the *Panchatantra*.)

Another such example is the story in *Chandogya Upanishad* about Satyakama Jabala, a young man of questionable birth, who is rejected by brahmin gurus because of his unknown parentage. However, he manages to learn transcendent truths from a bull, Agni, and the hamsa and madgu (diver) birds, who symbolize the elements of vayu, agni, Adityas (the sun and the moon), and breath/prana, respectively.

Thus, the *Panchatantra* clearly inherited the legacy of animal tales from India's various literary traditions, but its most obvious antecedent is the Jatakas, the Buddha's birth stories. In many of these tales, the Buddha reincarnates as various animals, and in each animal form he forebears the full gamut of the human experience. It is the same with the animal characters in the stories of the *Panchatantra*. Through the interplay of causality, didacticism about everyday life, and dialectics about values, ideals, karmic order, duties and responsibilities, and polity, they actuate worldly life.

Chandra Rajan, a Sanskrit scholar and a translator of the *Panchatantra*, believes that the 'animal characters are really people wearing animal masks. The use of masks is a distancing device that is more effective in conveying comments and criticism'. Hence, the wily jackal, the lofty but not so smart lion, the slippery snake, etc., are archetypes of human characteristics, and by employing these stock characters, the *Panchatantra* delivers its message about human behaviours with ease.

The *Panchatantra*'s use of animals to allegorize humanness is not just through characterization but also in the way it depicts a fully functioning animal world—'the world of parallel animal society built according to the same principles of government and political science as the human'. Hence, the forest is an equivalent of the city, with places of congregation, such as village squares and marketplaces, of the urban world replicated by riverbanks and bargad trees of the wilderness. That is why when animals wander from the city to the jungle, and vice versa (like the bull, the camel, and the blue wolf in the first tantra), they experience only a moment of culture shock before they adapt to the new way of life. They also learn to stay alive, while facing dangers and discrimination, by cohabiting with other species in the forest, just as people from all spheres and backgrounds coexist, in the ambience of the city. There is also oppression in both worlds. However, interestingly, the most feared oppressor in the forest is not an animal; it is a human—the fowler or the fisherman. This deviation from the seamless human–animal equation is an example of the subtle critique that the *Panchatantra* often makes against societal practices and afflictive human behaviours.

The cast of characters of the *Panchatantra* consists of lions, tigers, wolves, cats, tortoises, monkeys, deer, hares, snakes, crows, cranes, and various other birds, and water creatures, such as fish and crabs, etc. Most of these animals are portrayed in the image of how they are perceived in the human world; for instance, the donkey is foolish, the snake is sly, the lion is imperious, and the wolf is shrewd. There are also some human characters in the *Panchatantra*, such as weavers and barbers, fowlers and hunters, as well as wealthy merchants, kings' ministers, and kings, and, along with these, a smattering of brahmins. Thus, the stories cut a wide swathe, depicting as large a slice of life as possible, but without the hierarchy of caste or status. Both the lower echelon of the working class and the upper class of kings and brahmins are depicted in their raw humanness of desires and fears and contradictions.

MORALITY AND ETHICS

The tales of the *Panchatantra* are often called fables, simply because these are animal tales. However, unlike a traditional fable that uses animal characters to tell a story and to convey a moral, which is normally stated at the end, the *Panchatantra* stories lack a moralistic ending. But, because in 'the spirit of the apologue, the dramatis personae are moved by the same man-like traits which they acquired in the earliest examples of the fable', the text has been categorized as a book of fables.

In truth, the *Panchatantra* is not so concerned with morality. Patrick Olivelle, a scholar of Sanskrit literature, citing Hertel, states: 'Most of the stories remain true to the key-note of the book, its Machiavellian character; they are generally unmoral, and at times positively immoral, in the political lessons they inculcate'. In view of its quixotic nature of kings, shiftiness of ministers, faithlessness of wives, and hypocrisy of well-wishers, the *Panchatantra* does appear to be giving primacy to 'Machiavellian' tactics. But that is only one strain, just as niti is another strain. There is really no single theme that runs through the book. Moreover, its overall essence is actually ethical, drawing from the purusharthic ideals of dharma, artha, and kama, especially the latter two—the purpose and acquisition of wealth and the fulfilment of desires—because these promote a happy and fulfilled life. In fact, this imperative to live a happy life is the only connective; the weave of the fabric, so to speak. This ligature is not overtly stated, but most of the stories intrinsically tie into it and the accompanying verses make the bonds stronger. Moreover, without any authorial judgement on whether a character acts rightly or wrongly, the five tantras show multiple approaches to this imperative, and, through the experiential process of the characters, the readers are urged to figure out what ways are most practical for them in the pursuit of their own happiness. Thus, 'it is the truth value of the parables themselves that is put into focus, as well as how we deal with them'.

WORLD FAME

The spread of *Panchatantra* reads like the story of that star who, once discovered, has a meteoric rise to fame. Even though the Ur-Panchatantra was lost, perhaps in the sixth century, after it was first translated into Pahlavi for the Sasanian king, Khusru Anushirvan by his physician Burzoe, it began to permeate every corner of the world. At last count, there were at least 200 versions of the texts in more than fifty languages.

The Pahlavi text is also lost, but before it disappeared it was translated around 570 CE into Old Syriac by a Persian scholar, Bud, who knew Syriac, and it became part of early Christian literatures. This version, *Kalilag and Damnag*, is still extant and was rediscovered in 1870 in a monastery in Mardin, Turkey. Then, in about 750 CE, the Pahlavi version was translated into Arabic by another Persian scholar, Ibn al-Muqaffa. This translation, *Kalilah wa Dimnah* (Persianized names of Karataka and Damanaka, the jackal protagonists of the first tantra) is hailed as monumental; not only was it the first work of literary Arabic prose, but also '[it] was of central importance to the spread of the *Pañcatantra*, because it was the source, directly or indirectly, of all further translations into the languages of the Middle East and Europe'.

From the eleventh to the fifteenth centuries, this version was translated into Greek, back into Pahlavi, Old Spanish, Hebrew, Latin, and German. The latter, titled *Buch der Beispiele der alten Weisen* or *Book of Examples of the Old Ways,* was one of the first books to be published. Translations from the Hebrew version became more widespread in Europe, and in the sixteenth century, Czech and French versions were created. In 1552, Anton Francesco Doni published an Italian version, titled *La Moral Filosophia,* which became the source of the first English translation in 1570 by Sir Thomas North—*The Fables of Bidpai: Morall Philosophie of Doni.*

In the seventeenth century, the second Pahlavi version, *Anwar-E-Suhayli* was translated into Turkish, and 'by the end of the nineteenth century, well before the advent of modern publishing and distribution, the *Pañcatantra* as a whole, in part or as individual stories, was found in translation from Iceland to Bali, and from Mongolia to Ethiopia'. In other words, the *Panchatantra* is, perhaps, one of the most widely known works of literature—one which has played an important part in moulding the literatures of the world. Along the way, the *Panchatantra* itself changed, each version adapting to the culture of the retelling. From a book of stories guiding human conduct, it became a text of philosophy; from a tutorial teaching young princes about polity, it became a dialogue between a king and a philosopher; from its pedagogical purpose, it was given a didactic moralistic stance. Character names were changed, and frame stories were altered. Even the animals were substituted to include creatures that were native to the country of the translation. But whatever new avatara it was given, the *Panchatantra* never failed to mould.

THE INDIAN VERSIONS

In India and South and East Asia, there is evidence of *Panchatantra* recensions from Java to Thailand, present in both stone reliefs of Buddhist temples and storybooks. In India, there are twenty-five recensions that are considered 'official.' Two of these are prominent traditions—the Southern *Panchatantra* and the Northwestern or *Tantrakhyayika,* and each contains multiple manuscripts. The critical edition of the Southern tradition is short, about a third of the length of the Northwestern *Panchatantra.* However, Franklin Edgerton, the pioneer American linguist, who in 1924 reconstructed the 'lost' Southern recension, believed that it contains seventy-five per cent of the original prose.

The Northwestern tradition—*Tantrakhyayika*—was compiled in Kashmir, and Johannes Hertel published its critical edition in 1915. When he first discovered this text, Hertel thought he had found the Ur-text. Later, when he realized it was a recension, he declared that it was still 'the only version which contain[ed] the unabbreviated and not intentionally altered language of the author'.

The *Tantrakhyayika* itself bifurcated into two different compilations—one by a Jain monk who made all five tantras approximately of equal length by moving the stories around, and the second by another Jain monk, called Purnabhadra Suri, who, basing his compilation on the *Tantrakhyayika*, added stories to it from other versions. Hence, Purnabhadra's *Panchatantra*, also called *Panchakhyanaka*, is the longest of the recensions, and because there is written evidence about the compiler and the date of its compilation—Purnabhadra Suri, 1199 CE—this recension is considered most credible. Aside from that, Johannes Hertel believed Purnabhadra's work was 'approved by the most cultivated people of his own time as well as of later times,' because he was 'renowned for his *pāndityam*'. Hertel edited this version and published it in 1908 in the Harvard Oriental Series, Vol. xi.

A contemporary of Edgerton and Hertel was an Indian Sanskrit grammarian, M. R. Kale (Moreshwar Ramachandra Kale), whose version of the *Panchatantra* was very popular in India at that time and still continues to be the basis of many Hindi and vernacular translations and adaptations. Kale's version was not based on either of the critical editions; instead, it drew from the various prevalent iterations, and it also incorporated some other tales that may have been trending at that time, making them part of the Panchatantra corpus. This is the nature of dynamic ancient literatures, especially in cultures rich in orality and/or with a longstanding custom of interpolation; the texts constantly evolve to reflect shifts in ethos and socio-political climates. This is also what keeps them current and relevant.

In India, the Panchatantra tradition has passed through 'roughly 90 to 96 human generations'. Today, the *Panchatantra* has become an industry, but with mostly children as its target market. From an abundance of illustrated books and comics to cartoons on OTT streaming services; from block printing artwork 'potlis' on Amazon to interactive online games, the children of India are constantly and variously engaged with this legacy. On the other hand, people beyond school age have grown distant from it. The narrowed focus, relegating the text to just children's literature, has eclipsed its appeal for adults. However, the *Panchatantra* is a timeless book of wisdom for all ages, filled with astute tales laced with cogent witticisms, such as the following:

> Anger is a useless emotion for a man
> who cannot do anything about it.
> No matter how high a chickpea bounces,
> it cannot crack open the roasting pan.

(Tantra 1: 'The tale of how Dantika the merchant lost his reputation')

> If you cough all the time
> stop being a thief.
> If you fall asleep at night
> stop visiting prostitutes.
> If you are ill but want to live
> stop pleasuring your tongue.

(Tantra 5: 'The tale of the donkey who loved to sing')

> No one can see the anal hole of the peacock
> until he himself, lost in the music of rain,
> foolishly lifts his tail and begins to dance.

(Tantra 1: 'The tale of the crane who did not consider the benefit and harm')

AUTHOR'S NOTE

In this retelling of the *Panchatantra*, I have taken the liberties of a storyteller to create a work that is lucid, fluent, and engaging. However, while doing so, I have made every effort to keep the essence of this magnificent ancient literature intact and to remain honest to the *Panchatantra* tradition.

The following are the key alterations that a reader who is familiar with other versions of this text will notice:

TITLES OF STORIES

Most translations of the *Panchatantra* title the stories with just a reference to the key characters; for instance, 'The Brahman and the Goat', or 'The Turtle and the Geese', etc. Generic titles, such as these, fail to provide insights into the story. The most they do is hint at a narrative tension between the characters. I believe that the title of a story should be a bit more revealing of the story. Like a window that is slightly ajar, it should give the reader a peek at what the story promises or intends to do, while keeping a sense of mystery. Since the *Panchatantra* stories are about human behaviour and how characters experience success or failure due to their own choices, the accentuation of their actions becomes the intent of the story. Hence, moving away from the convention that was, perhaps, started by early Western translators, such as Arthur W. Ryder, who were used to the cryptic captions of Aesop's Fables, I have given the stories vivid titles that suggest the story's intent. For example, 'The Tale of the Jackal Who Faced His Fear' (rather than 'The Jackal and the War-Drum'—Ryder's title). Moreover, I think this is how Vishnusharma would have taught the princes: 'Now let's look at a story in which a jackal learns to face his fear.'

NAMES OF CHARACTERS

One of the most delightful features of the *Panchatantra* is its character names. Like the title, they give a glimpse into how the character will behave or why his behaviour will have a certain outcome. They are also pungent with irony and humour. Admittedly, some of them are quite a mouthful, such as Mandavisarpini (reference to a louse, who is 'slow-moving'), but their meaning is revelatory and apt, often resonating with cultural connotations.

Most English translations do not retain these original names. Normally, for the sake of accessibility, translators tend to translate the names as well, based on what the characters represent. For instance, in Chandra Rajan's excellent English translation, Damanaka, the jackal protagonist of the first tantra, is called Wily for being a 'mean and conniving rascal', and Karataka, his alter-ego, is called Wary, because he is 'shrewd, cautious, with good judgement'. Compare this to the meaning that the Sanskrit names connote: Karataka means 'a harbinger' or 'a crow', who in Indian folkloric culture is considered wise and judicious. And Damanaka is 'a suppressor' or 'tamer'. Hence, their names do not just describe their characteristics, but they are also predictive of how they will influence the story. Rajan herself admits in her introduction that neither of these names 'convey what the Sanskrit names express so well'. Hence, I have decided to use all the original Sanskrit names, and to aid the reader's understanding, I have provided the meaning in parentheses.

VERSES

As I mentioned in the introduction to the book, the *Panchatantra* is written in champu, a style that is a combination of prose and verse used in a way that the two not only flow into each other but also enhance each other. Ordinarily, in reading poetry, the mind learns to appreciate the creative syntax; however, in a work where one must constantly shift from prose to verse, and vice versa, unconventional syntax can hamper a smooth reading. While in the *Panchatantra*'s thousand or so stanzas in complex and cryptic Sanskrit syntax, the transition from one form to the other is seamless, in translation, this seamlessness is difficult to sustain, especially in metre. I have tried to retain the poetic rhythm of the stanzas, but in my effort to ensure that the verses do not obstruct the flow of the narrative, I have had to alter the syntax and line endings. Also, while it is customary to have quotation marks at the beginning of each paragraph when there are paragraphs of continuous dialogue, in the *Panchatantra* there are often extensive pages of dialogue and so in these instances I have done away with all but the opening and closing quotation marks.

TEXTS USED

The main text I have used for this retelling is a Sanskrit–Hindi version of the *Panchatantra* translated and edited by Acharya Guru Prasad Shastri and Acharya Sitaram Shastri, published in 2018 by Chaukhamba Surabharti Prakashan, Varanasi. I have also consulted these English translations: Chandra

Rajan's *The Pañcatantra,* based on the *Purnabhadra* recension and published by Penguin Books in 1993, Patrick Olivelle's *The Pañcatantra: The Book of India's Folk Wisdom,* based on the Southern recension and published in 1997 by Oxford University Press, and Arthur W. Ryder's *The Panchatantra of Vishnu Sharma* (1925), which is in the public domain and reproduced on many websites. In addition, I have had at hand M. R. Kale's 1912 *Pañcatantra of Viṣṇuśarman,* reprinted by Motilal Banarsidass, and Johannes Hertel's critical edition of Purnabhadra's *Panchakhyanaka,* published in the *Harvard Oriental Series* in 1908. My purpose in using these additional texts was not so much to adhere to the accuracy of Ur texts and the conventions of critical editions but to have access to other translations for reference, in case I needed help with some complex passage or other. More importantly, I wanted to have available as many stories as possible that come under the umbrella of the *Panchatantra* tradition, so that I could make an informed selection. I believe that folkloric texts like the *Panchatantra* gain from the interpolations that necessarily occur in their orality. Hence, I chose the Chaukhamba text not only because its Sanskrit version is produced from various popular *Panchatantras,* including those taught in schools and colleges, but also because its Hindi translation and annotations are rich with cultural meaning.

KATHAPITHA
(Preamble)

Extracting the summary of all popular Nitishastras of statecraft and polity, the learned Vishnusharma has utilized five devices to compose this delightful, edifying *Panchatantra* for the beneficence of humanity.

Here is the account of how this *Panchatantra* came about:

It is said that in the southern region there is a city called Mahilaropya—adorned with the attributes of women. Once, this city was ruled by the renowned Raja Amarashakti (undying power), who was accomplished in all learning and virtuous in every way, and whose generosity, like that of the wish-fulling tree, effectuated the desires of all petitioners. He was a lofty king, and the greatest kingly heads bowed before him, the rays from the precious jewels studded in their diadems illuminating his feet. Amarashakti had three sons: Bahushakti (powerful arms), Ugrashakti (forceful power), and Anantashakti (endless power). However, all three were unmannered and oafish, with not a whit of sense in their heads.

One day, Amarashakti called his ministers and said to them, 'My sons have no knowledge of shastras, and they are imbecilic, impetuous, and unrefined. Knowing this, I am constantly worried, and I feel no joy, even though I rule this vast kingdom. Someone has aptly said,

> There are three kinds of sons that give grief:
> sons yet to be born, sons birthed but dead,
> and sons who are fools.
> Sons dead and yet to be born are acceptable;
> their grief is short-lived,
> but foolish sons—they are the worst kind;
> their pain and anguish are felt through life.
>
> Better a pregnant wife miscarry.
> Better to distance a wife in season.
> Better the infant be stillborn,
> or the newborn die at birth.
> Better the foetus remains unborn.
> Better to have a daughter,
> or to have a barren wife.
> All these sorrows can be braved.

> But a son, even well-endowed and fair,
> if foolish, impudent, and illiterate,
> causes grief that cannot be endured.
>
> What use a cow who neither calves nor milks.
> What use a son who is neither learned nor virtuous.

Such a son is always a cause of embarrassment and scorn in learned gatherings. He causes shame in the same way as a child born from an adulterous relationship. Such a son disgraces his parents and himself. He even brings ignominy on his mother. But she whose son is respected in society and is a leader among men is considered a true mother of a son. On the other hand, she whose son has no name, fame, or position in society is equivalent to being barren. Therefore, find a way to shine the light of intelligence on my sons. There are five hundred scholars in my court, who depend on my beneficence to make a living. With their help, find a means to educate my sons.'

The ministers were sceptical about the king's demand and none of them could offer any advice. Then, one of the ministers spoke up and voiced what all the others were thinking, 'Maharaj, it takes about twelve years to learn just the science of grammar. After that, to gain knowledge, one studies the *Manusmriti* and other dharmashastras, such as Chanakya's *Arthashastra* and Vatsyayana's *Kamashastra*. It is only after reading these various shastras does one's intellect develop, and one becomes learned in all aspects. Therefore, to be educated, one requires a lot of time. It cannot be accomplished in the short time you envision.'

But among the king's ministers was one called Sumati (wisdom, good advice), and he said to the king, 'Maharaj, it is true that there is no end to the study of grammar and other shastras. They are prodigious and require intensive and extensive learning. On the other hand, human life is unpredictable and transient; it is also full of hurdles, like sickness. Therefore, I think the quickest and most efficient way for the princes to become learned would be through a summarized text that contains the key significant elements from all the shastras. Just like the hamsa bird separates milk from water to drink only the milk, the princes would be able to imbibe core learning, if they had access to such a text. In fact, in your royal court there is a brahmin scholar who can accomplish this. His name is Vishnusharma. He is well-versed in all shastras and has not only gained fame among peers but is also a talented teacher of young students.'

Amarashakti was thrilled to hear this, and he immediately summoned Vishnusharma. When the scholar arrived, the king said to him with utmost respect, 'I am honoured to welcome you. Please consider my request and do me the favour of teaching the princes so that they can become accomplished in polity and statecraft. In exchange for your service, I will gift you one hundred villages.'

'Maharaj,' Vishnusharma replied, 'I am not willing to sell my knowledge, whether it is for one hundred villages or more. This would mean that knowledge is for sale, and selling knowledge is a grave sin. However, I cannot refuse your gracious request. Therefore, I accept the task as a challenge to myself, and I say this to you: within six months I will make your sons scholars of statecraft, or I will change my name. Please know that I am not doing this for greed or money. I am eighty years old. What need do I have of wealth and money? Besides, I have renounced all material desires. I am accepting this task only because you have requested it, and I want to demonstrate to you the evidence of the Saraswati I have acquired. Therefore, please note today's date and my resolve: if within six months I am not able to make your sons extraordinarily brilliant in governance and statecraft, you can shame me by displaying your bare buttocks to me. This is my lion's roar.'

Hearing the brahmin's daunting self-challenge and willingness to be publicly dishonoured if he failed, the king and his minister were astounded. But, in his heart, Amarashakti welcomed the old man's words because they induced a burgeoning of hope. Thus, he was happy to entrust his sons to Vishnusharma, and he did so with a great sense of relief.

To instruct the princes, Vishnusharma composed five treatises of niti (customary and social laws, especially about conduct, that facilitate a happy life): Mitra Bheda (breach of friendship), Mitra Samprapti (acquisition of friends), Kakolukiyam (of crows and owls), Labdha Pranasham (loss of acquired gains), and Aparikshita Karakam (impetuous actions). By receiving education in these pancha (five) tantras, the princes became well-versed in polity and statecraft. This is how the *Panchatantra* became famous in the world.

Whoever reads or listens to this Nitishastra full of wisdom never faces defeat, not even from the ever-victorious Indra.

Thus ends the Kathamukha of the *Panchatantra*.

FIRST TANTRA
MITRA BHEDA
Breach of Friendship

From here begins the first tantra, 'Mitra Bheda', and here is its first shloka:

> A lion and a bull in the forest,
> bound by deep and fond friendship.
> A jackal full of malice and cunning—
> oh, how he severed their bonds of trust.

It is said that in the southern region, there is a city called Mahilaropya that is as beautiful as Amravati, the city of gods, and it graces earth like its crest jewel. A rich businessman named Vardhamana (increasing prosperity) lived in this city. He had earned his enormous wealth through rightful means. One night, lying in bed, he had these thoughts: although one may be wealthy, one must constantly think of means to increase one's wealth and safeguard it, because money is the key to achieving everything in this world.

> Whoever has money has friends, kin, and respect.
> A wealthy man is seen as learned and accomplished.
> Beggars heap on him accolades of knowledge,
> charity, craftsmanship, bravery, and resolve.

In this world, if a man has wealth, even his enemies treat him well; whereas, for an impoverished man, even friends turn into enemies. Hence, if one has a meagre fortune, one should employ all means to increase it and make it grow, just like an anthill. Once the wealth begins to accumulate, one must safeguard it, and then invest it to earn more.

> Water in a ductless tank spills over.
> Unused assets invariably go to waste.
> Wealth should beget more wealth.
> Tamed elephants lure wild ones into the pen.
> He who is wealthy, favoured by Fortune,
> but lacks the sense to employ his wealth,
> a bigger fool than him does not exist.

A wealthy man should use all means to gather wealth so that it accrues, just like rivers arising from mountains swell when rivulets join them. Money is what leads to everything else that is good in life. It is like the food one eats, which empowers one's senses and body. All the tasks in the world can be accomplished with money. In fact, money also affects one's appearance: a person who has money can keep himself youthful, even in old age; whereas, a destitute person is so plagued by worries, he appears older than his age.

There are six ways to obtain wealth: beg for alms, serve a king, do farming, get an education, lend money on interest, and engage in commerce. While all these methods help in gaining wealth, the last is the most profitable, because it is rightly said,

> Beggars there are aplenty.
> Kings do not pay one's due.
> Farming is a slave to rain.
> Education makes one serve a guru
> and abide by his rules and regulations.
> And lending money for interest
> can sink even one's principle.

Thus, commerce is the best possible way to make money, and in commerce, too, the best business is merchandising, especially of perfumes, oils, flowers, spices, etc., because one can purchase these from foreign lands and sell them at a hundred per cent profit.

Arriving at this conclusion, Vardhamana decided that the best way to make his money work for him would be to invest it in commerce. And the city he decided to use as his base would be the thriving metropolis of Mathura. Thereafter, he began to accumulate merchandise that included silks, spices, and fragrances, and when he had enough stock, he determined an auspicious date and, obtaining permissions from his parents and gurus, embarked on a journey to Mathura. The chariot he rode was yoked to his strong and trusted bulls, Sanjivaka (long life) and Nandaka (joyful), whom he himself had reared. The two bulls looked like two immense white clouds as they jauntily pulled Vardhamana's chariot, the golden bells around their broad necks, jostling and tinkling.

After they had travelled some distance, Vardhamana and his men came to the crossing of the Yamuna River at Kachha. As the chariot made its way across the bank, one of Sanjivaka's hooves got stuck in a soft, marshy patch. The charioteer urged Nandaka forward, hoping that the momentum would help Sanjivaka pull himself out. It did help, but, in the process, the bull's leg got badly sprained, and he came crashing to the ground, his fall breaking the yoke of the chariot.

Vardhamana quickly had the chariot repaired, but yoking Sanjivaka to it was not an easy task. He was clearly in tremendous pain. Seeing his beloved bull in this condition, Vardhamana decided to halt his journey and wait for him to heal. When five days passed with the bull showing no sign of improvement, Vardhamana's companions grew worried. 'O seth,' they said to him, 'why are you jeopardizing our lives and your own in this dangerous place surrounded by a forest full of wild animals, just for the sake of one bull. Someone has rightly said,

> The wise do not risk a large profit for a small gain.
> Hence, give up the meagre and protect the greater.'

Taking their advice, Vardhamana decided to proceed without Sanjivaka, and, appointing a few men to stay and care for him, he himself resumed the journey with the rest of his party. However, the men he appointed remained with the bull only for a few days, because they, too, feared the dangers of the forest. Leaving the ailing Sanjivaka, they took off and soon caught up with Vardhamana's party. 'Poor Sanjivaka passed away,' they lied to Vardhamana when they saw him. 'But rest assured, seth. Knowing your affection for him, we cremated him with full rituals.'

Grieving for his beloved Sanjivaka, Vardhamana the completed last rites for him and, bidding his soul a peaceful journey to the afterlife, proceeded to Mathura.

But Sanjivaka was definitely not dead. In fact, he was destined to live many more years. As he lay on the bank incapacitated, the cool, refreshing air of the Yamuna began to revive him, and soon he was able to pull himself out of the swamp and amble to dry land. There, on the river's edge, he found a plentiful supply of tender, emerald-green grass to graze on, and, in no time, he not only regained his health but also grew more robust and powerful than he had ever been before. His skin glistened and his hump became more pronounced and rounded. In fact, he looked so handsome that anyone could have easily mistaken him for Shiva's Vrishabha bull.

Free from all his constraints and responsibilities, Sanjivaka began to do whatever he desired, grazing to his heart's content and roaming on the river's bank, wherever he pleased. His favourite pastime was to dig his long horns into the base of anthills and uproot them with a loud roar.

> That whom God protects is safe even unprotected,
> and if God wills, even the protected is destroyed.
> A creature abandoned in the forest can survive,
> but when death comes, even his home is unsafe.

In that forest, near Yamuna's bank, lived the lion, Pingalaka (light reddish-brown in colour). One day, accompanied by his entourage of creatures, he arrived at the river's side to drink water, when, suddenly, he heard a tremendous roar in the distance. His heart pounding with fear, he somehow managed to compose himself and saunter to the large bargad tree under which he normally held court. However, this day, when he sat down, he made sure he was concealed by his retinue in a four-ambit formation around him: he in the middle, his most trusted ministers seated closest to him, followed by a ring of his special guards; then another circle, consisting of his spies and security personnel, and, in the outer circle, the other subjects that always lurk in the vicinity of a king, simply to be in the know.

> Pingalaka, king of the jungle—an epitome of a king.
> Honour and pride were his kingship, not pomp and show.
> No anointing was needed to make him king.
> No devious power played to secure his throne.
> He was a sovereign free, fearless, and indomitable.

Karataka (crow, harbinger) and Damanaka (suppressor) were two jackals, who used to be Pingalaka's retainers. They were sons of his old minister, but they had been dismissed from ministerial posts. However, they always hovered around Pingalaka in the hope of regaining his favour and their position. When Karataka and Damanaka saw Pingalaka return from the river without quenching his thirst, they knew something was not right. 'Our lord Pingalaka went to the Yamuna to drink water,' Damanaka said to Karataka. 'But what is the reason that he has returned thirsty and is sitting quietly and subdued under the bargad, within the protective circles of his followers?'

'It's none of our business what our king does,' Karataka replied.

> 'A person who interferes in someone else's business
> ends up dead, like the monkey who pulled out the wedge.'

'What is this story?' Damanaka asked, and Karataka narrated it to him.

THE TALE OF THE CURIOUS MONKEY WHO DIDN'T MIND HIS OWN BUSINESS

Once, a rich man was having a temple built in a forest, bordering a city. Trees had been cleared and a construction site had been set up, where artisans and carpenters worked every day, from morning till evening, except around midday, when everyone left the site to go to the city for lunch. One day, while they were gone, a troop of monkeys, leaping and jumping from trees, arrived at the building site and began to play with the construction materials. One of the artisans had been working on splitting a beam of wood from an arjuna tree. Before he left, he had inserted a long wedge of acacia near the top of the split. Noticing this half-split beam, a particularly curious monkey, whose death had come knocking, sat down on it and tried to pull apart the two sides. Suddenly the wedge came loose, and the two sides snapped together. The way the monkey was sitting on the beam, his scrotal sac was hanging in the split. You can just imagine what happened to him.

'That is why I say, don't poke your nose into someone else's business,' Karataka added. 'Or you will suffer the fate of that monkey. In any case, we have no reason to get involved. Our basic needs are already being met; we get to eat as much as we want from the kill that is left over after Pingalaka has had his fill. Then, why should we concern ourselves with anything else?'

'It seems that all you are concerned about is food,' Damanaka said. 'But that is not right. What about matters beyond the appeasement of hunger?

> What if one needs to help friends
> or to bring harm to one's enemies?
> One always needs the assistance of the king,
> for only the king can punish or reward.
> The educated, craftsmen, valorous, needy,
> and those who simply wish to serve—
> a king's patronage is sought by all.

There are some who, filled with conceit and the self-importance of belonging to a high caste or an upper-class family, think it below their dignity to serve a king. These people live their lives in penury, begging for their food. To live a good life, one needs to serve the king.

> Just securing one's food is no great feat.
> Even birds do that with just their beaks.
> To live a life of dignity, be it a short life,
> one needs science, chivalry, and wealth.
> These virtues make one successful
> and worthy of being remembered.

Otherwise, in this transient world, who doesn't live, and who doesn't die?

> Small rivulets overflow with just a downpour.
> A mouse's cupped hands fill with just a small offering.
> A lazy person is satisfied with just a bit of money.
> A dog is content with just a bone to chew.
> But a lion will toss the jackal caught between his paws,
> just so he can pursue a mighty bull elephant.

> Having stolen his mother's youth,
> causing her pain by being born.
> What use is that man's birth
> if he is not the flag on the pinnacle
> of his family's honour and glory?

Also,

> He who is without compassion
> for friends, relatives, the unfortunate,
> of what use is his life?
> The crow lives a long life
> on the pickings of others' sacrifice.
> But the reed on the riverbank
> lends itself to a drowning man.

> He whose life sustains others
> truly knows the meaning of living.
> Like sky-ranging clouds heavy with rain,
> he alleviates the suffering of people.
> Exemplary is the mother who bears
> a son with a generous heart and high ideals.

But he who is wealthy and powerful and doesn't use these achievements for the good of people, deserves only contempt. On the other hand, he who acquires wealth and gains fame and glory through his deeds, fulfils the purpose of his birth. He is the one who stands like a flag on the pinnacle of his family's honour.'

To this Karataka replied, 'But we have been dismissed from office and are now insignificant. We have nothing to do with these issues; moreover, we are in no position to do anything about it. People say, if a dismissed officer presents his views before the king without being asked, he is not only rejected but also ridiculed. As they say,

> Voice your views only to serve a purpose.
> Dye is permanent only on the colour white;
> it is futile to dye a fabric that is black.'

'I don't agree.' Damanaka said. 'Anyone who frequents court and tags along with the king, whether he is a dismissed minister or even a secondary subject, becomes important when the time is right. And even a person who is counted among the primary ministers can become secondary over time, if he distances himself from the king and doesn't remain his acolyte. The king favours those who stay in close proximity to him, even if they are uncouth or lack virtue. These are the beloved of the king, and it is to them that he offers his protection. But if a king is ill-tempered, he should be handled with discernment. For this king, a person should ascertain what pleases him and what angers him and then act to keep him happy. In this way, anyone can gain favour with an irascible king.

> People say it is difficult to manage a king.
> But if one can subdue poisonous snakes,
> ferocious tigers, lions, and elephants,
> one can also bring a king under control
> with diligence, motivation, and strategy.
> And the benefits of this are numerous:
> white umbrella, whisk, horse, and elephant.

I'm telling you, dear friend, I can have our king eating out of my hand again. I know he has been frightened by something, and I intend to investigate what it is. When I eliminate the cause of his fear, he will be so grateful that he will surely make me his minister.'

'How do you know he is frightened?' Karataka asked.

'A wise person can discern everything that is revealed, though it may be unspoken. I know that if Pingalaka was not afraid, he would not be sitting within his security circles.'

'That may be so, but you don't have much experience of serving, and you are hardly acquainted with courtly life. How will you coax him?'

'How can you say I don't know the ways of the court? I have been learning statecraft from the time I used to sit on my father's lap. When wise men visited him, I would listen to their conversations, and I have memorized every lesson.

> He who wants to curry favour with the king
> should liaise with men that he trusts
> and convey his messages through them.
> Only when the king grows eager to meet him
> should he respectfully present himself.
>
> A wise person should treat the king's relatives:
> his wife, his mother, his sons, and also
> his chief minister and priests with respect.
> And he should treat his enemies as his own.
>
> Always eager to serve, words like,
> "Yes Maharaj, it shall be done"
> should be flowing from his tongue.
> And if the king should reward him,
> with great humility and satisfaction,
> he should accept and strive for better.
>
> The ladies' palace is forbidden to him
> and alcohol should be like poison.
> In war, he must be at the forefront,
> in the palace, always behind the king.
> Such a person becomes a favourite of the king.

But a king's disposition also plays a big role in how one serves. Men should only put themselves in the service of a king who is prosperous and generous and is capable of recognizing his men's talents.

> Better to die of hunger and thirst,
> like a withering tree in adverse weather,
> than to serve a king who does not know

what is right and what is wrong and
treats his men with cruelty and disdain.

> Milkweed blooms pretty
> and it never fails to fruit.
> But none pick the flowers
> and none eat the fruit.
> Everyone knows its poison.'

Hearing Damanaka speak thus, Karataka was persuaded. 'All right,' he said. 'You've made your point. But what will you say to Pingalaka? How will you start the conversation?'

'Talented and sagacious people can tell whether a policy will be beneficent or detrimental, and they also know what makes a policy good or bad. Whoever has this talent should nurture it. I know what to say to him, and I can assure you my words will flow.

> After germination, seeds burgeon from seeds.
> In the same way words burgeon from words.
> The wise know the art of invoking conversation.
> Some, like parrots, can spout aphorisms with ease.
> Some never can, though they know them by heart.
> Others know them and can adapt them as needed.
> That is the talent possessed by a professional.

I, too, intend to be wholly professional when I talk to Pingalaka. And believe you me, I will be very careful with my words. Even the master of knowledge, Brihaspati—guru of the gods, who is the framer of sacred speech, needs to watch what he says. He, too, can be mocked if he speaks unprofessionally.'

'I believe you,' Karataka said. 'But it is so hard to gain the trust of kings.

> Like a rugged mountain inhabited with
> venomous snakes, tigers, lions, and dangers,
> kings are ringed by the wicked, evil, and glib.
> A king himself is like a serpent—coiled, undulating,
> deceptive in beauty, double-tongued, crooked-minded,
> but prudent and perceptive to the faults of others.
> Even by doing a king good, one burns—a moth in a flame.
> Just as brahmins are enraged by the slightest injury,
> a king becomes enflamed at the slightest insult.

> Kingship is difficult to obtain and protect.
> Hence, it is apt to keep it guarded,
> like water is safest when contained in a tank.
> That is why kings are difficult to approach.
> It is best to remain distant from a king.'

'You're not wrong, my friend,' Damanaka said. 'One must behave with people in a way that is most suited to their disposition. To engage with a king, one must know his state of mind. With such insight, even a rakshasa can be controlled.

> Laud an irate king.
> Love those he loves.
> Hate those he hates.
> Praise his charity.
> Tactics, not mantras
> control a monarch.'

'All right, my friend. If that is how you feel, then go ahead. Do as you wish. Go to Pingalaka. I wish you all the best. But just remember one thing. Both our lives depend on what you do; that is why you must be very careful.'

Bowing to his friend, Damanaka took his leave and went to seek Pingalaka.

When Pingalaka saw Damanaka approaching, he instructed his guards, 'Put aside your staffs. I see my old minister's son, Damanaka, coming this way. He should be allowed to enter unimpeded. Bring him here and have him take a seat in the second circle.'

The guards did as the king commanded and, allowing Damanaka to enter the formation, gave him a seat in the second mandala of the king's attendants. Damanaka bowed to Pingalaka, and the lion accepted his greeting by lifting his clawed paw and placing it gently on his head. 'Are you well?' he asked. 'I haven't seen you in a while. Where are you coming from?'

'Maharaj, I thought I would present myself to you. Although, you don't need anything from us, we live in the hope that you will call upon us from time to time. A king requires the services of all creatures, whether they are big or small, or of high, middle, or low status. It is said,

> Even a blade of grass is useful to a king
> to pick teeth, to scratch an itching ear.
> And he who has hands and speech—
> Can you imagine the use he can be put to?

We have been your servants for generations. In emergencies, we have always had your back. It is true that at present we are bereft of our rightful ministerial posts, but that doesn't mean Maharaj should forget us. Someone has rightly said,

> Servants and jewels—
> there is an apt place for each.
> "I am Lord, I can do as I please."
> Thinking thus, one cannot place
> a crest jewel at one's feet.

No matter a king's lineage, no matter his wealth, if he doesn't know the qualifications of each of his retainers, they will leave him. Even during an emergency, they will not serve him well.

> When a king treats his quality retainers
> the same as he does those who are unfit,
> he loses his most capable serving men.

> If a king, lacking intelligence, fails to assign
> appropriate tasks to the most qualified;
> if he appoints those who are accomplished
> to posts that are beneath their talents,
> his best retainers will resign from their jobs.
> And no one else but he himself will be to blame.

It is said:

> A gem worthy of studding in gold
> if embedded in cheap metal
> neither cries injustice nor loses lustre.
> The shame is of the jeweller's.

You asked me why you have not seen me in some time. Then please allow me to explain the reason.

> Servants refuse to serve in a house
> where the difference is not known
> between the right hand and the left,
> a gem is seen as just a piece of glass,
> and a piece of glass is seen as a gem.

In a country where jewels are not assayed, even pearls and precious stones have no value. For instance, you must have heard of Amir kingdom, where the valuable Chandrakanta gem sells for just three cowries. In such a country, where there is no distinction between a ruddy piece of glass and the Padmaraga gem, how can the business of gems be successful? In the same way, when a master treats all his retainers alike, those who are skilled, motivated, and capable of accomplishing difficult tasks become discouraged.

> Neither can a king live without retainers
> nor can retainers survive without a king.
> It is a mutual relationship, such as the one
> between the rim of a wheel and its spokes.

> Just as the fiery sun cannot shine on people
> without its rays
> A lustrous king cannot gain glory in the public eye
> without his working men.

Hence,

> The king should choose his retainers well:
> those who are wise, noble, brave, heroic, diligent;
> those who serve the king as their inherent duty,
> those who take on the most difficult tasks,
> simply because they will benefit their master.
> And never boast about their deeds.
> Those who are ever present to serve;
> those who, without being told, know
> what the king needs and what he doesn't;
> those who think it a privilege to protect
> the king and his kingdom from harm;
> those who, though disciplined by the king,
> never speak ill of him or wish him misfortune;
> those who, though honoured, never brag
> or, when insulted, never feel dejected;
> those who serve with no thought to their needs
> of hunger, thirst, sleep, heat, or cold.
> Only men with these qualities are worthy of serving the king.

Also,

> A king should carefully appoint ministers
> who have the skill to expand state boundaries,
> and he should dismiss those under whom
> the kingdom shrinks like leather shrivels in fire.

Maharaj, what I'm trying to say is this: it does not behove you to insult me by thinking, "He is just a jackal".

> Silk comes from a worm;
> gold from a rock;
> druba grass from cow's hair;
> red lotus from a marsh;
> moon from the ocean;
> blue beetle from cowdung;
> fire from wood;
> mani from a snake's hood;
> orpiment from cow's bile.

All these precious objects have unimpressive origins, but they are valued by everyone. A person's acclaim comes from his merits; it is not a result of his birth.

> A destructive mouse is shooed away,
> though it may be born in the house.
> Yet, an outsider cat is welcomed and fed,
> because it destroys the mouse that harms.
> Erand and aak woods, though large in quantity,
> cannot substitute for the durable wood
> that makes strong pillars of foundation.

Moreover, know that if a servant is dutiful but incapable of work, he is of no use; and what use is he who is capable, but harbours enmity? I am your dutiful and loyal servant, and I am fully capable; hence, it does not behove you to reject me.'

'Well,' said Pingalaka, 'let bygones be bygones. Whether you are capable or incapable is beside the point. The fact is that you are the son of my former minister, and I will listen to you. Say what you've come to say.'

'Maharaj,' Damanaka then broached the topic he had come to investigate. 'May I ask you a question?'

'Go ahead. Ask without hesitation.'

'Brihaspati has said that matters related to the king, even if they be minor, should never be discussed before everyone. Therefore, may I speak with you in private? It is said,

> Advice is advantageous only when heard by four ears.
> Heard by six, it spreads like a rumour everywhere.'

Pingalaka gestured to everyone, indicating that they should leave the assembly, and tigers, leopards, wolves, and all other animals instantly got up and left. Only those idiots who didn't catch the meaning of the king's gesture remained, and they, too, were thrown out by the soldiers. Once Damanaka was alone with Pingalaka, he started to speak: 'Maharaj, you went to Yamuna's bank with the desire to drink water. But without quenching your thirst, you returned here and sat down in an assembly. What could be the reason for that?'

Pingalaka was disconcerted by Damanaka's perceptiveness. Trying to conceal his reaction, he gave an embarrassed little laugh: 'No, no. No reason at all,' he said.

'If you don't want to reveal the reason to me, that is fine, and I'll leave. It doesn't matter, because someone has rightly said,

> Some matters should be concealed even from one's wife.
> Some matters should be concealed from friends.
> Some matters should be concealed from kin.
> Some matters should be concealed even from one's son.
> Though pressed even by someone great, one should
> only reveal what one can and conceal the rest.'

Listening to Damanaka, Pingalaka thought, he seems to be very intelligent and able; it may be worth my while to share my concern with him. It is said,

> A true friend, a loyal servant,
> a good wife, a faithful lover,
> and a compassionate king—
> confiding in them gives one relief.

Looking keenly at Damanaka, Pingalaka asked in a hushed voice, 'Can you hear this deep sound that is coming from somewhere?'

'Yes, Maharaj. I can certainly hear it. But how is this related to you?'

'Because of it, I'm thinking of leaving this forest and going elsewhere.'

'Why would you say this, Maharaj?'

'Because it seems that some extraordinary, terrible being has come here. If his roar is so horrific, imagine his strength and ferociousness.'

'Just by hearing a sound our lord and master has become afraid. This is not right. It is said,

> A bridge collapses with the force of water.
> Good advice is ruined by doubt.
> Love is destroyed by gossipmongers.
> He who loses heart merely at a sound
> is a coward who is easily overpowered.

This jungle is your inheritance, bequeathed to you by your ancestors. Losing courage and fleeing from it does not behove you. Besides, sounds can be produced by anything—kettledrum, flute, veena, mridangam, cymbals, conch—these instruments all create different kinds of sounds. Hence, one can't give in to fear simply by hearing a sound. It is said,

> A king who is unperturbed facing
> a powerful and ruthless enemy
> is impossible to defeat by anyone.
> Even Brahma's fierce form
> cannot destroy the courage of this king.
>
> In summer when rivers and rivulets run dry,
> the ocean becomes even more ferocious,
> causing its water to rise in tidal waves.
>
> He who is unaffected by calamity and joy;
> he who is fearless in battle—that unique son,
> can only be borne by a unique mother.
> He who lacks strength, masculinity, prowess;
> he who is not resolute before his enemies,
> that man is no better than a blade of grass.
> Just like glittery ornaments made of lac
> melt when brought near fiery flames,
> that man is only a shadow of a man.

Consider my words, Maharaj, and have courage. Don't be fearful of just a sound. There is a story:

When I first heard it, I thought
the kettledrum is flesh and blood.
When I entered it, I discovered
only its cover is made of skin;
inside it is hollowed out wood.'

'What is this story?' Pingalaka asked, and Damanaka related the tale.

THE TALE OF THE JACKAL
WHO FACED HIS FEAR

One day, a very hungry jackal, desperately searching for food, came to a forest, which had once been a battlefield. As he searched for anything that would serve as a morsel of food, he began to hear a sound he had never heard before—a strange rolling and drumming. It was a terrifying sound, which made the jackal stop in his tracks. Fearfully, he exclaimed, 'Oh, this sounds like my death is near. It seems that a powerful beast is waiting to devour me.' But then he thought, maybe, there's a way out. If I turn around and flee from this place as quickly as possible, I may be able to save my life. 'Wait!' he then said to himself. 'What am I doing? Before I do anything, I need to think this through. The wise say,

> When one is faced with fear or joy,
> one should examine the situation;
> that way calamities can be avoided.

I should investigate where this sound is coming from and who is making it, and only after that should I determine what further action to take.'

Feeling reassured by these thoughts, the jackal began to move stealthily towards the sound. As he drew nearer to it, his fears were further allayed, because lying on the ground among the bushes was just a drum. The wind passing through the bushes was smacking branches on its side and that is what was making the sound. Coming closer to it, the jackal saw that the drum's sides were covered with hide, and he hesitantly hit his own paw on one side. The sound it made was very much like the sound he had been hearing, except that it was fuller and louder. Now the jackal exclaimed in joy, 'Oh, that is a robust sound. I am so lucky. This thing is probably full of flesh and blood. After many days, I have finally found something that I can eat to my heart's content.'

Digging his teeth into the hide, the jackal tried to tear at it, but it was tough and unyielding. He broke many teeth and almost cracked his jaw, but he was finally able to pierce the hide and tear it. When he had a large enough opening, he stuck his head inside to see what there was to eat. However, what he found inside was only disappointment; the drum was completely empty. For a moment the jackal was dumbstruck. Then he began to laugh, and these are the words he said:

> What a loud, terrifying sound it made,
> like an immense creature of flesh and blood.
> But it is only skin on an empty wooden shell.'

'So, you see, Maharaj,' Damanaka said to Pingalaka, 'a sound means nothing. One should not fear just a sound.'

'That's all well and good,' Pingalaka replied. 'But look at my crew, my relatives, and my attendants. They are all afraid and ready to flee. How can I be calm?'

'Your followers can't be blamed. A servant follows what his master does. If you show you are fearful, your followers will also be afraid. If you are calm and courageous, your servants, too, will forget their fear. It is rightly said,

> Horse, sword, weapon, speech,
> instrument, follower, and wife—
> all learn abilities or inabilities
> from the one who wields them.

That is why you should not abandon your duty to your followers. I'll go and investigate what that sound is and who is making it. In the meantime, please be patient and wait here for me.'

'You have the courage to do this?' Pingalaka asked Damanaka in admiration.

'Maharaj, no task is impossible for a capable servant. It is said,

> At his master's command, a servant can
> thrust his hand into a snake's mouth,
> jump into a stormy sea, or fight lions,
> tigers, and maddened elephants, too.

In fact, if a servant hesitates to carry out a task commanded by his master, or he thinks a task is impossible, he should be thrown out, especially by a ruler who wants to work for the welfare of his people and achieve success.'

'My good fellow, if that is so, and you're not afraid to approach the source of that sound, then please go. May your path be safe and without hindrance.'

After Damanaka had left, Pingalaka began to worry: 'What have I done? Swayed by this Damanaka's arguments, I revealed myself to him. Is he colluding with my enemies? Has he been paid by them to destroy me? After all, I removed him from his hereditary occupation and ministerial status. I'm sure he hates me and has been looking for an opportunity to harm me. Who knows what's in his mind and what he intends to do? Maybe, the reason why he seemed so eager to find the terrible creature is to bring him here and have me killed. I should move away from here. Let me find a safe spot and wait for him there. It is said,

> A powerful foe can do no harm,
> even to one who is weak but mistrustful.
> The powerful, though, can be destroyed
> by a weak enemy who has been trusted.
>
> A man desirous of happiness, prosperity, and long life
> should not trust anyone, not even the divine Brihaspati.
> And in matters of the enemy—he should not be trusted,
> no matter how many oaths of friendship he takes.

Didn't Indra swear friendship with Vritra to secure his own position as king of gods? But when the opportune moment arrived, he treacherously killed him with his Vajra weapon. Also, didn't Diti, the mother of the daityas, trust Indra, who was her enemy? And what did Indra do? He entered her womb and cut her foetus into seven parts and each part into seven more. Thus, it is foolhardy to trust anyone; with cautious distrust, even the gods can be rendered powerless.' Thinking these thoughts, Pingalaka found a safe place and sat down to wait for Damanaka.

In the meantime, arriving on Yamuna's bank, Damanaka began to look for the source of the strange sound, and he discovered that it was just a bull. 'Aha,' he said to himself, quite pleased. 'What a great opportunity fate has given me. Using this bull, I can create a situation to manipulate Pingalaka. First, I will help the bull and him to become fast friends, and then I will make them enemies.

> A king disregards his ministers,
> be they wise, well-born, and well-wishing.
> But come a time of crisis or hardship,
> he gratefully follows their advice.
>
> A healthy man does not seek a doctor until he gets sick.
> A king doesn't need his ministers till he faces calamity.
> Thus, to manage a king, ministers wish for emergencies.'

With these thoughts percolating in his head, Damanaka returned to the bargad, looking for Pingalaka. When the lion saw the jackal searching for him, he quickly assumed an expression of nonchalance. Damanaka spotted Pingalaka sitting concealed behind dense foliage. Going to him, he bowed deeply and sat down before him.

'So, did you see the terrible beast that was making the sound?' Pingalaka asked.

'Yes, by your grace, Maharaj, I was able to see that terrible beast.'

'Are you being truthful?'

'Can anyone be untruthful before Maharaj?

> Who can lie to kings and gods?
> Utter destruction awaits him who dares.
> A king is seen as a god incarnate.
> The only difference between kings and gods is this:
> gods reward good or bad in the next life;
> the king's reward or punishment is immediate.'

'I do believe that you have seen that colossal, fierce beast, because you are here alive.

> Fierce winds uproot strong trees.
> They do not touch fragile undergrowth.
> The powerful, the exalted, the mighty
> do not demonstrate their might
> on merely the abject and lowly.'

'That maybe so, Maharaj. That beast may be mighty, and I may be lowly. But I have the power to lay the beast at your feet and make him your friend.' Damanaka replied.

'Can you really do that?' Pingalaka asked, intrigued by the prospect. 'Or are you just bragging?'

'What task in the world can't be accomplished with intelligence, Maharaj?

> Intelligent people can achieve the impossible
> simply in the course of a conversation.
> What weapons, elephants, horses, soldiers
> cannot accomplish, the intelligent can.'

'If that is so, and you accomplish this difficult task with your intelligence, I'll appoint you as the royal minister of rewards and punishment.'

Thrilled to hear Pingalaka's promise, Damanaka rushed to the bull with a plan in mind, and, as soon as he saw him, he began reprimanding him: 'O uncouth bull, why are you roaming around this forest, roaring without any reason? Come with me. Our lord and master, Pingalaka, wants see you.'

'Who is his Pingalaka?' Sanjivaka asked. 'And why does he want to see me?'

'What? You don't know who Maharaj Pingalaka is? Wait just a while and you'll find out yourself when your careless actions are duly punished. Look over there, behind the mighty bargad. Do you see our Maharaj Pingalaka seated there?'

Even though he only got a glimpse of the lion, Sanjivaka felt like he was looking into the mouth of death. Trembling in every limb, he said to Damanaka, 'Sir, you appear to be sagacious and kindly, and you have a clever way with words. Take me to the Maharaj if you must, but I beseech you, can you please ask your Maharaj to grant me the concession of safe conduct?'

'I hear what you are saying. And it is right that you ask for this protection; one never knows what to expect from a king. It is rightly said,

> Earth, sea, and mountain can be measured,
> but the mind of a king is unfathomable.
> No one, anywhere, knows its workings.

Wait here. I'll go to Pingalaka and request him for his word regarding your safety. Then I'll take you to him.'

Damanaka then went to Pingalaka and said to him, 'Maharaj, that creature is a bull, but he's not an ordinary bull; he seems to be the mount of Lord Shiva himself. He said to me that he's here, on Yamuna's bank, because of a reward from Mahadeva. The Great Lord himself gave him permission to feed on the rich grass here and to roam around in leisure.'

Hearing this, Pingalaka grew even more afraid: 'He's here by the grace of Shiva? Now I understand. Otherwise, which grass-eater would dare to come to this dense forest of meat-eating lions and tigers and roam around, fearlessly roaring and enjoying himself. What did you say to him?'

'I said to him, "O bull, this forest is ruled by Devi Chandika's mount, our lord and master, the lion. Hence, this is his domain, but you are welcome here as our guest. Please come with me to meet our king, Pingalaka, and like a loving brother, dine with him and stay here in comfort." He accepted my invitation and replied, "I am happy to meet your king, but please get me a promise of safe conduct from him so that I, as a bull, can feel safe in the presence of a lion." Maharaj, this is his situation. Please command me how you would like me to proceed.'

'Well done, dear Damanaka. Whatever you said to the bull are words straight out my own mouth. I grant him safe conduct. But please request him to also grant me the same favour, and once he gives his word, please bring him to me. I must applaud you for your intelligence and diplomacy, which are certainly worthy of note. Someone has rightly said,

> A strong, trustworthy, honest minister
> upholds a kingdom
> just like a sturdy, straight, termite-free pillar
> upholds a temple.

Also,

> Resolving a problematic situation
> is the true test of a minister's acumen,
> like treating patients with delirium
> is the real proof of a physician's skills.
> Anyone can be a pundit in ordinary tasks.
> A true pundit is he who takes on challenges.'

Respectfully bowing to Pingalaka, Damanaka returned to Sanjivaka. On the way, he gleefully thought to himself, how pleased the king is with me. I know he is gravitating towards me, and soon I will have him in my control. Surely, there is no one cleverer than I.

> Just like fire in winter is amrita,
> seeing a loved one is amrita,
> kheer included in a meal is amrita,
> so is respect from a king amrita.

Seeing Sanjivaka pacing the riverbank in agitation, Damanaka addressed him in a gentle, affable tone: 'Dear friend, I have acquired Pingalaka's promise of safe conduct for you. Therefore, please come with me to our Maharaj without any fear. Come with amicable intentions, adhering to the dharma of oath-keeping. Please don't act wilfully or be pompous with self-importance. I, too, will act in your best interest. In that way, we'll both be able to enjoy prosperity that the royal favour has granted us. You must have heard,

> As a hunter uses bait to round up game
> so as to shoot his target with ease,
> a shrewd man weaves greed and fear
> to fleece those caught in his web.

Men gain wealth and fame in the sport of hunting;
their game is not animals; it is unsuspecting people.

In a high position awarded by the king,
if one is intoxicated with his own importance,
he taints his own good name and loses respect
just like Dantika, the businessman did.'

'What is the story of Dantika?' Sanjivaka asked, and Damanaka told him the tale.

THE TALE OF HOW DANTIKA THE MERCHANT LOST HIS REPUTATION

On this earth is a beautiful city called Vardhamana. A merchant named Dantika lived there and traded in various kinds of merchandise. He was not only the leading businessman of the city but also the most respected. He was praised by both the people and the king, because, along with diligently serving the king, he earnestly carried out works of public welfare. It is said,

> Work for just the ruler
> and the ruled feel ignored.
> Work for just the people
> and the king is irked.
> He who keeps both ruler and ruled happy,
> such a working man is hard to find.

Dantika was just such a man.

Once, on the occasion of his daughter's wedding, Dantika invited Vardhamana's citizenry and all the king's officials to a feast in his house and showered everyone with gifts. He also sent a special invite to the king and queen and honoured them with elaborate rituals and a lavish spread.

Among the royal staff of Vardhamana was a sweeper, Gorambha, who used to clean the whole palace, including the king's rooms. He, too, received Dantika's invitation. On the day of the feast, arriving at Dantika's house, Gorambha found his way to the guest area and sat down in a vacant seat, not realizing that it was reserved for high officials. When Dantika saw the sweeper sitting there, he was livid. He harshly upbraided Gorambha for not knowing his place and pushed him out of the chair. Gorambha returned to his home feeling so humiliated that he was plagued by it day and night. All day he would sigh in dejection, and, at night, unable to sleep a wink, he would toss and turn, replaying the incident in his mind. All he could think about every minute of the day was how to avenge himself. 'I should discredit Dantika seth before the king,' he said to himself numerous times. But every time he thought this, the question arose in his mind: 'Who will believe me? I am just a lowly sweeper.'

> Anger is a useless emotion for a man
> who cannot do anything about it.
> No matter how high a chickpea bounces,
> it cannot crack open the roasting pan.

Thus, feeling powerless, yet burning with a fervent desire for revenge, Gorambha began to spend his time waiting for some opportunity to present itself. One early morning, he got his chance: as he swept the floors in the king's bedroom, he noticed that the king was just waking up. Seeing him hovering between sleep and wakefulness, an idea struck him. Moving closer to the bed, pretending to sweep under it, Gorambha began to mumble, 'Uff, that Dantika seth is something else. He's become so conceited that he has even started embracing the queen.'

When the king's ears caught these shocking words, he pulled himself out of the last vestiges of sleep and sat up. 'Arrey, Gorambha, is it true? Has Dantika really taken such liberties with my queen?'

'Maharaj, please pardon me,' Gorambha said quickly, touching his forehead to the floor. 'I don't know what I've been mumbling. You see, I was gambling all night and didn't get any sleep. I must have dozed off while sweeping.'

Jealousy coursed through the king's heart, and he became certain that what Gorambha had murmured in his sleep was, indeed, true. He is a sweeper, the king reasoned with himself. He has access to every room. That Dantika, too, visits the palace whenever he pleases. I'm certain he went into the queen's room, and Gorambha saw him there. What spilled out of his mouth unawares must really have happened. It is said,

> What a man wishes, sees, or does in the day,
> he repeats in the dreams of the night.
> And that which is harboured in his mind,
> even if it is buried deep as a secret,
> his mouth utters in sleep or inebriation.

This is amply true for women:

> Love talks with one, flirtation with another, pining for a third,
> but none of them are a woman's true love.
> For some, they smile with blush lips,
> others they gaze upon with lotus eyes.
> The generous ones they hold dear.
> But none of them are a woman's true love.

> The fool who thinks he has a woman enthralled
> becomes her captive like a parrot in a cage.
> He who lets himself be enamoured of women
> is mocked, mistreated, and trodden upon by them,
> like the henna they soak, squeeze, and put on their feet.

Thus, vilifying all women in his mind and lamenting his own susceptibility, the king distanced himself from Dantika that very day. He also barred Dantika from visiting the palace.

Perplexed at the king's sudden volte-face, Dantika began to think:

> Who doesn't become arrogant with wealth?
> Which worldly man has not experienced hardship?
> Whose heart has not wavered for women?

Also,

> Who is held dear by a king?
> Who is not shadowed by death?
> Who can escape the noose of evil men?
> Purity in a crow,
> truth in a gambler,
> forgiveness in a snake,
> satiation in a woman,
> patience in the impotent,
> mindfulness in a drunk,
> friendship with a king—
> who in the world has seen this?

'I have neither done nor ever wished any harm to the king or his relatives, then why has he withdrawn his favour and alienated himself from me?' Dantika asked himself and decided he would visit the palace to request the king for an explanation. However, when he got to the palace, the guards would not let him enter.

Just at that moment, Gorambha, the sweeper, was passing by. Seeing Dantika barred from entry, he laughed and made a mocking comment to the guards: 'This Dantika seth is a minion of the king. He has the authority to punish and reward as he pleases. If you heckle him, you'll also end up in a headlock, like me.'

When Danika heard Gorambha say this, it dawned on him that it was he who had, somehow, turned the king against him. It is common knowledge,

> Even a lowly dimwit, lacking respect, but
> in service of the king, is adored and revered.
> Even a coward cannot be defeated
> if he has the king covering his back.

Bemoaning his fall from grace, Dantika returned home, and that evening he invited Gorambha to his house. Honouring him with gifts of a dhoti and a shawl, he said to him, 'I know I insulted you at my daughter's wedding by throwing you out, and I want to apologize for that. But you were seated in a place reserved for the high brahmins. That was the only reason. I have no personal enmity with you. Please forgive me for any insult you may have suffered.'

Gorambha was pleased to receive the gifts and the apology from the seth. 'Sethji,' he replied. 'I appreciate this honour you have given me, and I forgive you. In return, I promise I will use some scheme to make the king change his mind about you, and soon you will be back in his favour.'

How right people are when they say,

> A pair of scales and degenerate menials are alike.
> Scales lift and fall with the slightest change in weight,
> menials puff up with the slightest honour.

After that, Gorambha carefully watched the king every morning, and the next time he saw him in a state of semi-wakefulness, he murmured, 'How ignorant is our king that as he empties his bowels, he eats raw cucumbers.'

The king sat up, shocked. 'Arrey, Gorambha,' he scolded, 'what rubbish are you speaking? Have you ever seen me eating cucumbers in the toilet? I should punish you for this offence, but I'm sparing your life, because you're my servant.'

'Maharaj, please pardon me. I was gambling all night and didn't get any sleep. That is why I dozed off while sweeping, and I have no idea what I muttered. I beg you to please have mercy on a sleep-deprived, poor sweeper and overlook my offence.'

After Gorambha left, the king started thinking: I have never in my life eaten cucumbers while using the toilet; yet this idiot sweeper is accusing me of it. Was he also making up false stories about Dantika? If so, then I have wronged that good man. Dantika is such a trustworthy and respected man; he could not have misbehaved with the queen. Besides, without Dantika, many programmes of governance and public welfare have stalled. I should reinstate him.

The king then summoned Dantika to court, and, giving him an honoured seat, removed his own royal shawl and ornaments and put them on him. 'Accept these honours and my favour,' he said. 'I reappoint you as my official.'

'Hence, I say again,' said Damanaka to Sanjivaka, 'a person of authority who does not respect people of both high and low status, faces the hardship that Dantika had to face.'

'I understand what you are saying and, wholeheartedly, agree with you,' Sanjivaka replied. 'I'll do exactly as you say.'

'I'm glad to hear that. Now, you must also give me your promise of safe conduct for Pingalaka, and then I'll take you to him.'

When Damanaka brought Sanjivaka to Pingalaka, the bull bowed meekly to the lion and sat down before him, trepidatious, even though he had the lion's vow that he would not harm him. Pingalaka peered keenly at Sanjivaka, his fear allayed at seeing with his own eyes that the bull posed no threat. Placing his right paw on Sanjivaka's broad and muscular withers in a gesture of geniality, Pingalaka greeted him, 'How are you? How did you happen to come to this dense forest that no man visits?'

Sanjivaka then related to Pingalaka the events that led up to his being abandoned by his owner on Yamuna's bank.

'Dear friend, Sanjivaka,' Pingalaka stated after hearing his tale, 'do not fear. Within the parameter of my mighty arms, you are safe. I will take care of you and protect you. Feel free to roam at will and enjoy your stay in this forest. But a note of caution: stay close to me, because this forest is dangerous. It is full of big, fierce carnivores and not the most congenial place for grass-eating beings like you.'

Sanjivaka profusely thanked Pingalaka, but the lion waved away his words of gratitude with a benevolence resulting from the confidence he had regained. Then he gathered his retinue around him and sauntered to the Yamuna to finally quench his thirst. On his return, he handed the responsibility of the kingdom to Damanaka and Karataka, intending to spend more time with his new friend, Sanjivaka.

The lion and bull became close friends. In fact, from their very first meeting, it appeared as though they had known each other for years.

> When true gentlemen meet each other,
> they naturally form an unbreakable bond.
> Thus it was with Pingalaka and Sanjivaka,
> they each benefitted from the alliance.

Sanjivaka was a wise bull, who had grown up listening to the shastras, and he began to mould the simple-minded Pingalaka into an astute and intelligent ruler. As a result, Pingalaka gave up violence and became more compassionate towards other creatures. Soon, Pingalaka and Sanjivaka built such a rapport that their friendship became exclusive, and they often sat in solitude, discussing matters close to their hearts. But, while the lion and bull formed their own little clique, the other animals and the king's ministers were left sitting at a distance, feeling rejected. Even Damanaka and Karataka couldn't enter that private circle. To add to everyone's consternation, Pingalaka also gave up hunting for prey; as a result, the other meat-eaters, including Damanaka and Karataka, who depended on him for their food, began to starve. Consequently, distraught with hunger pangs, many left Pingalaka to seek other providers. It is rightly said,

> Even a progressive and influential king
> will lose followers he cannot support,
> just as birds leave a dried and fruitless tree.

Also,

> Even the most honoured and devout retainers
> stay only as long as they receive regular wages.
> They can bear a king's ire
> not loss of their livelihood.

It is not just retainers in a king's service who stay for the promise of livelihood and money; this is, in reality, the nature of the world: ruled by the social laws of sama, dana, danda, bheda (persuasion, pay-off, punishment, and discord), everyone depends on one another, with each one looking out only for himself. There is, in fact, a pecking order of subsistence and dependence:

> The king on his subjects,
> the doctor on his patients,
> the businessman on his customers,
> the learned on the fool,
> thieves and robbers on the careless,
> alms-seekers on the householder,
> the prostitute on the libidinous,
> goldsmiths, carpenters, tailors on people.

Deprived of the lion's benefaction, Karataka and Damanaka discussed their plight. 'Dear friend, we have become secondary,' Damanaka said. 'No longer do we have any influence in the royal circle. Pingalaka is so devoted to Sanjivaka that he only listens to him now. As a result, he has forgotten his own enterprise of hunting and killing. All his followers have also left him in desperation. We are the only ones remaining. What do you think we should do?'

'Brother, I hear you.' Karataka replied. 'I think that even though the king doesn't speak with us or follow our advice, we should still try to talk to him and tell him about the situation. It is our responsibility as his ministers; otherwise, people will blame us for not doing our duty. It is said,

> The king may not follow his ministers' advice,
> but ministers should not stop advising him,
> or else they will be derelict in their duty.
> Just like Vidura kept advising Dhritarashtra
> even when the blind kind turned a deaf ear.

When a wealth-intoxicated king or a rut-maddened elephant go wayward, the ministers and the mahouts are the ones held responsible; their ineptitude is cited as cause. Besides, you are the one who introduced this grass-eating Sanjivaka to our king; you yourself have strewn embers in our path.'

'You're absolutely right,' Damanaka replied. 'It is my fault that I brought this grass-eater to our lion's attention. We can't blame Pingalaka for this. It is rightly said,

> A jackal caught in the battle of rams,
> a sanyasi caught in Ashadhabhuti's trap,
> a woman serving as emissary—
> all three were destroyed by their own actions.
> No one else was to blame.

'What is this story. Please tell me.' Karataka said, and Damanaka told him the tale.

THE TALE OF HOW THE SANYASI, JACKAL, AND EMISSARY CAUSED THEIR OWN SUFFERING

In a remote and beautiful place, there is a monastery. A sanyasi, called Devasharma, used to live there. He had a bundle of money that he had collected by selling the expensive clothing that the monastery received in charity. Ever since he acquired this money, he stopped trusting people and kept his bundle of cash clutched under his arm, day and night, never setting it down.

As they say,

> It is arduous to acquire money.
> It is even harder to protect it.
> To work for a livelihood is exhausting,
> and to spend money is also painful.
> Since having money means suffering,
> it is better that money be shunned.

One day, a thug, called Ashadhabhuti, saw Devasharma with his bundle of money and began to think about how he would rob it. He soon realized that he could only accomplish it if Devasharma put down his bundle, which he never did outside the monastery. And there seemed to be no way for Ashadhabhuti to gain entry into the monastery. Its walls were made of heavy stone; hence, it was impossible to bore a hole through them. They were also extremely high; therefore, scaling them was out of the question. Realizing that his only means of access to the money was through Devasharma himself, Ashadhabhuti came up with a plan to deceive him: he would meet Devasharma and convince him to make him his disciple, and, once he began to trust him, he would find some way to steal his bundle.

Someone has rightly said,

> He who lacks ambition cannot attain a high position.
> He who lacks desire cannot be fond of adornments.
> He who lacks wit cannot be a good orator.
> He who seeks rightfulness cannot be a thug.

Ashadhabhuti went to see Devasharma at the monastery, and, chanting the Shivaya mantra greeting, bowed to him by laying his head at his feet. 'O holy man,' he said with utmost humility and cordiality, 'this world is an illusion. Youth, too, passes swiftly, like a mountain river. Life is as fleeting as a fire burning hay. Material joys are as transient and scanty as the shadow of autumn clouds. Also, relationships with friends, sons, wife, servants, and others are like dreams that quickly end. I have understood this very well. Therefore, please advise me on what I should do to cross this worldly ocean.'

Very impressed with Ashadhabhuti's heartfelt thoughts about renunciation, Devasharma replied, 'Son, you are blessed for having such ascetic thoughts at such a young age. It is rightfully said,

> He who knows peace in his youth is truly at peace;
> for when the body becomes feeble with old age,
> who doesn't think about renunciation?
> The mind is the first to age, then the body.
> But for the lustful, the body ages; not the mind,
> forcing them to abjure sensual attachment
> because of the necessity of dulled senses.

You have asked my advice about a means to cross the worldly ocean. This is what I believe: initiated in the Shivaya mantra, wearing ashes and rudraksha, anyone, even a shudra, mlechchha, or chandala, can acquire the qualities of Shiva. And, if one is a brahmin, kshatriya, or any of the twice born, he only needs to offer a single flower with utmost faith on a Shivalinga to be liberated from the cycle of birth and rebirth.'

Ashadhabhuti then fell at Devasharma's feet in appeal. 'O holy one,' he said, 'please initiate me in the knowledge of Shiva and make me your disciple. I will be forever grateful.'

'Son, I will make you my initiate,' Devasharma replied. 'But you have to promise never to enter this monastery at night. The sadhus, renunciates, celibates, and ascetics who live here have vowed to remain aloof. You and I need to adhere to this rule. Wise people know,

> Associating with people destroys an ascetic,
> just like bad advice destroys a king,
> pampering destroys a son,
> lack of study destroys a brahmin,
> a bad son destroys a family,
> bad company destroys character,

> lack of trust destroys friendship,
> immoral behaviour destroys prosperity,
> a long-distance relationship destroys love,
> pride and beauty destroy a woman,
> carelessness destroys a harvest,
> wasteful spending destroys wealth.

So, my advice to you is to build a hut outside this monastery. After you have received the Shivaya mantra from me, we'll spend our days together, but, at night, you must stay in the hut.'

'Your words are my command,' Ashadhabhuti replied. 'Following your guided path will be my salvation. Therefore, I'm willing to do whatever you say.'

Receiving this promise, Devasharma taught Ashadhabhuti the Shivaya mantra and, anointing him according to the shastras, accepted him as his disciple. Ashadbabhuti also began to serve Devasharma like a true initiate, massaging his guru's feet, rubbing oil in his hair, and taking care of all his other needs. He was able to please his guru with his diligence, but the bundle of cash still remained under Devasharma's arm all day, depriving Ashadhabhuti of any opportunity to steal it.

After serving Devasharma for many months, when Ashadhabhuti still saw no possibility of bringing his plan to fruition, he got frustrated. 'Oh, this is impossible!' he said to himself. 'This man will never trust me. Not even for a moment does he part from his bundle. What should I do? Should I just kill him? I could stab him to death, or maybe I could poison him.'

As Ashadhabhuti was mulling over his next move, fate intervened: a son of one of Devasharma's former disciples arrived from out of town to deliver an invitation to him. His village was celebrating Shiva's grand festival, and they wanted him to come and perform the sanctification rituals to successfully conclude the festival. Devasharma happily accepted the invitation and set out on a journey to the village, accompanied by Ashadhabhuti, the master thug, who the poor ascetic thought was just a humble and virtuous disciple, and whom he had started to trust. Little did he know that he would soon be caught in the clever net that the man had been weaving for months.

When the sun set, Devasharma stopped near a river so that he could bathe and cleanse himself before he performed his evening puja. Just before he went into the forest to relieve himself, he tied up his bundle of money in a shawl and, handing it to Ashadhabhuti, said to him, 'Please guard this till I return. And be very careful. Shivji's sacred idol is wrapped in it.'

Ashadhabhuti received the bundle in his arms with his heart beating fast in excitement. He watched Devasharma walk away into the nearby forest and waited till the sanyasi was out of sight. Then he tore off the shawl and took off with the bundle of money.

In the meantime, as Devasharma squatted to do his business, he saw in the distance a flock of sheep, and among them, two rams fighting with each other, their horns locked in combat. Even as he watched, the rams disengaged, and, backing up a few steps, charged at each other again, butting heads. Then, they withdrew and charged again. In this way, repeatedly withdrawing and charging, their heads became so battered that blood began to pour down in rivulets. To his surprise, Devasharma then saw a jackal sneaking in through the flock and slinking up to the fighting rams to lick their dripping blood. What a foolish creature, Devasharma thought. Doesn't he realize that he can get caught in the middle of their fight? Enticed by the smell of blood, he is putting his life in danger. What an idiot. And, sure enough, as the rams charged at each other again, the jackal got smashed in the middle and died instantly. Saddened by this sight, Devasharma suddenly felt an unease about his money. Quickly finishing up, he ran to the spot where he had left Ashadhabhuti. But, of course, that thug was nowhere in sight, but the shawl in which Devasharma had wrapped his bundle was lying on the ground in a pile. Hurriedly washing his hands and mouth, Devasharma grabbed the shawl, hoping it still had the money, but, as he feared, there was nothing in it. Devastated, Devasharma fell on the ground in a faint, and when he regained his senses, he began to wail, 'Oh Ashadhabhuti, you thief, where have you have gone with my money? What am I to do now? Where do I look for you?'

Eventually, after he was able to gain some control over himself, Devasharma quietened down and got up to see if he could trace Ashadhabhuti's footprints, and, finding a faint trail, he began to walk in that direction. When evening descended, Devasharma found himself in a village. Just as he was about to cross a street, he saw a weaver leaving his house with his wife. They were talking about going to a liquor shop in a nearby town. Approaching him, Devasharma said, 'My good man, I have just arrived in this village, and I don't know anyone. I am a brahmin, and I am presenting myself to you as your guest. Please take care of me and avail yourself of this opportunity to gain some merit. The wise say,

> A guest who arrives at your doorstep at sunset
> is called a guest of the setting sun.

> Those who provide food and lodging to him
> make a path for themselves to heaven.

Also

> Whether one has food to share or not,
> but a mat to sleep on,
> a clean floor to rest on,
> water to wash and to drink,
> sweet welcoming words—
> these four are a must in civilized homes.
>
> With these four one should honour a guest.
> Agni is pleased by words of welcome to a guest.
> Indra is pleased by the mat he is offered for rest.
> Ancestors are pleased by the washing of his feet.
> Shiva is pleased by the honeyed water he gets to drink.

Hearing these words of virtuous behaviour, the weaver said to his wife, 'Take this guest and go home. Wash his feet, prepare him a meal, give him a mat to sleep on, and take care of him. I'll bring you plenty of liquor from town when I return.'

The weaver's wife, who was an adulteress, joyfully returned to her house with Devasharma.

People say,

> When the day is overcast with clouds, fog, rain, or snow,
> when the streets of a town are dark and deserted,
> when a husband is out of town, an adulteress is content.
>
> Beautiful bed with soft mattresses and silken sheets,
> handsome, well-built, and virile husband,
> palatial home with elaborate bedrooms—
> these hold no more value than a blade of grass
> for a woman addicted to clandestine excitements.
>
> Such a woman will accept everything—
> family's downfall, public censure, punishment,
> but she will not even consider mending her ways.

Bringing Devasharma to her house, the weaver's wife hurriedly gave him a broken, bare cot to sleep on, and saying to him, 'I'm going out to meet a friend and will return shortly,' she began to beautify herself. Then she left the house to go and meet her lover. However, just as she stepped outside, she saw her husband coming up the street, stumbling and staggering on his feet. His hair was open and wild, his clothes were dishevelled, and he was mumbling and cursing, while taking swigs from a bottle of liquor. Rushing back into the house, the woman quickly removed her adornments.

But the weaver had seen his wife all dolled up, and he had also witnessed her hasty return to the house. He had already heard rumours about her adultery; therefore, her behaviour that evening convinced him that what people said about her was true. Barging into the house, he shouted, 'You sinful woman! You slut! Tell me where you were going all dressed up?'

'What are you talking about? I didn't go anywhere. I've been sitting here since you sent me home. You're making baseless accusations because you're drunk. Someone has rightly said,

> Feeling restless, falling, stumbling, talking nonsense—
> all these are symptoms of delirium caused by liquor.

Also,

> Heading west at sunset,
> shedding clothes unbeknown,
> losing energy and strength,
> being flushed in the face—
> all are symptoms of drunkenness.

There's no doubt you're drunk. No wonder you're acting this way.'

'You whore!' the weaver shouted. 'Don't you dare try to shift the blame onto me. For months, I've been hearing people talk about your debauchery, and today I've seen it for myself.' Then he picked up a stick and began beating his wife. When she could barely stand, he dragged her to a pole and tied her to it as tightly as he could. Finally, exhausted, and still in a drunken state, he lay down nearby and fell asleep.

While all this was going on, a friend of the weaver's wife, who was the wife of the village barber, slipped into the house. She waited for the weaver to fall asleep and then came to her friend and whispered to her, 'That man whom you were going to meet tonight has been waiting for you at the assigned spot. Come with me quickly. I'll take you there.'

'Friend,' the weaver's wife replied, 'You can see what condition I'm in. I'm in no shape to go to him. Please go and tell him that we can't meet tonight.'

'He'll be so disappointed. How can you do this to him? You must have heard people say,

> The sweetest fruit grows in rugged and inaccessible terrain.
> One must be like a camel that thrusts its head through thorns
> to get to the succulents, even though other plants are close by.
> A wanton woman seeks men, though she may have a husband at home.
> This is the tenet of wantonness.

And also this:

> Who knows the hereafter?
> Gossip is full of truths and lies.
> What use is worrying about either.
> Take pleasure in your beloved,
> and gain praise for your pluck.

I can also tell you this:

> A lover whom she can meet in private,
> though he be ugly and unseemly,
> is preferred to a handsome man at home.
> Such is the fate of a wanton woman.'

'I hear you, but tied up with these ropes and my horrible, sinful husband sleeping right here—tell me, how can I go?'

'Your sinful husband is dead drunk and fast asleep. He'll probably open his eyes only when the sun's rays hit him in the morning. As for the ropes that bind you—I'll untie those. Once you're free, tie me up in your stead, in case your husband awakens in the middle of the night. Go and meet your beloved Devadatta, and when you return, we'll switch places again.'

Thus, the barber's wife freed the weaver's wife and took her place tied up to the pole, while her friend went to meet her lover.

A few hours later, the weaver, recovering slightly from his drunkenness, did, indeed, wake up. By this time, his anger, too, had abated a little. Peering in the dark at the bound woman, he took her to be his wife and muttered, 'O, cruel woman, if you promise never to leave the house, never to quarrel with me, and never to bombard me with your harsh words, I'll release you.'

The barber's wife heard him, but she couldn't respond, afraid that her voice would give her friend away. The weaver repeatedly asked her, and when he received no answer, he thought his wife was stubbornly ignoring him, which made him even more incensed. Getting up, he pulled out a dagger and cut off her nose. 'You whore!' he spat. 'Stay tied to the pole. I won't make any more concessions for you.' Then, lying down, he drifted off to sleep again.

Caught in the middle of all this, Devasharma, worried about his lost wealth, suffering intense pangs of hunger, and watching the character of wantonness play out before his eyes, didn't sleep a wink all night.

Many hours later, the weaver's wife, having visited with her lover, returned home and tiptoed to her bound friend. 'Is everything all right?' she whispered. 'I hope my sinful husband didn't awaken in the night.'

'All is fine,' the barber's wife replied. 'Except my nose, which he cut off. But whatever had to happen, has happened. Now quickly release me so that I can go back to my own house before your husband wakes up again.'

The weaver's wife quickly untied her friend and took her place against the pole.

Sometime after the barber's wife had left, the weaver awakened again and admonished his wife, 'You cheating whore, will you still remain silent? Are you waiting for more punishment? Shall I now cut off your ears, as well?'

'Shame on you, you fool,' his wife shouted back. 'I am a chaste woman. No one has the power to hurt me or cut off my nose and ears. I declare to the guardians of the world: O you Surya and Chandra, Vayu and Agni, Space, Earth, Water, Yamaraja, Day and Night, the two twilights of the day, and Dharma—all you just gods. If I am pure and chaste, if I have never ever sought another man, then restore my nose and make it as it was before. But if, even mistakenly, I have allowed a thought about another man to enter my mind, then burn me to ashes this instant.'

After that, she triumphantly stated to her husband, 'You cruel man. You sinner. Look! With the power of my merit my nose has grown back.'

The weaver lit a torch and brought it close to his wife's face. He was stunned to see that her nose was, indeed, exactly as it used to be, while on the floor was still a puddle of blood. Quickly untying his wife, he helped her to his bed, and, cajoling her with flattery and pleas of forgiveness, he was finally able to bring a smile to her face.

Watching all this, Devasharma was in disbelief. He concluded,

> Shambrasura, Namucchi, Bali, Kummini—
> all asuras are renowned for their maya.
> But in women maya is innate and a trap.
> A happy man happily gets entrapped,

a sad man sadly gets entrapped.
Ones they hate or one who abuses them
they also entrap with sweet words.
The maya of women is inescapable.

Also,

Shukracharya and Brihaspati
both know shastras as none other.
But compared to a woman, their intelligence
is perhaps, less, or equal, but certainly no more.
When such acute cleverness is at play
who can save men and how?

Women change untruth to truth, and truth to untruth so rapidly that even valorous men of patience are left flailing. Other learned men of policy have also warned men against women thus:

Never show them extreme love,
never increase contact with them,
never allow them too much power.
Like a crow toys with a parrot with shorn wings,
a woman toys with a man who is in love with her.

Sweet words flow from their tender lips,
striking with the honed sword of their heart.
Sweet nectar of amrita drips from their speech,
while horrific poison of Halahala burns in their heart.

Like bees desiring honey keep hovering over lotuses,
men caught by the taste of women's lips, stay in hot pursuit.
O men, in joining with a woman, drink the nectar of her lips,
but beat your fists on her chest for the poison in her heart.

A whirlpool of suspicion,
an abode of rebellion,
a city of audacity,
a treasure chest of faults,
a palace of a thousand treacheries,
a box of trickeries,
poison topped with amrita,
untameable by the best of men,

this device called woman was created
to destroy all dharma in the world.

Cruel breasts, capricious eyes,
lips uttering sweet, pretentious words,
entrapping tresses full of curls,
gentle gait, plump buttocks, weak of heart—
It is in their nature to deceive;
be it their own husbands.

They whose intrinsic quality is replete with such faults, though they may be doe-eyed and beautiful, are they worthy of man's love? Can they truly love someone? No! Never! Sometimes they laugh and sometimes weep, all to gain a man's trust, just to serve their own purpose. That is why, for his own well-being, a man of good character and noble birth should avoid women like he would the untouchable urns that hang from peepul trees in cremation grounds.

Tousled hair around the face like a lion's mane.
But, beware! each strand is a rivulet of intoxication.
Great men of high foreheads and intelligence
and heroes full of courage and valour—
all become prime cowards before women.

Till the time women do not have a man thoroughly enraptured, they flatter him and entertain him to his heart's content. But, as soon they see a man bound by desire for them, they reel him in like a fish caught on a bait hook, and, bringing him out of water, they fling him to the ground. Capricious by nature, like ocean waves, their love is transient, like wandering thin clouds of the evening sky. These women enter the simple hearts of men and intoxicate them. They ill-treat him, chastise him, and scream at him. Sometimes, they even please him; at other times, they make him weep; but oftentimes, it is their peevishness that men have to suffer. What else can be said about women. They put men through all kinds of hell; these femmes fatales are capable of anything.

Poisonous on the inside,
loving and pleasing on the outside;
like the scarlet ratti pea that looks pretty
but is deadly poisonous to eat.

Thinking these thoughts, Devasharma spent a difficult night.

Another person who had a stressful night was the barber's wife. She spent the night worrying about what she would do when her own husband returned. He had been away for a few days at the king's palace and was scheduled to return any time. She wondered how she would explain her slashed nose to him?

The barber arrived at his house early in the morning and began banging at the door. 'Dear woman, hurry and open the door,' he called. 'And bring me my barber's kit so that I can go to work.'

Afraid to show him her face, the barber's wife cracked open the door and threw out one of his razors.

Seeing just the one razor, the barber became angry and threw it back through the opening. 'I asked you for the whole chest of razors and instruments. What am I going to do with just this one razor? How many men can I shave with just this one? You know what I need. Bring it to me quickly.'

Suddenly the door swung open, and the barber's wife came out, screaming and wailing loudly so as to be heard by the neighbours: 'Look what this cruel, sinful barber has done to me—his faultless, virtuous wife. He has cut off my nose for no reason at all. Help me. Please help me. He's going to kill me. Save me, please.'

Hearing her, the neighbours quickly called the police, who arrived and beat up the barber. Then, they tied him tightly with thick ropes and took both him and his wife to court. 'Sir,' they announced to the judge, 'this barber has cut off his wife's nose for no reason. She is a beautiful, virtuous wife. Look what this man has done to her.'

'Why have you disfigured your beautiful, faultless wife's face?' the judge asked the barber. 'Has she committed adultery? Has she robbed anyone? Speak up. What crime has she committed to deserve such punishment?'

But the barber was in so much pain from the beating that he could not reply.

Taking his silence as his admittance of guilt, the judge came to the decision that the barber was guilty of ruining his wife's beautiful face without reason. 'It is clear from this man's demeanour that he is guilty,' he announced,

> 'His speech has changed,
> his face colour comes and goes,
> fear is shifting in his eyes,
> his intelligence is dimmed,
> and he has become bewildered.

When a person who has committed a crime comes before a judge, these signs give him away:

> Trembling legs, stumbling and staggering,
> with a pale face and garbled speech,
> a sweaty forehead he needs to mop,
> trepidation writ large on his face,
> and eyes that don't dare to look up.

An able and clever judge can recognize a criminal just by looking at him. On the other hand,

> An innocent man stands in court unafraid.
> Speaking clearly without hesitation,
> his eyes are focused and indignant.
> When questioned, he responds quickly
> and with courage and patience.

These are signs of a guiltless man. This barber, on the other hand, is nervous and unable to speak. It is clear that he has, indeed, committed a grave crime by cutting off his wife's nose and making her suffer. I declare that he be executed.' Announcing his verdict, the judge commanded the guards to take him away.

Devasharma had followed the barber and his wife to court. Watching the injustice of the trial, and hearing the underserved verdict, he was pained. Rushing to the judge, he appealed, 'This poor barber is being wrongfully executed. He's innocent. This is a grave injustice. He's a good man and completely without blame. Please listen to what I have to say.'

'Go ahead,' the judge gave him permission.

'By being caught in the middle of a combat of rams, the jackal was killed. I, too, was ruined by believing in that trickster, Ashadhabhuti. And this woman, the barber's wife, was hurt by doing her friend a favour. All three of us are to blame for our own suffering. No one else is at fault.'

Hearing these words from the ascetic, the judge, who was an adherent of justice, told the guards to wait. 'What are you saying?' he asked Devasharma. 'How did all this come about? Please tell me in detail.'

Devasharma then told him everything that happened to the jackal and to the barber's wife. Everyone in court was shocked at Devasharma's revealing account, and the judge ordered the guards to release the barber. He also declared, 'Brahmins, children, women, and sanyasis cannot be executed. This is the law. However, when they deserve punishment, they can be physically tortured. Hence, here is my final verdict: this woman, who tried to falsely implicate her husband, will have her ears cut off.'

Thus, it was that the barber's wife, already missing a nose, also lost her ears—all because she came in the middle of the conflict between a wanton woman and her husband.

Having witnessed these spectacles of life, Devasharma returned to his monastery, feeling sad about his money but the wiser for it.

'So, you see, my dear Karataka,' said Damanaka, 'how the jackal, the barber's wife, and the sanyasi were ruined because they came in the middle of someone's else conflict?'

'Then what do you suggest we do? Now that we have created this calamity for ourselves by putting ourselves in this situation with Sanjivaka and Pingalaka, what can we do to save ourselves?'

'Believe me,' Damanaka said, 'this disastrous situation will trigger a burst of inspiration in my clever mind, and I'll find a way to separate Sanjivaka and Pingalaka. Surely you must have heard,

> An arrow shot by a marksman can kill only one,
> and if it misses its mark, kill no one.
> But an intelligent man's shrewdness
> can destroy a king and his whole kingdom.

Watch me. I'll weave such a web of deception that I'll make Pingalaka and Sanjivaka turn against each other.'

'If Pingalaka finds out about your devious plan, or even if Sanjivaka learns about it, we both will be destroyed.'

'Don't doubt me, friend. Even when facing the gravest calamities, or fate's reversal, a master strategist never fails to use his brain. And if intelligence by itself fails to produce a desired result, one must be persistent till the end, because combined with either destiny's design or divine plan, intelligence can bring about desired outcomes. Take the example of the ghunakshara policy. The ghun or woodworm etches a word-like shape in the way that it eats the wood. This doesn't happen by design; it just happens naturally. In the same way, a simple plan can, by chance, succeed. That is why people say,

> Never lose patience.
> Tribulations pass,
> situations improve.
> Patience yields results.

Think about sea traders whose merchant ships are sometimes destroyed by storms. Yet, they attempt to cross the ocean by reconstructing a vessel using scraps of wood from the wrecked ship. Also remember,

> Wealth is obtained with constant effort.
> Only cowards and sluggards
> believe that fate brings fortune
> and that fate is supreme.

Hence, stop using fate as a crutch and work as hard as you can. And if, after all your hard work, you don't succeed, then you are not to blame.

> Even the gods come to the aid of those
> who are industrious and determined;
> just as Vishnu, Garuda, and Chakra
> all helped the weaver in his battle.

Besides, I am a craftsman and a strategist. With my keen intelligence, I'll weave such a net that both Pingalaka and Sanjivaka will not know what ensnared them. It is said,

> Well-crafted fabrications
> can dupe even Brahma.
> What chance do men stand?
> Hence, the weaver disguised as Vishnu
> enjoyed marital bliss with the princess.'

'What is this story?' Karataka asked, and Damanaka told him the tale.

THE TALE OF THE WEAVER WHO BECAME VISHNU TO WIN THE PRINCESS

In a town, a weaver and a carpenter were childhood best friends. When they were children, they played together and roamed wherever they pleased, and when they grew up, they still spent all their time together, gallivanting around and enjoying themselves.

Once, to celebrate some god, the town organized a big carnival. Hundreds of people, from the town and from out of town, came to attend it and enjoy performances by actors, dancers, and entertainers. The two friends also went to the carnival, and, as they were leisurely walking around, they spotted the most beautiful woman they had ever seen. She was a princess replete with all possible feminine endowments. She was riding a she-elephant and was accompanied by an entourage of soldiers and macebearers.

The weaver took one look at the princess he was struck with sharp arrows of love and desire. Then, like a person suffering from poison or possession by an evil spirit, he fainted.

Finding his friend in a dead faint on the ground, his friend, the carpenter, was very distressed, and with the help of some kind-hearted people, he brought the weaver to his house. There, by putting cold compresses on his forehead, while ojhas chanted mantras and waved whisks around him, he was finally able to revive his friend. As soon as the weaver opened his eyes, the carpenter asked him: 'Dear friend, how did you end up unconscious on the ground? Can you tell me what happened to you?'

'If you insist, I'll share with you the secret suffering that is torturing my heart. But, if you consider yourself my friend and well-wisher, start gathering wood to prepare a pyre for me so that I can end my life. And, dear friend, in all the years of our friendship, if I have inadvertently made you feel anything other than love and affection, please forgive me.'

His friend's words brought tears to the the carpenter's eyes. Swallowing the lump in his throat, he asked again, 'Dear friend, at least tell me the reason for your sorrow. I'm sure, we can find a remedy for it. It is said,

> Medicine, money, mantra and tantra, and sharp intelligence—
> No task in this world is impossible with the help of these four.

If your ailment is curable with the aid of these, I'll do everything in my power to help you.'

'Dearest friend,' said the weaver, 'none of these four remedies, or any thousands of others, can cure my affliction. The only thing you can do is quickly prepare for my immolation by gathering wood for my pyre.'

'Your affliction may be uncurable, and there may not be anything in the world that can help you, but at least tell me what ails you so that I can also understand why it is uncurable. Then, I, too, will climb into the pyre with you and give up my life, because I can't bear to live without you.'

The weaver then told his friend what ailed him. 'Remember the princess riding on the she-elephant we saw at the carnival? I took one look at her and Kamadeva assailed me with his torturous arrows. I can't bear this agony of desire any more. I can only wish what one poet has aptly said:

> When will I, just for a moment,
> ensconced in the embrace of her arms,
> lay my breast against her bosom,
> fragrant with sandal paste and swollen
> like the forehead of an intoxicated elephant.

Also,

> When I think of
> her lower lip as red as bimba flowers,
> her breasts rising in the pride of youth,
> her deep navel and slim waist,
> her hair whose nature it is to curl,
> I feel tortured and distraught because
> these are all devious and prideful; not she.
> Her true character is innocent, soft, and pure.
> It is my own torturous desire that degrades her.'

The carpenter burst into laughter at the weaver's words. 'Friend,' he said, 'if this is the only reason for your suffering, then I'm glad, because our object is clear and achievable. I promise you that today itself you will be able to enjoy a union with her.'

'How is this possible?' The weaver sat up in disbelief. 'In a palace where nothing except air can enter, where security is as thick as walls, how can I meet her, let alone engage in sexual union with her? Why are you trying to delude me with these lies?'

'Just watch the power of my talents and intelligence, and stop worrying,' replied the carpenter. Then he got to work. Using the tools of his trade, he quickly crafted a mechanical flying Garuda bird of strong varuna wood, along with a conch shell, chakra, mace, lotus, four arms, diadem, Kaustubha gem—all of Lord Vishnu's attributes that are visible on his physical form. When he was done, he helped the weaver put on a dhoti and pitamber, like Vishnu's, and, seating him on the wooden Garuda's back, he arranged the four arms and other objects on his person. Then, giving him the key to operate the Garuda vehicle, he advised him, 'Fly to the princess's palace tonight.' 'And make sure that you land directly on the veranda of the seventh floor, that houses the princess's rooms. That way you will evade all security guards. Also make sure that she sees you with these accessories of Vishnu. Get close to her and entice her with all sorts of sweet talk, and then, following the custom of Vatsyayana's *Kamasutra*, enjoy your union with her.'

Bursting with nervous excitement, the weaver flew to the princess's palace that night, dressed as Vishnu. Just as his friend had advised, he entered her bedroom through the seventh-floor veranda and approached her as she slept. 'Dear princess,' he whispered in her ear, 'are you asleep, or are you awake? Look! Leaving Lakshmi in Kshirasagara, I have come to you, captivated by your love. Come, get up and embrace me.'

The princess woke up to see Lord Vishnu, mounted on his Garuda, resplendent with four arms and diadem, chakra, and Kaustubha gem, standing beside her. Jumping out of bed in amazement, she bowed deeply with folded hands. 'O Deva, you are lord, and I am a mere mortal, as insignificant as a moth. I am impure, and you are the purest in all three worlds. You are venerated by Indra and all the gods. How can I consider myself worthy of your love? You say you have left Lakshmiji to come to me. I am nothing in comparison to Lakshmiji. How can I even think of a union with you?'

'O fortunate one,' the weaver replied, 'what you say is true, but when I was in my Krishna avatar, you were Radha, my first wife. This is your rebirth. That is why I have left Lakshmi and come to you.'

'If this is so, then lord, please ask my father for my hand in marriage. Knowing who you are, he will not refuse.'

'Dear, fortunate one, I keep myself invisible to humans; talking to them is out of the question and asking a human for something—that is unthinkable. Therefore, if you want me to be your husband, you'll have to offer yourself to me in a gandharva marriage. If you refuse to do this, it'll make me very angry. And who knows what will be the consequence of my anger? I may curse you and also burn your father and your whole family to ashes.'

'I'll do whatever you say, lord,' the princess said in a trembling voice.

Dismounting from his Garuda, the weaver took the princess's hand and drew her to him, even as she held herself back in apprehension and modesty. Then, embracing her, he lay down with her on her bed. All through the night, the weaver fulfilled his heart's desire and stopped only when the sun began to rise. Then, kissing his princess, and promising to return at night, he quietly left the palace on his Garuda. In this way, the weaver began to visit the princess every night, and, at dawn, before her attendants awoke, he flew home.

These clandestine meetings continued until that day when the attendants noticed love bites on the princess's neck and breasts. Shocked, they discussed the matter with the security guards: 'Surely the princess has been meeting a man at night,' they exclaimed. 'But how is it possible for any man to enter this secure palace. Haven't you been guarding the gates day and night?'

Ultimately, the attendants and guards decided that the king should be informed. 'Maharaj,' they all said to the king, 'we guard the princess's palace with utmost diligence. Yet, it appears that a man has been visiting the princess. But we have never seen him. We don't know who he is, how he comes in, and how he leaves. Please command us. What should we do?'

The king was dismayed to learn about his daughter's liaison, and his thoughts turned to the woes of parenthood.

> A daughter's birth comes with worry.
> As she grows, fathers worry
> whom to pick for her husband.
> When she marries, fathers worry,
> is she happy or unhappy
> in her husband's house?
>
> Women and rivers are alike—
> rivers have shores
> and women their families
> of birth and of marriage.
> Rivers with their force
> cut and deplete shores.
> Women with their misconduct
> tarnish the good name of families.

Moreover,

> A daughter brings her mother sorrow
> just by being born. As she grows older
> the suffering of her parents increases.
> When she is married to her husband,
> parents fear she will bring disgrace.
> And after she has been married
> parents worry if she is unhappy.
> Hence, this peril called daughter is unending.

Plagued with these thoughts, the king went to discuss the situation with his queen: 'Go and find out what is going on,' he said to her. 'What these attendants and security guards are saying is unbelievable. Who is this man? Look at his courage—taunting Yamaraja and inviting death?'

The queen, too, was equally shocked to hear about her daughter's clandestine lover, and she hurried to the princess's palace to find out the truth. When she saw for herself the brazen display of love bites and nail scratches on her daughter's neck and breasts, she was livid. 'Sinful girl!' she screamed. 'Besmircher of the family's repute! Why have you abandoned your modesty and virtue in this way? Who is this man that comes to meet you? Who is it that has called the wrath of Yamaraja on himself? Tell me the truth right now!'

Hearing her mother's reproach and seeing her angry visage, the princess cowered in fear, and, lowering her face in shame, she replied, 'Dear mother, don't be angry with me. I didn't give up my virtue to an ordinary man. Lord Vishnu himself comes to me every night on his Garuda. He has accepted me in gandharva marriage.'

'What?' the queen said in disbelief. 'How can that be? Are you lying to me, girl?'

'No, mother. I'm telling you the truth. It is Lord Vishnu. If you don't believe me then come here at night and see him with your own eyes, resplendent in his dhoti and pitamber; his luminous face and four hands; his lotus and chakra and Kaustubha gem.'

Believing the earnestness in her daughter's eyes, extreme joy coursed through the queen's body, and she rushed to her husband. 'Congratulations, Maharaj!' she called to him. 'The lord, Shri Vishnu himself, comes to meet your daughter every night. In fact, he is her husband. He celebrated a gandharva marriage with her.'

The king, too, was in disbelief at first, but when his queen told him everything that the princess had said, he began to believe it. 'Tonight, you and I will hide somewhere near our daughter's room and witness the Lord's glorious form with our own two eyes,' the queen said. 'Imagine what it will be like to behold a form that no ordinary man can see.'

After that, the king and queen spent all day in a heightened sense of excitement, impatiently watching each hour pass like a hundred years. As soon as night fell, they rushed to their daughter's palace and, hiding themselves in an alcove near her veranda, began to watch the sky. Soon, they saw Lord Shri Vishnu on his Garuda descending on the veranda. And, just as their daughter had described, he was resplendent in his diadem and Kaustubha gem and was holding the conch shell, chakra, mace, and lotus in his four hands.

The king was so gratified and he felt such a sense of exaltation, it was like he had taken a dip in an ocean of amrita. Filled with elation, he said to his queen, 'There cannot be any one in the world as fortunate as you and I. Lord Vishnu himself has accepted our daughter. It feels like all our desires have been fulfilled. Now, with the influence of my son-in-law, who is the Lord himself, I will subjugate the whole earth.'

The very next day, the king severed all his alliances with the neighbouring kingdoms and issued a declaration of war. Subsequent to his act of defiance, those rulers formed a union and mounted an attack on his kingdom.

When the first battle started, the king sent his queen with a message to the princess: 'Dear child, how can the neighbouring rulers dare to fight me when I have a daughter like you and a son-in-law like Shri Narayan? Please talk to your husband about this and tell him to destroy my enemies.'

That very night the princess appealed to the weaver Vishnu, 'Oh Lord, it is not right that despite having you as a son-in-law, my father should suffer defeat by the neighbouring rulers. I beg you to destroy all my father's enemies.'

'O dear one, your father's handful of enemies are nothing,' the weaver replied in a cavalier fashion. 'I can cut all of them to smithereens with my chakra, just in a blink of an eye.'

However, other than uttering such boasts, there was nothing he could do. In the meantime, the enemy rulers kept advancing, and in no time, they had control of the kingdom. All that remained was the king's fort, where the king and queen and the people of the kingdom had taken shelter, But the king remained hopeful. Every night, he sent his son-in-law expensive gifts of camphor, saffron, fragrant incense, and perfumes; clothes of brocade and silks; garlands of exotic flowers; delicacies made of milk and butter, and the best liquor. And, every day, he told his daughter to beg Lord Vishnu for help. Then, one night, the message he sent was of extreme urgency: 'O Lord, it appears that tomorrow morning, our last refuge, this fort, will also be stormed by the enemy. We are out of provisions, and we have lost most of our soldiers. Those that remain are badly wounded and in no shape to put up any sort of defence. We're losing hope, and this may be the very last night before we fall. If you don't help us now, we will be lost.'

When the weaver arrived that night and heard the king's message, he thought, if the fort falls, I, too, will lose my princess. How will I live without her? I must do something. But what? Perhaps, if I show myself to the enemy, dressed the way I am, they'll think I am the real Vishnu, just as the princess thought. And, when they see that I, the Lord Vishnu, am supporting the king, perhaps they'll lose confidence and flee from the battlefield. Then the remaining soldiers of the king will be able to rout them and destroy them. After all, it is said,

> A cobra who has lost his venom
> should still flare his hood and hiss.
> Who will know the truth?
> Just the flared hood of a cobra
> is enough to instil in people
> fear that will make them flee.

Following that, another thought struck him: what if someone decides to shoot at me and I die? But then he reasoned with himself, so what if I die? It is said,

> Whoever sacrifices his life protecting
> cows, brahmins, king, master, wife, and home
> receives the highest honour in the afterlife.

Also,

> In the dark night of the new moon,
> the moon takes refuge in the sun's orbit.
> When Rahu threatens to consume it,
> Surya fights Rahu to protect the moon.

It is praiseworthy when someone who is powerful protects someone who is seeking sanctuary. Disguised as Vishnu, I have the power to protect these people; therefore, it is right that I should do everything I can to protect them.

With these thoughts playing in his mind, the weaver completed his toilette and, resolutely going to the princess, told her, 'Dear one, I vow that today I will not have a morsel to eat until all your father's enemies have been destroyed. Go to your father and tell him to gather as much of a force as he can and mount an attack on the enemy outside the city limits. Tell him to battle fearlessly, because sitting on my Garuda in the sky, I will render the enemy powerless, and he will have no trouble destroying them. You see, I, myself, can't kill these men, because death at my hands means an afterlife in my realm of Vaikuntha, and none of these men are worthy of that. In fact, tell your father that when they begin to flee, strike them from behind so that they will die a cowardly death and not reach heaven at all.'

The princess rushed to her father and repeated what the weaver had said. Believing the words to be Vishnu's, the king enthusiastically started preparing for battle. Gathering his remaining soldiers, he marched out of the city at the crack of dawn, feeling confident of victory. The weaver, too, donned in Vishnu's paraphernalia, mounted his Garuda, and flew up into the sky, but unlike the king's, his heart was pounding in his ears with fear, although he was prepared to accept death, if it came to that.

In the meantime, the real Vishnu, the knower of everything in all pasts, presents and futures, sat in his Vaikuntha, watching the earthly drama unfold. When he saw the weaver rise into the sky, he summoned Garuda in his mind, and when that heavenly bird became present, he said to him with an amused smile: 'Do you know, dear Garuda, that a weaver, impersonating me, riding a wooden Garuda operated by machinery, has been visiting a princess in her palace every night?'

'Yes, Lord,' Garuda replied. 'I know everything about this weaver and his activities. Please advise me, what should be done about him?'

'Well, it appears that this weaver is prepared to die. He has sworn that he will break his fast only after he has destroyed the king's enemies. In fact, he has just left for battle. This is what concerns me—what if some marksman in the enemy force shoots an arrow at him and kills him? Then he and his Garuda will come crashing down. Can you imagine what people will say when they see this Vishnu-looking weaver die at the hands of a mortal man? They will say that if Vishnu and his Garuda can so easily be killed by brave kshatriya soldiers, what divine power do they have? After that no one on earth will worship us. And, anyway, since you and I will be considered dead, why would they offer us any worship? So, you see, Garuda, this does not bode well for us; that is why, we must do something to salvage this situation.

Why don't you go and enter that wooden mechanical Garuda? I will have my chakra, too, enter the weaver's fake chakra, and I, myself, will infuse some of my power into the body of the weaver. This way, the weaver will be able to destroy the king's enemies, and people will think we have brought about the destruction. That will also increase our glory among mortals.'

'It will be as you command, Lord,' Garuda said and infused a portion of himself in the weaver's mechanical Garuda. Vishnu's chakra, too, permeated the wooden chakra, and Lord Vishnu himself imbued the weaver with a little bit of his power. Thus, the weaver, stationed directly above the battling forces, wielding his chakra and bow and arrow and, riding his mechanical Garuda, was able to render the foe powerless in an instant. Then the king's men surrounded the befuddled enemy soldiers and made short work of defeating them. Soon, word spread across the land that this king was able to destroy his enemies in a matter of moments, because helping him was his son-in-law, who was no other than Shri Vishnu himself.

Hence, when the incredulous but relieved weaver brought his Garuda to the ground, and alighted, his father-in-law's minister and subjects all gathered around him, vying with each other to get a close-up look of the Great Vishnu. However, as soon as they drew close to him, they saw that this Vishnu looked very much like the weaver who lived in their city. 'What is this farce?' they all exclaimed, confronting him.

The weaver then related the whole tale from beginning to end—how he fell in love with the princess at the carnival, how he visited her every night dressed as Vishnu, and how, determined to die for her and her father, he decided to delude the enemy into thinking he was, indeed, Vishnu so that they would flee the field in fear.

The weaver's deception irked the king, but he was also impressed at his courage. Moreover, since it was the weaver's audaciousness that had brought him victory over his enemies and gained him respect and fame in the whole world, he forgave him and accepted him as his son-in law. The princess's wedding to the weaver was celebrated with great festivities, and the king gave his daughter part of his kingdom as dowry. Thus, living with his beloved princess, enjoying all kinds of sensual and material pleasures, the weaver began to live his days in happiness.

'So, you see,' Damanaka said to Karataka. 'As I explained to you, a well-thought-out strategy evades even Brahma's detection.'

'I hear what you are saying,' Karataka replied. 'But I'm still afraid, because

Sanjivaka, the bull, is very smart, and I fear that he will see through your scheming. And you know our lion, Pingalaka. He is aggressive and vengeful. If he discovers your plot, we'll be dead instantly. I admit that you have a brilliant mind, but I still don't think you'll be able to separate Pingalaka and Sanjivaka.'

'Even though it appears that I, myself, don't have the ability to make this scheme work, I can assure you that the means I employ will ensure its success,' Damanaka replied. 'People say,

> When skill does not work
> a clever ploy may.
> The crow killed the snake,
> And all it took was a golden chain.'

'How does that story go?' Karataka asked, and Damanaka told him the tale.

THE TALE OF THE CROW'S SCHEME TO KILL THE WICKED SNAKE

In some forest was a great big bargad tree. A crow and his wife lived in it. They had a happy marriage, but there was relentless sorrow in their lives. In that tree also lived a wicked black snake. Every time the she-crow laid eggs, he would emerge from his hole, slither up to the birds' nest, and eat their eggs.

The crow couple lived in constant fear and grief. They tried to think of ways to stop the snake, but no matter how much they wracked their brains, they couldn't come up with a sure-fire solution. Finally, desperate to save their babies, they decided to get advice from their friend, the fox, who lived in a burrow near the roots of another tree.

'Dear friend,' they called to the fox, alighting on the branches of his tree, 'we need your advice.'

'How can I help?' the fox said, emerging from his burrow.

'There is an evil-minded, wicked black snake who lives in the hole in our tree,' the male crow explained. 'Every time my wife lays eggs, he comes up to the nest and gobbles them up. What should we do? How can we rid ourselves of this constant threat? It is truly said,

> The farmer whose land is on a riverbank,
> the husband whose wife has a lover,
> the householder whose home is invaded by a snake—
> how can anyone in such plights live in peace?

Besides, living in a house with a snake is, in itself, like courting death all the time. When a snake is discovered near any village, that whole village is deemed dangerous. You can just imagine the condition in which my wife and I are living; not only are we constantly fearful for our own lives, but we also dread the birth of any children because of the certain death that looms over them.'

'My sympathies, dear friend,' the fox said. 'But try not to worry. I promise I'll think of some solution. It's clear that this greedy, evil-minded black snake is not someone we can get rid of with conventional means. What we will have to do is come up with some astute scheme. As people say,

Strategy works where weapons don't.
Small in stature though one may be,
a clever scheme defeats the biggest enemy,
just like the greedy crane lost his life
to the clever plan of the cunning crab.'

'What is that story?' the crow and his wife asked the fox, and he narrated the tale.

THE TALE OF HOW THE GREEDY CRANE WAS KILLED BY THE CLEVER CRAB

In a verdant area watered by many streams, there was a large lake. In that lake lived an old crane, who was so decrepit that he could not catch fish any more to feed himself. One day, standing by the lake, feeble with hunger, he began to cry, his tears falling to the ground like a string of pearls. Seeing him in such distress, a crab who lived in the lake swam to the side and asked him: 'Uncle, why you are you not catching fish today? Instead, you are standing here, quietly weeping. What's wrong?'

'You have correctly surmised my state of mind, nephew,' the crane replied. 'I have become extremely weary of killing fish to feed myself. In fact, I have decided to renounce food all together and give up my life. That is why I'm not attempting to catch even those fish that swim within my reach.'

'What is the reason for this apathy, dear uncle?'

'Nephew, I'm just saddened at the thought of what will happen to this lake and the creatures that live in it. I was born near this lake, and my life has been sustained by it. Now I hear there will be a terrible famine that will last twelve years, and this lake will dry up.'

'Who told you this?' the crab asked worriedly.

'I heard it from astrologers. I heard that Shani will pierce Rohini nakshatra and collide with Mangal and Shukra. The result of this configuration is a twelve-year disaster. You see, when Surya's son, Shani, pierces Rohini nakshatra, Indra holds back his rain from earth for twelve years, and so the earth dries up and becomes barren, causing a famine that brings death to many. This lake of ours is already shallow, and I fear that lack of rain and the sun's scorching rays will dry it in no time. Can you imagine what will happen to all the fish and other creatures who live in it? I have grown old with all these creatures. They are my companions. I have sported with them and celebrated with them. Their death will devastate me.

In other lakes and ponds, creatures are already aware of this astrological event, and they are moving to larger waterbodies by themselves, or with the help of other creatures who are bigger and can transport them, such as crocodiles and porpoises. But the creatures in our lake are oblivious to the impending disaster. This makes me cry, because I know they will be wiped out, and I can't imagine life without them. That is why I've decided to just end my life by fasting till death.'

The crab was stunned to hear what the crane had to say. For a moment, he just stood there petrified, then he dived into the lake and hastily gathered as many of the inhabitants as he could to tell them what the crane had said. The other creatures, too, were struck by fear, thinking about the impending famine and devastation. Then, together they swam to the crane. 'Uncle,' they entreated, 'is there a way we can escape this calamity?'

'Yes, there is a way,' the crane replied. 'Very near here, there is a much bigger lake. Its waters are clear and sweet, and it is always covered with lotuses. It is so deep that even if the drought and famine last for twice its estimated time, it will not dry up. If you want to save your life, you should leave this lake and move to that one at once, by whatever means available to you. I, too, can help carry some of you to that lake.'

All the creatures quickly gathered around the crane, pleading, 'Take me! Take me!'

The cunning crane happily agreed. After that, every day, he took a few of the creatures on his back on the pretext of transporting them to the big lake, and, in a hilly area at a little distance, he smashed them on a rock to kill them and had a sumptuous meal. In this way, his days began to pass in the contentment that comes with a full belly.

One day, the crab came to the crane and pleaded with him: 'I was the first one with whom you shared the news; yet, you have been taking all the other creatures to safety, while I remain in this lake scared to death. Today, you must take me to the other lake and save my life.'

The crane had become a little bored with eating fish, and savouring crab meat for a change appealed to him very much. 'Come, nephew, I'll take you today,' he said and, putting the crab on his back, flew to the rock which had become his feeding ground.

As the crane neared the rock, the crab started to see piles of bones on the ground. Fearfully, he wondered what place this was. 'Uncle, you must be tired from flying such a distance with me on your back,' he said to the crane. 'How far is this lake that you're taking me to?'

'There is no other lake, you fool,' the crane replied. 'Look down there. Do you see those bones? They belong to your companions. And this is what I intend to do with you, as well. I'll fling you on a rock, and you'll perish. Then I'll eat you.'

Terror gripped the crab, making him shake so much that he almost fell off the crane's back. He cursed the day he had listened to this crafty old crane and believed him.

> Enemies become friends
> and friends become enemies,
> all to the purpose of one's own gain.
> Only the wise can discern
> who is friend and who is foe.
>
> Better to be in the company of a snake.
> Better to invite a thief into your home.
> But shun an evil friend who is two-faced.

Thinking these thoughts, the crab became determined to destroy the crane.

> When danger is impending, fear it.
> When you are face to face with it
> fight it with all your faculties.

Crawling up the crane's back, the crab extended his pincers and sunk them into the crane's neck, slitting it from side to side till it tore right off. Then, carrying the severed head, he began to make his way back to the lake. It was a long and toilsome trip, but he didn't give up, and, as soon as he reached the lake, he gathered all the other creature around him to tell them how the crane had lied to them and tricked them. 'There is no big lake,' he informed them. 'Nor is there an impending famine. It was all a ploy—an easy way for him to kill us and feed on us. After killing me, he would have returned to kill the rest of you, but I stopped him. Here is his head. Now we are all safe from that selfish, cruel, deceiving crane. Do not fear any more.'

'So, you see how the crane's greed caused his downfall and how he was killed by the smart crab?' the fox said to his crow friends.

The crows nodded. 'Then tell us how we can kill the snake who is devouring our babies.'

'Here's the plan: go to the capital city and find a wealthy man there—a king's minister, or even the king himself—anyone who is careless with his wealth and jewellery. Watch this person carefully. When he sets aside a gold necklace, or a string of pearls, or any such valuable ornament, grab it in your beak and fly to where the snake lives. Then drop it near his hole. When the officials come searching for it and see it lying near the snake's lair, they'll believe he stole it and kill him.'

The crows liked this plan and immediately flew to the capital. On the way, they saw the king's wives bathing in a lake, their belongings lay on the shore. Quickly, the she-crow dived down and, picking up a gold necklace with her beak, flew towards the bargad tree. The queens' guards saw the crow take the necklace, and they ran in hot pursuit, brandishing their staffs. But the crow did not panic. With courage and persistence, she flew to the tree and flung the necklace into the hole, and then went and sat on a high branch in another tree. The guards had followed the crow and had seen the hole in which she had thrown the necklace. When they peered inside it, the snake peeped out, hissing and flaring his hood. Instantly, the guards rained down blows on his head and killed him. Then they retrieved the necklace and returned to the lake.

After that, the crow couple had many chicks, who grew up to be healthy adults, and they all lived a happy and peaceful life.

'Hence, I say,' Damanaka concluded,

> What can be accomplished easily with ploy
> cannot be achieved with weapons and war.
> For the wise, no task is impossible.

Also,

> He who is wise is powerful.
> He who is a fool has no power.
> The arrogant lion in the forest was
> brought down by a wise little hare.

'What is this story?' Karataka asked, and Damanaka related it.

THE TALE OF THE DIMWIT LION AND THE WISE HARE

In a forest lived a lion called Mandamati (dullard). He was intoxicated with his own strength and took pride in slaying hapless animals. Every day he would go on a rampage, slaughtering numerous deer, boars, bulls, and hares and still be restless for more. The creatures of that forest lived in constant fear and were sick and tired of the lion's ceaseless and purposeless killing. One day, conferring with each other, they decided on a system that would give them some modicum of peace. Going to Mandamati, they said to him: 'Maharaj, you needlessly kill countless animals every day, even though your hunger is appeased with just one kill. That's not right. Therefore, if you promise not to go on a killing spree, we ourselves will select an animal every day from different species and send it to you as your prey. That way you will not have to put in any effort to procure your food, and we will not live in fear of being randomly slaughtered by you. You are a king; you must observe a king's dharma.

> Just as a healthy body is gradually built
> by eating daily a fixed dose of nutrients,
> a wise king who uses the kingdom's resources
> in measured amounts, builds a strong kingship.

Also,

> a king who takes care of his subjects
> secures for himself heaven in the other world
> and praise, fame, and wealth in this world.

Moreover,

> As a cowherd feeds his cow to her satiety
> to milk her from time to time for his need,
> so should a king's care satisfy his people
> to receive from them their sincere service.
> This is the just law of kingship.
> The foolish king who, like a butcher

slaughters his subjects like goats,
profits only the one time, and no more.

The king who desires his kingdom's growth
should provide for his subjects,
like a gardener nurturing a sapling.

Just as the lamp burns on oil,
but only the flame is visible,
a good king should use his people
in a way they don't feel depleted.

Like a cow is fed at a given time,
and it is milked at a fixed time;
like a fruiting tree is watered every day,
and its fruits are plucked at the right time;
subjects taken care of in a timely manner
become felicitous when the time is ripe.

Rulers who nurture their subjects with loving care
grow prosperous day by day.
Rulers who afflict their subjects with suffering
beget their own sure downfall.'

Hearing these words from the animals, Mandamati acquiesced. 'I'll accept your system,' he said. 'But be warned that the day I don't receive my daily meal of one animal, I will kill all of you.'

Swearing to keep their end of the bargain, the animals returned to the forest, freed from their fear of the lion. Every day, one of them, no matter his or her age, circumstance, or family commitment, was selected according to species and sent to the lion at his scheduled time of feeding.

One day, it was the turn of a hare. With words of praise and gratitude from the other animals ringing in his ears, the hare, with a heavy heart, began to slowly make his way to the lion's den. He wished he could, somehow, escape the lion and kept thinking of ways to do it. But the more he wished and thought, the slower his feet moved, till he was quite late. Suddenly, he come upon a well. When he looked down into the water and saw his own reflection, an idea began to work itself in his mind. After that he hurried to Mandamati's den, but by that time, it was well past the lion's feeding time, and he was raging with hunger and licking his chops, thinking about going into the forest and killing every single animal.

The hare warily approached the lion and bowed.

'O evil hare,' thundered the lion, 'in the first place, you are so tiny that eating you will hardly satisfy my hunger, and then you have the audacity to come late. Today, I will eat you, and tomorrow, I will go into the forest and kill all the other animals and eat them.'

'Maharaj,' said the hare in a voice that sounded like a cracked instrument, 'pardon me for being late. But this is neither my fault nor the fault of the other animals. Will you please listen to the reason for my delay?'

'Hurry up and tell me,' the lion roared. 'Before you find yourself a pulp between my jaws.'

'Maharaj, because today the hares were selected for you, the other animals, knowing that one of us would not be enough to satisfy you, actually sent five of us. As we five were on our way to you, another lion emerged from his cave and accosted us. "Where are you all going?" he said. "Think of your guardian gods one last time, because I'm going to eat you."

"We're going to our Maharaj, the king of this forest, Mandamati," we told him. "As per our agreement with him, one animal goes to him voluntarily, every day. Today five of us are going, because we are small, and our Maharaj has a big appetite."

"Is that right?" he said. "But this forest is mine. I am the king here. Therefore, you animals should make an agreement with me and send me an animal every day; not that Mandamati. Besides, he is a thief. He has robbed me of my forest. Who is he to take an oath from my animals? And if that Mandamati has any problem with this, he should sort it out with me in a show of strength. Go and call him. Leave your four relatives with me as a guarantee, and go and fetch Mandamati. I'll fight him, and whoever wins will eat the five of you."

'So, you see, Maharaj, this is the reason for my delay. I came as fast as I could to tell you what the other lion said. Please do whatever you think is right.'

'O hare, take me to that thug lion right away. I will destroy him,' Mandamati thundered, shaking his mane. 'That is the only way I can appease my anger. It is said,

> Kingdom, friends, and gold—
> these three are rewards of war.
> Lacking prospects of at least one,
> no wise person would start a war.
> With no chance of a reward

and no threat of disrespect,
only a fool would trigger a war.'

'You're absolutely right, Maharaj,' the hare said. 'A kshatriya fights either for a kingdom or to maintain his good name. But I think you should know that that lion lives in a fort. We saw him come out of it when he accosted us. An enemy ensconced in his fort is difficult to subjugate. It is rightly said,

> A fort in a war can accomplish
> what thousands of elephants
> and lakhs of horses cannot.
> Just one archer behind a fort's wall
> can kill a hundred enemies outside it.
> The wisdom of a fort is praised
> by every master of statecraft.

In bygone days, fearing daitya Hiranyakashipu, Indra, advised by Guru Brihaspati, had Vishvakarma build a fort for him, and he was so pleased with it that he gave a boon to all kings on earth: "If you have a fort, you will celebrate victory." Since then, thousands of forts have been built on earth and will continue to be built as long as there are kings, and the kings have enemies.

> Just as a serpent without fangs
> and an elephant without madness
> can easily be brought under control,
> so can a king unprotected by a fort.'

'Even if this thug of a lion is hiding in a fort, you must take me to him,' Mandamati roared. 'I will destroy him in his fort. It is said,

> A new disease and a new enemy
> should be rooted out without delay.
> A disease can sap one's strength,
> and the enemy's strength can grow.

Also,

> One should never underestimate a rising enemy.
> Wise men equate him to an advancing disease.
>
> Blinded with self-importance, men make assumptions,
> while a weak enemy, once easy to defeat, gains power,
> like a new ailment, once negligible, begins to worsen.'

'What you say is right, Maharaj. But I want to warn you that the other lion is not weak by any means. In my humble opinion, you should not challenge him without first assessing his strength. People say,

> One who challenges another,
> only too eager with excitement
> and assesses not the opponent's strength,
> crashes to the ground like a kite on fire.

And,

> By mounting an attack on an enemy strong
> without careful thought and strategy,
> even if one is powerful, one loses face,
> like an elephant who charges a stronger foe
> and returns with broken tusks and in pain.'

'Why are you concerned with these matters of an enemy's strength or weaknesses?' Mandamati asked, irked. 'Stop talking and just take me to my contender.'

'Then follow me, Maharaj,' the hare said and led Mandamati to the well. Halting near the parapet, he turned to the lion and stated, 'No one can withstand your magnificence, Maharaj.' 'Look! Just by seeing you from a distance that coward lion has gone into hiding in his fort. Come. Step closer. I'll show him to you.'

As Mandamati came close to the well and looked down, he saw his own reflection and thought it was another lion. When he roared, the sound echoed in the well, and its reverberations were much louder than his own roar. Eager to fight his adversary, Mandamati jumped into the well, and, needless to say, he drowned.

Ecstatic at the lion's demise, the hare ran back to the forest to give the good news to all the other animals. Everyone praised the hare for his brilliant mind, and they thanked him profusely. From that day on, they all lived in the forest in peace. 'That is why I say to you, whoever is wise and possesses wisdom is truly powerful,' Damanaka concluded. 'Therefore, if you agree, I'll go to the lion and the bull, and, with my wisdom, I'll try to destroy their friendship.'

'If you are that confident about your wisdom, then go,' Karataka replied. 'May you be successful, and may you not encounter obstacles.'

From that day on, Damanaka began to wait for an opportunity to catch Pingalaka alone. Then, one day, seeing the lion sitting by himself, he went to him and, bowing with respect, sat down beside him.

'Dear friend, I haven't seen you in a while. I hope all is well,' Pingalaka greeted him.

'Maharaj has no need of us any more,' Damanaka said. 'That is why I have stayed away. But my heart burns at the thought that Maharaj may be in danger. Therefore, I had to come. As they say,

> A good person cannot bear
> to see someone else harmed,
> whether he be friend or foe.
> He says what needs to be said,
> pleasing or displeasing, sweet or bitter.
> His sole purpose is the other's benefit.'

Hearing Damanaka's words of selfless geniality, Pingalaka became curious to know what danger he was implying. 'What is it that you have come to tell me. Speak without hesitation,' he said.

'This bull, Sanjivaka, is not your friend, Maharaj. In fact, he is planning a coup against you. The other day, thinking that I am his confidant, he told me, "Now I know this Pingalaka's capabilities—his strengths and his weaknesses. Using that information, I plan to kill him and become the king. Then, I will make you my minister."'

These words of betrayal struck Pingalaka like a lightning bolt, and he passed out. Seeing this extreme reaction, Damanaka realized how very attached the lion had become to Sanjivaka. 'This does not bode well for the lion,' he said to himself, because it is known,

> When the king depends on one minister
> and makes him his be all and end all,
> puffed up with self-importance and pride
> that one begins to resent his servitude
> and seeks to be fully autonomous,
> even at the expense of the king's life.

'In this situation, what is the best course of action?' Damanaka asked himself. Even as he was trying to figure out what to do next, Pingalaka regained consciousness and said, 'What you say, pains me. Sanjivaka is dearer to me than my life, and he serves me with such love. This makes me wonder if what you are saying is true. I don't think he is even capable of a disloyal thought, let alone treason.'

'Maharaj, a loyal servant will remain a loyal servant forever; that is a misconception. You must have heard it said,

> There is not a person in the world
> who does not wish to be king.
> It is their inability that forces them to,
> instead, be in service of a king.'

'I know what you are saying, but both my mind and heart refuse to believe such a change in Sanjivaka. I have full faith in him. I know he can't harbour any evil thoughts about me. I firmly believe this. Someone has rightly said,

> One's body may be riddled with diseases,
> but one loves it because it is one's own.
> In the same way a dear one remains dear
> even if he happens to err and take missteps.'

'Maharaj, it is because he knows you love him that he has dared to make such a move. As you know,

> A man, whether of low birth or high,
> who becomes the object of a king's affection
> also gains the grace of Goddess Shri.

This Sanjivaka has no good qualities to commend him, yet you keep him by your side. Now, if you were to think, "This Sanjivaka is a big bull. His body is strong and full of muscle. I can use him to destroy my enemies," it would make sense for you to have him beside you. But this will never happen, because he is a grass-eater, and he cannot kill any meat-eater. Therefore, you will never use him to destroy your enemies. My advice to you is to get rid of him. Accuse him of some offence, hold him accountable, and then kill him.'

'How can I do that?' Pingalaka replied. 'They say,

> The one you have called gifted and deserving in court,
> how can you call him an undeserving offender
> without negating your word and showing bad judgement?
> Such wavering and double talk is unworthy of a king.

Besides, I promised Sanjivaka safe conduct on your advice; now, how can I break that promise and kill him? Moreover, I think of that bull as my friend and well-wisher. I have no anger or resentment towards him. With what motive can I kill him? Think of it this way:

> It was Brahma who infused Tarakasura with power.
> To kill the daitya, he needed some one other.
> This daitya is of our very own making.
> How can we then kill him ourselves?
> When, with one's own hand, one plants a tree
> and nurtures it with love and care into full foliage,
> how can one cut it down, poison though it may be?

In the same way, it is I who have elevated Sanjivaka to such heights; that is why even if he is villainous, his destruction can't be by my hands.

> One must not so easily vow love to someone,
> but if one does, that love must not decrease.
> Loving someone and uplifting him
> and then flinging him down in rejection—
> how shameful is such behaviour?

Also,

> Already on the ground, one has no fear of falling
> but raised up high, a fall to the ground is terrifying.

> There is nothing special about being charitable
> towards those who themselves are charitable.
> But he who shows beneficence to the unkind
> is truly the one who possesses charity.

That is why I will not hold any ill feeling towards Sanjivaka, even if he is plotting against me.'

'But, Maharaj, to forgive a traitor is against a king's dharma. It is said,

> He who is an equal in wealth,
> he who is an equal in power,
> he who knows the king's intimate secrets,
> and he who shares an equal repute—
> if the king does not destroy him in time,
> he will destroy the king when he can.

And I must say, Maharaj, and pardon me for saying this, but after forming a friendship with this Sanjivaka, you have forgotten all rajadharma. And because of that, your entire official circle of servants, ministers, and advisers is crumbling. Estranged from you, they are leaving to go elsewhere. What else can they do? Sanjivaka is a grass-eater. Your associates are all meat-eaters, like you, and they depend on you to provide them food. But, influenced by Sanjivaka, you have stopped hunting; hence, your associates have no choice but to leave you. In fact, some of them believe that you, too, have become a grass-eater. I believe that this is another reason that will lead to your destruction. You must have heard,

> Whomever we associate with, whomever we serve,
> in their company, we become like them.

One's own qualities change from inferior to mediocre to superior, depending on the company we keep.

> If water is sprinkled on hot iron,
> it ruins the iron forever.
> If water is sprinkled on a lotus leaf,
> the drops shine like pearls.
> If it falls in the ocean in the belly of oysters
> a single drop of water becomes a true pearl.

Also know that:

> Good people are ruined in the company of bad people,
> just as Bhishma Pitamah, the best of all men,
> influenced by Duryodhana, stole Raja Virata's cows.

That is why the advice of the wise is to distance yourself from the contaminating influence of rogues. It is rightly said,

> If you are unsure of someone's ethics,
> don't give him refuge in your house.
> Because of the bedbug's fault
> poor Mandavisarpini had to die.'

'What is this story?' Pingalaka asked Damanaka, and Damanaka narrated the tale.

THE TALE OF HOW THE BEDBUG'S SELFISHNESS COST THE LOUSE HER LIFE

There was a king who ruled over a beautiful kingdom. He lived in a gorgeous palace and slept in a charming bedroom. His bed had soft makhmal sheets, and a quilt that was covered in pure white cotton. In the creases of the makhmal, enjoying its luxurious feel, lived Mandavisarpini (slow-moving), the louse. In the morning, she gambolled around in the fabric, and, at night, she crawled onto the king's body and gently sucked his blood, and this is how she lived her days in peace.

One day, a wandering bedbug, named Agnimukha (fire mouth), showed up in the king's bed. He was scooting around in the sheets, thanking his stars for landing him in such a princely place, when the louse saw him.

'What are you doing here?' she demanded to know. 'This is my place of living. You can't just take up residence here! Besides, if anyone sees you here, you'll surely get into trouble, and I may end up suffering your fate. So, please leave before you are spotted.'

'Dear lady,' said Agnimukha. 'Consider me your guest. It is said,

> Brahmins revere fire.
> People revere brahmins.
> A wife reveres her husband.
> But guests are revered by all.

Even if someone undesirable comes to your house, he is still a guest, and you should still welcome him. That is dharma. You should not insult him and shoo him away. Besides, I have a great desire to stay here. I have tasted numerous kinds of blood—bitter, salty, even tart—all depending on the food habits of the person. But I've never tasted sweet blood. This king's blood must be so sweet, because he gets to eat the most delicious of food and mithai. I would really like to taste his blood. Even though they say,

> A king and a pauper are no different
> in how they taste different foods.
> Both of them have taste buds,
> and both enjoy delicious food.

But it is also said,

> In this world, the tongue's taste is the key to living.
> It is for the tongue that people work so hard.
> If there was no need to gratify the tongue,
> no need to satiate the stomach with food,
> no one would be subservient to another.

In this world, people will do anything to fill their stomach—lie, serve an unworthy person, travel overseas, and suffer other indignities. Hence, dear lady, I am presenting myself to you as a hungry guest, who is only requesting food. Therefore, please let me remain and feed on the king's delectable blood.'

'Fine,' said Mandavisarpini. 'But listen up. I bite the king only when he is in deep sleep, and, that too, so gently that he hardly feels it. I hear that your mouth is like fire, and your bite is fiery. You better be very careful when you bite him. It would be best that you wait until he is in deep sleep. But I fear you are unpredictable. Promise me that you will wait here with me. I don't want you to bite the king while he is still in the first stage of sleep. Don't be impatient. It is rightly said,

> One who doesn't see time and place,
> or know what is right and wrong;
> one who acts without thinking,
> loses all chances of success.

So, if you want to taste the king's blood and not lose your life, wait here till I tell you it is time.'

'I'll do as you say, dear lady,' Agnimukha replied. 'I'll wait for you to first bite him before I begin sucking his blood. I swear to you that I will not bite him first.'

As the two were talking, the king came into his room and lay down on the bed. The bedbug got so excited at the feel of his body that he was unable to control his salivating tongue and fiercely dug his bloodsucking beak into the king's arm, even before he could fall asleep.

> Advice cannot change someone's nature,
> like water that returns to its coolness,
> no matter how much it is heated.
>
> Fire may turn cold, the moon may burn,
> but the nature of people will never change.

The bedbug's bite pricked the king like a sharp needle. He instantly jumped out of bed and summoned his servants. 'It seems that a bedbug or louse is hiding in this bed, because I got bitten. Find it and kill it right away.'

The servants began to inspect every finger's width of quilt and sheet with a keen eye. The quick-moving bedbug slipped out of the quilt and scooted into a crack in one of the bedposts; however, the slow-moving louse, who was sitting in the seam of the quilt, couldn't go anywhere. The servants spied her and pulled her out triumphantly, and then they killed her.

'That is why I am telling you, Maharaj,' Damanaka said to Pingalaka, 'Don't give refuge to someone whose nature you don't know. Please think deeply about what I am saying. Kill him, or he will find an opportunity to kill you. It is said,

> One who distances himself from his well-wishers
> and embraces those he does not know
> dies like Raja Kukudhrum, that fool Chandrava.'

'Tell me that story,' Pingalaka said, and Damanaka told him the tale.

THE TALE OF HOW THE BLUE JACKAL WAS REALLY JUST A JACKAL

In some jungle lived a jackal called Chandrava (one who howls at the moon). One day, plagued by hunger, he found his way into some town. When the street dogs in that town saw him, they surrounded him, barking and snarling. Somehow, he managed to escape from the circle of dogs, and, looking for a place to hide, ran into the open doorway of a house that belonged to a washerman. As he rushed in, he accidentally fell into a large trough of indigo dye. He struggled out of the trough, but when he emerged, he was completely blue, from head to toe.

After waiting in the house for some time, Chandrava ventured into the street again, hoping the dogs would be gone. They were still there; however, when they saw Chandrava this time, they hardly paid him any attention and soon wandered off. Chandrava was amazed at this sudden transformation in the dogs and wondered what could have caused it. Then it struck him: it was the colour of his coat. The dogs didn't recognize him in blue. A strange excitement began to course through Chandrava, and he decided to head back to the forest to see how the other animals would react to his new appearance. It is said,

> The colour blue is indelible. Also,
> cement, fools, women, crabs, fish,
> crocodiles, drunkards—all of these,
> if they seize, they never let go.

Seeing Chandrava dyed in indelible blue, the color of Kalakuta poison that was lodged in Shri Mahadeva's throat and earned him the title of Neelakantha (blue-throated), the other animals, too, did not recognize him. 'This is some strange, new being that has come into our forest,' they said to each other. 'He may be dangerous,' some said. 'It's best to stay away from him.' 'What nature of an animal is this?' others speculated. 'Perhaps, he's not an animal at all, but some form of man. It's better to avoid him.'

The wise say,

> Putting your trust in someone who is not known to you,
> whose caste, lineage, ability, and business are unfamiliar.
> is putting your wealth and well-being in jeopardy.

Seeing the other animals running helter-skelter in fear and agitation, Chandrava was emboldened, and a plan took shape in his mind: 'Why are you running away from me in fear?' he called gently to the animals. 'Don't be afraid. I have been sent to you by Brahmaji himself. He said to me, "The wild creatures in the forest have no king. I am anointing you as their king, and from today your name will be Raja Kukudhrum. Go to the earth and take care of your subjects." Therefore, from today, all animals, including lions and tigers, must be allegiant to me. I, Raja Kukudhrum, am the sovereign of all forest creatures in all the three worlds.'

Believing the jackal, the animals began to form a circle around him. Then all of them, including predators, such as lions and tigers, bowed before him and said, 'Lord, we are your servants. Command us.' Elated at their obeisance, Raja Kukudhrum selected his ministers: he picked the lion to be his prime minister and assigned the duty of guarding his bed to the tiger. The leopard became in charge of his betel box, and the wolf was given the duty of guarding the door. As for the jackals—he refused to even look at them. In fact, he had all the jackals thrown out of his court.

Chandrava, alias Raja Kukudhrum, now began to live a life of a sovereign. The lion hunted for him, bringing him whatever prey he killed. From this, the jackal first ate to his heart's content, and then he divided the remaining meat among the other animals.

In this way, much time passed. One day, Raja Kukudhrum was sitting in his court, with his followers assembled around him, when, far in the distance, a pack of jackals howled. Hearing that beloved sound, Chandrava's mind and body were filled with the joy of it. Instinctively, he stood up and, raising his head to look at the moon, let out a long, loud howl.

The lions and tigers and leopards sitting around him looked at him in shock. 'A jackal? We have been serving a lowly jackal?' they exclaimed.

Hearing their exclamations, Chandrava realized what he had done. He immediately ceased his howling and loudly cleared his throat, pretending that the howl had been no more than a faulty expulsion of sound, but the animals were on to him. He tried to flee, but they pounced on him and wasted no time in tearing his body apart.

'So, you see, Maharaj,' Damanaka said to Pingalaka. 'The king who leaves his own trusted people and appoints strangers as his retainers dies the death of Kukudhrum.'

'What proof do you have that Sanjivaka harbours this enmity towards me?' Pingalaka asked.

'Maharaj, he swore to it in my presence that tomorrow, at dawn, he will attack you. In the morning when you see him looking at you red-eyed, ruddy-faced, lips trembling in rage, and eyeballs darting from side to side, know these to be signs of antagonism, proving the truth of my claims that he wants to kill you. I have told you all I know. Please do whatever you think is right.'

Having incited Pingalaka against Sanjivaka, Damanaka went to see the bull. Approaching him with halting steps and a sad face, he greeted him quietly and sat down beside him. Seeing his friend looking so dejected, Sanjivaka welcomed him with love and warmth: 'Hello friend. I haven't seen you in a while. How are you? Tell me if there's anything I can do for you—anything at all. It is said,

> That man is blessed, that man is wise,
> that man is respected and hailed by all,
> whose house is frequented by friends
> when they need help and advice.'

'How am I, you ask?' Damanaka replied. 'How can a servant be?'

> To serve a king one must be prepared,
> to relinquish claims to one's own wealth,
> to give up peace of mind and leisure,
> to put one's life in constant danger.

Also,

> A man's life is full of sorrow and pain.
> Then poverty takes its own toll.
> To top this is a life spent in serving.
> Oh, the custom of servitude is endless.
> How pained and helpless one feels in its bind.

Moreover,

> The impoverished, ailing, foolish,
> those who live in a foreign land,

and those whose livelihood is to serve—
they have no life, though they live,
says Vyasa in the Mahabharata.
This also is the conclusion the wise draw.

A servant never eats what he wants,
never does he satiate his hunger.
Hesitant speech, disturbed sleep,
constantly in fear of his master—
a life of servitude is hardly worth living.

When people say a serving life is a dog's life,
they do not know the truth of this statement.
A dog has the freedom to go where he pleases,
a servant is bound by his master's command.

Sleeping on the ground, remaining celibate,
eating meagrely, keeping a body lean and thin.
This regimen of a servant is also that of an ascetic
But while one is a sinner, the other follows dharma.

A man bears heat, cold, and other miseries in servitude.
If he were to bear just a fraction of those for dharma,
he would be liberated and on his way to moksha.

Even the softest, sweetest, moist laddu
received in bondage is bitter in taste.
And even a dry roti of independence
is like the most delicious delicacy.'

'What is the matter, dear friend? There is clearly something you want to tell me through all this preamble. What is it that you want to say?' Sanjivaka said to Damanaka.

'What I'm trying to tell you is this:
the rightness of place and time,
the acquisition of friends,
the balance of gains and losses,
knowledge of one's own strengths,
and commitment to pursue goals—
all are matters one must often review.'

'I still don't understand what you are saying. Please tell me clearly.'

'Dear friend, a king's trusted minister should not reveal the king's secrets from the counsel the king has sought.

> If a minister selected to advise the raja
> exposes the reasons of the raja's counsel,
> not only does he kill the king without weapons
> but also, he himself ends up in the darkest hell.

However, dear friend, because of my love for you, I have come to reveal to you the secret plans that Pingalaka is making. You came into Pingalaka's royal circle because I brought you into it, and you trusted me. It is said,

> If a person puts his trust in someone,
> and that results in that person's slaying,
> the sin of it falls on the one he trusted.
> This is what Manu says about matters of trust.

To say it bluntly, that Pingalaka has turned against you and wants to kill you. He told me in private, "I will kill that Sanjivaka at sunrise and, after a long time, enjoy bull's meat with my meat-eating subjects." "Maharaj," I said to him, "it is not right to kill a friend to feed your own belly." People say,

> After murdering a brahmin
> one can be absolved through rituals,
> but killing a friend is unforgivable.

"You scoundrel," he chided me. "Sanjivaka is a grass-eater, and we are meat-eaters. Our enmity is of nature's own making. And an enemy must be destroyed with any means possible. Also, there is no sin in killing an enemy.

> A kshatriya facing an enemy in war
> does not think if killing is right or wrong.
> His dharma is to annihilate the enemy
> with whatever means available to him.
> Didn't Drona's son, Ashwatthama,
> kill Duryodhana while he was sleeping?"

Realizing what Pingalaka intends to do, I have come to you. I know I'm betraying Pingalaka by doing so, but I'll leave it to you to judge whether I'm right or wrong. You should take whatever actions you can to save yourself.'

Damanaka's words delivered a cut to Sanjivaka's heart that was as deep as a sword's, and he staggered from it. Then, in a despondent and weary voice, he said: 'Someone has rightly said,

> Women are most attracted to rogues.
> Kings often favour the unworthy.
> Money finds its way to the miserly.
> Clouds shower often on mountains and forests,
> while farming fields remain needful of rain.

The fool who thinks, I have an affinity with the king, and he loves me, is as ridiculous as a bull without horns. I made a grave mistake when I made Pingalaka my friend.

> When two people have equal wealth,
> they have similar lineage, and matched strength,
> their friendship or enmity makes sense.
> How can a rich man and a poor man,
> a man of power and a weakling,
> a man of high caste and low caste
> forge a friendship or enmity that lasts?

> Deer move in company of others of their own species.
> The same is true of cows and horses and other animals.
> Fools, too, can be found in the company of other fools.
> So also is true of those who nurture the intellect.

Why am I surprised at Pingalaka's intention? We are worlds apart. Now, even if I go to Pingalaka and try to please him again, he will not be pleased, because, as they say,

> If someone has a reason to be angry,
> he can be appeased by removing the cause.
> But if he harbours anger and hatred without cause,
> how is that person to be appeased?

> One may serve the king with utmost devotion,
> but there is no guarantee the king will be pleased.
> Another may blatantly do him a disservice,
> yet his work may be appreciated by the king.
> A king's moods are varied and indiscernible.
> His mind is as hard to read as it is to know dharma.

But really, Damanaka, my friend, I'm sure you will agree with me that:

> Calamities strike without cause.
> Anger can rise without reason.
> Friendships should not be abandoned
> without examining all the facts.

I think I know what happened—why I fell out Pingalaka's favour. All those sycophants who resented my friendship with him finally managed to persuade him to kill me.

> Sycophants can't bear to see their lord
> drawing close to another, no matter his qualities.
> Just like a wife, unable to bear her husband's co-wife
> finds fault even in her best talents and qualities.

You see, Damanaka, the ones who lack merit can't bear to be in the presence of the meritorious, because they know that no one will pay them any attention. Hence, they burn in jealousy. As is well known,

> A lamp glows beautifully in the dark,
> but as soon as the sun rises, its beauty fades.'

'Friend, if what you say is the reason for Pingalaka's displeasure, then you have nothing to worry about,' Damanaka said. 'If you think someone has bad-mouthed you and discredited you before Pingalaka, all you have to do is to remove his doubts and show him your devotion. That should put you back in his favour.'

'You're right. It's tiny doubts and suspicions that plague a man the most. While each of them, individually, may be small, when they are put together, they can compound to a degree that can destroy him. As it is said,

> Corrupt, petty, evil people,
> though singly inconsequential,
> can together wreak big damage,
> just like the crow and others teamed up
> to kill that unsuspecting camel.'

'What is this story?' Damanaka asked, and Sanjivaka told him the tale.

THE TALE OF THE HOW THE CAMEL WAS DECEIVED INTO SACRIFICING HIMSELF

In a forest lived the lion, Mandotkata (the vigorous and arrogant one). He had three lackeys: a tiger, a crow, and a jackal. One day, as the four of them were wandering in the forest, they saw a camel, who had wandered away from a caravan of businessmen. Mandotkata had never seen a camel before.

'What a strange creature this is?' he said to his toadies. 'Find out who he is and what is he doing in our forest.'

'Maharaj, this is a camel,' said the crow who had seen many creatures in the course of his flights. 'You can make him your prey since he is a grass-eater.'

'I would never kill anyone who has come into my forest as a guest. Don't you know,

> He who kills a guest that is sheltering in his home,
> feeling fearful yet trusting to be free of danger,
> incurs the sin of killing a hundred brahmins.

Therefore, you three should go to this camel and bring him to me, after giving him my promise of safe conduct. I want to ask him why he has come here.'

The tiger, crow, and jackal went to the camel and, promising him safe conduct, brought him to Mandotkata.

The lion gestured to the camel to be seated and asked him gently, 'Dear guest, who are you? Where have you come from? And why have you come to this forest?'

'I am a camel, and my name is Kathanaka (storyteller). I work for a Vaishya who travels for business. He loads his heavy baggage on my back, and we cross vast distances to faraway lands so that he can sell his merchandise and make a profit. Our caravan was in the process of crossing this forest, and we had set up camp for the night. At dawn this morning, while everyone was still sleeping, I wandered off to find something to eat, but by the time I returned, my caravan had left. Now I'm thinking of going to the next village to see if I can find my owner there.'

'O Kathanaka, why would you go looking for your owner to be burdened by his heavy loads again? You are free now. Stay here in this forest, free of care. The grass here is as green as emerald and it grows everywhere. Graze where you please and spend your time with me,' Mandotkata said to the camel.

The picture of life that Mandotkata painted was very appealing to Kathanaka, and he agreed to remain in the forest as his friend, under the protection of his promise of safe conduct. From then on, wandering leisurely, savouring the abundant green grass, and breathing the air of freedom, Kathanaka began to live a peaceful and contented life.

One day, Mandotkata got into a fight with a huge, intoxicated tusker who gored him in many places with his massive, pestle-like tusks. Badly wounded and in tremendous pain, the lion staggered to his den and lay down. Many days passed. His followers—the tiger, crow, jackal, and camel—came to see him numerous times and to urge him to get up and hunt, but the lion just could not muster enough energy. Soon, without their daily sustenance, which the lion used to provide, the other meat-eaters became lean with hunger. Seeing the desperation on their faces, Mandotkata said to them. 'Bring me an animal. Even in my state, I can kill him, and then you all can eat.'

So, the four—the tiger, the crow, the jackal, and the camel—went in search of an animal they could bring back to Mandotkata. However, their search proved futile, and after many hours of trying to catch prey, they started back for the lion's den, feeling quite dejected. Then, the crow and the jackal, who had drifted a bit away from the others, began to talk:

'I see no point in wandering any more,' the jackal said to the crow. 'I doubt if we'll find anything. But we have the camel. Why don't we take him back as prey?'

'I agree with what you're saying. But how can we do that to Kathanaka? Our king has given him an oath of safe conduct.'

'I have a plan,' the jackal said. 'I'll create a situation where our lion will himself kill this camel.'

'What is your plan?' the crow asked, and when the jackal shared it with him, the crow approved.

As everyone drew near Mandotkata's den, that jackal requested the others to wait outside, while he went in to talk to him. Then, approaching the lion, he said, 'Maharaj, we have been wandering the forest for hours, but there is not a single animal to be had. What should we do? We are so hungry that even putting one foot in front of the other is becoming impossible. Besides, we must arrange some food for you, as well. I have a suggestion, if Maharaj will allow me to make it.'

When the lion nodded, the jackal continued, 'Why don't we eat the grass-eater among us—that Kathanaka, the camel?'

The lion was enraged to hear the jackal's uncivil and cruel proposition, 'You evil-minded jackal, shame on you. If you ever make such an evil suggestion again, I'll kill you and eat you. I have given Kathanaka my word, promising him safe conduct. How can I kill him? The wise have said,

> Neither the giving of nine cows in charity,
> nor the giving of earth or grain
> is superior to bestowing fearlessness.'

'This is true, Maharaj. If you yourself kill someone on whom you have bestowed fearlessness, then it is a sin, but what if he himself were to come to you and sacrifice himself at your feet? Surely that is acceptable and not a sin. What if he insists that you kill him? Will you then do it? Also, I have everyone else's word that if Kathanaka doesn't offer himself, you can kill one of us without hesitating. What is the use of our life if it doesn't serve you? You must appease your hunger, or your health will further deteriorate. In any case, if anything happens to you, we, too, will end our lives by burning in your pyre. How can we live without you? It is said,

> The chief who rules the clan
> must be protected at all costs.
> If he dies, the clan is wiped out.
> A wheel rotates because of the axle
> not because of its spokes.'

'If that is how you and the others feel, then do as you wish,' Mandotkata replied.

Receiving the lion's permission, the jackal rushed back to the others and told them, 'His condition is not good at all. Without him we'll be without protection, and we might as well die. Let's go in there and give ourselves to our king. That way we can pay our debt to him. It is said,

> A servant should take care of his master
> as long his heart beats with life.
> If he just looks on while his master is dying,
> he embarks on the path to hell.'

The other three nodded their assent and, following the jackal inside, went to the lion with moist eyes and sat down beside him.

'Have you brought me prey?' Mandotkata raised his head a little and looked around. 'I don't see any.'

The crow spoke: 'Maharaj, we searched the whole forest, and we couldn't find a single creature. But Maharaj, I am here. Please eat me and satiate your hunger. Your life will be saved, and I will achieve heaven. It is said,

> By sacrificing his life for his master,
> a servant is freed of old age and death,
> and he starts on the path to moksha.

Therefore, Maharaj, don't hesitate to kill me and eat me.'

'No. no.' the jackal interrupted the crow. 'Look at your size. You are too small. Your meagre flesh will not even serve as sustenance on his way to the afterlife,' he said. 'Maharaj, eat me and save your life. That way, not only will I gain praise and fame in this life, but, in the other life, I will go straight to heaven. It is said,

> The life of a servant belongs to his master,
> bought in exchange of the food and wealth he provides.'

'Dear Jackal,' the tiger said. 'You have certainly demonstrated your noble character by offering yourself to our lord and master. But your body, too, is small, and you hardly have any flesh. Maharaj will not be able to appease his hunger on your meat. Also, you are armed with claws, so you are related to his species. It's not right to eat someone related to you. So, please step aside and let me offer myself.' Then bowing to the lion, the tiger begged, 'Please allow me to sacrifice myself, Maharaj, and bestow the privilege of heaven on me. This world, too, will remember me as a devout servant. Don't hesitate now. Strike me without another doubt. I am your prey. It is said,

> The devoted servant who gives up his life
> so that his master can achieve his goals
> is promised an eternal life in heaven
> and everlasting fame and glory on earth.'

Watching the crow, jackal, and tiger spout such praiseworthy words, the camel thought, the lion didn't eat any of them, but they have proved themselves as self-sacrificing and loyal. Let me do the same. I, too, will offer myself. Just as he didn't hurt the others, he will not eat me, and I'll gain his gratitude.

Stepping forward, the camel nudged the tiger away. 'You too are armed with claws, and you use them to hunt, dear Tiger. Therefore, you, too, are related to our Maharaj in that sense, which makes you unsuitable prey.' Then turning to the lion, he bowed and said, 'Maharaj, instead of the crow, jackal, and tiger, eat me, and save your life. Let me achieve heaven with my sacrifice.'

As soon as the camel said this, the lion gestured to the others. The tiger and the jackal then jumped on him and tore into his sides, and the crow plucked out his eyes. Thus, the camel died, and the cunning animals ate him and appeased their hunger.

'So, you see, friend, how even inconsequential people can wreak havoc when they team up?' Sanjivaka said to Damanaka. 'You know, I've realized that your king has surrounded himself with lowly followers; that's why he's not worthy of being served by the high-minded. Everyone knows that the king whose coterie of officials and circle of followers are of low morals, his subjects can never be happy. In fact, influenced by them, he himself ends up committing immoral acts. It is said,

> If the king is ignoble like a vulture,
> but his officials are noble like hamsa birds,
> service under that king is still possible.
> But if the king is of high character like a hamsa,
> and the officials are loathsome like vultures,
> one should not be in service of that king.

I'm certain that evil-minded followers have turned Pingalaka against me and have incited his anger toward me. That's why he is considering this evil action of killing me. It is not surprising. Even great minds get swayed when they are influenced by others.

> When soft, fluid water can abrade and break
> mighty, impervious rocks in a mountainside
> by simply flowing against it day by day;
> just imagine what the constant tattling
> of a malicious tattler can do to a mere mortal.

Also, this:

> Whoever steps on a snake or strikes it
> is the one in whom the snake sinks its fangs.
> But see the mysterious power of backbiters,
> while they tattle in one person's ear,
> someone else's life gets wrecked.

So, dear Damanaka, advise me as a friend. In such a situation, what should I do?'

'In a such a situation, you should just leave this forest and go somewhere else. It is not worthwhile to serve a weak-minded overlord. The wise say,

> Even a guru, arrogant and misleading,
> who lacks duty but upholds misdeeds,
> should be abandoned without fear of sin.'

'I don't think it is wise for me to leave the forest and go elsewhere while Pingalaka is so upset with me,' Sanjivaka stated. 'I'll find no peace, even if I am living in another place. It is said,

> Having offended your superiors,
> don't live under the misconception,
> "I am far away and unreachable."
> Powerful people adept in statecraft
> have hands that reach as far you can go.
> They will strike you down wherever you are.

That's why, I think the only option for me is to fight Pingalaka. Live or die—that is the honourable thing to do. It is said,

> In the desire of heaven
> people go on pilgrimages.
> They do rigorous penances.
> They live a good and moral life.
> Yet heaven remains unattainable.
> But for those who fight in wars
> with valour, courage, and resolve,
> unafraid to sacrifice their lives,
> the gates of heaven open wide.

Besides, he who loses his life in the battlefield not only achieves heaven in the afterlife but also glory in this life. Thus, heroes achieve rare rewards in both the worlds.

> When, from a hero's head wound
> blood trickles into his mouth,
> it is like the elixir of soma
> taken with mantras and rites
> as a reward from a soma yajna.'

This eventuality had not occurred to Damanaka that Sanjivaka would begin to prepare for battle, and with such eagerness. He had thought that he would be able to persuade him to leave the forest. Now he thought, what if he is able to fatally gore Pingalaka with his sharp horns and kill him? That would be catastrophic. 'I must convince this bull to give up the thought of battle and go away,' he said to himself. 'That is the best solution, and that is what I had hoped to accomplish.' So, looking sceptical, he said Sanjivaka, 'I hear what you are saying, friend. But how can a retainer and a king battle against each other? People say,

> A wise man keeps his anger in check
> on seeing an enemy more powerful.
> Like cool rays of a winter moon,
> his demeanour changes to peaceful.

Also,

> A person who challenges an enemy
> without assessing his strength and prowess
> is defeated, as the mighty ocean was by a titihari.'

'What is this story?' Sanjivaka asked, and Damanaka told the tale.

THE TALE OF HOW THE TITIHARI BIRD DEFEATED THE MIGHTY OCEAN

In a place near the ocean lived a titihara couple. They had been married for many years, but they had no offspring, which tinged their happy married life with sadness. Then, to their great joy, the she-bird conceived. When it was time for her to lay her eggs, she said to her husband, 'Dear husband, my time to deliver our babies is close. Please find us a suitable place where I can safely lay the eggs and hatch them.'

'Dear wife, this ocean shore is a beautiful and romantic spot. Why don't you lay your eggs right here?'

'Yes, it is very romantic. But on a full moon's night, the tide is so powerful that it can take with it a full-grown elephant. My little eggs don't stand a chance.'

'I disagree,' the titihara said with a fond laugh. 'No one, not even this mighty ocean, has the power to take my children.

> Who will dare jump into a forest fire,
> whose smokeless flames reach the sky,
> lapping at gods and birds alike?
>
> Who will dare to lie down to rest
> in the shade of a maddened tusker,
> even if the summer's heat is intense,
> and the wilderness terrain is treeless?
>
> Who wishes to die and go to Yamaloka
> by rousing Yamaraja—the fearsome lion?
> Who can split the forehead of maddened elephants
> and then just fall asleep after the exertion?
>
> Which sensible person knowing right and wrong
> will take a cold-water bath to remove the jitters
> after walking in dawn's bone-chilling wind?

What I'm saying, dear wife, is that to meddle with me is to come face to face with Yamaraja. So don't worry. You go ahead and deliver your babies here without any fear. Besides, you know what they say:

> He who relinquishes his place and flees
> in fear of being overthrown by the enemy
> shames his own birth and his mother.
> For such a one the mother herself
> feels pained like a barren woman.'

While the titihara was going on and on about his abilities, the ocean was listening to him with incredulity. 'How could an insignificant little bird issue such a challenge to me? What arrogance!' the mighty ocean thought. It is truly said,

> Self-importance can fill anyone with hubris.
> Even the little titihara sleeps with its feet up
> thinking that if the sky falls, he will push it back.

'You boastful little titihara,' the ocean said. 'Bring it on! Let me see what you will do when I take away your eggs.' Now the ocean was eager for the mother bird to lay her eggs, and when she finally did, in a spot she thought was safe, the ocean swelled and swept the eggs away with its huge waves. At the time, the tithari had been away, gathering food. When she returned and saw her eggs missing, she was beside herself with grief. Weeping and lamenting, she rushed to her husband and screamed at him, 'You fool. I told you that the tide washes over this whole bank, and it's dangerous to lay eggs here, because the water sweeps everything away. But your head was so swollen with self-importance, you refused to listen to me. Someone has rightly stated,

> He who does not pay heed to words of well-wishers
> dies the same way as the foolish tortoise that fell.'

'What story is this?' the titihara asked his wife, and she related the tale.

THE TALE OF THE TORTOISE WHO DID NOT HEED THE ADVICE OF WELL-WISHERS

In a lake lived a tortoise called Kambugriva (conch neck). He had two hamsa bird friends, Sankata (risky) and Vikata (knotty) who loved him deeply. Every day, the three friends would meet at the edge of the lake and spend their time talking to each other and telling spiritual stories about gods and holy men. At night, the hamsa birds would fly off to their nests and the turtle would swim to his home in the water. In this way, they passed their days in happy camaraderie.

Once, the rains failed to arrive, and the lake began to dry up. 'Friend,' the hamsas said to the tortoise, 'your lake has become like a marsh. How are you living here? We feel your pain. Tell us what we can do to help.'

'You're right,' the tortoise replied. 'It really is becoming impossible to stay in a lake that has no water. I've been thinking about what can be done. It is rightly said,

> One should not lose heart even in adverse situations
> but seek a way out with patience and forbearance.
> Patience breeds sensible thought, which finds solutions,
> like seamen after a shipwreck find driftwood
> to keep afloat and paddle across the water to safety.

When someone is in a dire situation, his friends and relatives should do everything they can to help him. I am very lucky to have you two as my friends. So, here's my plan: first, find out where is the nearest lake that is still full of water. Then, find me a sturdy rope or even a light piece of wood. I'll grab the middle of the wood or rope with my teeth while you two hold its ends and fly me to that lake.'

'Of course, friend Kambugriva,' the hamsas said, 'we'd be happy to do that. But you'll have to be very careful. You must promise to remain quiet throughout the journey, with your teeth clamped tightly. Don't open your mouth, no matter what happens, or you'll fall.'

'Of course, I'll be careful,' the tortoise said, dismissively.

The hamsa birds found a lake nearby and, on their way back, they also picked up an appropriate piece of wood. Kambugriva clamped his teeth around the wood, while Vikata and Sankata grabbed its ends with their beaks, and the three of them flew off into the key, with the tortoise hanging between the birds. They were quite a sight to behold, and as they flew over a town, the townspeople stood and watched them in awe. 'Look at those hamsas flying side by side, carrying a piece of wood. But what is that round object attached to the bottom of the piece?' they asked. 'What an amazing sight!' many said, looking up and pointing at the sky.

The noise below reached the tortoise, and he looked down to see what was going on. When he saw that people were pointing at him, he realized that he was the centre of attention. He wanted to ask his friends if they could make out what people were saying, but as soon as he opened his mouth, he came tumbling down to the ground and died instantly.

'So, you see, husband,' the titihari said to her mate, 'he who does not pay heed to what his well-wishers advise, falls to the ground like the tortoise.

Then there's also this tale: Anagatvidhata and Pratyutpannamati live happily and prosper but Yadabhavishya does not fare well.'

'Tell me that tale,' the titihara bird said to his wife, and she narrated that story.

THE TALE OF THE FISH WHO LEARNED IT IS BETTER TO ACT THAN TO DEPEND ON FATE

In a lake lived three fish, Anagatvidhata (forethought), Pratyutpannamati (one who thinks on his feet), and Yadabhavishya (whatever happens, happens). Their personalities were suited to their names.

One day, fisherman passing by that lake saw that it was brimming with fish. 'Why have we never fished in this lake?' one of them said. 'It looks like we will have a very good catch. We should cast our nets here.'

'How about tomorrow morning?' another one suggested. 'We have enough of a catch for today, and the sun is also about to set. So, let's come here tomorrow morning.'

The creatures of the lake heard the fishermen and were struck dumb with fear. Then, chaos erupted as they all tried to find a way to escape the impending doom. Finally, Anagatvidhata called a meeting. 'You heard what these killers of fish intend to do tomorrow,' he said. 'I suggest that we all leave this lake tonight. The wise say,

> In the face of a powerful enemy,
> the weak should flee to save their lives,
> or hide in some secret hidden place.
> For the weak, there is no other choice.

Before those fishermen come tomorrow morning with their nets, we should find a new place to live. It is also said,

> If you can find livelihood and be happy
> in a new place where you can go,
> wisdom is in leaving your land
> rather than seeing your kin destroyed.'

Pratyutpannamati found Anagatvidhata's words to be very wise. 'I agree with you whole-heartedly,' he said. 'We all must leave this place as soon possible. People say,

> Those who fear leaving their land,
> such as the prideful, domesticated,

impotent, cowards, crows, and deer
end up suffering and dying in that land.

In my opinion, a talented man can live successfully anywhere, in any country.'

Hearing what Anagatvidhata and Pratyutpannamati had to say, Yadabhavishya burst into laughter. 'How is it acceptable to leave the land of your fathers and grandfathers?' he asked. 'And only because you happened to hear some fishermen discuss a vague plan. For all we know, it could've been idle talk. Besides, if our end has arrived, then no matter where we go, death is inevitable. And if it is our fate to live longer, then even if we stay here, no one can touch us. It is said,

> One who is unprotected
> is made secure by the gods.
> But if the gods are inimical,
> all means of protection are futile
> and destruction is inevitable.
> An orphan abandoned in the forest
> will survive if fated to do so.
> And even if someone is at home,
> protected by a lakh efforts,
> if death has come knocking, he'll die.

Hence, I will not leave this place. You all do what is best for you.'

That night, all those who agreed with Anagatvidhata and Pratyutpannamati gathered their families and left the lake and found other water bodies. Whereas, all those who sided with Yadabhavishya stayed in the lake. The following morning, when the fisherman came and spread their nets, they were all caught and killed.

'So, I'm telling you, husband,' the female titihari said, 'he who recognizes a calamity about to happen and finds a way to protect against it, even before it happens, lives a life of peace and happiness. And he who looks towards fate to make his decision for him is destroyed.'

The male titihara was hurt by his wife's taunt. 'Do you think of me as a slave to fate like that Yadabhavishya? You have not seen my mettle and the power of my intellect. I can dry up this ocean just by using my beak.'

'What are you saying?' the female titihari scoffed. 'How can you compare yourself to the mighty ocean? A battle between you and the ocean is unthinkable, so stop puffing yourself up with indignation. It is said,

> Those who have unrealistic notions about themselves
> end up getting hurt with their own rising anger,
> just as an iron vessel sitting on a burning fire
> gets hot and hotter, making its own backside burn.

Also,

> One who mounts an attack on an enemy
> in a rush of impatience and ignorance,
> lacking sense of his own and the enemy's ability,
> burns to ashes, like a moth caught in flames.'

'Don't speak like that, wife,' the male titihara said. 'One whose spirit is indomitable, even if he is diminutive in size, can tackle anyone, of any size. That is why people cite this example:

> Even though the moon is full
> Rahu does not hesitate to attack it.
> We see this during every lunar eclipse.

Also, this:

> The mountainous elephant is bigger than a lion,
> and his forehead becomes darkened with madness.
> For that very reason, the lion strikes him and fells him.

And more:

> Those born radiant and courageous—
> what meaning does age have for them?
> Dawn's rays touch the heads of mountains and kings
> even though at that time the sun is only newly born.

And consider,

> An elephant is strong and enormous,
> yet it is controlled by the goad.
> Does that mean the goad equals the elephant?
> No, it does not mean that at all.
> The dark is dispelled by a small diya.
> Is the light only as little as its flame?
> No, it eliminates a roomful of darkness.
> Great mountains are shattered

by the strike of Indra's lightning.
Is a lightning bolt as big as a mountain?
No, it is nowhere close to that size.

That is why, one who is brilliant and courageous is always bigger; size doesn't matter in the least. You want me to show you what I can do? I'll empty the ocean and make it as dry as this sandy bank.'

'My dear husband,' said the female titihari, 'the ocean in which Ganga ji and Sindhu rivers assimilate, each with their nine hundred tributaries, making it swell everyday with water from eighteen hundred sources, how can you, a tiny bird with a beak that can pick up no more than a drop of water at a time, empty it of water and make it dry?'

'Dearest,' said the male titihara to his wife, 'not declaring a loss right at the outset is the first principle of gaining wealth. Don't underestimate my beak; it is like a beak of iron that never wears out. Also, know that the quantity of time is relative. Sometimes, even the time that stretches between a day and night can be immense. Everyone knows,

> Unless one puts in the effort
> and does not shy from taking risks,
> success and progress do not happen.
> Even Suryadeva must climb the scales of Libra
> to win victory over rain clouds.'

Seeing her husband so adamant, the titihari gave in. 'Dear, if you are bent on battling the ocean, then go ahead. But please heed my advice and take the help of other birds and our friends and relatives, because it is said,

> When weak individuals gather as one,
> they form a group strong and invincible,
> just as a strand of hay, though insignificant,
> when woven with other strands, becomes
> a rope that can bind powerful elephants.

It is also said,

> Together, the sparrow, woodpecker, bee, and frog
> took on the maddened elephant and killed him.'

'Tell me this story,' the male titihara asked, and his wife related the tale.

THE TALE OF HOW THE SPARROW, WOODPECKER, BEE, AND FROG TEAMED UP TO KILL THE ELEPHANT

In a forest, on a tamala (Indian bay leaf) tree, there lived a sparrow couple. Once, when the female sparrow had just laid eggs, an intoxicated, wild elephant, exhausted and sweating from the heat, came and stood under the tree. In his madness, he wrapped his trunk around the branch on which the sparrows were nesting and broke it. All the eggs smashed on the ground, but the sparrow couple somehow survived. The bereaved mother sparrow was beside herself with grief, and all she could do was weep and lament. Her friend, the woodpecker, who saw the tragedy, could hardly bear her heart-wrenching sobs and tried to console her, 'Hush, my friend. Stop crying. Your tears will not bring your babies back. The wise say,

> People who have the ability to think logically
> do not bemoan the lost, the dead, the past.
> This is how a fool and an intelligent person differ.

Besides,

> All creatures in this world
> are mortal and evanescent.
> It is foolish to weep for them.
> He who grieves for the perishable
> sinks deeper into his own grief.

Also, think about this:

> The spirit of the departed
> must drink the tears of the bereaved,
> It is not tears the departed need
> but death rites and proper rituals
> that will benefit the soul's afterlife.'

'You're right, dear friend,' the sparrow said to the woodpecker. 'But how can I forgive this wicked elephant who destroyed our offspring in a fit of madness. If you consider yourself my friend, then help me think of how I can get my revenge. Only by killing him will I feel consoled and find peace.'

'I know what you mean,' said the woodpecker.

> 'A true friend comes to your aid in times of need.
> Everyone can be your friend in times of prosperity.
> Need is what brings people together, not caste similarity.

It is also said:

> A friend who helps in need is a true friend indeed.
> A son who is devoted to his parents is a true son indeed.
> A servant who fulfils his duty is a true servant indeed.
> A wife whose husband is happy is a true wife indeed.

Now, watch me. See how I punish that elephant who killed your children. I'll enlist the help of my friend, the bee, Veenarava (hum of a veena).'

Hence, the woodpecker took the sparrow with him to meet the bee. 'This is my friend, Sparrow,' he said to Veenarava. 'A wild, mad elephant smashed her eggs on the ground and didn't even apologize. She is feeling very dejected and disrespected. Can you help us punish that elephant?'

'Need you even ask? Veenarava said. 'Your friend is dearer to me than even you. Because it is said,

> Friends helping friends is merely
> a give and take of friendship.
> But to help a friend's friend—
> now that is true friendship.

But wait, I, too, have a friend—a frog. His name is Meghanada (music of the clouds). Let me call him as well. Together, we will come up with the best strategy to destroy that wicked elephant. As they say,

> The remedy that one concocts together
> with noble, educated, and wise men,
> who wish well and are well-intentioned,
> that remedy is faultless and appropriate,
> and it rarely ever fails to be effective.'

So, the three of them—the sparrow, the woodpecker, and the bee went to meet Meghanada, the frog, and apprised him of the situation.

'That intoxicated elephant will be reduced to nothing by our combined effort,' the frog promised after hearing the whole story. 'Here is what I suggest we do: O bee, go and gently buzz in his ear. Hearing your sweet hum, the elephant will get drowsy and close his eyes. O woodpecker, after that, it's your turn. Once the elephant goes to sleep, you will peck his eyes out and blind him. When he gets up, he will be thirsty, but blindness will make him disoriented. I will then go to a dark pit and begin croaking. Following my frog sound, thinking it must be from a nearby pond, he will stagger towards me and will inevitably tumble into the pit and die. Thus, we will all form a group of avengers and avenge the death of Sparrow's babies.'

The four avengers then followed the plan: Veenarava, the bee, flew to the elephant and began to hum a lullaby in his ear. As soon as he fell asleep, the woodpecker poked his eyes out with his beak. When he woke up and began lurching around, looking for water, Meghanada, the frog, found a deep pit and began croaking from its edge. Following that siren sound, the elephant tumbled into the pit and died.

'So, you see', the titihari said to her husband, 'how tiny creatures, like the sparrow, woodpecker, bee, and frog came together with a common goal and managed to destroy the immense elephant?'

'Dear one, I'll do exactly as you instruct. I'll talk to our friends and relatives, and we'll deal with the ocean together.'

Hence, the male titihara visited each of the bird species—cranes, herons, peacocks, etc., and, sharing with them his and his wife's grievance against the ocean, requested them to join him in his quest: 'Dear friends, my wife and I are not only grieving the death of our children, but we are also feeling insulted. Hence, do you see why I must teach the ocean a lesson by drying up its waters? Can you help me?'

The birds conferred and then responded to the titihara's request: 'We are not capable of drying up the ocean's water. In fact, we think that it is futile to even try. It is said,

> The weak one, who, drunk with vainglory,
> mounts an attack on an enemy more powerful
> suffers immense pain and a shameful defeat,
> in the same way that an intoxicated tusker
> has his tusks crushed if he battles a mountain.

Thus, we can't attack the mighty ocean and hope for victory. We are too weak. But here is what we should do: our king and lord is Garudaji. Let's go to him and tell him what the ocean has done to you, and how its actions have insulted the whole bird community.'

'Okay,' the titihara nodded. 'But what if he does nothing?'

'Even if Garudaji does not agree to help us get revenge, or if he listens to us in silence and offers no advice, it will be our gain, because people say,

> Intimate friends, talented, respectful servants,
> a like-minded wife, and a strong and able king—
> confiding in these people makes one feel supported.

Therefore, the birds all went to Lord Garuda to request his help. Arriving in his palace, with sorrowful faces and tearful eyes, they began to beseech him, 'O Lord Garuda, our king. We have come to tell you about a matter of grave injustice that has been meted out to one of us. How can such a thing happen when you are our king?'

'Please tell me what has happened?' Garuda asked.

'The innocent titihari couple had their eggs stolen by the ocean. If crimes such as this continue to occur, all species of birds will be wiped out. In this instance, the ocean is the culprit, but soon there will be other copycats who will carry out similar crimes against birds. It is said,

> When one man does a bad deed,
> others are sure to follow suit,
> because that is the nature of man.

Also,

> Thugs, thieves, and robbers,
> flatterers, cheats, and deceivers—
> it is the king's duty to protect subjects
> from the acts of such criminals.

It is said,

> The king who protects his subjects well
> receives one-sixth share of their dharma.
> The king who fails to protect his subjects well
> receives one-sixth of the sin incurred
> by both his subjects and the criminals.

Also,

> The suffering of subjects generates a fire so destructive,
> it can turn to ashes the king's wealth, family, and life.
> and it cannot be doused till the king's all is destroyed.

> The king hoping to share in his subjects' prosperity
> must nurture people, like a gardener does his plants.
> He waters them, feeds them, and protects them,
> till seeds burst into tender sprouts and flower.
> In the same way, subjects nurtured and cared for
> reward their king with fruits borne by his care.

The king's wealth, his gems and jewels, and his money to buy material comforts are all generated from his subjects. That is why a king whose subjects are happy is called a wealthy king.'

Hearing the birds' lament, Garuda was saddened. He was also angered by the ocean's arrogance. Even as he as he was debating about how to punish the ocean, Lord Vishnu's messenger came to summon him. 'The Lord needs to travel to Amaravati, the region of the gods, and he wants you to come quickly to Vaikuntha—the abode of Vishnu.'

Being summoned by Lord Vishnu always filled Garuda with a sense of pride for being the Lord's mount, but this time he saw it as an opportunity to enlist the Lord's help in fulfilling the birds' request. 'Tell Lord Vishnu that I am unable to go,' he said to the messenger. 'In fact, tell him that I resign from my duties, and he should employ another mount.'

'What are you saying?' the messenger was shocked. 'How can you refuse the Supreme Lord. Besides, he is your lord, and you are his servant.'

Garudaji's response was:

> 'If an employee's talents are unrecognized,
> he should leave that employer and seek another.
> That employer will never help him progress,
> just as a barren field will yield no grain,
> no matter how much one works to till it.

Also, tell Vishnuji that his attendant, the ocean, has stolen the eggs of the titihari bird, who is one of my subjects. Unless the Lord does something about this and punishes the ocean, I cannot work for him.'

When Vishnu heard Garuda's passionate response to his summons, he recognized the trust hidden in Garuda's refusal. 'He is rightfully angry. I should go myself and talk to him,' he said.

> 'For his own welfare and prosperity,
> an employer should respect and love
> an employee who is devoted to him.

Also,

> A king pleased with his servant only
> rewards him with money or promotions.
> But a servant who is respected and content
> is willing to give up his life for the king.'

Thinking these thoughts, Lord Vishnu rushed to Rukmapura, Garuda's city. When Garuda saw Lord Vishnu at his doorstep, he lowered his gaze in embarrassment for having been so presumptuous. 'Lord,' he said to him, 'I am honoured that you have come yourself to enquire about my reasons for refusing your summons. But, your attendant, the ocean, has dishonoured me by stealing the eggs of one of my subjects. Due to my respect for you, I have not punished him thus far, otherwise, in no time at all, I would have dried him up and changed him into land.'

> A respectful servant should never do anything
> that pains his master, even if it means his own death.

'You are right, my dear Garuda,' Vishnu replied. 'A master is responsible for his servants' wrongdoing, and even more than the servant, it is the master who should be ashamed of the wrongful action. Therefore, I am truly to blame for what the ocean has done. But I'm here to remedy the situation. Let's go and get the titihari's eggs back from the ocean and then head to Amaravati.'

Standing at the water's edge with Garuda, Lord Vishnu first chided the ocean, and then, mounting the fire missile arrow on his bow, he threatened him, 'Wicked being. Return the titihari's eggs right away, or I will make you as dry as the earth.'

Trembling in fear, the ocean immediately brought the eggs to the bank. The titihara, who was waiting nearby with bated breath, quickly collected them and flew home to his wife to hand them over to her.

Hearing this tale, Damanaka said to Sanjivaka, 'That's exactly what I was telling you. It is not wise to attack an enemy whose power and strength one does not know. But a person should never give up the effort or stop working towards goals. Just like the titihara did not stop at anything to get his eggs back.'

'I know what you are saying,' Sanjivaka replied. 'But it's hard for me to comprehend that Pingalaka is upset with me. For days, he has only showered me with love, and he has always been gracious about showing me how happy he is with me. Also, I have never seen him upset at me, or even witnessed any signs of anger. Then tell me why I should think that he is now my enemy and plans to kill me? And why should I make plans to kill him for my protection?'

'If it is signs you're looking for, then I'll tell you what they are. Next time you see him, notice if he looks at you with reddened eyes. Also, see whether his forehead is creased in a frown, and if he is licking the corners of his lips. When he displays any of these signs, know that the lion is readying to lunge at you. If you don't see any of these signals, then disregard what I have said and continue being his friend. But now I must go home. Just promise me that you will not share with anyone what I've said to you. And take my advice: if I were you, I would get out of his forest this very night. It is said,

> If an individual's death saves a family,
> it is better to kill the individual.
> If a family's destruction saves a village,
> it is better to destroy the family.
> If eliminating a village saves a township,
> it is better to eliminate the village.

In other words, if the destruction of one can save many, then it should be done. But if the matter is of one's own life, then all bets are off and nothing else matters. It is said,

> Protect your wealth for emergencies,
> but spend the wealth to protect your wife.
> and to protect yourself, give up both wealth and wife.

Also,

> If one's enemy is strong
> it is politic to either leave town
> or to make friends with him.

That is why I'm telling you that to save yourself, you should leave the forest and go somewhere else. But if you don't want to leave, then you should at least try to make that lion favourable towards you again, perhaps by flattering him. The wise say,

> One should try to do whatever possible—good or bad
> to save oneself from poverty and distress.
> Dharma comes later, when one has the means.

Also, do consider:

> It is foolishness to cling to wealth
> when one's life is in grave danger.
> Once life goes, what use are money and wealth?'

With that last thought Damanaka bid Sanjivaka farewell and returned to Karataka.

As soon as Karataka saw Damanaka, he asked him, 'Tell me what you have done.'

'I have sowed the seed of division; now let's see what fruit it bears. I've done the work; let's see what fate will bring us, because it is said,

> Even if fate is unfavourable,
> one must continue the effort
> for one's own self-affirmation.

Also,

> Lakshmi goes to him who works.
> Fate and luck are excuses of the lazy.

'But do tell me what divisive game you have played. What did you say? What did they say?' Karataka asked, anxiously.

'I told each one about the other's intention to kill him and created such a rift between them that I guarantee will never be bridged. You'll never see them sitting together, or talking, or conferring.'

'Oh, this is not good. By making them suspicious of each other, you have pushed two beings, who were happy, into an ocean of bile. You have not done a good deed. It is said,

> The evil person who creates distress and grief
> in the lives of those who bear no enmity
> and are happy and content in their world,
> finds no happiness in his life and goes to hell.

Also, the fact that you are patting yourself on the back for turning them against each other is just not right. You see, it's easy to cause harm, and once that downward slide begins, it's hard to stop it.

> Causing ruin is not a difficult feat,
> but very few know how to construct.
> The wind has the power to only fell trees,
> it does not have the power to re-erect them.'

'My dear friend,' Damanaka replied, 'you don't know the secrets of Nitishastra, the system of politics and statecraft; that is why you speak like that. Nitishastra says that the man who does not get rid of an enemy or a disease at its very outset will one day be killed by one or the other, no matter how powerful he is. And this Sanjivaka is certainly our enemy; he is stealing our ancestral ministerial posts from us. Besides, I'm the one who brought him to Pingalaka with an oath of safe conduct. I thought he was just an ordinary bull, and the two would just meet and greet and then part ways. How was I to know that he would make such an impression on the lion and sabotage our own positions? People say,

> If a good man, out of a goodness of heart
> shows his high position to an evil man,
> beware! That evil person begins to plot
> how to destroy and replace the good man.

Hence, wisdom dictates not allowing any evil person into your home or business. That is why I've had to plan Sanjivaka's ruin. Either he'll leave town, or he'll get killed. But listen, dear Karataka, no one knows this secret plan, except you, so please keep it that way. And I assure you that this is the best plan for both of us. It is said,

> Making your heart stony and ruthless
> but your tongue as sweet as sugar,
> you should kill the one who wrongs you.
> What is the point in dithering about it?

Besides, think about this: once this Sanjivaka dies, he'll also become our food. In fact, there are so many benefits of his death—firstly, we'll avenge ourselves for what he has done to us; secondly, we'll regain our lost positions; and thirdly, his meat will satisfy our hunger. A triple reward! I can't believe you are rebuking me for accomplishing all this. You truly are a fool, and you have no idea about politics. Whereas, I am like the man who can achieve multiple goals with one action.

While hurting the enemy, he makes gain for himself,
yet no one sees how shrewdly his mind works.
Just like Chaturaka the jackal, who no one knew,
rid himself of the enemy, made personal gain,
and managed to secure food for many days.'

'What is that story?' Karataka asked, and Damanaka began narrating it.

THE TALE OF THE CLEVER JACKAL WHO SCHEMED TO ELIMINATE THE COMPETITION

In the deepest part of a forest lived a lion called Vajradanshtra (teeth like lightning bolts). He had two attendants who always stayed by his side—a jackal called Chaturaka (very smart) and a hyena named Kravyamukha (one who eats carrion). One day, the lion saw a pregnant camel, who was writhing in the last throes of labour pains. She was probably left behind by her caravan because of her state. The lion leapt on the defenceless animal and killed her. When he tore open her belly, a little calf, who was still alive, fell out. Since the camel's meat was enough to satisfy the lion and satiate the hunger of his followers, the lion saw no reason to kill the calf. And, since the baby had nowhere else to go, he brought it home to his den. 'Listen child,' he said to him, 'you have no one to fear in this forest. Roam around as you please and consider this den your home. I will also give you a name. Since you have straight and sharp ears, like nails, I'll call you Shankukarna.'

From then on, the camel calf began to live fearlessly in the forest, and soon he joined the jackal and hyena in attending to the king, and the four of them became inseparable. As the calf grew into adulthood, he became so attached to the lion that he refused to leave his side, even for a moment.

Once, the lion battled a wild tusker whose vicious attacks gravely wounded him, tearing open his sides and breaking one of his paws. Limping and bleeding profusely, the lion managed to return to his den, but he did not have enough strength to go out and hunt for food. Day by day, his throat grew dry like the desert and his stomach ached with hunger. Finally, one day, he said to his trusted companions, 'Just go and catch a creature and bring him here to me, and I'll kill him so that we can all eat.'

The hyena, jackal, and camel roamed all day in the forest, but they were unable to catch a single animal. When, at sundown, they were headed back to the lion's den, Chaturaka, the jackal, began to think: what if we kill this Shankukarna? That way, the rest of us can eat his meat for a while. But then he thought that the lion would never kill him. Not only did Shankukarna stay in his den, but also, he loved him like a son. 'Maybe I can persuade the lion to kill Shankukarna,' he said to himself. 'After all, it is said,

Nothing is impossible for a smart man.
No path is inaccessible; no task is impossible.'

With a plan hatching in his mind, Chaturaka went to the camel and said to him, 'Our Maharaj, the lion, is starving. His hunger might kill him, and if he dies, we'll all be without protection. Hence, for the welfare of our Maharaj, I want to say something to you; please listen carefully.'

'Tell me quickly, Chaturaka, my friend,' Shankukarna said. 'If I can do something for the welfare of our Maharaj, it'll make me feel like I have done a thousand good deeds.'

'Give up your body for our Vajradanshtra, and you'll get back a body twice its size. This way, our Maharaj will be saved, and you'll also reap benefits from it.'

'If what you say is possible, then what a fantastic deal it is. Go and tell our Maharaj that I'm willing to give up my body, but he must guarantee it, with dharma as witness, that I'll get back double my body.'

'Yes, yes, of course, he will guarantee it,' Chaturaka promised.

Then, accompanied by the hyena and the camel, he went to the lion and said, 'Maharaj, we searched the whole forest, and we couldn't catch a single animal. But there is a solution. Our Shankukarna will give up his current body for your consumption, provided you make him a promise, with dharma as witness, that he will get back double his body.'

'Oh really?' said Vajradanshtra. 'This is wonderful news. If Shankukarna is willing to give up his body, with dharma as witness to this debt, then, so be it.'

No sooner had the lion said these words than the jackal and the hyena fell upon the camel and tore him apart, and, as soon as he breathed his last, they stepped away so that Vajradanshtra could begin feeding. The lion got up, groaning in pain, but, instead of eating, headed out of the den. 'I must bathe and pray to the gods before I eat,' he stated. 'Chaturaka, please watch my food until I return from the river.'

As Chaturaka sat watching the camel meat, his mouth began to water. 'I wish this camel meat were all mine,' he muttered to himself. 'What can I do to make it so?' Playing out various scenarios in his mind, he settled on one plan and decided to execute it. Waiting for a while, allowing the lion enough time to finish his bath, he called Kravyamukha and said to him, 'You look really hungry, dear friend. Why don't you begin eating the camel? I'll keep watch while you do. As soon as I see the lion, I'll let you know, and you can stop. I'll even engage him in such a way that he won't question why some of the meat is gone.'

The hyena gave Chaturaka a grateful look and then dug his teeth into the meat. However, he had hardly taken one bite, when Chaturaka warned, 'Stop! The lion is coming.' The hyena immediately jumped away, licking his lips.

When Vajradanshtra saw a bite-sized chunk missing from the camel, he knew that someone had started eating it. 'Who has touched my meat?' he roared. 'Tell me quickly and I will make him my food, as well.'

Kravyamukha glanced at Chaturaka, beseeching him to remain quiet.

'Why are you looking at me now,' Chaturaka said with an uncomfortable laugh. 'First you begin eating the camel without telling me, and then you expect me to help you. Now suffer the rewards of your greedy action.'

Kravyamukha was shocked to hear Chaturaka's words and was hurt by his deceit, but there was nothing he could do. With the lion eyeing him wrathfully, all he could do was flee as quickly as he could.

Having rid himself of one contender, Chaturaka now wondered how he could make the lion give up the kill, as well. Then happenstance worked in his favour. Just as Vajradanshtra sat down to eat, a strange sound, like a ringing of a bell, came from the forest. The lion leapt away from the meat and hid himself. 'Find out what that sound is,' he whispered to Chaturaka. When the jackal went to investigate, he was met by a sight that delighted him. A caravan with several camels was crossing the forest, and the camel in the front had a large bell around his neck which rang as he plodded along. Rushing back to the lion's den, Chaturaka shouted, 'Run, Maharaj! Run!'

'What is it? Vajradanshtra asked fearfully. 'You're scaring me. Tell me what you saw.'

'Maharaj, remember you made dharma your witness when you killed Shankukarna? It seems that you angered Dharmaraja by killing him, and he himself has come to punish you. He has bought with him a whole herd of camels along with Shankukarna's father, grandfather, and great-grandfather from the other world. They are all coming this way. The camel in the front is wearing a big warning bell, and that is what you hear ringing. Run, I say. That's the only way you can save yourself.'

Stepping close to the entrance of his den, Vajradanshtra saw the truth of Chaturaka's words. Then, without so much as a glance at Shankukarna's meat, he took a long leap out of his den and fled the forest.

And that is how Chaturaka was left with the whole camel, which he ate for many days with much relish.

'So, you see, Karataka,' Damanaka said. 'As I was telling you, just like this Chaturaka, who was able to get rid of his contenders with just talk, I too am adept at weaving a web of deceit, and no one will be able to see truth through it. This is how our purpose will also be realized.'

In the meantime, after Damanaka had left, Sanjivaka had started to think: what a fool I am and what terrible error in judgement I have made. I am a grass-eater; yet trusting that meat devourer, Pingalaka, I became his minister. Someone has rightly said,

> That dimwit who visits those who shouldn't be visited,
> who serves those who are not worthy of being served,
> summons his own death like the mule mare does
> when it conceives, only to expire after childbirth.

What am I to do now? Where should I go? How do I save myself? Then he thought, what if I go to Pingalaka and throw myself upon his mercy? Perhaps, if I seek his refuge, he'll feel dharma-bound to protect me. Then he won't kill me. It is well known that

> Just as fire burns the skin
> heat from the fire cures the burn.

But it is also well known that:

> Every being in this world is living out
> his good and evil karma of a past birth
> by engaging in tasks good and bad.
> Whatever good and evil he incurs
> inevitably gets him equal and fair rewards.
> There is no doubt about this cycle of life.

Finally, Sanjivaka accepted the situation and told himself that there was no point in worrying; whatever had to happen would happen. Even if he left the forest and went far away, it wouldn't make a difference, because if he were to be eaten as prey, then it would happen, no matter where he was.

Thinking these thoughts, Sanjivaka started walking with trembling legs and faltering steps in the direction of the grove where Pingalaka was holding audience. In his mind, he was chanting the following shloka:

> When one enters a king's beautiful palace,
> teaming with schemers, liars, and thugs
> and men who are cruel and ruthless,

> one is fearful, baffled, and hesitant,
> in a way that one would be if one entered
> a welcoming house where a snake resides,
> or a verdant forest that is engulfed in flames,
> or a glorious lake that is covered with lotuses
> but is filled with ferocious, devouring beasts.

As Sanjivaka drew near to Pingalaka, he saw what Damanaka had warned him about: the lion's eyes were red, and there was a deep frown on his forehead. Seeing these signs, such terror struck his heart that he could not even bow to him in greeting. Cowering, he found a place in a corner, quite at a distance from the lion. Pingalaka, too, looked at the bull and saw what Damanaka had warned him about: his eyes were red, his lips were trembling, and his eyeballs were darting from side to side. 'That traitor,' Pingalaka muttered, and, unable to suppress his rage at the bull's treachery, he leapt at him, drawing his sharp claws all the way down his back, tearing through skin and flesh. Swinging around, Sanjivaka thrust his horns in the lion's belly, and soon the two of them were locked in combat. Before long, they were both covered in so much blood that they looked like palash trees in full bloom. Still, they fought, tearing and biting and goring. Seeing them battle, Karataka chided Damanaka, 'By provoking these two to fight, you have done a terrible deed. You think you know Nitishastra; you don't even know the basic principle of policy. You are a complete fool.

> The basic tenet of policymaking is this:
> great rewards seized from battle,
> from bravely attacking another,
> from strenuous effort of combat,
> can easily be gained by the policy
> of love, patience, and negotiation.
> True ministers know this learning.

On the other hand, ministers who, willy-nilly, invoke violence and mete out cruel punishments at the smallest provocation, jeopardize the king's name and wealth. Think, if Pingalaka is killed in this battle, what'll be the benefit of your policy of divisiveness? And if Sanjivaka is not killed but is heavily wounded, he'll suffer in prolonged pain, through no fault of his own. What good-willed and just minister orchestrates such situations? How do you even aspire to a ministerial post, when you have no idea how to resolve matters in a peaceful manner? One who incites people to war and violence can never be a successful minister. It is said,

> There are four ways to accomplish a task:
> Sama, dana, bheda, danda. (conciliate, compensate, cause dissent, and punish)
> Brahmaji himself has established these.
> Out of these, danda is only the last resort,
> to be used when no other method works.

Also,

> If a task can be accomplished with sama,
> the wise would never employ danda.
> If heat rash can be cured by eating sugar,
> why would one eat the bitter leaves of parwal?

That is why a smart scholar first employs sama, because a task accomplished with agreement and assent rarely ever fails. On the other hand,

> Enmity is such a darkness that nothing,
> not even the rays of the moon or the sun,
> or the light from a fire can dispel.
> Darkness that spreads from enmity
> negates any possibility of an accord.

Let me tell you that you are completely unsuited for the post of a minister, because you really have no idea what the duties of a minister are. A minister's counsel is of five kinds: the process to begin a task; analysis of the money and people to be employed in that task; the division of labour, time, and task; a plan of recourse in place, just in case a fault arises, or something doesn't go as planned; and a clear certainty of expected results. Good counsel of a good minister takes all this into account.

But look what your counsel has done; it has brought our king and his minister to the verge of death. Now, if you are capable, think about how to rectify this situation. A test of a wise adviser is how he resolves an issue gone wrong. But I can tell you, you evil fool, that you are incapable of resolving this matter. It is aptly said,

> The wisdom of a minister is tested
> when he finds a solution to problems.
> A doctor's acumen and skill are tested
> when he treats a patient with delirium.

> Who isn't a pundit in humdrum tasks?
> Even housewives have home remedies
> to cure ordinary, everyday sicknesses.

Lowly people always like to ruin other people's projects, but they don't know how to resolve matters.

> A mouse can only spill and gnaw a basket of wheat.
> He cannot clean the spill and repair gnawed holes.

But you know what, Damanaka, I can't really blame you. The fault is actually our king's, the lion who trusted you and believed your lies. It is rightly said,

> Kings who trust the lowly
> and let them be their guides,
> ignoring the wise and noble,
> end up trapped in such prisons
> of calamity and enmity
> from which there is no release.

And, unfortunately, by some twisted quirk of fate, if you do manage to become Pingalaka's minister, I can tell you that no noble being will serve him, because it is said,

> A king may have the best qualities,
> but if his minister is ignoble and evil,
> no noble person will benefit from him.
> like a lake that may have the purest water,
> but if it has crocodiles swimming in it,
> no sane man will step into it to bathe.

Thus, when refined men stop visiting this king, his failure as a monarch is imminent. It is said,

> The king that entertains retainers
> who only make sugary conversations
> of flattery, flummery, and gossip,
> with no skill of how to pull a bow string,
> opens his kingdom and wealth to enemies.

It is useless to give advice to idiots like you; in fact, it is downright harmful.

A wood incapable of soaking water
can never become moist.
A knife cannot cut stone.
This is what Suchimukha learned:
when one counsels someone
who has not asked for counsel,
that counsel falls on deaf ears.

'What is this tale?' Damanaka asked, and Karataka told him the story.

THE TALE OF HOW THE NAGGING NEEDLE-BEAKED BIRD LOST HER LIFE

In a mountainous region lived a troop of monkeys. One winter, the weather suddenly became severe with gusts of icy cold winds and snow and hail, followed by torrential rain. The monkeys were caught unawares. Their bodies beaten by the slapping winds, and their furs knotted with icicles, they searched everywhere for shelter.

Suddenly, a few of the monkeys came upon a bush of gunja fruits, and thinking their bright red colour were sparks from a fire, they sat down around it, blowing on it, hoping for the sparks to flame. Watching these monkeys from a tree was a weaver bird, Suchimukha (beak like a needle's eye). He called down to the monkeys, 'You all are dimwits. Don't you see that these are not sparks of fire? They are gunja fruits. No matter how hard you blow on them, they're not going to catch and create a flame. You can't warm yourself on these. If you want to escape the cold, then find a cave or a crevice in a mountain, or some other spot that will shield you from the wind. If I were you, I'd hurry, because it appears that it'll rain again. The sky is still covered with heavy rain clouds.'

The monkeys listened to the bird with annoyance, and an old monkey among them, replied, 'What business is it of yours what we do? Who are you to lecture us? Go. Be on your way. It is said,

> One who wishes success in an endeavour
> should refrain from talking to anyone
> who has failed numerous times himself,
> or anyone who gambles and takes risks,
> or one who constantly tries to catch a prey,
> but not a single animal can he catch,
> or one who is stuck in misfortune himself.
> Conversing with them is an exchange of insults.'

Suchimukha paid no heed to what the old monkey had to say; instead, he continued to call the monkeys fools, reiterating that their efforts would yield no results.

Tired of his constant jabbering, one of the monkeys grabbed him and smashed him on a rock. Suchimukha died instantly.

'That's why I said to you,' Karataka said to Damanaka, 'just like it is futile to moisten dry wood or cut a stone with a knife, it is futile to give advice to a fool. Also,

> Advice makes a fool angry,
> it disturbs him even more,
> just like giving milk to serpents
> increases their venom.

And,

> Never give advice without thinking.
> By giving the foolish monkey advice,
> the beautiful bird had its nest destroyed.

'Tell me that tale' said Damanaka, and Karataka related the tale.

THE TALE OF THE CHATAKA BIRD'S UNWANTED ADVICE

In a forest was a shami (also known as banni) tree with very long branches. In one of the branches, a chataka (cuckoo) couple had made their nest, and they lived there happily. One winter day, it began to rain. As the clouds opened up, temperatures fell, and the air became chilly. A monkey, caught in the downpour, his body trembling like a blade of grass in the wind, and his teeth chattering like an instrument, found his way to the tree and sat down among its roots, huddling as close to the trunk as possible to shield himself from the wind and rain.

Seeing him in this condition, the female bird called down to him: 'Brother, you have able hands and feet, and you seem to have a face like man's; however, you're suffering in this freezing rain. You look like a fool. Why don't you make a dwelling for yourself so that you can shelter in it during weather such as this?'

The monkey became irritated at the bird's advice: 'Why don't you just mind your own business and sit quietly in your nest?' he said to the bird. 'Who has asked for your advice?'

'I'm just telling you what a waste it is to have able limbs and not to put them to good use.'

I can't believe this bird's wickedness, the monkey thought. She's mocking me at a time like this. This evil, lowly scut, who thinks she knows it all. Jabbering away, non-stop. Not afraid of me at all. Doesn't she realize, I could climb up this tree and strike her dead in an instant? Maybe that's exactly what I should do. 'You stupid bird,' he called up to her, angrily, 'what is to you whether I'm happy or suffering. Mind your own stupid business. Who are you to tell me what to do? Haven't you heard,

> Advise someone who respects you,
> and only if he insists,
> and only for his benefit.
> Without respect, advice is as useless
> as weeping in an empty forest.

So, shut up. I don't need your advice.'

'I'm just saying....' the bird began, but the monkey had had enough.

'Let me show you what happens to those who recklessly spew advice,' he said, climbing the tree in two bounds. Then, reaching into the branch, he grabbed the nest of the chataka birds and tore it to pieces.

'Poor bird. She became homeless simply for giving unwanted advice. That is what I'm telling you,' Karataka said. 'Your advice can be the cause of your own harm. I told you not to interfere in their business, but you didn't listen to me. My words just go in one ear and out the other.

> A learning mind learns a given lesson.
> What good is it to teach a closed mind?
> It is like a lamp placed in a deep hole
> that cannot dispel the darkness outside.

In your arrogance of being a know-it-all, you never listen; hence, you never see the harm you are doing yourself or others. This is the conclusion I have drawn about you: either you have no sense at all, or you're just downright wicked.

It is aptly said:

> Books of social law
> talk about four kinds of sons:
> he who has the qualities of his mother,
> he who has the qualities of his father,
> he who surpasses his father in qualities,
> and he who lacks all qualities of his parents.

Also,

> Wicked people are happy
> at other people's misfortune,
> even if they themselves suffer loss.
> In war, a headless body dances,
> because it can still slice off other heads.
> "My own head is gone, so what?
> as long as other heads fall,
> I will dance, dance, and rejoice."

I know two friends, Dharmabudhi and Paapabudhi.

> Paapabudhi's cleverness
> caused his father to suffer:
> he choked on smoke
> and died in a fire.'

'Tell me this story,' Damanaka said, and Karataka told him the tale.

THE TALE OF HOW PAAPABUDHI'S CLEVERNESS KILLED HIS FATHER

In a town lived two friends, Paapabudhi (evil-minded) and Dharmabudhi (dharma-minded). Dharmabudhi was an intelligent man, who achieved success in all his endeavours. On the other hand, Paapabudhi was an impoverished dullard. One day, Paapabudhi came to the realization that to change his financial situation, he needed to go to a foreign land and start a business there. 'I'll request my friend, Dharmabudhi, to come with me so that we can use his business sense,' he said to himself. 'And once we've made enough profit, I'll come back here and live a life of comfort.'

Hence, Paapabudhi went to Dharmabudhi and said to him, 'Dear friend, you should really travel to foreign lands, otherwise when you're old, you won't have any exciting stories of adventure to tell your children and grandchildren. People say,

> He who hasn't travelled far and wide
> and hasn't seen different ways of dress,
> or has no knowledge of different languages
> has not achieved the full benefit of his birth.

Besides,

> Unless one visits foreign lands,
> one does not gain knowledge, wealth,
> and appreciation of art and culture.

Dharmabudhi was persuaded by Paapabudhi, and he obtained permission from his parents and teachers to travel. The two friends then determined an auspicious date and started on their journey. They found a prosperous city in a faraway land, and that's where they set up their business. Using Dharmabudhi's business acumen and intelligence, both friends, very quickly, made plenty of money, and, after some years, they grew eager to return home. It is truly said,

> People who go to foreign lands
> and gain both knowledge and wealth

> are so impatient to return home,
> even one kos distance to them
> seems like four hundred kos.

As they neared their hometown, Paapabudhi began to wish that he didn't have to share the money with Dharmabudhi, and he began to devise ways to keep all of it for himself. 'We are carrying a lot of money,' he said to Dharmabudhi. 'I don't think we should take it all home. Our relatives will pester us to share it or to lend it to them. I think we should bury most of it here, in a safe place, and take with us only as much as we need immediately. And when we need more, we can come back here and get it. You've heard what people say,

> Even if a man has little money,
> he should not show it to anyone.
> The sight of it can change the saintly,
> let alone the mind of ordinary men.

Also,

> Just as in water, a fish eats smaller fish,
> on earth, predators eat cats and dogs,
> in the sky, eagles eat crows and other birds,
> in the same way, many kinsfolk lie in wait
> to gobble up those who have money.

Paapabudhi's suggestion appealed to Dharmabudhi, and he agreed to his suggestion of hiding it somewhere safe. Hence, the two friends found a suitable spot in the jungle and, digging a hole, buried their wealth in a vessel. Then they returned to their homes and began to live happily, spending the portion of money that they had brought with them. Then, one night, Paapabudhi went into the jungle by himself and dug up the vessel. Taking all the money, he put the empty vessel back in the ground, filled up the hole, and smoothed the dirt around it, making it look exactly as it was before. After a few days, he went to Dharmabudhi and said to him, 'Dear friend, I'm running out of money. As you know, I have a wife and children, and my money runs out fast. Come with me to our secret spot so that I can take out some more for our use.'

Dharmabudhi accompanied him to the jungle, and the two of them started digging in the spot where they had buried their earnings. However, when they pulled out the vessel, Dharmabudhi discovered that all the money was gone. 'What happened to our money?' he exclaimed. Paapabudhi, too, pretended to be shocked. 'Oh no! It's gone. How did that happen? Who took it?' Then, turning to Dharmabudhi with accusing eyes, he said, 'You took it, didn't you? You stole our money.'

'What are you saying?' Dharmabudhi was hurt by Paapabudhi's accusations. 'I didn't steal it. Maybe some thief....'

'If it was a thief, why would he take the time to fill up the hole and leave it exactly as it was? He would have run away right after the deed. It had to be you. You didn't want me to find out; that's why you made sure that the spot looked untouched. You took it. I have no doubt. Now, hand over half that money—my share of it, or I'll have no choice but to take the matter to court.'

'Watch what you're saying,' Dharmabudhi warned. 'I did not steal that money. I am Dharmabudhi, I wouldn't commit such adharma. Haven't you heard,

> For a follower of dharma,
> all women except his wife
> are like his mother.
> For a follower of dharma,
> someone else's money
> is like a pile of mud.
> For a follower of dharma,
> hurting another being
> is like hurting oneself.'

'Just because your name is Dharmabudhi doesn't mean you can do no wrong,' Paapabudhi scoffed.

'I never said that. But I didn't take the money. Maybe you took it, and you're trying to put the blame on me to cover your own tracks.'

Thus, flinging insults at each other and questioning each other's honesty, the two reached the king's court. Even after they presented their case to the judges, they continued to accuse each other in voices that grew louder and more vitriolic. The judges tried to figure out from their heated exchange who was at fault, but they could not make any sense of the case. Hence, in the interest of justice, they commanded them both to take the fire trial. In this test, each accused made Agni his witness and held a smouldering piece of wood on a peepul leaf in the palm of his hand; if his palm remained unharmed, he was considered innocent, and if his palm burned, he was declared guilty.

'But that is not justice,' Paapabudhi objected.

> In a dispute, solid proof is key—
> papers, documents, and all.
> If no documents are to be had,
> an eyewitness serves as proof.
> Only when there are no documents
> and not a single eyewitness
> should the truth test decide the case.

The truth test of fire is only administered when there is no clear decision after the witnesses have been heard. In my case, I have a witness.'

'You do?' said the judges and Dharmabudhi, surprised.

'Yes, of course, I do. The god in the tree that is standing near that spot is my witness. He was present right there when we buried the money, and he was present when the money was stolen. I'm certain that he'll be able to tell us, without a doubt, who is the thief and who is innocent.'

'You're right,' the judges declared. 'If there is a witness, we can't ask for a truth test. It is said,

> In a dispute, even the hangman as witness is worthy.
> His proof is more just than the justice of the truth test.
> And when the gods themselves are called as witnesses,
> how can a truth test be an undisputed decision-maker?

Besides, your declaration that the tree god is an eyewitness has intrigued us,' the judges said to Paapabudhi. 'We would like to see how you call this god as witness. Therefore, tomorrow, the two of you will accompany us to the spot, and truth and lie will be decided right there. Now, stop fighting and go home, and wait for tomorrow.'

Paapabudhi rushed home to his father. 'I need your help,' he said to him urgently. 'If you help me, I'll make you rich.'

'What are you saying?' said his father. 'Explain to me in detail.'

'I stole money that belonged to both Dharmabudhi and I, but with one small lie from you, I can be exonerated, and this money can belong to both of us. If you don't help me, we will not only lose the money but also our lives.'

'What do I need to do? Tell me quickly. How can I help secure this money and make sure we get to keep it and be at liberty to enjoy it?' his father said.

'In the spot where Dharmabudhi and I buried the money, there is a huge shami tree, and in the trunk of that tree is a big hollow. Go there tonight and hide in that hollow. Tomorrow morning, when I come there with Dharmabudhi, and the judges, and ask the shami tree to tell the truth about who stole the money, I want you say, "It was Dharmabudhi." That is all you need to do.'

That night, Paapabudhi's father went and hid in the hollow in the shami tree, and in the morning, when Paapabudhi and Dharmabudhi, arrived there, accompanied by the judges, Paapabudhi drew close to the tree and said loudly,

> 'Sun, moon, air, fire, sky, earth, water, heart,
> Yamaraja, day, night, the two twilights,
> and dharma—all these elements know the truth
> about men's actions and behaviours.

Hence, I call on the god of the tree as my witness. Whoever is the thief between Dharmabudhi and I, please declare it.'

'Dharmabudhi!' declared a thunderous voice from the tree.

Everyone was flabbergasted to hear the tree speak. But, while all the judges were still trying to gather their wits, Dharmabudhi went around the tree and saw the hollow. He quickly gathered dry wood and began piling it at the base of the tree. Then, he sprinkled it with inflammable oil and lit it. As soon as it caught fire, loud screams came from the tree and, suddenly, to everyone's surprise, Paapabudhi's father spilled out of it. His body was half burnt, his eyeballs had burst, and he had lost all his hearing.

'Oh!' exclaimed the judges. 'Who are you?'

But the old man was in no condition to respond. He fell on the ground, writhing in pain, and soon died. Weeping over his father's body, Paapabudhi then confessed everything to the judges. The verdict that the judges pronounced for Paapabudhi's crime was death by hanging from that very shami tree. Thereafter, declaring Dharmabudhi innocent, the judges said,

> 'When a wise person thinks of a solution,
> he first thinks of the harm it could bring.
> By not considering the benefit and harm
> side by side, see how the stupid crane
> could not stop the mongoose from killing
> all the other cranes one by one.'

'What is this tale?' Dharmabudhi asked, and the judges told the story.

THE TALE OF THE CRANE WHO DID NOT CONSIDER THE HARM WITH THE BENEFIT

In a forest there was a large bargad tree on which several cranes used to roost. That tree had a massive trunk with a small hollow near its base. In that hollow lived a black snake. Every time the female cranes laid eggs and the chicks hatched, the snake would slither up to their nest and eat them, even before their wings sprouted. Thus, while the cranes suffered grief, the snake lived happily, feeding on the delicious tender meat of chicks. One day, a male crane, witnessing the snake devour his chicks before his eyes, couldn't bear it any more. Flying to the ocean shore, he sat down in the sand with his head hanging low and large teardrops falling from his eyes. Seeing him so grief stricken, a crab came to him and asked, 'Uncle, why are you crying?'

'Dear nephew, I'm ill-fated. A black snake, who lives in a hole in my tree, has eaten all my chicks, and I'm devastated. I don't know what to do. If you know of a way that I can kill this snake, do tell me.'

The crab thought, the crane is an enemy of water creatures. Why should I help him? But, perhaps, I can use this opportunity to help my brethren in the water. I'll come up with some scheme that will sound harmful for the snake, but, in actuality, it will destroy the cranes. The wise say,

> Making your tone sweet and soft,
> but firming your heart inexorably,
> give such counsel to the enemy
> that his whole clan is wiped out.

Thinking these thoughts, the crab said to the crane, 'Uncle, I can tell you an excellent way to kill that snake. Find a mongoose's burrow nearby, and then scatter pieces of fish all the way from the burrow to the snake's hole in the tree. The smell of fish will bring the mongoose out, and he will follow the trail of fish food, till he reaches the snake's hiding hole, and, finding him there, he will destroy him.'

The crane liked the crab's plan and did exactly as the crab suggested, creating a trail of fish food for the mongoose from his burrow to the snake's hole in the bargad. Smelling the fish, the mongoose emerged and, eating the pieces of fish, reached the snake and tore him into pieces. Then he climbed the tree, and, one by one, killed all the cranes, as well, and ate them.

'That is why we advise that in finding a solution, one must also consider the harm that could result from it,' said the judges. 'In an attempt to get away with his theft, this Paapabudhi employed his father to pretend to be a tree god. It was a good scheme, but he didn't, for a moment, consider what would happen if his scheme failed—what harm it could do. Well, we saw how the scheme failed and what the harmful consequences were: his father burnt to death and he himself was hanged.'

After telling this story, Karataka said to Damanaka: 'You imbecile, like that thief Paapabudhi, you also only thought of a scheme to achieve a desired result, but you did not give one thought to the harm that scheme could do. You are even more of a villain than that Paapabudhi, because with your plan, you jeopardized the life of our own food provider. You are not only an evil-minded villain, but you have displayed your own villainous nature. Somebody has rightly said,

> No one can see the anal hole of the peacock
> until he himself, lost in the music of rain,
> foolishly lifts his tail up and begins to dance.

If you can put your own lord and master in a such a precarious situation that even his survival is in jeopardy, how can you be trusted with others. So, please leave. Get away from me. And stay away. People say,

> Where mice can eat an iron scale,
> weighing one thousand palas,
> what is the wonder if there
> a falcon grabs a boy to eat?'

'What is that story?' Damanaka asked, and Karataka narrated it.

THE TALE OF THE IRON-EATING MICE AND THE BOY-DEVOURING FALCON

In a town lived a businessman, named Jirnadhana (depleted wealth). Over the years, he suffered several business losses, and his money depleted, till his situation became dire. Hence, he decided to go to a foreign land and try his luck there. He thought,

> In a place where a person has enjoyed
> the rich rewards of his labour and effort,
> how can he then live a respectful life,
> when his money begins to diminish?

He also felt dejected because,

> When a man lives in a town for many years
> with head held high in pride and esteem,
> he loses all respect of people he knows,
> if his status becomes meagre and pitiful.

'It is best for me to leave town and try to rebuild my wealth in another town,' he said to himself and, packing up everything, vacated his house. However, he had in his house a heavy iron scale, weighing about one thousand palas, that he had inherited from his ancestors, and he didn't want to sell it or give it away. Therefore, before leaving town, he went to a fellow businessman and acquaintance and requested him to keep his scale safe, promising him that he would come to get it when he returned.

Jirnadhana spent many years abroad, and when he returned, he went directly to his businessman friend's house to retrieve his scale. However, when he asked him for it, the response he got was: 'Dear man, we have searched everywhere for your scale, but it is nowhere to be found. It appears that mice may have eaten it.'

Jirnadhana was shocked to hear this, but, he quickly concealed his reaction and said to the businessman, 'Sethji, if my iron scale was eaten by mice, then it is not your fault, because this is how the world is. Nothing lasts forever. Everyone and everything is transient and has to leave this earth. If the scale has left, then what is the surprise in that? Be it so. But I have a small favour to ask. I've just returned from overseas, and I need to go and bathe at the river. I request you to please send your youngest son with me with a change of clothes, soap, oil, towel, etc.'

The businessman was a little taken aback by the request, but he figured that he owed the man at least that much, after robbing him of his scale. So, calling his little boy, Dhanadeva (lord of wealth), he instructed him: 'Boy, this is your uncle. He needs to go to the river for a bath. Go with him and take the items he requests; then stay there till he brings you back home.'

Oh! Someone has rightly said,

> True devotion or respect is never the cause
> for why someone would do another's work.
> It is fear or greed, or some such thing
> that propels people to help others.
> Proof of this can be found in flattery;
> no one flatters another out of devotion.
>
> When one receives
> utmost deference without cause,
> one should look at it with suspicion.
> It disguises deceits and treacheries,
> which will be revealed at the end.

The little boy gathered the items and accompanied Jirnadhana to the river. Telling him to sit by his clothes, Jirnadhana took a long bath, and, thereafter, taking the boy by the hand, he led him to a cave in the mountain. 'Stay here, son,' he said, gently. 'Don't be afraid. I'll return shortly.' Then he covered the mouth of the cave with a rock and went to the see the businessman.

Seeing him return alone, the businessman asked him, 'Where is my son. I sent him with you to the river. Why hasn't he returned with you?'

'Sethji,' said Jirnadhana, 'as the boy was sitting on the bank, a falcon swooped down and grabbed him and flew away.'

'What?' said the shocked businessman. 'You liar. What are you saying? How can a falcon carry away such a big boy?'

'O truthful seth, just as a falcon can't carry away a boy, mice can't eat a massive iron scale. If you want your son back, return my scale,' said Jirnadhana.

The two businessmen then began hurling insults at each other and their quarrel escalated to such an extent that they ended up in the king's court.

'I'm devastated, Maharaj,' said the father of the boy. 'This wicked man has kidnapped my son. Please order him to return my child. How can such a heinous act be allowed in your reign?'

The magistrate turned to Jirnadhana and asked him, 'Where is the boy, and why did you kidnap him?'

'Maharaj, I did not kidnap him. As the boy was sitting on the bank, a falcon suddenly swooped down and grabbed him. I saw it with my own eyes, but there was nothing I could do. It happened so suddenly.'

'What you are saying is obviously not true,' the magistrate said sternly. 'How can a falcon carry away a boy?'

'Maharaj, in a place where an iron scale, weighing thousands of palas can be eaten by mice, there, a falcon can certainly carry away a boy. Believe me. There is no doubt about it.'

'Explain yourself,' the magistrate asked Jirnadhana, and he related the whole tale from beginning to end.

Hearing the story, everyone in the court began to laugh. The magistrate then ordered the businessman to return Jirnadhana's scale and for Jirnadhana to return the boy.

'That is why, I'm telling you,' Karataka said, 'that where mice can eat an iron scale, a falcon can carry off a boy. In other words, since you can jeopardize our king's life for your own benefit, you will have no compunction about doing the same to others. The fact is that you were resentful of Pingalaka's kind regard of Sanjivaka; you couldn't bear it; you were burning up with jealousy. That is why you sowed this seed of dissension between them. Somebody has rightly said,

> The noble are vilified by the ignoble,
> the most loved wife by her co-wives,
> the charitable one by the miserly,
> a simple soul by the manipulative,
> the wealthy by the impoverished,
> beautiful people by those who are ugly,
> a pious one by someone who is impious,
> and a scholar of shastra by the ignorant.

Also,

> The ignorant hate the knowledgeable.
> The poor hate the rich and wealthy.
> Those who break dharma laws hate adherents,
> and prostitutes hate women in matrimony.

'That is why, you dull brain, with your stupidity, harbouring the illusion of helping our king, you hurt him. People say,

> A learned enemy is preferred to a senseless well-wisher.
> A devoted but moronic monkey killed the king,
> while a learned thief saved four lives with nobility.'

'What is this story?" Damanaka asked, and Karataka told him.

THE TALE OF THE SENSELESS MONKEY AND THE INTELLIGENT THIEF

A king had a monkey. The animal was very devoted to the king and would not leave him even for a moment, not even when he went to his innermost chamber. The king trusted the monkey, utterly; hence, he appointed him his bodyguard.

Once the king was sleeping peacefully and the monkey was waving a fan over him to keep him cool, when a fly came and sat on the king's forehead. The monkey made numerous attempts to shoo the fly away, but it kept coming back to sit in the same spot. The monkey became so frustrated that he pulled out his sword and brought it down on the fly. The insect got away, but the king's head was split in half.

'Therefore, the wise say,' said Karataka, 'if one wants to live safely, one should not hire idiots as attendants. Now let me tell you the story of a learned thief.'

A prince of a certain kingdom had two close friends; one was the son of a merchant, and the other the son of a scholar. Every day, the three of them would get together and spend their time in leisurely, pleasurable activities, such as strolling in gardens, partying with friends, tasting various varieties of food, and other such entertainments. The king was distraught at his son's disinterest in princely pursuits of hunting, archery, horse riding, and other such character-building activities. One day, he reprimanded his son and ordered him to do his duty. The prince was very upset by his father's censure. Going to his friends, he complained to them, and the three of them decided to leave town and travel to another place, preferably where they could acquire a lot of wealth. And so, they set off.

As luck would have it, when they were climbing up a mountain, they each found a valuable gem.

'Fate is favourable to us, but how do we protect our new-found wealth?' the merchant's son asked his friends. 'It's dangerous to travel with such valuable gems. What if we are accosted by robbers? They'll not only take the gems but will also kill us.'

'I have an idea,' the scholar's son said. 'Why don't we swallow our gems?'

'What do you mean? How would that help?' the prince asked.

'It is known that if you have nothing of value, robbers will leave you alone. So, if robbers can't see our gems, they'll think we have nothing. If we carry the gems in our luggage or even hidden in our clothes, someone is sure to find them. But if we carry them in our body, who will be able to see them?'

The other two agreed that this was a brilliant idea, and that night, after their meal, they each swallowed a gem.

Listening to these three friends was another traveller, a brahmin scholar, who, due to the karma of a former life, was a thief in this one. Intending to rob these three, he decided to join them so that, somewhere along the way, he could kill them, cut open their bellies, and steal the gems.

With this plan in his mind, he came to the three friends and began reciting various shlokas in a melodious voice. As he had anticipated, they were soon quite enraptured by his erudition. When they expressed appreciation, the brahmin asked them if he could accompany them. It is said,

> Adulteresses are more bashful;
> brackish water is cooler;
> hypocrites are more discerning;
> thugs and robbers are more sweet-tongued.

The three friends readily agreed to have the brahmin join their group and the four of them began to journey together. One day, as they were passing through a settlement of Kiratas, the crows in that village began to call out: 'O Kiratas, catch these men. They are carrying valuable gems.' The people of the village understood the language of the crows. Hence, commanded by their leader, they caught the four travellers and brought them to the chief.

'Search their baggage and clothing and find the gems,' the chief ordered his men.

However, despite a thorough search, the men found nothing resembling a gem in the travellers' possessions, or on their person. They were perplexed; the crows had never lied to them before, but what could they do, except to let the travellers go.

The friends had hardly gone a short distance, when the crows began calling the Kiratas again: 'Catch them! They are carrying valuable gems.'

The chief had the travellers captured again and brought to him, and again he had them strip-searched, this time turning all their clothing inside out to make sure nothing was concealed in the seams. However, as before, nothing could be found, and the chief had to release the young men. But no sooner had they left when the crows started cawing raucously, 'Catch them! Catch them! They are carrying valuable gems.'

This time, when the Kirata men brought the four travellers to the chief, he said to them, 'You are obviously carrying gems. Our crows have never lied before. Since, they're not on your body, they must be inside your body. Tonight, you'll spend the night in the dungeon, and tomorrow, at dawn, I'll split your bellies to find the gems.'

Sitting in the dungeon that night, the brahmin thief began to think: tomorrow morning that Kirata is going to kill all of us. When he splits the belly of one of the men, he'll find the gem, and then he'll kill all of us, one by one, thinking that each of us has a gem in his belly. Since, I'm going to die anyway, I might as well do a good turn and save these three. It is said,

> Life is transient in any case.
> But if in one's dying breath,
> one can do good in the world,
> one is immortalized as a noble soul.

Also, the wise say,

> Child, what's the point of fearing death?
> Death is so inexorable and cold-hearted,
> it'll kill you even if you are afraid.
> It is inevitable—today or in a hundred years.

Hence, in the morning, when the Kiratas come to get us, I'll beg the chief to kill me first. When he splits open my belly, he won't find a thing, which will make him think that the others have nothing as well, and he may let them go.

Thus, at dawn, then the four were dragged out of the dungeon and brought to the chief, the brahmin thief said to him, 'None of us are carrying any gems. But if you need proof of that, then kill me and see. Why commit a sin of killing all four of us, when only one death can prove to you that we have no gems. I can't see my friends die, so please do me a favour and kill me first and get your proof.'

The Kirata chief then ordered his men to kill the brahmin and split open his belly. But when they found no gems, even after they shredded his entrails, the Kirata chief felt deeply regretful. 'What have I done?' he wailed. 'I should have believed him, instead of those stupid, lying crows.' Then he let the others go.

The three friends quickly left the Kirata village, grieving for their brahmin friend and thanking the day they had met him.

'That is why I tell you, Damanaka, a stupid person is dangerous, even as a friend, and a noble one is safer, even as an enemy.'

Castigated by Karataka, Damanaka slunk away to see how Pingalaka and Sanjivaka were faring. He arrived at the scene just as Sanjivaka, badly wounded from the assault of Pingalaka's sharp claws and teeth, fell to the ground, breathing his last. Seeing him in the throes of death, Pingalaka was suddenly hit by what he had done, and he was overcome with grief. Remembering his friend's good qualities and lamenting over his wounded body, he wailed, 'Oh what a terrible thing I have done. What a sin I have committed. I'm the one who gave him the boon of safe conduct, and after he began trusting me, I killed him. Can there be a bigger betrayal than mine? It is said,

> As long as the sun and moon shine
> betrayers, ingrates, and slanderers
> will live their afterlives in hell.

> Lost land is destructive for a kingdom,
> as is the loss of wise ministers.
> But these two losses are hardly similar.
> Land can be regained; not wise ministers.

I, myself, praised Sanjivaka in my court, and look how I have rewarded him for his good qualities. It is rightly said,

> Having praised someone as talented and valuable
> in court or in an open public assembly,
> a wise man should not then call out his faults.
> It would be like breaking his own oath,
> and oath-breaking is as ugly as sin.

Hearing him lament, Damanaka went to Pingalaka and admonished him. 'O king,' he said. 'What are you doing? Laments are a sign of weakness and cowardice. You killed a traitor and enemy grass-eater, and you're weeping for him? This behaviour does not behove monarchs. It is said,

> Even if a father, brother, son, wife, or dear friend
> becomes treasonous and threatens the king's life,
> the king will commit no sin in killing that traitor.

Also,

> A king showing mercy to the criminal,
> a brahmin who eats indiscriminately,
> an immodest wife, an evil-minded person,
> a traitorous friend, impudent servant, ingrate,
> and an official who is negligent and careless—
> it is best not to keep company with these.

Besides,

> A king's policies change form like a courtesan.
> She is truthful when she wishes and lies for gain.
> She harshly extracts money and sweetly flirts.
> Sometimes she is violent and sometimes kind.
> At times she is greedy and, at times, miserly.
> At other times her generosity knows no bounds.
> Her expenditures are varied and excessive.
> And her money-making means are also numerous.

What is ironic is that,

> One who lives a straightforward life without rebellion
> is never revered or even remembered by the world.
> Serpents, though, are rebellious and feared by all,
> and look how they are worshipped in the world.
> But Garuda, killer of serpents and greater than them,
> simply doing his ordained duty, receives no prayer

In the meantime, Karataka, tired of waiting for Damanaka to come back and relay to him the latest report of the fight between Pingalaka and Sanjivaka, decided to go himself and see the outcome of the fight. Arriving there, he saw the dead Sanjivaka on the ground, and Damanaka sitting close to the weeping Pingalaka, consoling him and giving him advice. Karataka quickly went to the lion and said to him, 'Maharaj, don't listen to Damanaka. He has no idea what statesmanship is. Dissension among friends is a policy that only brings destruction. Also, a wise official should never fill the mind of his king with suspicion that leads to war. There are other, more effective ways to resolve a dispute and clear doubts; for instance, negotiations, conciliation, giving of gifts, etc. As it is said,

> Even Kubera, Indra, Vayu, and Varuna
> suffered losses in bitter disputes.
> Victory and defeat cannot be predicted
> whether you live in heaven or on earth.

However,

> Abandoning statesmanship to start a war
> is not what the wise sages would advise.

Therefore, ministers who claim to be wise should refrain from advocating war to their monarchs.

> Enemies will never defeat a king
> whose ministers are free of greed.
> With their wisdom and integrity,
> they only wish the king's interest,
> even when planning to meet his foes.

That is why the wise say:

> Give honest and helpful advice
> even if it sounds harsh.
> When ministers only speak nice,
> O king, beware! Danger lurks nearby.

Also, on matters of importance, the king should consult with multiple ministers, not just one, and then, taking all counsel into consideration, he himself should decide what is the best course to follow. Sometimes, due to confusion and misconception, things are not as they appear. For instance,

> The firefly looks like a flame,
> and the sky appears like a flat roof;
> whereas, in truth, the firefly is not a flame,
> and the sky is neither flat nor a roof.

If the king listens to just the counsel of one minister, he may be deceived, because that minister may be serving his own purpose and lying to the king to that end. Therefore, a king must keep in mind,

> Any plan should be carefully examined,
> by oneself and by one's trusted friends.
> And it should be executed with care.

> One who has the discernment to do this
> earns not only respect but also fortune and fame.

Thus ends Mitra Bheda, the first tantra of *Panchatantra*, whose opening shloka is as follows:

> A lion and a bull in the forest,
> bound by deep and fond friendship.
> A jackal full of greed and cunning—
> oh, how he severed their bonds of trust.

SECOND TANTRA
MITRA SAMPRAPTI
Acquisition of Friends

Let us begin the second tantra, Mitra Samprapti. Its first shloka goes like this:

> Lacking resources and facilities,
> the wise and sagacious still manage to
> accomplish the most difficult tasks
> with ease and expeditiousness,
> just as the crow, tortoise, deer, and mouse
> accomplished what they needed to do.

People say that in the southern region is a city called Mahilaropya. Near it is an immense bargad tree, so abundantly laden with figs that it feeds all the birds of various species that dwell in it. In its holes and cracks live numerous insects, and its heavy branches provide shade to hundreds of travellers every day. It is rightly said,

> The tree in whose shade deer sleep in peace,
> whose fruit and leaves many birds consume,
> in whose holes dwell varied types of insects,
> in whose thick branches monkeys frolic,
> whose nectar of flowers intoxicates bees—
> such a tree is praiseworthy, that, in its entirety
> provides happiness and refuge to various beings.
> If not like this, a tree is like a burden on earth.

Once, on this great bargad tree lived a crow called Laghupata (small-winged). One morning, as this crow started on his flight towards the city to search for food, he saw a dark, ugly man with dirty, thick feet and cracked heels, long, spiky hair, and a fearful countenance, hastening to the bargad, like an emissary of Yamaraja, carrying a net in his hand. Seeing him, the crow became agitated. 'Why did my day have to begin this way—seeing this fowler first thing in the morning near my home?' he muttered to himself. 'Who knows if the birds that live in the bargad will live or die today. But, at least, I should inform them of the impending calamity.' Hence, the crow flew back to the tree and, perching on a high branch, called, 'Listen up, dear tree-mates, I just saw a bird-catcher headed this way, carrying a net and a bag full of rice. When he spreads the rice on the ground and invites you to come and eat it, don't listen to him. Don't go to pick the rice. Think of it as poison. If you descend to pick so much as one grain, it will be the end of your life.'

Even as the crow was issuing this warning, the fowler came and spread his net under the bargad. Sprinkling rice all around, he called to the birds and then went and hid behind another tree. But the birds had heeded Laghupata's warning and, despite seeing the enticing rice, which shone as pure white as the nirgundi flower, they knew it was as deadly as poison and did not even venture outside their nests.

However, it so happened that at that time, the king of doves, Chitragriva (with a neck as beautiful as a painting) was flying across the sky with his flock of a thousand. Searching for food, he was looking down, and he spotted the rice on the ground. As he began to descend, Laghupata tried to warn him, but the king of doves paid him no heed, because at that time, he and his flock could only think about the taste of food on their tongue. Inevitably, as soon the doves touched the ground, they were caught in the net.

Someone has rightly said,

> Those who only think about food
> are caught by the hook like fish in water.

> How did a great Vedic scholar like Ravana
> commit the grievous adharma of taking Sita?
> How did he not consider the wrongfulness of it?
> Rama too chased the gold deer knowing well
> that such a deer does not exist. Why did he do it?
> If he had refrained, Sita would have been safe,
> and Ravana would not have abducted her.
> And Yudhishthira, the incarnation of dharma—
> how did he get caught up in the throw of dice,
> putting in calamity his brothers and wife.
> If only he had refrained from gambling,
> the Mahabharata war would not have been.

Thus, one can surmise:

> When a calamity is impending,
> a man's mind shuts down.
> Then fate and impaired judgement
> make him act contrary to himself,
> causing adversity for years to come.

And

> Those whose minds are filled
> by the fear of death's noose,

> or thoughts of fate's doom,
> though they are thinking men,
> their power of logic is thwarted,
> and the wrong path appears right.

Very pleased at having caught the whole flock of doves, the fowler stepped out from behind the tree and advanced toward the net, wielding his staff to beat the birds to death. Seeing him approach, the doves began to screech in panic.

Chitragriva calmed his flock. 'Don't be afraid,' he said. 'We'll find a way to escape. It is said,

> If your mind is not impaired by calamity,
> it can employ fortitude and intelligence
> to arrive at the other end of misfortune.
>
> If you can remain steadfast
> in both fortune and misfortune,
> like the sun that remains ruddy
> in both its rising and setting,
> you will surely achieve success.

Therefore, listen to my plan. Together, with all our strength, we'll lift up in the air, taking this net with us. Once we are out of the fowler's sight, we'll find a way to get rid of the net. Be brave now. And don't lose heart. If you allow fearfulness and thoughts of defeat to fill your mind, you will fail to join in the effort of lifting this net, and then, we'll all surely die. It is said,

> Thin, weak, breakable threads
> join and become a sturdy rope
> that can bear the heaviest weight
> and bind even an elephant.
> The same applies to people and beings.'

Following Chitragriva's advice, the doves, in one big heave, took off in flight, carrying the net with them. The fowler was flabbergasted, to see his catch suddenly soar and fly away. He began to race after his flying net, with his head thrown back and his eyes glued to the sky, telling himself,

> 'The birds in unity are flying away with my net,
> but when they begin to fight each other,
> they will come crashing to the ground,
> and I will gain both my net and my catch.'

Witnessing this scene, Laghupata the crow forgot his foraging and began to follow the flying net, curious to see what the doves would do next. 'What will they do?' he said to himself. 'How will they get that net off?'

On the ground, when the fowler could no longer see the net, he sat down, disappointed. Then, to console himself, he said,

> 'What is not meant to happen
> will never happen
> no matter the effort.
> What is meant to happen
> will certainly happen
> without any effort.
>
> What is not ordained by fate
> will be lost even after it is acquired.

Also,

> If fate is not in your favour,
> but, somehow, wealth comes to you,
> you will, more than likely, lose it
> and along with it your other wealth,
> like Shankha Nidhi which brings wealth
> that cannot be used, and when it goes,
> it takes with it other accumulated wealth.

I am a perfect example of this: trying to catch doves, I made an excellent catch, but not only did it all disappear, but it also took with it the net which was my livelihood. If this is not misfortune, what is?' Thus, lamenting his fate, the fowler decided to head home.

Seeing him leave, Chitragriva sighed with relief. 'Dear doves, the fowler has left. We are safe,' he said to his flock. 'Now all we have to do is find someone who will rid us of this net. Stay with me and do as I say, and I promise you, we will be free and safe. With patience and forbearance, help me fly this net to the city of Mahilaropya. There, in the forest, I have a friend—a mouse called Hiranyaka (golden). At my request, he'll cut this net and free us. It is true what they say,

> In this world when you need help,
> only a friend comes to your aid.
> Others, even if they are under oath,
> are likely to turn away if they can.'

Thus, rallied by Chitragriva and bolstered by his words, the flock of doves exerted one last effort and, holding the net with their beaks, flew it to the forest near Mahilaropya, where Hiranyaka the mouse lived, and brought it down outside his hole. Hiranyaka had secured his hole like a fortress, and he lived a carefree and peaceful life inside it. Someone has rightly said this about creatures like Hiranyaka.

> Anticipating danger and misfortune,
> a person well versed in Nitishastra
> secures his fortress with a thousand gates,
> as Hiranyaka the mouse had done with his hole.
>
> Just like a serpent without venom
> and an elephant without madness
> are easy to bring under control;
> so is a king without a fortress
> easy to subdue even by a weak enemy.

Also,

> A thousand elephants and lakhs of horses
> cannot provide a king the protection
> he can receive from just one secure fortress.

Standing at the entrance of Hiranyaka's home, the king of doves called loudly, 'O friend, Hiranyaka. Please come out as quickly as possible. I am in a desperate situation.'

The mouse responded from the safety of his hole: 'Who are you? Why have you come here? And what is this desperate situation?'

'I am your friend, Chitragriva, the king of doves.'

Recognizing his friend's voice, Hiranyaka scurried out of his hole, eager to see his dear friend.

> Beloved, bringing joy to the heart and eyes—
> only the noble and lucky are visited by friends.
>
> Sunrise, tobacco, the story of Mahabharata,
> beloved wife, and a true and most loved friend—
> these five, even though part of everyday life
> always give one happiness never felt before.

Those who are visited by friends experience a unique happiness that nothing else in the world can provide. That is why when Hiranyaka emerged from his hole and saw his friend, Chitragriva, and his doves caught in a net, his body shuddered with shock. 'What has happened?' he cried. 'O friend. Who has done this to you?'

'When you can see with your own eyes, friend Hiranyaka, why do you ask?' Chitragriva said,

> 'From whomever, whenever, whatever,
> to whom, how much ever, wherever,
> a man has to pay in sorrow or happiness
> in equal measure of his past karma.
> In return he will receive the exact equivalent
> from whomever, whenever, wherever,
> in the same way, in the same measure.

I, too, am paying for being consumed by the taste of my tongue, disregarding prudence about what is right and what is not. That is why I have come to you. Please help free me and my doves.'

'My friend,' said Hiranyaka. 'Don't fear. I'll help you. But I must say,

> It is ironic that the bird
> who can see its prey from
> a hundred or so yojanas away
> misses the net laid a few feet away.

But also,

> Seeing the sun and moon eclipsed,
> the maddened elephant captured,
> the fearful snakes ensnared,
> the sky-ranging birds entrapped,
> and great intellectuals impoverished,
> I can only say: fate is all powerful!

Besides,

> Birds that fly at the speed of wind,
> alone and high in the limitless sky
> can also meet with accidents.
> Able fishermen can catch fish
> even from the fathomless ocean
> with their relentless nets.

> That is why no place is good or bad
> or safe or unsafe in this world.
> Great time can spread its hand
> to catch one even in a faraway land
> that is inaccessible and secure.'

Saying this Hiranyaka the mouse began to gnaw at the corner of the net that was caught around Chitragriva's neck like a noose.

'Wait, dear friend,' said the king of doves. 'Before you cut me loose, please free my subjects.'

'No. I don't agree,' Hiranyaka chided. 'Only after the master can his attendants be considered.'

'No, my dear friend. That is not right. All these doves are dependent on me. They have all left their families to serve me. It is said,

> Servants respected and cared for by their king
> happily and willingly serve him at all times,
> and never leave him, regardless of their own
> situation of financial hardships and danger.

Also,

> The core foundation of wealth is trust.
> This trust is what puts the tusker
> in the centre of all other elephants.
> And it is the lack of trust that makes deer
> avoid the lion even though he is their king.

Besides, what if something untoward happens as you are cutting my binds? Your teeth could break, the fowler could show up, or something else prevent you from freeing my subjects. Think about the sin I would incur; it would be enough to send me to hell. It is said,

> If virtuous and able attendants suffer,
> and the king does not alleviate their pain,
> while he himself continues to enjoy himself,
> his life and his afterlife are both doomed.'

Hiranyaka's heart filled with pride at his friend's views and about how responsible he felt for those who served him. 'I know what you are saying, and I'm so pleased to hear you say it,' he said. 'I was testing your allegiance to your subjects, and I'm happy to know that you are a worthy king. I wish you success and prosperity. With your ideals, I have no doubt that you will be successful in everything you do. A king such as you rules the three worlds. And now, without wasting time, let me cut the bonds of your subjects.'

Soon, Hiranyaka was able to free all the doves. As they shook out their wings and readied themselves to fly off again, Hiranyaka bid a fond farewell to his friend, Chitragriva, and assured him that he would always be there for him. 'If you ever find yourself in a precarious situation again, don't hesitate to call upon me,' he said. Then, wishing all a safe journey home, he returned to his own home in the ground, while Chitragriva and his doves returned to live happily with their families.

It is rightly said,

> People who have close friends
> accomplish the most difficult tasks,
> exercising the least amount of effort.

In all this time, Laghupata the crow was watching the interaction between the doves and the mouse, and he was amazed by Hiranyaka's selflessness. 'I'm in awe of his strength of character,' he said to himself. 'The way he released those doves from the intricate net is a true example of how the vows of friendship are fulfilled. And his fortress, too, is a wonderous thing. I don't normally trust others, because I know myself and how unpredictable I am. But I really want to make that Hiranyaka my friend. It is said,

> Even if one lacks nothing
> and feels completely fulfilled,
> friends and soulmates are a must.
> True friendship makes one wise.
> The ocean, though replete in itself,
> awaits his friend, moon, at every dawn.'

Thus, desiring Hiranyaka's friendship, Laghupata flew down from the tree, where he was perched, and hopped to the entrance of Hiranyaka's hole fortress. Then, imitating Chitragriva's voice, he called out, 'O Hiranyaka. Come out please. As soon as you can.'

Wondering why Chitragriva had returned and why he needed his help again, Hiranyaka quickly came out of the hole. Seeing a crow instead of his friend, he was taken aback. Retreating a few steps, ready to scuttle back into his hole, he said angrily to the crow, 'Who are you, and why did you call me, sounding like my friend?'

'I am Laghupata the crow,' Laghupata replied.

Hiranyaka moved back a few more steps. 'What are you doing here?' he asked. 'Tell me quickly and then please leave.'

'I've come to discuss a very important matter with you—a matter that is very close to my heart,' Laghupata said.

'I have no urge to talk to you or to discuss anything with you.'

'I saw how you released Chitragriva and his doves from the net. My heart is filled with awe and love for you. If, some day, I am caught in a net, like the doves, I hope to have you there to help me. That is why I've called you. I request you to please make me your friend.'

Hiranyaka laughed. 'My dear crow,' he said. 'I am your prey, and you are my devourer. How can there be friendship between us? It is said,

> Friendship and marriage are best between people
> who are from a similar financial and social status.
> Rich and poor, strong and weak, high and low—
> if alliances happen between these opposites
> they are sure to end in conflicts and hurt feelings.

Also,

> That fool who makes friends with someone
> dissimilar to him—less or more than him—
> becomes a laughing stock among people.

Therefore, I say again, please leave.' Hiranyaka stated.

'I'm not leaving,' Laghupata replied. 'I'm sitting right here in front of your mousehole. And if you don't make me your friend, I vow that I'll die at your doorstep.'

'Why don't you understand?' Hiranyaka said in frustration. 'Your kind and my kind are sworn enemies; we have been for generations. How can we be friends? People say,

> Do not form an alliance with a known foe,
> even if his deal sounds fair and you know him.

There are two kinds of enemies: one, a natural enemy; and the other, an unnatural one—created due to circumstances. You are my natural enemy. About the latter, it is said,

> Circumstantial enmity can be resolved
> once the circumstance is removed.

But natural enmity has no circumstance.
It persists through life and remains till death.'

'Please tell me the characteristics of both types of enmities,' Laghupata asked Hiranyaka.

'Circumstantial enmity is due to some acrimonious situation, or even a misunderstanding. And it can be resolved with some negotiations, apologies, and good turns.

> Natural enmity can never come to an end.
> Snake and mongoose, grass-eater and carnivore,
> fire and water, devas and daityas, cats and dogs,
> rich and poor, wife and co-wife, elephant and lion,
> hunter and deer, fool and pundit, righteousness and evil,
> those who work and those who are lazy,
> a virtuous wife and an adulteress,
> These are all natural enemies.

For them:

> Even when no one has killed the other,
> or, no one has wronged the other,
> each is ready to take each other's life.
> That is why it is called natural enmity.'

To this, Laghupata replied: 'This animosity makes no sense. There has to be a reason for friendship and animosity. There is no reason for the two of us to be enemies. Surely, it is not wise to consider someone your enemy without justification?'

'You don't understand. Let me explain to you the principle from Nitishastra.

> Animosity once created
> cannot be uncreated.
> Renewing that association
> or trying to forge a friendship
> can be an invitation to death,
> like the female mule who dies
> just as soon as it conceives.

Also, one can't walk around thinking, I'm a good person. I have no acrimony toward anyone; I am friendly with everyone; hence, why would anyone feel animosity towards me?

> Even Panini, the creator of grammar laws
> was killed in the forest by a lion,
> and Jaimini, the author of Mimansa
> was trampled to death by an elephant.
> Pingala, who authored *Chhandashastra,*
> was devoured by a crocodile on the seashore.
> Thus, knowledge and virtue are meaningless
> to ignorant creatures filled with fury.'

To this, the crow replied: 'You're right, of course. But listen,

> People form friendships variously.
> They can do good deeds for each other.
> Animals and birds can also be friendly.
> Fools can become friends, as well,
> due to their own fear and greed.
> The noble need only look upon each other
> to form deep bonds of friendship.
>
> Friendship with a villain is like an earthen pot,
> ruining quickly and hard to repair.
> Friendship with a noble person is a gold pot,
> difficult to ruin and easily repairable.
>
> Just as sugarcane gets sweeter
> from node to node, top to bottom,
> friendship with virtuous people
> becomes more pleasurable with time.
> And the exact opposite is true
> with friends who are villainous.

Someone else has also said:

> Friendship with the unrighteous
> is like one's shadow early in the day.
> It is full, long, and extended,
> But, as the day progresses, it lessens,
> till nothing remains of it by the end.
> But friendship with the righteous
> is like the afternoon shadow;
> it starts small, then slowly develops,

and by the end, it becomes full size.

Please know, O Hiranyaka, that I am a righteous being, and if you become my friend, I know our friendship will deepen,' Laghupata said. 'I call upon all the gods as witness and vow that you will be safe with me, and I promise you that I will never do you any harm.'

'How can I believe you and your vows?' Hiranyaka replied. 'It is aptly said,

> A thousand vows an enemy can take
> but he cannot be trusted.
> The example is in the Puranas:
> Indra took a vow of friendship
> and built trust with Vritasura.
> Then he used his Vajra weapon
> to tear Vritasura to pieces.

Also,

> When one trusts an enemy,
> one's ruin is imminent.
> The gods themself exemplify this:
> Indra made Diti trust him.
> Then he entered her womb
> to destroy her foetus with his vajra.

A wise person, desiring happiness and a long life, should not trust anyone, not even Brihaspati, the guru of the gods. People say,

> All an enemy needs is a tiny opening.
> Once inside, he plants his feet
> and brings about total destruction,
> like water trickling in through a hole
> slowly fills the ship and sinks it.

So, the lesson to be learned is this,

> One who cannot be trusted should never be trusted.
> But also be wary of those who can be trusted,
> because when trust is broken, it cuts to the root.
> As long as you remain mistrustful, no one,
> not even the strongest enemy, can hurt you
> no matter how weak you yourself are.

> But once you begin to open yourself to trust,
> even the weakest enemy can hurt you,
> no matter how strong you yourself are.'

Rendered speechless with Hiranyaka's knowledge of human behaviour and books of social law, Laghupata the crow thought to himself, this Hiranyaka mouse is so wise, it makes me even more eager to gain his friendship. So, he said to the mouse, 'The wise say,

> Friendship with noble souls is formed
> just by walking seven steps with them
> Seven steps and seven words is all it takes.

And we have already walked those seven steps with our discussion, so, from now on, I will consider you my friend. Let me just say one thing: don't trust me if you don't want to. But converse with me, even if it is from the security of your holed fortress. Talk to me about right and wrong and tell me enchanting tales. I've never met anyone as wise as you.'

Laghupata's humility and openness appealed to Hiranyaka. 'He seems really smart and honest,' he said to himself and thought that it would not be such a bad thing to make friends with him.

'Fine,' he said to Laghupata. 'But I warn you, don't ever enter my hole, not even by accident.'

'I promise you that I'll never attempt to enter your fortress,' Laghupata assured Hiranyaka.

The mouse then came forward and embraced the crow, and from that day on, they became the best of friends. They began to spend a lot of time together, chatting about life, matters of polity and philosophy, and this and that. They enjoyed each other's company and often demonstrated their affection for each other through friendly gestures. For instance, once Laghupata came upon a buffalo, freshly killed by a tiger, and picking the juiciest bit in his beak, he brought it for his friend. Another time, Hiranyaka gathered rice and grain and, piling it outside his hole, invited his friend, Laghupata, for a treat. They liked doing these things for each other. It is such actions that build a friendship. As people say,

> Giving and receiving,
> sharing joys and sorrows,
> revealing one's secrets,
> eating and inviting—

these six are symptoms
of friendship and fondness.

Without such expressions of kindness, affection does not grow. In fact, gift-giving is appealing to the gods, as well, and they reward you by fulfilling your desires.

In this world friendships lasts
only as long as one gives.
Even a calf stays with his mother
only till she can provide him milk.

Gift-giving is miraculous. Even an enemy can be instantly won over with a gift. Let alone people, animals, too, love receiving; sometimes, even at the expense of their own offspring. Consider, for example, the cow who gives up all her milk to the one who feeds her oil cakes, not leaving so much as a drop for her calf.

Thus, like nail and flesh, the crow and mouse became inseparable, and their love continued to grow strong. In fact, over time, they became so attached that the mouse often sat nestling in the crow's feathers.

One day, Laghupata came to Hiranyaka with tears in his eyes and a lump in his throat. 'Dearest Hiranyaka,' he said. 'I can't stay in this land any more. I must leave and go elsewhere.'

'Why? What has happened? Why do you want to leave?' Hiranyaka asked, his heart breaking at the thought of separating from his friend.

'As you know, it hasn't rained for a long time. This land is experiencing an extreme drought. The fields have dried up, and there is no yield. Now people are starving. Not only have people stopped putting out feed for us, but they are also trapping us for food. I almost got caught in a net today, but somehow escaped. That is why I've become weary of this land and would like to go and live elsewhere. I held out as long as I could, but I can't bear the drought any more. And the thought of leaving you is wrenching my heart; that is why I'm crying.'

'Where will you go?' Hiranyaka asked.

'In the southern region is a dense forest in which there is an immense lake. In that lake lives one of my dearest friends, perhaps even dearer than you—a tortoise named Mantharaka (slow). When I go to live with him, he'll feed me pieces of fish, which I enjoy very much. Eating juicy pieces of fish, being in the company of a good friend, I'll spend my time in happiness. I'll miss you very much, but if I stay here any longer, I'll surely be caught and become some starving person's meal. The wise say,

> When drought hits one's place of living
> and wheat and grain are destroyed,
> those who can leave before witnessing
> their homeland beggared and loved ones dead
> should consider themselves fortunate.

Besides,

> What is impossible for the able-minded?
> Which country is too far for the enterprising?
> For the talented and scholarly, what is foreign?

But this gives me hope:

> The king and the scholar are not alike:
> the king is adored only in his land;
> the scholar is respected everywhere he goes.'

'Then take me with you,' Hiranyaka said to his friend. 'I, too, am not happy here.'

'Oh, really? Why are you unhappy?'

'It's a long story. I'll tell you when we get there,' Hiranyaka replied.

'But, friend,' the crow said. 'I fly in the sky, and you walk on the earth. How can we go together?'

'If you want me to come with you, then carry me on your back. Otherwise, I won't be able to go.'

The mouse's words made the crow very happy. 'I will be honoured to carry you on my back,' he said. 'That way my happiness will be doubled, having both you and my friend, Mantharaka with me. Did I ever tell you that I am an expert flyer? I know all eight types of flights.'

'What are the eight types of flights?' Hiranyaka asked.

'Sampata (even), vipata (rapid), mahapata (long and sustained), nipata (swooping down), vakrapata (curvaceous), tiryaka pata (slanting), udharva (upwards), and laghu (small and light),' the crow replied.

Hiranyaka then jumped onto Laghupata's back, and the crow began flying in sampata speed, keeping it even and smooth to ensure Hiranyaka's comfort. Flying over nine countries, they arrived at the lake Laghupata had described.

Mantharaka the tortoise saw the crow with the mouse on his back from afar and, thinking this to be a strange sight, he jumped into the water to see what would happen next.

Alighting on a tree near the lake, Laghupata deposited the mouse in a safe hole and flew to perch on a branch. Then he called his friend, 'O Mantharaka, dear Mantharaka, come out. Look who is here. I, your friend Laghupata. I've been meaning to come and visit you for some time, and, finally, I decided to make the journey. Come out and embrace your old friend. People say,

> Not even sandal mixed with camphor,
> nor cooling ice in a drink of khus khus
> is more appealing than a friend.
> A friend's embrace can't be equalled
> even by the sixteen divine arts of Krishna.

Someone has rightly said,

> A friend constitutes two amrita-like qualities:
> He is a buffer against adversity.
> He is an antidote for sadness.'

Mantharaka, the tortoise, carefully listened to the crow's voice and sharply inspected him, and only when he was convinced that this was no other than his dear friend, Laghupata, he emerged from the water. Seeing the crow, his heart was filled with love, and his eyes became moist. 'Come, dearest friend,' he said. 'Come. Let me embrace you. It has been too long. That is why it took me some time to recognize you, and I went into the water. I was following Brihaspati's advice:

> If you do not know someone's strength,
> background, business, and work,
> stay away from them until you know.'

Laghupata flew down from his perch and wrapped Mantharaka the tortoise in his wings and held him to his heart, his eyes brimming.

> The happiness one derives from being soaked in amrita
> does not equal the joy one gets from embracing a friend.

Feeling replete with love, the crow and tortoise sat down under the tree and began to catch up with each other's lives. Seeing them in such happy camaraderie, Hiranyaka the mouse stepped out of his hole and quietly sat down at Mantharaka's feet.

'Oh! Who is this mouse?' Mantharaka asked Laghupata. 'Is he your prey? Then how is it that you were carrying him on your back?'

'Dear friend, this is Hiranyaka. He is my friend; dearer to me than life.

> Just as it is impossible to count
> raindrops falling from clouds,
> stars shining in the sky,
> grains of sand on the beach,
> the qualities of this great soul,
> Hiranyaka, cannot be counted.

He has become disenchanted with the land where we lived; that is why I have brought him here to you.'

'Why is he feeling this way?' Mantharaka asked.

'I asked him the same question,' Laghupata replied. 'But he told me that it is a long story, and he'll tell it to me when we arrive at your lake. Well, here we are, dear Hiranyaka. Now, please tell us the reason for your despondency.'

Hiranyaka then related his tale.

THE TALE OF HOW HIRANYAKA THE MOUSE WAS OUSTED FROM HIS HOME

There is a city called Mahilaropya in the southern country. In this city is a Shiva temple with a monastery. A sanyasi called Tamrachura used to manage that monastery, but his real livelihood was begging for food. From the food he received in alms every day, he would eat half, and the other half he would store away in his begging bowl, which he would hang from a nail in the roof's rafter, just before he went to sleep. In the morning, he would take that food and distribute it among the sweepers of the monastery as payment for their work.

One day my friends and relatives came to me and told me about Tamrachura's hanging begging bowl. 'He puts all his leftover food in it,' they told me. 'But he hangs it so high that no mice can get to it. We've all tried to reach it; none of us can jump that high. But we know that you can. We know that jumping up to the hanging begging bowl will be an easy task for you. So, we've decided that today we'll take you with us to his hut. Instead of foraging for food today, we want to eat the food from the sanyasi's begging bowl.'

To honour their request, that night I went with the mice to the monastery, and they led me to the sanyasi's room. I saw his begging bowl hanging from the rafter and jumped on it right away. It was hardly a challenge for me. When I climbed into the bowl, I discovered that it was full of delicious food. I feasted on it myself and shared it with my friends and relatives. After everyone had had their fill, we went home. From that day on, the sanyasi's room became our regular nightly haunt, and his begging bowl became our bowl of plenty. I would jump onto it and throw down the food to my clansmen. We would eat as much as we could and then return home to sleep the sleep of those whose bellies are full.

Naturally, the sanyasi noticed that his food was being eaten by mice. Every night he tried very hard to stay up and guard his bowl, but, eventually, he would fall asleep, which was my cue. While he slept, I raided his food.

One day, to protect his food, he came up with a harsh plan. He found a thick bamboo staff, and, all night, he beat that on the begging bowl at regular intervals. After that, every time I attempted to get to the food, I had to jump out and run away for fear of getting smashed with the sanyasi's bamboo staff. Time passed, and even though it became more difficult to get to the sanyasi's food, I was still able to feed myself and my friends and relatives quite well.

Then, one day a friend of Tamrachura's visited him. He was another sanyasi called Brihatisfak (one with a big backside). He was on his way to a pilgrimage and was at the monastery to visit his friend. Tamrachura welcomed his friend warmly and invited him to sleep in his room.

As the two sat on kusha grass on the floor, chatting about this and that, Tamrachura kept beating on the hanging begging bowl, even in the midst of a conversation. He was so focused on his begging bowl that his responses to Brihatisfak were monosyllabic, 'hm', 'hm'. This annoyed Brihatisfak very much and he said to Tamrachura, 'Today I've realized that our friendship is waning. That's why there is no excitement in our conversation; you are not even responding to my questions; all you're saying is "hm", "hm" to everything I say. I don't want to stay here any more. I want to leave. One should only go to the house of those friends who welcome you with warmth and sweet words: "Come, sit on this seat. I haven't seen you in such a long time. How are you? You look too thin. Is everything okay? I'm happy to see you, and other pleasantries, such as these.

> If you visit a house where the host
> shows no interest in you.
> He doesn't meet your eye,
> looks down, looks away,
> looks distractedly all around,
> then you are a bull with no horns and tail.

> The wise do not visit a house,
> even if it is raining gold in it,
> where the host neither rises in welcome
> nor greets you with pleasantries
> or exchanges of joys and sorrows.

Tamrachura, you have become so full of yourself on acquiring the management of this tiny monastery that you have forgotten how to be gracious to friends. Don't you know that by becoming the prefect of this monastery, you have bought an invitation to hell? It is said,

> If you want to be on the straight path to hell,
> serve as a presiding priest for just one year.
> And if you wish to get there sooner,
> serve as a monastery's prefect for three days.
> Just three days will give you all you need for hell.

Therefore, you fool, instead of feeling dismay at being given the responsibility of the monastery, you are walking around proudly. Shame on you. I am so offended by you that I want to leave this instant.'

Hearing this tirade from Brihatisfak, Tamrachura was very aggrieved, and his body started trembling in agitation. 'Please don't say this,' he begged his friend with folded hands. 'You are my best friend, and I don't want to lose you. At least listen to the reason for my distraction and my apparent disinterest in our conversation. The thing is, there is a mouse who comes to my hut every night and jumps so high that he reaches that begging bowl hanging from the roof. Because he eats up that food and contaminates the rest, I can't give it to the servants and sweepers of the monastery. Hence, I have nothing to pay them for their work; therefore, no work gets done. It is to scare the mouse off that I constantly beat a bamboo stick on the begging bowl. That is why I seemed distracted. I wasn't disregarding you. It is also not my pride or any such thing. It is this this evil mouse who seems to be more adept than even a cat or a black-faced monkey.'

Hearing his friend's explanation, Brihatisfak calmed down a bit and took a breath. 'Oh, I see,' he said. 'Well, maybe I can help you figure out a plan to get rid of the mouse. Where is its hole? Do you know?'

'Not really,' Tamrachura replied.

'It is most likely where there is a buried treasure,' Brihatisfak said. 'The warmth of that treasure is putting that spring in his jump. Just as that boy said,

> Mother, why would this woman, Shandili
> give away hulled sesame for unhulled seeds.
> She must have a special reason for doing it.'

'Please tell me that story,' Tamrachura asked his friend, and Brihatisfak told him the tale that he himself had witnessed.

THE TALE OF SHANDILI AND HER HULLED SESAME SEEDS

Once upon a time, during the Chaturmasya Vrata, I was visiting a village, where I requested a brahmin for a place to stay. He not only gave me a place but also took responsibility for caring for my needs for those four months. Hence, I began to live happily in that house, engaged in work and austerities. One day, I woke up at dawn, disturbed by some whispering. Straining my ears, I heard the brahmin and his wife talking. The brahmin said, 'Today is Dakshinayana Sankranti, which means that this morning is a big day for charity. That is why I'm going to the next village to receive alms. I want you to observe the day by inviting one brahmin to the house and feeding him, as is the custom.'

The brahmin's wife replied in an angry voice, 'Where is there food for charity in this house, you impoverished no-good husband? Aren't you even embarrassed to ask me to do this? I haven't seen a single day of happiness since I married you. Never have I tasted mithai or eaten any delicacies. Never have you given me a single piece of jewellery to wear around my neck or wrists.'

The brahmin was distressed by this wife's tirade and, trying to calm her, said in a strained voice: 'It's not right that you should say such things to me. It is said,

> If you have one bite of food
> give half of it to a beggar.
> Who has wealth enough
> to give away in charity?
> So, give what you have.

> The merit a king or a rich man receives
> from giving money, jewels, gold, and land
> is the same merit the poor can receive
> by giving just one cowrie in alms.
> This is what the shastras say.
> A giver, no matter how small, is adored.
> A miser, no matter how wealthy, is ignored.
> A small well with sweet water, even shallow,

can make people happy and contented. Whereas,
a sea of saline water cannot quench anyone's thirst.

People love the sight of clouds,
because they shower down rain.
None likes to look at the sun
whose rays are spread out like hands.

Therefore, I tell you, wife, that even the poor should attempt to give to others whatever little they are able to. It will be rewarded manifold. Besides, it is said,

One's desire must not exceed bounds,
but one should not give up all desire.
He who desires excessively, suffers
and develops a lump on his head
like the jackal who desired too much.'

'What is this story?' the brahmin's wife asked, and the brahmin narrated the tale.

THE TALE OF THE JACKAL WHO DESIRED TOO MUCH

In a forested region there lived a hunter. One day, on a hunt, he saw in the distance a wild boar as black as Kala Naga, the highest peak in the Saraswati mountain range. Stealthily drawing close to the animal, the hunter mounted an arrow to his bow. The boar heard the twanging of the bow and arrow and saw the hunter, but, instead of fleeing, he kept advancing towards the hunter. Surprised, the hunter said,

> 'This boar is not afraid of my arrow
> nor of my bow mounted with the arrow.
> Instead, he is walking fearlessly towards me.
> Clearly Yamaraja himself has sent him as my kill.'

Convinced of this, he pulled the string to his ear and released the arrow. The boar was fatally hit, but he kept approaching, snarling, baring his teeth that were sharp and curved like crescent moons, and sank them into the hunter's stomach. The man died instantly. And the boar, after staggering around for a few moments, crashed to the ground, and also died. A little while later, a hungry jackal wandered that way. His death must have been hovering close, because when he saw the man and the boar dead on the ground, he rushed to them in excitement. All that food—he could hardly believe his eyes, and he thought,

> Good or bad rewards of past karma
> manifest themselves as though fate,
> and they are received without any effort.

Someone has rightly said,

> In whatever country,
> in whatever time,
> in whatever situation,
> in whatever way,
> whoever has performed
> whatever good or bad karma,

he reaps rewards in the same way
at a time that has been ordained.

I was fated to get all this food today, and I did. I should consume it bit by bit so that it lasts many days. Let me start by eating this string lying beside the man, which is probably an entrail. The wise say,

> Money earned by your own hand
> should be consumed bit by bit,
> like small doses of medicine.
> Do not spend it quickly and rashly.

And so, the jackal stepped towards one end of the strung bow and put it in his mouth to eat the string. Suddenly the string snapped, and the bow's pointed end went through the roof of his mouth and, piercing his head, came out at the other end, like a protrusion on his head. Needless to say, the jackal died instantly.

'That is why I say, a person should not desire excessively. Otherwise, he may end up like the jackal with a lump on his head,' said the brahmin to his wife. 'It is said,

> Lifespan, livelihood, wealth, education, and death—
> these five factors of life are determined by fate,
> even as one develops in the mother's womb.'

The brahmin's wife was persuaded by her husband's arguments, and she said to him, 'Fine. I have some sesame seeds stored away. I'll crush them and make a meal of them to feed a brahmin for Chaturamasa.'

Satisfied that his wife would observe the beginning of the sacred fast, the brahmin went away to the other village to receive whatever alms he could. At home, his wife washed the unhulled sesame in warm water and then, removing the hulls, crushed and ground the seeds on a grindstone. Then she took the sesame flour outside and spread it on a low parapet near her hut so that it could dry in the sun. After that, she got busy with her chores. Sometime during the day, a dog passing by stopped near the parapet and, raising its leg, urinated on the drying sesame. The woman saw it all from the window. 'Oh, my ill luck,' she lamented. 'All I had was this handful of sesame seeds, and now, even these are ruined. What should I do? I promised my husband that I would feed a brahmin today. From where can I get more sesame?' Then a thought came to her: Why not go into the neighbourhood and see if anyone would exchange ground sesame with whole seeds. 'I think many would be happy to take the ground seeds, because they won't require much work,' she convinced herself.

Then, spreading the sesame on a winnowing fan, she left the house and began to roam around the neighbourhood, calling, 'Exchange your unhulled sesame with ground seeds.'

'That morning I had gone out to beg for alms,' continued Brihatisfak. 'The housewife who was serving me at the door heard Shandili's call and became interested in making the exchange. She called Shandili to her door and, telling her to wait, went inside to bring the unhulled sesame. But her young son, who was reading Kamandaka's *Nitishastra*, told her to stop. 'I don't think you should take these ground seeds,' he said to his mother. 'The woman put in a lot of effort to hull the seed and grind the sesame. Then why is she willing to take unhulled seeds for the hulled and ground seeds? There must be a reason she is making this uneven exchange.'

The son's logic dissuaded the woman and she refused Shandili's deal.

'That is why I am saying to you,' Brihatisfak said to his friend, Tamrachura, 'This mouse is jumping so high; there must be a reason for it. Let me ask you, do you know the path this mouse takes when he comes into your hut?'

'Yes, in fact, I do know the path, because he never comes alone. He is always accompanied by a nest of his clan, and they all wander around my house, fearlessly. Then, after eating my food and making mischief, they all leave together. That's why I am familiar with his comings and goings.'

'Aha!' exclaimed Brihatisfak. 'Do you have any tool for digging, my friend?'

'Yes, I do,' Tamrachura replied. 'See there, I have an iron shovel.'

'Good. Tomorrow morning, come with me to track the path of these mice. We need to leave really early, while the tracks are still fresh.'

'When I heard those sadhus,' Hiranyaka said to Mantharaka. 'I was certain that I was going to die. The way that guest sadhu was talking, it appeared to me he meant business. I feared that just to as he had surmised there was buried treasure under my hole, he would soon locate my fortress, as well. It is said,

> A wise man needs just one look
> to determine the quality of a man,
> just like a savvy merchant

> who can hold an item in his hand
> and judge its weight without a scale.

Also,

> The desires a man has in this life
> indicate the good and bad actions
> of his births in the past and the future,
> just as watching the enchanting stride of a
> peacock's chick, people know it is a peacock
> though the chick's feathers are not yet sprouted.

That is how I deduced that the sadhu was a fearsome and ruthless man who did what he said he would do, and this caused me great anxiety. So, that day, after we left the brahmin's hut, I led my family through a different path. But we had hardly gone a short distance, when, suddenly, a big cat appeared before us. Seeing so many of us together, he leapt on us and smacked down several of us in one fell swoop. After that, it was a massacre.

"Why did you make us leave our safe, easy path and lead us into this danger?" my surviving relatives wailed, blaming me for the death of our brethren. Those of us who could still walk, managed to find our way back to my fortress, even though we were badly wounded and covered in so much blood, we were soaking the earth red. Someone has rightly said,

> Through bad luck a deer was caught in a net,
> and when he managed to cut the net,
> he fell into the pit dug to catch deer.
> When he pulled himself out of the pit,
> he got snared in a trapper's hanging noose.
> With great effort, he broke the noose and fled,
> only to be engulfed in a tremendous forest fire.
> When he found his way out of that alive,
> hunters shot at him to kill him for his meat.
> Fleeing from the hunters, he made a long leap
> and fell into a well, where he drowned.

When your fate is not in your favour, no efforts or tasks meet with success. Just like this deer, who, despite so much effort, ended up dead in a well. Therefore, it can be concluded that you can only be successful in your efforts when fate is favourable.

Trying to escape the cat, veering away from my normal path, I found a different hole to hide in. But my remaining friends and relatives all went back to our fortress and scuttled inside. Following the trace of their blood, the determined sanyasi found the place and began digging there. As he had expected, he soon struck the buried treasure. This wealth was the reason for my confidence; its warmth was why I was able to jump so high and reach even the most inaccessible stores of food. Discovering my wealth, that cruel sadhu became very pleased with himself, and he said to his friend, "Tamrachura, now you can sleep peacefully at night. That mouse who used to jump so high and steal the food from your begging bowl no longer has the wherewithal to jump." Taking my treasure, both brahmins then returned to the monastery.

I watched them go with a sinking heart, and then, I, too, returned to my fortress home that was now not only empty, but it had also become unwelcoming and unexciting. I couldn't stay there any longer. My mind just felt too unsettled and agitated. Then I started to think: what should I do? Where can I go? How can I find peace again? Caught in the circle of these thoughts, I somehow passed that day, and, as soon as night fell, I took my remaining mouse companions and went to the monastery to see if I could still secure some food, even though my mind was not in it.

Tamrachura must have heard us enter his hut, because he picked up the bamboo staff and began beating his hanging begging bowl.

"My friend, why don't you sleep in peace now?" Brihatisfak said to him.

"I can't. That evil mouse has returned with his family. I need to keep him away from my food."

Brihatisfak then said with a laugh, "His power and energy have all gone, along with his treasure. This is what happens. Losing wealth can break anyone.

> Those with happy faces, full of enthusiasm,
> who walk around with an air of superiority,
> thinking of others as though they are nothing—
> these are the ones who are riding high on wealth.

This mouse is no longer riding on wealth. You don't need to fear him any more."

Listening to him talk about my defeat, I was filled with rage, and, just to show him, I pulled together all my energy and jumped to reach the hanging bowl. But, of course, I couldn't reach it and came crashing down to the floor. Hearing me fall, my enemy, that Brihatisfak, burst out laughing. "See?" he said to his friend. "Take a look at this spectacle. In this world, whoever is powerful is so, because he has wealth. It is wealth that makes people pundits and wise. See, because he has lost his wealth, this mouse has become like everyone else in his community, and the special ability he had of jumping so high has vanished? So, my friend, don't worry and sleep in peace. That which caused this mouse to jump is in our hands. Now we don't need to fear him. Someone has rightly said,

> A serpent without fangs and
> an elephant without madness
> are fierce in name only.
> A man without money is also
> the same way; he's only a name.
> Losing the support of his money,
> he has no strength or talent."

These words of the sanyasi struck the final blow, and I began to think, he's right. I don't have the strength any more to jump even a finger's length. Truly, cursed is life without wealth. And it is rightly said,

> Without having the means,
> a man's intellect and ability
> to think and act are destroyed.
> All his efforts are thrown awry,
> just as rivulets that flow in the hills
> dry up in the summer heat.

> Just like wild barley and sesame
> are barley and sesame in name only,
> because their kernels are empty,
> yet they are still called by their name;
> in the same way a poor man is called
> a man only because he is a man.
> He cannot accomplish anything worthy.

> A poor man may have other good qualities,
> but even they lose their lustre in poverty.
> As the sun illumines all things mobile and immobile,
> wealth illumines all qualities and talents.

> He who has always been destitute and poor
> knows not the pain of impoverishment,

as much as he who has had wealth and lost it.

A dried, insect-ridden, burnt-out tree
standing in barren ground, unproductive,
can sprout new shoots and be born anew.
But an abject, beggarly man's birth
will always be futile and meaningless.

A destitute man is always suspected,
even if his intention is to do good.
"He's surely come to ask for something,"
people think and turn their faces away.

A poor man has many desires
that rise and vanish in his heart.
They never achieve fulfilment,
like the breasts of a widow
that never garner male attention.

A person covered with the darkness of poverty
is invisible to all even in the brightness of day,
no matter how hard he tries to attract attention.

Looking longingly at Tamrachura's unreachable begging bowl and then despondently at my treasure lying under his pillow, I bewailed my fate. I had no other choice but to return home, starving and empty handed. Seeing me, my servants were equally dejected. "Oh, this master has become unable to feed us," they said. "It is better leave him. In fact, if we stay here, we may have to suffer the attacks of cats and mongooses, who will surely be looking for him.

> If serving a master reaps
> calamities and misfortune,
> instead of desired benefits;
> better to leave that service
> and find work elsewhere."

Trying to turn a deaf ear to such degrading and hurtful comments from my servants, I entered my fortress. No servant came to serve me, no relative came to greet me. That is when I decided, this abject poverty be damned. And, that night, lying in bed, I began to plan: what if go to that evil brahmin's house again and, sneaking under his pillow, gnaw the box that has my treasure and bring my wealth back to my fortress, piece by piece? That way I could regain my influence and power. It is said,

> Poverty is the greatest grief.
> A poor man is treated as dead
> by his friends and relatives.

Also,

> A man blackened by the sin of poverty
> becomes an object of people's pity,
> an easy target for all sorts of insults,
> and a host for unending misfortune.
>
> When a person has not a cowrie to his name,
> friends and relatives are ashamed to talk to him,
> hiding from the world their relationship to him.
> Friends become enemies and vilify him to others.
>
> Just as people avoid dust from the feet of sheep,
> and the dust rising from a sweeping broom;
> just as they fear the shade of a diya or a cot,
> portended by dharmashastras as bad omens—
> certain to be the cause of losing wealth,
> so do they fear a person without means.
>
> A man with no means is ashamed.
> Shame leads to loss of self-worth.
> Loss of self leads to loss of honour.
> Humbled, he becomes despondent.
> Sadness follows, clouding intelligence.
> And with a weak mind, he wastes away.
> Ah, poverty is the root of all misfortunes.

That is why I had to get that wealth back, I was even ready to die in the effort. In any case, it is better to die than to lose your wealth, because it is said,

> The man who watches his wealth stolen
> and doesn't do everything to save it,
> be it the sacrifice of his own life,
> is a pariah even to his ancestors,
> who refuse to take his ritual water.

It is said,

> To save a cow and a brahmin,
> to fight for and give up one's life,
> to save a woman and one's wealth,
> to die fighting an enemy in battle—
> these lead to eternity in Brahmaloka.

Thus, full of conviction about what I had to do, I went to the monastery again that night. The evil brahmin, Tamrachura, was sleeping peacefully, with my wealth under his pillow. So, I climbed on to his bed and crept under his pillow. But, as soon as I began to gnaw a hole in the treasure box, he woke up and, picking up the bamboo staff, struck me hard on the head. I almost died from the blow and only survived because there was still some time left in my life span. It is said,

> If someone is meant to get something,
> he is sure to get it; no doubt about it.
> Even the gods cannot prevent this.
> That is why I do not think and worry,
> nor am I surprised when I get something,
> because what is mine will remain mine.
> Its acquisition will be mine, no one else's,
> just as Sagaradatta's son believed all his life.'

'What is this story?' the crow and tortoise asked Hiranyaka, and the mouse told them the tale.

THE TALE OF THE MAN WHO RECEIVED WHAT HE WAS MEANT TO

In a city lived a businessman named Sagaradatta. He had a son who once bought a book for a hundred silver coins. In it was written just one verse:

> Whoever is meant to get something, will get it.
> even the gods can't prevent this, let alone men.
> Therefore, it is futile to bemoan a loss
> or be prideful of acquiring something,
> because what belongs to you and is yours,
> how can that belong to someone else?

When Sagaradatta saw the book in his son's hand, he asked him: 'How much did you pay for this?'

'One hundred silver coins,' replied the son.

'You idiot,' the businessman shouted. 'Shame on you. You paid a hundred pieces of silver for a tiny little book in which there is just one verse. With this kind of meagre intelligence, how will you ever earn money, let alone make a profit? I'm ashamed to call you my son. I disown you. Leave my house and never come back.'

The young man was very sad at being thrown out of his father's house. Nevertheless, he left town and went to live in another city.

One day, someone in that city asked the young man, 'Where are you from? What is your name?'

'Praptavyamartha labhate manushya,' (every man will receive what he is meant to obtain) replied the young man.

Sometime later, another man asked him, 'What is your name?' And he gave the same answer—'Praptavyamartha labhate manushya.' In fact, this was his stock response to anyone who asked him about himself. Therefore, he became known in that city as Praptavyamartha (what he is meant to obtain).

Once, there was a large fair in the city, and everyone came to attend it. The kingdom's princess, Chandravati, whose youth was blossoming and beauty was stunning, also came to it. As she was walking to the fairground, she saw a very good-looking prince and was struck by the arrows of desire. Appealing to her friend, she said, 'I must meet this handsome prince today, no matter what. Therefore, please arrange a meeting, however you can.'

The friend went to the prince and said to him, 'After seeing you, the princess has been suffering from the pain of Kamadeva's arrows; if you don't go to her immediately, she'll have no choice but to end her life.'

'If that is the case, tell the princess that I'll go to her as soon as possible,' said the prince. 'Can you tell me how I can enter the princess's palace?'

'Tonight, a thick rope will be lowered from the wall of her palace. Climb the rope, and it will take you directly into the princess's rooms.'

'Please tell the princess that I will be there tonight,' the prince promised.

When the friend informed Chandravati of the prince's intention, she was ecstatic. All day she waited impatiently for night to fall, her anticipation increasing with each passing hour. On the other hand, the prince began to have second thoughts. He told himself that clandestinely meeting the princess of the land was really not a prudent thing to do.

> Sleeping with the daughter or wife of
> a guru, friend, king, master, or servant
> is equivalent to the sin of brahminicide.

Also,

> That action should never be committed
> which brings dishonour in this life,
> and suffering in the next life,
> prohibiting one from entering heaven.

Thinking along these lines, the prince, ultimately, decided not to visit the princess that night. Moreover, fate had something else in mind. That night, walking near the palace was Praptavyasmartha, the businessman's son. Seeing a rope hanging down the palace wall, he became curious to find out its purpose, so he climbed up it and stepped into the princess's room.

In the shadowed lamplight, Chandravati mistook him for the prince she had seen that morning and warmly welcomed him with a scented bath, delicious food, and fine clothing. Then, asking him to lie down on the bed that was made with silken sheets, she embraced him. Trembling with excitement, she said to him, 'As soon as I saw you, I became enchanted and lost myself. I give myself to you, wholeheartedly. From today, I'll consider you my husband. But why are you so quiet? Why are you not talking to me?'

'Praptavyamartha labhate manushya,' said the businessman's son.

The princess jumped out of bed in shock. 'Who are you?' she cried. 'You are not the prince I saw this morning.' And, calling the guards, she had him thrown out.

Trying to find his way back to the city, the young man became quite tired. Then, by chance, he came upon a dilapidated temple of the god Khandoba and decided to spend the night there.

Just as he entered the temple, a police chief also came in. He was following the instructions of a courtesan, whom he was to meet there. Seeing the young man, he halted, afraid that his secret would be revealed. Therefore, he asked the young man in a no-nonsense voice, 'Who are you and what are you doing here?'

'Praptavyamartha labhate manushya,' replied the young man. 'I was looking for a place to spend the night, and I came upon this temple.'

'This is a vacant, abandoned temple,' the police chief said. 'It is not a fit place to spend the night. Since you are a visitor here, I can offer you shelter. Go and sleep in my house. No one is there, because I am here. So, feel free to make yourself comfortable in my bed.'

The young man gratefully accepted the chief's offer and went to his house; however, looking for the chief room, he accidently ended up in the wrong room, and since there was a large bed there, he lay down in it. By this time, he was so exhausted that he didn't even check to see if the bed was occupied. It so happened that the police chief's daughter, Vinayavati, was lying in that bed, waiting for the young man with whom she had an assignation. This was the first time she had invited him to her bed; hence, in the darkness, she did not realize that the man who had slipped into her bed was not her lover. Her face beaming like a lotus, she quickly declared that she accepted him as her husband and embraced him. Then she said to him in a cajoling voice, 'I want to hear sweet love words from you. Why aren't you talking to me? Is something the matter?'

'Praptavyamartha labhate manushya,' replied the businessman's son.

Vinayavati knew that this was not the man she had been waiting for. Oh, she thought, this is exactly what occurs when a task is done in a hurry, with no thought put into it. Feeling regret at what she had done, she asked the young man to leave her house.

As he stepped out of the police chief's house, the businessman's son encountered a wedding barat of a young man called Varakriti, and he joined the dancing and singing baratis. After winding through a number of streets, the barat reached its destination—a merchant's house elaborately decorated with lights and flowers. Inside the house a beautiful mandap was set up and sitting before it in full bridal finery and expensive gold jewellery was the merchant's daughter.

Just as the baratis entered the house, a musth elephant suddenly crashed his way in. The frightened baratis scattered, running in every direction, trying to escape him. When the elephant turned towards the mandap, everyone who was there, also scooted. The poor bride was left all by herself, trembling like a leaf, looking with fear-filled eyes at the advancing beast.

Seeing her alone and in danger, the businessman's son rushed to her. 'Don't be afraid,' he said. 'I'm here. I'll protect you.' Taking her right hand in his right hand, he pulled her out of the elephant's path, and calling out to him in a firm, commanding voice, he brought him under control. Then steering the animal away with calming gestures, he directed him out of the wedding mandap. In all this commotion, the auspicious time of the wedding ceremony passed.

When the groom, Varakriti, his relatives, and the girl's family came out of hiding, they saw the bride's hand in the hand of a strange man and were outraged. 'You have wronged me,' Varakriti accused his would-have-been father-in-law. 'You promised me your daughter and then you gave her hand to another man.'

'I didn't do this,' the father of the bride tried to explain. 'Like you, I, too, ran away from the crazed elephant. I, too, have just come here.' Then, turning to his daughter, he scolded her, 'Daughter, why have you married another man, when I promised you to Varakriti? You have not done a good thing.'

'Father, this man saved my life,' the daughter replied. 'How can I exchange ritual water with another man in this life? Now, only this man is entitled to my hand. I can't marry another.'

This acrimonious exchange between the bride, her father, and the groom-that-would-have-been went on till dawn, and a crowd began to gather outside the wedding house. Hearing about the pandemonium, the princess Chandravati also arrived there, as did the police chief's daughter, who heard about the events of the night from someone in her neighbourhood. As the crowd swelled, traffic came to a halt, and the king was informed.

Arriving at the house, the king asked Praptavysmartha: 'Young man, tell me, without fear, everything that happened here.'

'Praptavyamartha labhate manushya,' replied the businessman's son.

Remembering that she had heard these words the night before, princess

Chandravati exclaimed, 'Every man will receive what he is meant to obtain, just as he obtained me last night.'

Then that police chief's daughter added, 'That is why I neither worry about my situation nor do I rejoice in it. What is to happen will happen.'

'What is mine is mine, and it can't belong to anyone else,' the merchant's daughter joined in.

Thoroughly confused about what was going on, the king commanded each of the young women to relate her version of the events. Finally, when it all became clear to him, he praised Praptavysmartha for his bravery and for his comprehension of how fate operates. Then, he rewarded him with a thousand villages and married his daughter to him, providing her with a dowry of horses and elephants and maids and valuable gems and jewels. He also announced that Praptavysmartha would be his heir apparent. The police chief, too, gave his daughter to Praptavyamartha in marriage, along with a hefty dowry of gold and jewels.

The businessman's son then called his parents and relatives to this city and settled down with them and lived a happy life.

'Brothers, that is why I say, if someone is supposed to get something, he'll get it, and not even the gods can prevent this,' Hiranyaka said to Laghupata the crow and Mantharaka the tortoise. 'But do you see now, Mantharaka, why, having experienced a life of joys and sorrows, I felt disillusioned? That is why I accompanied my friend, Laghupata, and came all the way here to live with you.'

'Dear Hiranyaka, Laghupata is certainly your true friend. Even though you are his prey, he carried you on his back for the whole journey. He must have been hungry and thirsty on the way, yet he didn't harm you. This has proved that he is truly your friend. It is said,

> He whose body and mind do not covet
> even when he sees objects of his desire;
> he who remains a friend when needed,
> whose friendship is the same in joy and sorrow,
> he is worthy of being called a friend.

Also,

> The wise should test friends the same way
> that brahmins test the colours of homa fire.

Just as it is said:

> A friend during adversity
> is a true friend indeed.
> In times of prosperity,
> even the evil and wicked
> call themselves your friend.

Moreover, the way this crow has taken care of you in your time of need has increased my own trust in his friendship. Otherwise, you know what the Nitishastras says: water creatures like us have no business being friends with meat-eating creatures like Laghupata, because the two are natural enemies. Someone has rightly stated,

> No one is an enemy forever,
> and no one is a friend forever.
> Those who help are friends,
> and those who harm are enemies.
> To decide if someone is friend or enemy
> let his actions show the truth.

And the actions of Laghupata have shown you that he is certainly your friend. That is why, dear Hiranyaka, I am your friend, as well. My house is behind this lake, and I welcome you to it. Please consider it your own and be comfortable, and know that I am always here and ready to help you. I realize that you have lost all your wealth, and you have had to leave your homeland. But don't be sad about that any more. It is said,

> Shade from clouds,
> affection from the wicked,
> cooked food,
> women of beauty,
> youth and wealth—
> all these last just a short time.

Besides, wealth is so quixotic; it comes and goes and never stays permanently with one person. This is what the wise say,

> Always accumulated, never spent,
> protected more than one's life,
> unused even for creature comfort,
> what use is such cold-hearted wealth that

it doesn't walk with you even five steps,
when you leave to go to Yama's abode.

Also,

> Just as a piece of meat is eaten
> by the fish in the water,
> by dogs, cats, and tigers on earth,
> by eagles and crows in the sky—
> to eat the wealth of a rich man
> people are waiting everywhere.
>
> Even if a wealthy man is innocent,
> the king and his police heckle him
> for this offence or that offence,
> simply to fleece him of some money.
> A poor man may commit a crime
> but no one bothers to question him.
> What can one gain from the destitute?
>
> It is painful to grow wealth.
> To safeguard it is also not easy.
> If it gets destroyed or is spent,
> sorrows assail one's heart.

The effort that people expend to acquire wealth—if they put in even one hundredth of that effort into achieving moksha, they would be liberated.

I'm also sorry that you have had to leave your homeland, and now you'll have to live in a foreign land. But don't feel bad about that, as well. The wise say,

> What burden is too heavy for the able?
> What land is too far for the enterprising?
> For the wise what is a foreign place?
> For the sweet-spoken, who is a stranger?

Besides, you are an ocean of wisdom. You are no ordinary being who will have problems acclimatizing in a foreign land. Also know,

> Lakshmi herself seeks out those
> who are lively and expeditious,
> who know the way things work,

> who stay away from substances,
> who are brave and appreciative,
> who know how to keep a friendship.

Furthermore, acquired wealth is sometimes lost. That object which is not ours can't be used by us even for a moment. If, by accident, we receive something that isn't ours, destiny instantly snatches it away.

> Riches you have grown yourself
> cannot be used unless fate allows,
> just as the hard-earned money
> of the foolish Somilaka vanished
> every time he entered the deep forest.'

'What is this story?' Hiranyaka asked, and Mantharaka began the tale.

THE TALE OF SOMILAKA AND THE VANISHING GOLD

In a town lived a talented weaver called Somilaka. The colours and images he wove into his silk and brocades were extraordinary and worthy of royalty. However, despite being so accomplished, he could barely eke out a living. Unlike him, the other weavers in that town, who were not as talented and could weave only ugly, thick cotton were becoming wealthy from their trade. Unable to comprehend this inequity, Somilaka said to his wife one day, 'Do you see, dear, how these inferior weavers are accumulating gold and silver and becoming rich by making thick cotton garments; whereas, I continue to be stuck in poverty, even though my weaving is far superior, and the silk and brocade garments I can weave are worthy of a king. I feel like this town is not for me. Maybe, if I go to a different place, my skills will be appreciated, and I'll be paid accordingly.'

'I don't agree with that,' the weaver's wife said. 'I don't believe in such talk—that a town doesn't suit me and another one will. It is said,

> An object could be flying in the sky,
> penetrating the netherworld,
> roaming till the ends of the world.
> But one cannot obtain this object
> if it hasn't been prepaid in a past birth.

Just as someone has said,

> What is not destined
> will never happen.
> And what is destined
> will happen without effort.
> An object not in your destiny
> will vanish even from your hand.

> Destined karma is like a calf.
> Just as he follows his mother and finds her,
> though she may be among a thousand cows,
> karma follows one through many births,

attaching to the doer, till it is spent.
It sleeps when the doer sleeps.
It walks along wherever he walks.
It sits and stands when he sits and stands.

Hence, dear one, my advice to you is to earn your livelihood right here in this town. Whatever has to happen will happen.'

'I don't agree with you,' the weaver replied. 'Because without effort, even karma doesn't come to fruition.

> Just as in the act of clapping
> one needs both hands,
> to receive karma's reward
> one needs to put in effort.

It is said,

> By luck you may have food,
> But, unless your hand
> puts it in your mouth,
> you cannot eat it.

Someone has rightly said,

> Lakshmi comes to one who works hard.
> Only cowards say, "It is a matter of luck."
> Instead of depending on mere luck,
> focus on your strength and industry.
> Only when your efforts prove futile
> should you blame it on bad luck.

As it is said,

> Only effort accomplishes a task.
> Mere desire doesn't produce results.
> A deer does not himself walk into
> the mouth of a sleeping lion.
> Even a lion must put in the effort
> to kill so as to appease his hunger.

That is why, dear wife, I have decided that I'll go to another town and keep working hard. I'm certain my effort will pay off.' Having made this decision, Somilaka the weaver left for the city of Vardhamana. There, he worked very hard and was duly rewarded. In three years, he accumulated three hundred gold mohurs and then decided to return home.

On his way, about halfway home, as he was crossing a dense forest, night fell. Fearing tigers and other predators, he climbed up a big bargad tree, and, sitting safely in its thick branches, he soon fell asleep. Around midnight, he had a dream in which he saw two fearsome men engaged in a conversation. The first man said, 'O lord of Doers, you know very well what is written in Somilaka's fate; he will only have enough money for food and day-to-day living; nothing more. Then why did you give him three hundred gold mohurs?'

'O Fate,' said the second man, 'People who work hard, I reward them with money. To determine what the outcome of that money will be is your domain. Do whatever you have to.'

At this juncture, Somilaka woke up. For a moment he thought it was only a dream, but when he checked the bundle in which he had kept his hard-earned gold mohurs, he found it empty. The mohurs had vanished.

Somilaka was shattered. Damning fate, he began to lament, 'I can't believe this. Where did all my money go? It took me three years to earn it. And I worked myself to the bone. This is unfair. Now, how can I return home? What face will I show my wife and my friends?'

And so, deciding not to go home, Somilaka got down from the tree and returned to Vardhamana. This time, in only one year, he was able to accumulate five hundred gold mohurs. Securing them in a bundle, he once again started on his journey home, and, as before, when he started across the dense forest, night fell. However, remembering his last experience, and fearing that if he slept, he would lose his money again, he was determined to press on, even though he was weary and fearful of wild animals.

As Somilaka made his way through the trees, he suddenly came upon two fearsome-looking men who were deep in conversation. The first man was saying, 'O lord of Doers, why did you give this Somilaka five hundred gold mohurs? Don't you know that he is fated to have only enough for food and the basic necessities, and no more than that?'

To this, the second man replied, 'Dear Fate, I always reward those who work hard. But what happens to that reward is your business.'

Somilaka quickly opened his bundle. Sure enough, it was as he feared: all the mohurs were gone; not even one remained. Feeling devastated and disheartened, he said to himself, 'My life is futile without money. And since it seems to be written in my fate that I'll never have money, I might as well hang myself.' With this resolve, Somilaka gathered strands of kusha grass and, braiding them into a rope, made a noose to put it around his neck. As he strung the rope from a tall tree and began to tighten it, he suddenly saw a big, fearsome man in the sky, who said to him in a booming voice, 'O brave Somilaka, stop what you are about to do and go home. I am the one who stole your money. Because you are not supposed to have more than what you need for bare necessities, I had to take it. But I am impressed by your bravery. That is why I will give you a boon. Ask me for anything.'

'Loads of money; that is what I ask for', Somilaka replied immediately.

'What will you do with money that you are not fated to have? Even if you have loads of money, you will not be able to use it.'

'I understand that. Give it to me anyway. It may be unusable, but I still want it. As you know,

> If someone possesses money,
> though he be miserly and ignoble,
> people serve him and flatter him
> in the hope that he will share it.

It is said,

> I have waited fifteen years
> for the loose, hanging, big, round
> testicles to fall, thinking,
> today they will fall, now they will fall,
> tomorrow, they will fall, any moment....
> But they have not fallen.
> How much longer must I wait?'

'What is this story?' the man in the sky said, and Somilaka told him the tale.

THE TALE OF TIKSHANA VISHANA AND HIS LOOSE-HANGING BALLS

In a town lived a hulking, weighty bull by the name of Tikshana Vishana (sharp horns). Conceited and haughty about his size and strength, he left his herd to do whatever he pleased: amble here and there, dig up sand on the riverbank, and graze on emerald-green grass wherever he saw. When he reached the forest, he began to wander around there as well, uncaring of its dangers.

In that forest lived a jackal called Pramolaka. One day this jackal was sitting on the riverbank, enjoying his leisure with his wife, when Tikshana Vishana came to the river to quench his thirst.

Seeing his huge scrotum, the jackal's wife said to her mate, 'O husband, look at his massive, fleshy testicles. They are hanging so loosely that it appears they may fall any moment. Why don't you follow him, and, as soon as they fall, grab them. What a meal they'll make.'

'Dear wife, who knows when they'll fall, or, if they'll fall at all. Don't make me work futilely for something that may never happen. Let's just sit here by the water and catch the mice that come by to drink water. I've heard that this is the path the mice take. If I leave this spot and begin following that bull, some other jackal might take my place. That way I may not get the bull's balls, and I'll lose out on my mouse meal as well. It is said,

> He who leaves a thing of certainty
> and runs after something uncertain
> loses both the certain and the uncertain.'

'You're such a coward,' the she-jackal said to her husband. 'Satisfied with just meagreness when you can be going after plenty. It is said,

> Just like a small mountain river
> fills to the brim with a little water,
> and the cupped hands of a mouse
> get filled with a just little bit of grain,
> a coward is content with just a bit of riches.

That is why a man should always be motivated to achieve more. It is said,

> Enthusiasm initiates many new ventures.
> Where sloth is nowhere to be found
> and ability and work ethic are employed,
> there Lakshmi makes her permanent residence.

Also,

> Those ill-fated ones
> content with a little wealth
> lose the little they have,
> let alone gain more wealth.

And your wishy-washy opinion about the bull's testicles—whether they will fall or not; that, too, is questionable, because it is said,

> Men with strong resolve
> are big men in the truest sense.
> Big stature does not make a big man.
> The chataka bird may be small
> but its will is so unyielding,
> Indra himself pours water in its beak.

Besides, I'm tired of eating mouse meat. I really do think that the bull's testicles are on the verge of falling. Please do what I'm asking you to do and follow that bull.'

Listening to his wife, the jackal gave up catching mice and got up to follow the bull, Tikshana Vishana. Someone has rightly said,

> A man is independent and free to do what he wants
> till sharp words of his wife prick him like a thorn.
> Then he is like an elephant with a thorn in his foot.

> Inspired by his wife, a man considers
> a task that cannot be done to be doable,
> an inaccessible path as reachable,
> inedible food as worthy of eating.

Thus, persuaded by his wife, that jackal, accompanied by his wife, began following the bull. The two of them followed him for fourteen years, but that sac of testicles did not fall. When the fifteenth year was ending, the jackal said to his wife in frustration, 'Watching the loose-skinned and low-hanging, big balls of the bull, I've spent fifteen years thinking, now they'll fall. When will they fall? Will they ever fall? Caught between hopefulness and hopelessness, I've waited fifteen years, but they haven't fallen. And no one knows if they'll fall in the future. But now I'm done waiting. Come on. Let's go back to our spot by the river and catch mice.'

'That is why I tell you that people will become my followers just in the hope that I may decide to give them a portion of my wealth,' Somilaka said to the man in the sky. 'This means that only when there is money do people wait on you. Whether the money is for use or not is not the point.'

'If this is so,' said the man in the sky, 'then go back to Vardhamana and pay a visit to two men. One of them has accumulated a lot of wealth, but he keeps his money in a safe and spends his life safeguarding it; and the other man only has consumable wealth, and he likes to spend it. Watch the men and see which lifestyle suits you better, and which kind of wealth you want. That is the boon you should ask for, and I will fulfil it. If you want money that you cannot spend, but money that people respect, then I will give you a secret stash. But if you want to use your money for your own comfort and to give away in charity, then I will give you that.'

With these words, the sky man vanished. Somilaka was astounded by this incredible encounter and was not sure whether to believe it or not. But he decided to return to Vardhamana and visit the two men. By the time he got to the city, the sun was setting, and he was exhausted. After, asking around, he found the house of the rich man who had accumulated wealth, and, pushing open the door, stepped in.

'Who are you and what are you doing in my house?' the man of the house asked him. But Somilaka did not respond; instead, he entered the house. The man, his wife, their grown children—all asked Somilaka who he was and what he was doing in their house, but he didn't respond and kept advancing into the house. When they tried to push him out, Somilaka stubbornly sat down in one corner and refused to leave. Finally, the family just let him be, and when it was time for the evening meal, they gave him a few dry rotis, disregarding all rules of hospitality. Sitting there in the cold corner, Somilaka fell asleep, and, around midnight, he heard the same men from his earlier dreams:

Fate said, 'O lord of Doers, how did you get this miser to spend money on feeding Somilaka. He has spent a bit more today than he does on other days. This does not bode well.'

'O Fate, it is not my fault,' the lord of Doers said. 'You know I reward according to how much a man toils. This Somilaka worked hard for his food. Now what happens to that reward is your business. If you think the rich man has overspent, then you can punish him.'

After this the two men vanished and Somilaka went back to sleep again. When he woke up in the morning, he found out that the rich man had become sick with cholera. He remained sick for a while, but then he got better. When he started eating again, another bout of cholera hit him and he had to go on a fast.

Observing the man whose wealth was locked up and unusable, Somilaka left that place and sought out the house of the man who had money to spend. At this man's house, Somilaka was treated like a guest. At dinner, he was served varied, delicious dishes, and at bedtime, he was given fine clothes and a comfortable bed. His belly full, and his body snug in the comfort of soft sheets, Somilaka soon fell asleep, but in the middle of the night, he was woken up by the sound of talking; it was those two men again.

Fate was saying, 'O lord of Doers, this man of consumable wealth has spent a lot of money on Somilaka's hospitality. You know he borrowed that money from the moneylender. How will he pay off his debt?'

The lord of Doers replied, 'O lord of Destiny, to make a man spend money is my job, but what happens to the man after that, is your responsibility.'

The next morning, Somilaka woke up to someone knocking at the door of the house. It was a king's man who had come to give the businessman some kind of reward money from the king. With that money the man paid off his debt to the moneylender.

Somilaka left that house, thinking, this man does not have accumulated money; however, whenever he needs money, he, somehow, gets it. Nothing in his life is hindered by lack of money. He not only eats well himself, but he also feeds others well. That is why this man is so much better off than that other man who has loads of hidden wealth, but doesn't spend any of it on enjoying life. This man, on the other hand, has no wealth to speak of, yet he lives like a rich man and deals with others with a big heart, and he lives a happy life. It is said,

> The reward of learning the Vedas:
> knowledge of yajnas and fire rituals.
> The reward of learning shastras:
> virtuous and courteous behaviour.
> The reward of marriage and a wife:
> an able son worthy of your name.

> The reward of having money:
> give and take and enjoyment.

His decision made, Somilaka wished to have consumable wealth and that is what Fate bestowed on him. From that day on, he began to eat and enjoy, without worrying about having money, or its lack, thereof, because whenever he needed it, he acquired it in some way or other.

'That is why I tell you,' said Mantharaka the tortoise, 'that even after you acquire money, there is no guarantee that you'll be able to use it, unless fate dictates it, just like Somilaka realized when he was crossing the forest. Therefore, Hiranyaka, think that it's all a matter of fate and stop grieving for your lost wealth. Also, think that even if you had retained the money and had been unable to use it, it would have been equivalent to not having it. It is rightly said,

> If someone thinks he is wealthy
> because he has wealth buried in a hole,
> that wealth belongs to everyone,
> because no one is putting it to use.

Someone has said,

> Giving away accumulated wealth
> is the best way to safeguard it;
> Just like a lake is preserved
> by letting it stream into a dugout.
> Stagnant water always gets dirty.
>
> Money should be used for charity,
> and money should be used to live well.
> But money should never be hoarded.
> Look at the bee and its hoarding of honey.
> All of its life's work that others steal away.
>
> Wealth has three channels:
> charity, consumption, and destruction.
> Those who neither give money in charity,
> nor consume it for enjoyment,
> channel their money towards destruction.

That is why a person is wise when he doesn't acquire wealth only to hoard it, because this money will only bring grief. It is rightly said,

> It is fools who look for happiness and peace
> in the attainment of money, wealth, and sons.
> Hoping for coolness in the torment of heat
> is to invite heat to become more fiery.
>
> Snakes eat only air,
> yet their bodies keep plump.
> Elephants eat grass,
> yet they are strong and robust,
> and they also appear to be happy.
> Forest-dwelling rishis stay healthy
> by eating only tubers and fruits.
> The happiness you can attain
> eating the amrita of contentment
> can never be attained
> by those who hunger for money.
>
> Just like the rays of the sun
> are covered by the clouds,
> the senses are curtailed
> by restraining the mind.
>
> Great souls and great rishis
> say the restraining of desire
> leads to health and quietude.
> Desire cannot be fulfilled by money
> just like fire cannot quench thirst.
>
> The desire of money leads people
> to condemn even the righteous,
> or praise those who are unworthy.
> Thus, for money people will not stop
> at anything, even if it is wrongful.
>
> Seeking money for dharma too
> is not a desirable pursuit.
> Renouncing desire is dharma.
> What is the point of doing this—
> first muddying your feet in a swamp

and then washing them after?
Desiring money and attaining it
through evil actions, and then
using the money in dharmic ways
to wash away the evil of one's actions—
isn't it better to just not desire?

There is no treasure like charity.
There is no enemy on earth like greed.
There is no ornament like modesty.
There is no wealth like contentment.

The true image of poverty is wanting,
not paucity of money and wealth.
Shiva's only wealth is an old bull,
yet he is the lord who gives to all.

When good people happen to fall
by chance of dictate or fate,
they drop like a ball and bounce back.
But whenever the wicked fall,
they drop like a heavy clod of clay.
Thus, though the good suffer bad times,
it is only a brief phase in their life.'

'Dear friend,' said the tortoise to the mouse, 'considering the pros and cons of this situation, you should be grateful rather than upset at losing your wealth.'

The crow, too, said to Hiranyaka, 'Do pay heed to the advice Mantharaka has given you, and try not to dwell on the past and on your losses. Somebody has aptly said,

O king, there are many who flatter
with sweet-sounding words.
But few are those who speak
harsh but beneficial words.
And few are those willing to hear
words that benefit but are harsh.

Those who speak harsh words
that are only for your welfare
are your true and caring friends.

> Others are just friends in name
> who may actually be enemies.'

As the mouse, crow, and tortoise were talking, a deer called Chitranga came dashing towards the lake. Startled by his sudden arrival, Laghupata the crow rose up in a flutter of wings and alighted on a branch of the tree. Hiranyaka the mouse jumped into a clump of grass that was growing nearby, and Mantharaka the tortoise jumped into the lake.

Watching the deer's agitation, as he drank loudly and thirstily from the lake, Laghupata called out to the tortoise, 'O dear Mantharaka, it appears that this deer is here only to quench his thirst. We don't have any reason to fear him. Please do come out.'

'Actually, from the way he is breathing deeply and constantly turning his head to look behind him with frightened eyes, it appears that he is not thirsty but terrified. I'm certain that he is being hounded by a hunter. Can you come down and find out from him if, indeed, a hunter is following him? It is said,

> When a man is frightened,
> his breathing quickens,
> his gaze darts all around,
> and peace and quiet evade him.
> These are the signs of fear.'

Mantharaka's wise words reached the deer's ears as well, and he felt compelled to respond. 'O gentle sirs, you have accurately guessed the reason for my anxiety. I was being chased by hunters. Dodging their lethal arrows, I have managed to escape. I was with a herd, but I'm certain that the hunters have killed all the others. My name is Chitranga, and I have come to seek refuge. Please help me and give me shelter and protection. I need to hide somewhere safe.'

'O Chitranga, allow me to tell you what the Nitishastra says,' Mantharaka said.

> Confronted by the enemy,
> there are only two ways out:
> use your hands to fight,
> or use the speed of your feet.

It appears to me that the best course for you is to use the latter. My advice to you is to hide. This is a vast and dense forest. You can hide anywhere, and don't come out till the hunters are gone.'

Then Laghupata surveyed the forest from his perch up in the tree, and he saw the hunters, carrying heavy loads of carcasses, head out toward the city. Flying down, he hopped closer to the other two and informed them, 'I just saw the hunters leave the forest. Therefore, Chitranga, you don't need to hide. You have nothing to fear now.'

Chitranga thanked both Mantharaka and Laghupata for their assistance and advice, and he greeted Hiranyaka, who had also emerged from his hiding place.

'Have some water from this sweet lake,' Mantharaka said to the deer. 'Relax in the shade of these trees. You're welcome to stay here with us, if you like.'

Chitranga was feeling quite comfortable in the company of these three and wondered why it was so. Then the answer came to him: the tortoise lives in water, and the crow and mouse eat small dead animals. He had nothing to fear from them. 'I think I'll stay here with you and live in the forest,' he said to them. 'Thank you for inviting me.'

'If you don't mind, do tell us why you left your forest and ran all the way here,' Mantharaka asked him.

'The forest in which I lived was a constant venue for hunters. I grew tired of being hounded by them and their hunting dogs. That's why when I fled from there, I knew I'd never go back. My burning throat brought me to this lake, and, as soon I stopped here to drink, I felt a sense of peace descend on me. I would like very much to stay here with you all, if you will allow me. Will you accept me as a friend?'

'We are small creatures compared to you,' Mantharaka said. 'It is said that friendship is most successful when one friend can help another in time of need. What help can we be for you?'

'Why do you point out such differences between us and disparage yourself by saying you are small. It'll be an honour for me to call you my friend. You must have heard the saying,

> Make friends with the powerful,
> but also make friends with the weak.
> It was tiny little mice that freed
> the mighty elephants from their bonds.

'Please tell us that tale,' Mantharaka said, and Chitranga related it.

THE TALE OF THE MICE THAT FREED THE ELEPHANTS

There was a town somewhere that had been abandoned by people. As a result, all its houses, temples, and buildings had fallen into disrepair. However, while the people had left, the land's old inhabitants, the mice, had made themselves even more comfortable there. For generations, they had lived there—great-grandfathers, grandfathers, fathers, sons, and their sons, too—all celebrating life in all its aspects—births, marriages, deaths, shradhas, and various other sacred rites. Along the way, they also increased their colonies in every direction. Every night they retired to their homes in the nooks and crannies of the buildings and in the crevices of floors and ceilings. And, during the day, they roamed without a care in the streets of the unpeopled town.

One day, a king of a thousand elephants, having heard about a cool, sweet water lake on the other side of this town, led his herd through the town's streets. As the elephants passed through, hundreds and thousands of mice were injured and thousands were crushed under their massive feet. In fact, there was not one mouse family that remained untouched by that tragedy.

Those who survived called a council. 'What if the elephants return?' they said, fearfully, 'We'll be wiped out. We must find a way to save ourselves. It is rightly said,

> An elephant can kill just by its touch.
> A snake can kill just by its sniff.
> A king can kill with his smile alone.
> The evil kill in the guise of sweet talk.

The mice elders advised that the matter had to be brought to the attention of the elephants themselves; hence, it was decided that a few of the elders would go to the lake and talk to them.

'If it pleases you, Maharaj,' the elders who had come to the lake, squeaked as loudly as they could to get the elephants' attention. However, they had to make many attempts before they could be heard. When the king of elephants finally looked down and saw the mice, the elders made their plea: 'We have been living here for generations,' they said. 'We have prospered and propagated, and our children and their children have inherited this land. However, Maharaj, today your clan came through our town and destroyed countless of our clan. They were trampled under your feet. If Maharaj returns with his herd and comes through our town again, we will be wiped out. Therefore, we beg you to use another path to the lake that doesn't go through our town. This request may sound presumptuous to Maharaj, coming from little creatures like us, but even small creatures can be of big use when the need arises. Please call on us if you need us.'

The king of the elephants heard the plea of the mice with empathy and agreed that an injustice had been done. 'Fear no more,' he said. 'We will find another path so that no other mice are hurt by us.'

Much time passed. Then, one day, the king of a certain region ordered his men to acquire more elephants for his royal stables. Following his orders. his men constructed a decoy water tank and trapped the entire herd of elephants that had passed through mouse town. Binding them with thick ropes, the men dragged them to the forest and tied each one to a tree. Feeling defeated and helpless, the king of elephants wondered how he could save his clan. Then he recalled the promise that the mice had made. Calling a young cow elephant, the only one who had escaped capture, he told her to go and summon the mice. 'Tell them, "Dear friends, we need your help, and it is a matter of urgency."'

The elephant rushed to mouse town as fast as she could and relayed to the mice the predicament of the elephant herd, conveying to them the urgent message that the king of elephants had sent. Eager to return the favour that the elephants had done them, the mice all scampered to the forest and got to work. They climbed the trees and gnawed at the ropes that bound the elephants and soon freed the whole herd.

'So, as I said before,' said Chitranga, 'make friends with the powerful but also with the weak, because even the smallest of creatures can be of the biggest help, just as the mice freed the elephants.'

Hearing that tale, Mantharaka, Laghupata, and Hiranyaka were happy to invite Chitranga into their circle of friendship. From that day on, the four friends began to spend all their time together, lying in the cool shade of trees, conversing with each other, and simply enjoying each other's company.

One day, as the friends gathered at an assigned spot, Chitranga failed to show up. The other three waited for a while, their concern growing with every passing moment. All kinds of worrisome thoughts crossed their minds:

has he been attacked by some wild, ferocious creature? Has he been killed by a lion? Is he caught in a forest fire? Did he slip and fall into a deep pit trying to reach a patch of fresh green grass? Is he lying wounded somewhere, struck down by a hunter's arrow? Not knowing what had happened to him, filled them with anxiety. Someone has rightly said,

> Even when friends, children, dear ones
> go into the garden outside the house
> and are delayed in their return home,
> one begins to have all sorts of doubts:
> did he fall? Is he hurt? What happened?
> And when friends, children, and dear ones
> go into a deep, dark, dangerous forest
> the doubts one has increase manifold.

Thus, the three friends became apprehensive about Chitranga, who had become very dear to them. When more time passed with still no sign of Chitranga, Mantharaka said to Laghupata, 'Someone needs to go and search for him. Hiranyaka and I obviously can't do it, because we move slowly and on the ground. You, on the other hand, can fly up in the sky and get an aerial view of a large area. Go and survey the forest and see if you can find Chitranga. It'll be such a relief if you see him alive.'

Laghupata the crow nodded and flew up into the sky. He had gone only a short distance when he saw Chitranga beside a small lake, caught tightly in a hunter's noose. Deeply distressed by the sight, the crow quickly flew down and, hopping close to the deer, asked him in a whisper, 'Oh, dear friend, how did this happen?'

Seeing Laghupata, Chitranga burst into tears. This is normally what happens:

> Even if a sorrow has lessened or has been forgotten,
> on a seeing someone loved, it is renewed, often heightened.

After weeping his heart out, Chitranga wiped his tears and said to Laghupata, 'Dear friend, it appears that my time on earth has come to an end. At least I was able to see you before I go. I'm grateful for that. It is said,

> At the time of passing,
> if one is able to see a friend,
> the sight gives two comforts:
> its joy lasts till one's dying breath,
> and its peace stays with the soul.

If, any time during our friendship, I inadvertently said anything to you that hurt you, please forgive me and know that it was only out of love and affection. Also, please say this to Hiranyaka and Mantharaka on my behalf: "Dear friends, knowingly or unknowingly, if I have said anything hurtful, please forgive me out of the goodness of your heart and the love and affection you hold for me."'

Laghupata's eyes brimmed with tears at Chitranga's heart-rending words. 'Dear friend, stop this talk,' he gently chided. 'Nothing will happen to you. With friends like us, you have nothing to fear. We will not let anything happen to you. I'll go this instant and bring Hiranyaka here so that he can gnaw through your noose. Remember that those who are good and virtuous don't let anything break them, even if the situation is dire. It is said,

> He who is not elated by wealth
> or dejected by impoverishment,
> and he who is fearless in battle—
> such a one is like an auspicious tilak
> on the forehead of the three worlds.
> A mother rarely births such a son.

'So, be brave and wait for us,' Laghupata said to Chitranga. 'I'll be right back with the others.' Then, flying rapidly to where his friends were waiting to hear about Chitranga's whereabouts, he told them everything he could about the deer's plight.

'I can certainly cut his noose,' Hiranyaka stated. 'Can you take me to him?'

Laghupata then took the mouse on his back and flew to Chitranga. When the trapped deer saw the crow with the mouse on his back in the sky, he took a deep breath of relief, and his heart filled with hope. He said,

> Wisdom is in making friends true and noble.
> They destroy hardships that come your way.
> Without the help of friends, no one in this world
> can free himself from the assault of adversity.

As soon as Laghupata landed with Hiranyaka, the mouse rushed to the deer: 'Dear friend, you are so wise and smart, and you're so well-versed in the Nitishastras, how did you get trapped in this common net that hunters often lay to catch deer?' he asked.

'I'll tell you later,' Chitranga replied. 'Right now, there is no time. The hunter will be returning shortly. Do you think you can quickly gnaw through the nooses around my feet?'

'Are you still afraid?' Hiranyaka asked his friend with a laugh to instil courage in him. 'Don't be. I'm here. I just mentioned the Nitishastras, because I myself am losing my faith in their wisdom. If someone like you, who knows the law well, can get trapped, then what use is their advice?'

'The law books are not to blame,' said Chitranga.

'Sometimes, in some precarious circumstances, people forget all learning. Call it fate. But that doesn't mean that you should lose faith in the law books. That's why people say:

> Bound in the noose of Yamaraja,
> mind and heart dulled by fate,
> even the wisest in such situations
> lose their sense and follow a path
> that leads them deeper into adversity.
>
> What Fate has written on one's forehead
> not even the wisest of wise can erase.'

As the three were assessing Chitranga's situation, they saw Mantharaka crawling towards them.

'Oh, no! This is not good.' Laghupata exclaimed.

'What is not good?' Hiranyaka asked him.

'Mantharaka shouldn't have come here. When the hunter returns, I'll fly up in the sky, you'll jump into some hole, and Chitranga, freed from his trap, will leap into some bush. But Mantharaka is a water creature, and there's no waterbody nearby. How will he escape? This is what worries me.'

By this time Mantharaka had reached his friends, and Hiranyaka said to him: 'You shouldn't have come here, dear friend. The hunter will be returning any time. Then what will you do? Please go back to your lake as quickly as you can.'

'What could I do? I was burning in the fire of worry for my friend who is trapped in a hunter's noose. I couldn't bear the thought of it, and that's why I had to come here. It is said,

> Words of consolation from our dearest friends
> are the panacea that helps us bear all sorrows:
> from losing dear ones to losing wealth.

I came to offer some solace to our dear Chitranga.

> It is better to lose your life
> than to separate from a true friend.

> Life can be regained in the next birth,
> but true friends once lost are hard to find.'

Just then, the hunter arrived, his bow to his ear, the bowstring pulled, and the arrow mounted on it, ready to be shot. Hiranyaka the mouse quickly cut the deer's noose with his very sharp teeth. Freed from his trap, Chitranga leapt in the air and sped away, as swift as the wind. Laghupata, in a flutter of wings, flew up and perched on a high branch of a tree, and Hiranyaka scampered away into a nearby hole in the ground.

When the hunter saw that his noose was cut, and the deer he had trapped had escaped, he was very disappointed. 'All that effort, gone to waste,' he muttered to himself. But then, as he looked around, he saw a tortoise slowly crawling away. 'Aha,' he said with a smile. 'I may have lost the deer, but it seems that Fate has sent me this tortoise, instead. Today, its meat will feed my family.'

He then braided blades of grass to make a rope and, tying the tortoise's legs with it, hung him from the end of his bow.

Seeing his friend tied up and hanging from the hunter's bow, the mouse began to lament:

> Oh, what woe!
> My sorrow was already deep and vast like an ocean,
> and now this new pain of separation from a friend.
> Truly, when bad times come into a man's life,
> one hardship follows on the heels of the other,
> all piling up into a mountain of sorrow and woe.
>
> A man walks along happily on even ground.
> Once he trips, he stumbles at every step.
>
> A sturdy, malleable bow, friend, and wife
> are the rarest gifts that fate bestows.
>
> The trust one has in intimate friends
> cannot be surpassed even by one's trust
> in one's mother, wife, brother, and son.

As it is, bad luck had already robbed me of my wealth, my family, and homeland. Why, oh, why did it also deprive someone like me, who is already exhausted from suffering the calamities of life, of a true friend, as well? Perhaps, in the future I'll have other friends, but I know I'll never find a friend like Mantharaka. Who else will help me in my time of need? Why is it that I'm always the one on whom misfortune showers its sharp, calamitous arrows? It is aptly said,

> Men's bodies are constantly decaying,
> their wealth and joys are transitory,
> meetings are harbingers of separation.
> All men have to part from friends one day.

But as it is also said,

> A wounded spot on the body
> is susceptible to new wounds.
> Poverty heightens hunger pangs.
> Adversity increases antipathy.
> One mistake breeds many more.
> Bad times bring with them
> all kinds of misfortunes.

> The one person who stands
> between you and adversity
> is a mitra—a two-syllable word
> created by the Creator.'

While Hiranyaka was thus lamenting, the other two friends, Laghupata and Chitranga, also arrived at the spot. Seeing them, Hiranyaka wiped his tears and fixed his resolve. Turning to his friends he declared, 'There is no point in wailing or lamenting. We must do something to free our friend. It is said,

> If a person is struck
> by disaster and misfortune,
> and all he does is weep and lament,
> his weeping and lamenting will go on—
> endlessly—for the rest of his life.

> To survive misfortunes
> pundits of Nitishastra prescribe:
> start working doubly hard,
> let go of regrets and what ifs.

Also,

> The true solution mantra
> should guard acquired wealth,
> ensure prospective good fortune,
> and secure release from hardship.

Hearing Hiranyaka's wise words, an idea began to form in Laghupata's mind. 'Dear friends, I have a plan,' he said. 'Let me tell you what it is: Chitranga, you should go to the lake that is further up, and the hunter will cross on his way. Go and lie there beside it, pretending to be dead. I'll sit on your head and pretend to peck into your eyes with my beak to show him that you are, indeed, lifeless. Seeing this sight, that cruel hunter will put down his bow, along with our friend Mantharaka, so that he can get to the deer. Hiranyaka, this will be your moment to cut the rope that binds our friend. Once he is free, he can jump into the lake and swim away.'

'Oh, what a brilliant plan!' Chitranga exclaimed, congratulating Laghupata. 'I have no doubt that it'll work. I can already see our friend Mantharaka free. It is said,

> Readiness of mind and body,
> or lack thereof, is indication
> of the success of a task or its failure.
> But only the wise can discern this.
> Not all men have this ability.

Your plan has instilled all of us with a new zeal, and we are ready. That's why I feel strongly that we will succeed. We'll do exactly as you have told us.'

Then that deer sped towards the path that the hunter had taken and, seeing a lake in the distance that he would cross, he lay down beside it, as though dead. The crow then flew to him and, perching on his head, began to gently dig into his eyes with his beak.

In due time, when the hunter came to the lake, he saw the deer he had caught in his noose lying on the ground, quite clearly dead, because a crow was pecking at its eyes. He was thrilled, and thought with satisfaction that even though he escaped, the wounds from the noose must have weakened him. He had just enough life left in him to come to this lake. 'I already have a tortoise,' he said to himself. 'I can't lose it, because it is securely tied to my bow. Now Fate has dropped the deer at my feet, and I can take him, as well. Today, Fate seems to be favouring me.'

Hence, placing the tortoise on the ground by the water, he walked with quick steps towards the prone deer. In the meantime, Hiranyaka went to work and, with his strong, razor-sharp teeth, cut through the rope that tied Mantharaka to the bow. As soon as the tortoise was free, he jumped into the lake. As for the deer—even before the hunter could reach him, he got up and ran away, with the crow flying over his head.

Embarrassed at himself for mistaking a live deer for a dead one and disappointed that he had lost the deer for the second time that day, the hunter returned to the spot where he had left his bow and the tortoise. The bow was still there, but there was no tortoise; and on the ground were pieces of the shredded rope. 'What is this trickery?' the hunter wailed, sitting down with his head in his hands in utter disbelief. Then, filled with dejection, he spoke the following words:

'O Lord of Doers and Destiny, you had already snatched from me my best net and the fat, healthy deer. Now you have also taken the tortoise; at your dictate, it, too, has slipped out of my hand. Here I am, tired and hungry, wandering aimlessly in the forest, away from my wife and children. If there is any other hardship left in my share, why don't you go ahead and send it to me. What choice do I have but to bear it all? I have no control over you. People rightfully say, Fate is all powerful.'

Thus, bewailing his fate, the hunter started on his way home. When the four friends were sure that he would not return, they came back together, whooping with joy. Then they embraced each other gratefully, feeling like they had been born again. After that, they went back to their own lake, where, once again, they began enjoying the pleasure of each other's company, chatting, frolicking around, and debating issues of life, philosophy, and polity.

> That is why I say to you,
> with the help of true friends,
> you can overcome any hardship.
> That is why wisdom is in making friends
> and never deceiving or cheating them.
>
> If four-legged creatures can
> have the wisdom for friendship,
> imagine how much intelligent men
> can gain from making friends.

Thus, we come to the end of the *Panchatantra*'s second tantra, titled, Mitra Samprapti, whose opening verse was,

> Lacking resources and facilities,
> the wise and sagacious still manage to
> accomplish the most difficult tasks
> with ease and expeditiousness,
> just as the crow, tortoise, deer, and mouse
> accomplished what they needed to do.

THIRD TANTRA
KAKOLUKIYAM
Of Crows and Owls

Here is the first shloka of the third tantra, titled, 'Kakolukiyam'.

> Don't trust an enemy of yore
> even if he comes as a friend.
> Heed! A cave full of owls,
> all burnt alive in a fire
> set aflame by the crows—
> present friends but past foes.

The tale is told by old folks in this way:

In the southern region is a city called Mahilaropya. Near the city is an immense bargad tree that has countless branches, all laden with leaves and fruits. In that tree used to be a strong, impenetrable fort of the king of crows, Meghavarna (cloud colour). He lived there happily with thousands of his kinsfolk.

Nearby, in a mountain cave, lived the king of owls, Arimardana (destroyer of enemies) with his clan of owls. Every night, Arimardana would go to the bargad and, circling it, kill any crow that he saw outside the fort.

These crows and owls had a long-standing vendetta.

Owls are blind in the light of the day. That is why the king of owls carried out his attacks on the crows in the darkness of the night, when the crows become blind. In this way, by killing a few crows every night, Arimardana was slowly but surely reducing the number of the enemy.

If an enemy's hostile acts are ignored, the consequence can be disastrous. It is said,

> Whoever intentionally ignores
> an enemy advancing on all sides,
> or carelessly ignores sickness,
> strengthens the foe and the disease
> and invites his own death at their hands.

Also,

> He who does not destroy
> an enemy or disease
> as soon as it originates
> will be killed by the foe
> or die from the illness
> even if he is strong and healthy.

One day, Meghavarna, the king of crows, called all his ministers and said to them: 'Oh, this enemy of ours is too fierce and assiduous. He also knows how to use the time of day to his advantage; that is why he's growing so powerful. Every night he comes and kills more of my crows. How do we resolve this situation? What can we do? How can we retaliate? He strikes at night, and we can't see at night. We can attack the owls during the day, but we don't even know where they live. As you know, there are six ways to deal with enemies. Think about these and tell me which one should we employ? Let's take action as soon as possible and rid ourselves of this constant threat.'

'Maharaj,' the ministers replied, 'You have asked a very strategic question. It is said,

> Advisers should advise
> even without the king's asking,
> and if the king does ask,
> sound and beneficial advice
> is what advisers must provide,
> though it may not be to his liking.

> An adviser who does not provide
> counsel that will result in good,
> and spouts only words of flattery
> is not the king's well-wisher.
> He is a foe in the guise of a friend.

That is why, Maharaj, you should discuss this issue with each one of us individually so that we can give you an impartial opinion without being influenced by the others.

Heeding his advisers' suggestion, Meghavarna invited each of his five advisers—Ujjivi (reborn), Sanjivi (able to revive the dead), Anujivi (lives dependent on someone else), Prajivi (lives like a parasite), and Chiranjivi (long-lived), to talk to him.

Meeting with the first adviser, Ujjivi, Meghavarna asked him: 'O minister, what do you think is the best way to deal with this problem of the owl king's daily killing of our crows? What should we do?'

'Maharaj,' the adviser responded, 'one should never declare war on a powerful foe. And our enemy, this king of owls, has a lot of power, because he waits for an opportune time and only attacks at night. We can't see at night, which makes us weak. So, I would say that our enemy is strong because time is in his favour. The wise say,

> Just as rivers never flow against their current,
> that king who deals with a powerful enemy
> in a gentle manner, negotiating a treaty, and
> waiting to wage a war only when the time is right,
> retains his kingship and his kingly wealth.

Also, as someone has said,

> Dharmic, high-minded,
> supported by friends and family,
> victor of many wars—this is strength.
> Do not take such an enemy to war.
> Negotiate a peace treaty with him.
>
> And if your life is in danger,
> make a treaty and save yourself,
> even if the enemy is low caste,
> because if life is safe, all else is safe.
> Hence, an alliance with a low caste
> is much preferred to losing your life.

Our enemy, the king of owls, is also known to have defeated many in war. Therefore, my advice to you is to sign an accord with him. It is said,

> Forming an alliance with a brave king,
> well known for his many victories in war,
> influences one's other enemies, as well.
> They come and bow to you out of fear.
>
> Also form a treaty with one's equal,
> because in war victory is uncertain,
> since both sides sacrifice many lives.
> One should never do anything uncertain.
> Brihaspati himself has said this.
> Therefore, an alliance is better
> even with a foe of equal power.
>
> The king who is too prideful
> to form an alliance with a foe
> whose power is equal to his own
> and decides to attack instead
> destroys both himself and foe.

>Just as when two clay pots collide,
>they both shatter and break,
>when equally matched foes battle,
>the result is the destruction of both.
>
>To declare war on an enemy more powerful
>is to issue an invitation to your own death.
>Just as when a clay pot clashes with a stone,
>the stone utterly smashes the pot;
>when the weak battle the strong
>annihilation of the weak is the outcome.

Also,

>Territory, friends, and wealth—
>these three are the prizes of war.
>If even one of these is not assured,
>war should not be an option.

Besides,

>If a lion digs in a mousehole
>on a stony mountain side,
>either his fearsome claws break,
>or his kill is just a tiny mouse.
>Therefore, war for a trifling matter
>is foolhardy and a waste of time.
>That is why there is a saying:
>dug a mountain, found a mouse.
>
>Where no substantial gain is promised
>and war seems to be a futile effort,
>one should not provoke a conflict there.
>
>If a king wants his kingdom's prosperity,
>and he is attacked by a strong enemy,
>his attitude should be of appeasement
>not of a hissing cobra with a flared hood.
>
>A wise king attacked by a strong enemy
>should be like a tortoise—retreating
>and bearing all strikes in silence.

> But he should rise when the time is right
> and strike like a deadly black serpent.
>
> Even if war is inevitable, knocking at your door,
> stay calm and try to delay it as long as you can.
> Don't lose patience and join the fray.

Someone has said,

> "Fight the powerful!"
> But there is no example of this anywhere.
> Clouds never oppose the direction of wind.
> Similarly, men never confront a strong enemy.
> It is better to sign a treaty of peace with him.'

In this way, Ujjivi advised the king to consider a strategy called sandhi—treaty or alliance—as opposed to declaring war.

Meghavarna then called his second minister, Sanjivi, and said to him: 'Ujjivi suggests we sign an accord with the owls. What is your advice in this matter? What should we do to stop the owl king from killing our crows?'

'O king Maharaj, I am not in favour of bowing before the enemy and signing an accord, because it is said,

> Even if one knows one's enemy well
> and his manner is acceptable,
> one should not get into an alliance.
> Even when water is as hot as fire,
> if it falls on fire, it will still extinguish it.

I've heard that the king of owls, Arimardana, is cruel and greedy, and he knows no dharma. Therefore, you should never sign a treaty with him. It is said,

> Never sign an accord with an enemy,
> who lacks both truth and dharma.
> When the treaty is signed and locked,
> he will revert to his destructive ways.

Therefore, my advice to you is to fight with the owl king and destroy him, and it won't be difficult, because people say,

> Ruthless, greedy, lazy, untruthful,
> careless, cowardly, quixotic, foolish,

> one who circumvents going to battle—
> such an enemy is easy to kill in battle.

Besides, that king of owls has already shown us that he has the upper hand. If you decide to sign an accord with him, he'll think he has defeated us, and we fear him. Consequently, he'll increase his violence against us, because he'll feel empowered by our attitude. He will then make us suffer even more. It is said,

> The enemy that can only be quelled by war
> will not listen to any talks of peace;
> instead, peace talk will embolden him.
> A rising fever needs to be sweated out.
> No wise person will cool it with cold water.

Also,

> To talk peace to a furious foe
> is to make him even more irate.
> It will be like sprinkling cold water
> on hot ghee to make it sizzle.

I know Ujjivi must have said to you that the enemy is very strong, therefore, we are better off with an accord. But I don't think that the strength of the enemy is necessarily a reason for an accord. It is said,

> If one has zeal, one can face any enemy.
> Even if the zeal is dwarfed by strength,
> it can destroy the biggest of enemies.
> A lion is small before an elephant,
> but he can tear open the largest of the herd.

> The foe that can't be killed with strength
> through deception should be destroyed,
> just like Bhima killed the powerful Kichaka,
> duping him in the guise of a woman.

> When the king fights like a warrior,
> and his punishing rod deals death,
> enemies all fall at the king's feet.
> When he is tender-hearted and clement,
> his foes see him as paltry as a weed.

The king whose lustre is dulled
by the magnificence of another—
was the only purpose of his birth
the ruin of his mother's youth?

Just as a woman beautiful and fair
but unadorned with cosmetics
has no appeal for the connoisseur,
a king not covered in vermilion blood
does not appeal to the high-minded.

What praise for a king whose land is not irrigated
with enemy blood and the tears of enemy wives?'

In this way, Meghavarna's second minister, Sanjivi, gave him the advice of vighraya—declaration of war.

The king then called his third minister, Anujivi, to ask him his opinion on how to thwart the owls.

'Maharaj, this Arimardana, the king of owls, is very cruel and powerful. He is not the kind to adhere to any policy or treaty. Therefore, I would advise against both an accord and declaration of war. It is said,

Fiercely powerful, ruthless, lacking decency—
if an enemy demonstrates such traits,
it is ill-advised to either war or seek accord.
Better to just walk away and find another land.

The walk of war has two forms:
flight for the sake of one's life and
the march into battle for victory.
Marching into enemy land is best
in the Kartika or Chaitra months—
not too hot and not too cold,
clear roads and standing crops,
rivers all flowing at their pace.

But for a surprise attack
any time is a good time.
When the foe is in hardship,
when the land is in chaos—
a surprise attack at such a time

> will surely lead to victory,
> no matter who the enemy.
>
> Desirous of conquering a kingdom,
> a king should secure his own land,
> appoint the bravest of brave guards
> and strongest of strong soldiers.
> Spreading a network of spies,
> knowing the right time to strike,
> accompanied by valorous warriors,
> he should mount a deliberate attack.

But also note:

> When a king attacks a land,
> he must ensure a regular supply
> of provisions: food and water,
> back-up troops and weapons,
> or else he will never see his homeland.

Therefore, Maharaj, in my opinion, at this time, you should think about ways to save yourself. That's why I think you should use the strategy of yana—moving or marching. Leave this bargad tree and make your home elsewhere. Powerful and ruthless, as well as untrustworthy as our enemy is, I don't think we should go to war with him or invite him to discuss an accord. I think we should retreat until the time is right. That is the only prudent action at this time. It's wise to wait for the opportune time, because it is said,

> When a ram retreats from a fight,
> not fear but strategy is the cause.
> He will charge with double force.
> When a lion steps back from a hunt,
> not fear but anger is the cause.
> He will strike with all his might.
> The wise bear enemy strikes
> with some strategy in their mind,
> nurturing hostility in their heart.

Also,

> If the enemy is strong
> migrate to another land

> and you will keep living
> to return and fight again,
> just as Yudhishthira did
> after thirteen years of exile.

Besides,

> A king who attacks a foe
> to massage his ego and pride
> fulfils the desire of the foe.

Maharaj, your enemy is very powerful, and he has started a campaign against you. That is why the best strategy for you right now is to leave your home. This time is for saving your life; not for battle and not for accord.'

Thus, Anujivi gave Meghavarna the advice of withdrawal, perhaps, to return later at more favourable time. After hearing what he had to say, the king called his fourth minister, Prajivi. 'Wise minister, the first three ministers have advised accord, war, and retreat. Please tell me what you think should be done about the situation,' he asked him.

'Maharaja, I don't agree with any of these solutions. I think it is best that we fortify ourselves and use the strategy of asana—sit inside a secure fort. It is said,

> Crocodiles and sea creatures,
> when at home in the water,
> can catch and drag in elephants.
> Once they leave the water for land
> even a dog can harass them.

Also, the wise say,

> When under attack from a strong enemy,
> O king, shut the gates of your fort and wait.
> Also send a message to allies for help.
>
> And the king who, flustered with fear
> runs away on hearing, "The enemy is near,"
> can never return to his land to rule again.
>
> Just as a snake without his fangs
> and an elephant without madness
> can easily be put under control,

> a king away from his fort is easy
> to defeat, restrain, and suppress.

So, Maharaj, secure yourself and your subjects in your fort; don't flee.

> Safe within the fort,
> even if you're alone,
> and the enemy is strong,
> you can fight thousands.

Therefore, O King, make the security in your fort as tight as possible, and fully prepare for war. Make arrangements for ample provisions of food and water. Ensure that there is a stockpile of projectiles and weapons. Strengthen the wall and clear the pits. Then sit tight and keep the conflict going from the behind the fort's wall. If you survive and win, you'll rule the earth. And if you die in battle, your sacrifice will take you to heaven. This is a win-win situation. You can't go wrong. As the adage goes: you have laddus in both your hands.

It is well known:

> When the small and weak band together,
> no enemy, no matter how strong, can destroy them,
> just as when little vines and other plants entwine,
> no wind, no matter how gusty, can uproot them.

> Even our big, mighty bargad tree—
> if it stood here by itself, all alone,
> would be uprooted by a stormy wind.
> But since there grows a line of trees,
> standing together with it as its buffer,
> not even a vicious gale can break them.
> In the same way, a solitary person,
> no matter how brave or valorous,
> can be suppressed by the enemy,
> or even killed at the enemy's whim,
> if he lacks support from others.

Therefore, I advise following the strategy of asana. Stay in the fort, along with your brave soldiers, and continue to fight from within its safety.'

Having heard the advice of four of his ministers, Meghavarna called the fifth minister, Chiranjivi, and asked him, as well, what he thought should be the crows' strategy in the matter of the owls.

'Maharaj,' said Chiranjivi, 'Instead of the solutions of sandhi, yudha, yana, asana, I suggest using samashraya—taking help from an ally. I think seeking help from a powerful friend and ally is the best way out of this situation. It is said,

> A man may be brilliant, diligent, and able,
> but without help, what can he do by himself?
> Fire, though flaming, still needs the aid of wind,
> if it is by itself, it just extinguishes after a while.

> For men, association with others is gainful,
> especially if those others are like-minded.
> Rice must be covered with husk to grow.
> Without husk the kernels don't swell.
> Rice and husk are of the same mind.

That is why, Maharaj, I advise that you stay in your fort but contact a close friend and ally who is powerful and able to help you. If you leave this place and go elsewhere, you may not receive that help, because it'll weaken you even more. It is said,

> A forest fire is fierce in itself,
> and the winds make it stronger.
> But the wind doesn't help a diya;
> instead, it extinguishes its flame.

In other words, no one wants to help the small and weak. Everyone wants to befriend the strong.

Moreover,

> Calling on multiple helpers is also wise;
> though small, together they can be a force.

It is said,

> Because bamboo grows in clumps,
> it is not easy to uproot or cut.
> A king surrounded by his allies,
> though small, cannot be destroyed.

And if you get the help of someone noble and strong, it's even better. It is rightly said,

> Who does not gain from association with the noble?
> It is like a drop of water gracing a lotus leaf.

That is why, O King, I believe you will not be successful unless you take the help of a strong friend.'

Thus, Chiranjivi gave Meghavarna the advice of samashraya.

After listening to all his advisers, the king summoned his long-time and aged minister, Sthirajivi. He trusted this minister the most, because he had been his father's adviser as well, and he was thoroughly familiar with all the tenets of Nitishastra.

When Sthirajivi arrived in the court, Meghavarna respectfully bowed to him and said, 'Dear uncle, I called my five ministers to assess the efficacy of their advice. Each one of them offered a different perspective. Now, I ask you to please consider our situation with the owls and advise me on how to suppress them.'

'Dear son,' Sthirajivi said, 'the views that your five ministers presented are all in accordance with the laws of Nitishastra. Each of those suggested solutions can prove beneficial in the right situation. However, now is not the right time to use any of those strategies, singly. At this time, you should employ dwaidhibhaga—the two-pronged strategy. It is said,

> If the enemy is strong and ruthless,
> talk with him about accord but
> secretly prepare for a full-on war.

And never trust the enemy that is both ruthless and powerful, like the owls. That is why the two-pronged strategy will work best in this situation. Hence, my advice is, sign an accord with the foe and give him every reason to trust you, while distrusting him. Entice him, and then, when the time is right, strike. The surprise attack will destroy him. It is said,

> The enemy that must be felled
> elevate him once, say the wise.
> Inflation makes him easy to kill.
> To cure congestion, physicians
> first increase phlegm with sugar,
> then its medicine begins to work.

Someone has said,

> Single-minded devotion to a woman, enemy, deceiving friend,
> and especially to a prostitute is a sure way to death's door.

The only ones who are worthy of single-minded devotion and trust are the gods. For everyone else, man should use the two-pronged strategy. But his distrust should not be obvious. His actions should demonstrate that he trusts, but in his heart he should question everything, and his eyes should be carefully observing everything.

> Devotedness is the pursuit of sadhus and yogis,
> it does not suit kings in pursuit of progress.

Anyone who is pursuing wealth and prosperity must employ strategies of diplomacy and also astute manoeuvres. That is why, O King, by using the dual strategy gambit not only will you be able to reside safely in your fort, but also, by giving the enemy an illusion of an accord, you will be able to sack him, when the time is right. Moreover, in the process, if you see cracks in the enemy's defence, you can take advantage and destroy him.'

'But uncle,' Meghavarna said, 'I don't even know where our enemy lives, how will I see the cracks?'

'Let me send my secret agents,' Sthirajivi replied. 'They will gather intelligence, not just about the owls' residence but also about their weaknesses. It is said,

> Dogs and other animals recognize through smell.
> Brahmins discern through Vedas and shastras.
> Kings view through information gathered by spies,
> And all other people see by using their eyes.

The shastras say,

> The king who knows the running of all his offices,
> is especially familiar with matters concerning enemies,
> and also knows the errors of high ministers in charge,
> never suffers unexpected hardships or setbacks.'

'Uncle, who are considered high officials, and how many high officials should a king have? Also, how should he select secret agents? Please tell me all this clearly.'

'Narada Muni advised Yudhishthira thus: the high officials to watch in enemy ranks should be eighteen, and one's own officials of consequence should be fifteen. Each of these officials have three secret agents, and the king should be regularly informed by these agents. That is how he will always remain in control. This is what Narada said to Yudhishthira:

"O King,
do you know the faults of each of the high officials
in your enemy's camp and in your own charge?
Do you know the abilities that make them well-suited?
Do you keep yourself informed about these officials
through the three secret agents that they work with?"

The consequence of secret agents that don't provide optimal intelligence can be perilous for the king. On the other hand, if the agents are working at their best, without deterrents, like bribery and theft, then the king will see progress and success.

Here are the eighteen high officials in the enemy camp: chief minister, chief priest, commander-in-chief, crown prince, chief usher, chief of the palace guards, chief of the guards of the women's palace, commissioner of revenue, keeper of stores, chief justice, manager of the royal stables, manager of elephants, minister of defence, chief marshal responsible for soldiers, chief marshal of soldiers at the border, superintendent of forests, general of security officers who guard the fort, and secretary of the king. If you can cause dissent among these enemy officials, or disrupt their operations, the battle is already won.

Now, let me tell you about the fifteen officers of consequence that should be in the king's own camp: queen, queen mother, keeper of the royal household, keeper of gardens, keeper of royal beds, superintendent of spies, keeper of the king's wardrobe, royal astrologer, royal physician, royal cupbearer, keeper of tobacco and betel nut, royal guru, chief of the royal bodyguards, keeper of the royal umbrella, and chief of the courtesans.

About secret agents it is said,

Physicians, astrologers, and teachers
can be appointed spies in disguise as
snake-charmers, magicians, and madmen.

Spies need to be smart and sharp-brained,
who can plumb the depth of the enemy camp
and give a full account of it to the king.'

'Thank you, uncle, for educating me about such matters of polity in dealing with the enemy. Now I have another question. It is something I have always wanted to know. Please tell me how did the crows and owls become such bitter enemies?'

Sthirajivi then told Meghavarna the story of how the enmity began.

THE TALE OF HOW THE CROWS AND OWLS BECAME ENEMIES

Once upon a time, many birds, including hamsas, parrots, cranes, cuckoos, owls, peacocks, pigeons, pheasants, and others gathered to discuss issues of their protection. The complaint that all the birds had was that Garuda was their king, but he was so devoted to Lord Vishnu that he could barely spare any time for them and their protection. 'What is the use of such a king,' they complained mournfully. 'He doesn't do anything to protect us from the nets of fowlers and arrows of hunters, and other such dangers that we face every day. What use is such a king?

> The king who does not protect
> fearful and suffering subjects
> is Yamaraja incarnate, not a king.
> Without a king's protection
> the lives of subjects are in danger,
> like a boat without a boatman,
> sinking in the middle of the ocean.
>
> Just like a broken ship abandoned in the ocean,
> these six kinds of men should also be abandoned:
> a teacher who does not teach,
> a Vedic seer who does not chant mantras,
> a king who does not protect his subjects,
> a quarrelsome wife who speaks harshly,
> a cowherd who does not graze his cows,
> a barber who does not provide shaves.'

Therefore, the birds decided that it was best for them to give up hope in securing Garuda's help and find another, more able king. Having come to a consensus about this, they then chose a king from amongst themselves—the beautiful, white-faced owl. Thereafter, all the other birds began to prepare for the owl's coronation.

They accumulated the required items for the ceremony: water from all the pilgrimages, one hundred and eight medicinal herbs, a map of the seven oceans and continents with the earth's mountains and rivers drawn on it, a golden pot filled with holy water, diyas to light every direction, musical instruments to play festive music, a mirror to prevent manglik Vaastu dosh, Gorochana placed nearby, and singing minstrels and bards. Then they installed the throne and, with Vedic brahmins chanting mantras in unison, they began the ceremony. The chief queen of the owls, a Krikalika (a type of owl smaller than the Ullu and able to see during the day) was brought in and seated, and, finally, the owl was invited to sit on the throne. However, just as he was approaching it, a crow came flying into the congregation. 'Oh! How unusual for all these birds to gather like this,' he said. 'I wonder what's going on.'

Seeing the crow amongst them, the other birds began to twitter: 'How fortuitous that the crow has joined us. Aren't crows supposed to be the most intelligent of birds? It is said,

> Among men a barber is wily and clever.
> Among birds it is the crow.
> Among the meat-eaters, the jackal.
> Among sadhus, it is the Shvetambara Jains.

We should have consulted him before picking a king. People say,

> A course of action discussed with many,
> considered from every possible angle,
> vetted by the wise and worldly
> is neither fruitless nor wasteful.'

Even as the birds were considering whether to talk to the crow or not, the crow himself approached them and asked, 'Why are all the birds gathered here today? Is it a celebration of some sort?'

'We birds felt that we needed a king who cared for us. That's why all the birds decided to make the owl our new king. You've arrived here at an opportune time. We were just about to crown the owl. What do think about our decision? Do you agree with it?'

The crow laughed. 'How could you all decide that? You made a bird who is blind in the day and ugly of face our king, especially when you could have picked any of the other great birds, like the peacock, hamsa, koel, parrot, cockatoo, crane, green pigeon. So, no, I don't agree with you all. I don't agree that the owl should be put on the throne. Look at him:

> Hooked nose,
> wide, cruel eyes,
> ghoulish to look at.
> Such is his happy face.
> When he is angry
> how terrifying will he be?

Also,

> Ferocious and dreadful,
> cruel by natural instinct,
> his hoots harsh on the ears.
> Why make him our king?

Besides,

> Garudaji is our god-ordained king.
> Why replace him with this blind owl?
> Moreover, coronating another king,
> while already allegiant to a king
> is neither right nor gainful.

It is said,

> Only one lustrous king is needed
> for the welfare of the kingdom.
> Multiple kings prove ruinous,
> like the rising of many suns
> is annihilating during pralaya.

Also think, just by the fact that Garudaji is our king, no one dares subjugate us. Someone has rightly said,

> Only the mention of your glorious king
> should protect you from the evil-minded.
> Just naming the great one has the power
> to help you accomplish anything with ease.
> See how the mere mention of the moon
> saved the rabbits from losing their homes?'

'What is this story?' the birds asked, and the crow told the tale.

THE TALE OF HOW THE RABBIT IN THE MOON SAVED HIS RELATIVES

In a forest lived a towering elephant called Chaturadanta (four tusks). He was the overlord of a large herd. At that time, the region was suffering a calamitous drought, because it hadn't rained there for many years. As a result, all the streams, lakes, and other water holes had dried up. The elephants said to their overlord, 'O Gajaraja, many of our mates and little children are dying from lack of water, and many others of our clan have already died from unbearable thirst. Please look for water so that our wives and children can moisten their parched throats. That is the only way we will survive.'

Hence, Chaturadanta dispatched his scouts in every direction to search for a lake or waterbody that was not too distant and still had enough water from which the whole herd could drink. The agents who went in the easterly direction came upon a lake that was on the other side of the forest. It was a glorious lake, brimming with clear water and dotted with lotuses and geese, cranes, and ducks. All around it were blossoming trees, whose flower-laden branches tilted towards the water, sprinkling fragrant petals into its sweetness. Gentle breezes wove themselves with the waves, creating a ripple of music. The lake was called Chandrasarovara and it was being fed by Patala Ganga.

Rushing back to Chaturadanta, the scouts excitedly told him about the heavenly lake they had found.

'Let's all go there now,' Chaturadanta declared, and the elephant herd began its journey east. It took them five days and five nights of arduous trekking, without water, but, finally, they reached the lake, and gratefully dipped their trunks into the cool water to drink their fill. Then, all day, they bathed themselves and each other and sported in the water, and when evening came, they reluctantly left the lake and went into the forest to find a place to rest for the night. What the herd didn't realize was that near the edge of the lake, in the water-softened soil, were hundreds of rabbit holes, which they trod upon, as they crossed over to the forest. Many of the rabbits were crushed to death and many more were badly injured with broken backs and limbs.

Once the elephants had retired to the forest, the surviving rabbits hobbled to a place of assembly to discuss the situation. They were a tragic sight to behold, bleeding profusely, arms and legs broken, backbones crushed, dead children in their arms, tears streaming down their faces. Devastated and fraught with anxiety, they said to each other: 'We'll all die. Now that the elephants have discovered this lake, they'll come here every day, because everything else is dried up. How long can we dodge their pestle-like feet? Sooner or later, we'll all be crushed to death. We must think of some way to escape these elephants.'

One rabbit said, 'What is there to think about? We should just leave this place and make a home elsewhere. The great sages Manu and Vyasa have said,

> To benefit the family, give up one person.
> To benefit a community, give up the family.
> To benefit a village, give up the community.
> To benefit a region, give up the village.
> And to benefit oneself, give up the whole world.
>
> Even if a land is flourishing and prosperous,
> even if it yields ample grain and rice,
> even if it is congenial to animal welfare,
> a king should leave it to save his life.
>
> A king should safeguard wealth
> to be used for emergencies,
> to be used to protect women.
> But himself he must protect
> from both wealth and women.'

Another rabbit then said, 'But it's not easy to just abandon the land of our forefathers. What we need to do is to somehow scare the elephants away so that they don't return. Haven't you heard,

> A serpent may have lost his venom,
> but to save himself he should still hiss,
> he should still raise his dreaded hood.
> Venom or no venom, just the hood
> and the hiss are enough to frighten.'

A third rabbit added, 'If this is so, then I can suggest something that will certainly terrify the elephants and keep them away. But to make it work, we'll need a very clever and eloquent messenger, because the message he will take is related to our lord, Swami Shashakaraja Vijayadatta, who lives in the moon. This messenger will have to convince them that he is Vijayadatta, the king of rabbits, and the moon himself has sent him.'

'What will the message be?' the rabbits asked with bated breath, as though they were truly receiving a message from the moon.

'This is what the messenger will say: "I am Shashakaraja Vijayadatta, the king of rabbits, and I reside in the moon. Chandra deva has sent me to tell you that Chandrasarovara, the lake you visited today, is his lake, and it is forbidden to you from now on. At the edge of the lake live thousands of my kin, and your coming and going across their homes is sure to bring them great pain and suffering."'

Among the rabbits was one who was eloquent and convincing. His name was Lambakarna (long ears) and he was selected to be the envoy. It is said,

> A king's messenger should be
> pleasing of appearance,
> clever in conversation,
> well-read in the shastras,
> and intuitive to others' thoughts.

Also,

> The king that appoints
> a foolish, greedy envoy,
> especially one who lies,
> cannot ever achieve success.

All the other rabbits agreed with this plan and wished Lambakarna success. Following the trail of the elephants' footprints, Lambakarna crossed the forest and arrived at the place where the herd was resting. Then, climbing to a high point on a nearby hill, he addressed Chaturadanta, the king: 'O wicked elephant, why did you take your herd to Chandrasarovara and sport in and around it, unrestrained? After today, you are forbidden to go there. Return to where you have come from.'

'Who are you?' Chaturadanta asked the rabbit who was issuing such haughty commands.

'I am Shashakaraja Vijayadatta, the king of rabbits. I live in the moon. Chandra deva himself has sent me to you as his envoy. I have brought you a message from him.'

'O Shashakaraja,' Chaturadanta said, respectfully, 'we'll obey Chandra deva's command instantly. Please tell us his message.'

'This is the message: "O king of elephants, when you and your herd came to Chandrasarovara, you killed many rabbits and their children, and you destroyed their homes. Do you not know that rabbits are my special attendants? By hurting them, you have angered me. If you want to keep your life and save the lives of the members of your herd, do not ever go back to Chandrasarovara—for any reason at all."'

'O king of rabbits, please tell me where Chandra deva is right now,' Chaturadanta asked Lambakarna.

'He is actually at Chandrasarovara today, consoling those grieving rabbits who lost their loved ones under the cruel feet of your trampling herd. I have come from that very place.'

'Please take me to Chandra deva, so that I can offer my apology to him in person. After that, I'll take my herd and leave this place.'

'All right,' said the rabbit. 'You alone can come with me. I'll take you to Chandra deva, and you can meet him.'

Lambakarna then took the king of elephants to the lake. By the time they reached the lake, it was dark, and he told the elephant to follow him to the edge of the water. There, pointing to the reflection of the moon, he said, 'See our lord Chandra deva? He is sitting in the water in quietude. So, just bow to him from here, without disturbing him, and then leave. If he is disturbed while he is in meditation, he will be very irate.'

The king of elephants had no wish to anger Chandra deva any further. Therefore, quickly bowing to him from the water's edge, he turned around and returned to his herd, and that very night, the elephants left the region of Chandrasarovara.

'So, you see, that is why I say,' said the crow to the birds, 'just by mentioning the names of very important dignitaries, one can accomplish a lot of difficult tasks. Besides,

> Never make him a king who is
> petty, lazy, and mean-spirited,
> who is an ingrate, a coward,
> an addict, addict, and a slanderer.

Because this is how,

> In bygone days,
> hoping to get fair justice
> from a petty-natured judge
> the hare and the bird lost their lives.'

'What is this story?' the other birds asked, and the crow told them this tale.

THE TALE OF HOW THE CLEVER CAT ATE THE GULLIBLE HARE AND BIRD

Sometime ago, I used to live on the top of a tree. At the bottom of the tree was a hole in which a chataka bird called Kapinjala (partridge), had made a nest. We became very good friends, meeting every evening on a low branch of the tree to tell each other ancient tales about gods and goddesses, composed by rishis and maharishis. Sometimes, we would describe to each other all the wonderous sights we had seen in our daily pursuits. Those were good times, and we spent them in happiness.

One day, without informing me, Kapinjala joined a flock of chataka birds to fly to another land that had abundant rice fields. I waited for him all evening, and when, by nightfall, he still hadn't returned, I became worried. What could have happened? I wondered. Is he sitting in some hunter's cage? Is he dead? Because if he were alive, he would have been home by now. I knew he couldn't stay away from me for very long.

Caught in this vortex of anxiety, my heart sinking with each passing hour, many days passed. One evening I saw a hare called Shighragati (fast speed) enter the hole in the tree where Kapinjala's nest was. By this time, I had given up all hope of my friend's return, so I did not object to the hare living in the hole. However, it so happened that many months later, Kapinjala showed up. He looked robust and plump from having gorged himself on fresh wheat and rice, but now he wanted to come back to his nest. It is true,

> Even heaven doesn't provide the comfort
> one feels in one's land and one's own home,
> no matter how beggarly it may be.

When Kapinjala hopped into his hole and saw that it was occupied by the hare, he became irate. 'O hare,' he shouted, 'this my home. You can't just come in here and make it yours. Leave, this instant.'

'How is this your home?' Shighragati asked. 'It is, in fact, mine. Why are you accusing me? It is rightly said,

> A stepwell, well, lake, temple, and tree
> once given away can never be reclaimed.

Also, it is said:

> Ten years of occupation
> of a field or piece of land
> means full ownership
> of that field or piece of land.
> Proof is in the possession.
> No need for papers and witnesses.

The law of possession for human beings has been established by the great rishis who composed the Dharmashastras. And the law of possession for animals is this: as long as an animal stays in a place, that place is his; once he leaves it, he has no right over it. You not only left this place, but you were also gone for months. Therefore, this is now my place, because I live here. You have no right to this place.'

'O hare,' Kapinjala stated, trying very hard to remain calm. 'If you are citing the Dharmashastras, then come with me. Let's actually go to some Dharmashastra scholar and ask him to decide for us, according to the shastras, who is the rightful owner of this hole. Whoever he pronounces as rightful, will live here.'

Shighragati acquiesced, and the two of them went in search of a Dharmashastra scholar. A jungle cat heard about their dispute and, taking advantage of the situation, waylaid them on the bank of a river. They saw him standing on one foot, his hands raised, one of them holding kusha grass, his face turned up to the sun, spouting dharma wisdom: 'Oh, this world is meaningless, life is transient, and the company of loved ones is untrue, like a dream. Even family, home, and household are just a magician's illusion. Dharma is the only truth, the only protection, the only liberation. It is said,

> This body is short-lived.
> Wealth, too, is not forever.
> Death is a constant shadow.
> Keep adhering to dharma.
> He whose days come and go
> without accumulating dharma
> is breathing like a smithy's bellows,
> sustaining a body that has no life.
> Like a dog's tail that just hangs,
> neither covering his testicles nor
> flicking away mosquitoes and flies,

is useless; so is a wise man's wisdom
that is not used to follow dharma.

Also,

Just like shrivelled rice grain is discardable,
moths and mosquitoes are insignificant,
men without dharma are of no consequence.

A tree's quintessence is fruit and flowers.
Butter's quintessence is ghee.
Sesame's quintessence is oil.
A human life's quintessence is dharma.

Like animals who eat and defecate,
their purpose in life no more than
to carry heavy loads for others,
dharma-devoid men, too, eat and defecate,
their purpose in life no more
than to work for others for their food.
Dharma is the special something
that makes man different from animals.

Dear people, what is the use of elaborating? Let me give you the essence of dharma in a few words. Hear it from me and employ it in your life, as you please.

What pains us, pains others.
Knowing this, do not do unto others
what you do not want done to you.'

When the hare and the bird heard the wild cat spout such knowledge about dharma, they were thoroughly impressed. 'Hey, Kapinjala,' the hare said to the bird, 'this ascetic, standing on the riverbank, is surely a scholar well-versed in dharma. Let's have him decide our dispute.'

'But he is our natural enemy.' Kapinjala was not as trusting. 'We can ask him, but let's do it from a distance. If we come closer, who knows if he'll suddenly abandon dharma and jump on us. Maybe he's just pretending to be an adherent of dharma.'

The hare agreed with Kapinjala, and, standing at a distance, they addressed the jungle cat: 'O dharma preaching sanyasiji, we have a dispute about our place of residence. Please resolve this for us using the laws of the Dharmashastras.

And whichever one us is lying, you have our permission to eat him.'

'Dear good souls, I have renounced the path of violence, which only leads one to hell. Non-violence is the path to heaven. To never kill another is my dharma goal. The wise and scholarly say,

> Non-violence is the true way.
> Even the tiniest of creatures,
> lice, bedbugs, and mosquitos,
> are protected by dharma,
> as are animals that prey.
> Killing any creature, good or bad
> is a grave sin that only leads to hell.

In fact, even those who sacrifice animals for the purpose of yajnas don't actually know the true meaning of the Vedas. The Vedas ascribe, "perform yajnas with Aja". Foolish people understand "aja" to mean goat, when, in fact, it means rice that is seven years old. Also,

> If, by cutting trees,
> by killing animals,
> by bloodying the earth,
> one can reach heaven,
> Who then will go to hell?

That's why,' said the jungle cat, 'I have no intention of eating anyone. But I can certainly help you resolve your dispute. I'll be happy to tell you who has won, and who has lost. However, I'm old, and I can't hear you when you stand so far away. So, come closer and speak into my ear, as you tell me your side of the argument, so that I can hear every word and am able to make an accurate and fair decision based on the tenets of dharma. It is said,

> He who passes judgement
> with anger, ego, greed, or fear
> passes an inaccurate judgement.
> False judges, witnesses, and claimants
> are all candidates headed to hell.
>
> In a dispute about animals, he who
> knowingly passes wrong judgement,
> incurs the sin of killing five animals.
> In a dispute about cows, he who

knowingly passes false judgement
incurs the sin of killing ten cows.
In a dispute about women, he who
knowingly passes wrong judgement,
incurs the sin of killing a hundred women.
In a dispute about men, he who
knowingly passes false judgement,
incurs the sin of killing a thousand brahmins.

A claimant should always be truthful in court,
and a claimant who lies should be dismissed.

Therefore, noble souls, without any inhibition or fear, come close to my ear and tell me your side, truthfully and clearly.'

'What more can I say about this tale,' the crow said. 'That jungle cat convinced the hare and bird so effectively that they went and sat in his lap. And the cat wasted no time in gobbling them up right away. That is why I say that installing a small and lowly creature on the king's throne will benefit no one. And I warn you that if you make this day-blind owl your king, he'll wait till night when you all can't see, and then he'll kill you, like the jungle cat killed the foolish, trusting hare and chataka. Therefore, think carefully about what you are about to do, and proceed only after you have thoroughly considered the pros and cons.'

After listening to the crow, the birds began to re-think their decision, and they concluded that the crow was right. 'Let's delay the crowning of a king and reconvene later,' they said and flew off to their nests. Only the owl remained, still seated on the throne, unable to see anything but keenly attuned to the sounds of birds taking flight.

'Where is everybody going?' he asked. 'Why aren't we getting on with the coronation?'

'Dear husband,' said Krikalika, 'your coronation is not going to happen. The crow came and put a stop to it. All the birds have left and gone to their homes. Only the crow is still sitting here, and I have no idea why. Now, get up, let me help you home.'

Infuriated by what his wife told him, the owl shouted, 'O wicked crow, what harm have I ever done to you that you have come here and put an impediment to my acquiring kingship? I declare that from today till forever, we are enemies, and this enmity will continue through our progeny. It is rightly said,

> A wound from an arrow heals with time.
> A wound from a sword also heals with time.
> But a wound to the heart from abhorrent words
> never closes, never heals, never stops bleeding.'

Saying this to the crow, the owl left with his wife. As for the crow—the owl's words struck fear in his heart, and he began to worry. I have created bad blood for no reason at all, he thought. Why did I even interfere in this imbroglio? I had no reason to say what I did. And now that owl feels such rancour towards me. I have earned his hostility through my own fault. People say,

> He who speaks, without considering
> the propriety of time and place,
> words that hurt in consequence,
> words that show his own pettiness,
> words that are hard and bitter—
> his words aren't words; they are poison.
>
> No matter how able or powerful one is,
> knowingly creating an enemy is asinine.
> Which wise person will eat poison,
> just to prove that he has good doctors?
>
> The wise and noble know
> never to criticize anyone in public.
> Truth it may be, but made public,
> the truth dulls, and word-blades cut.
>
> He who acts only after
> taking friends' advice and
> considering all perspectives
> is wise, indeed, and also favoured
> by wealth, fame, and prosperity.

'With these disquieting thoughts, the crow, too, left that place. And from that day on, the crows and owls have been enemies,' concluded Sthirajivi.

'Now I understand the reason behind the hostility,' said Meghavarna. 'And it seems that it can't be resolved. Therefore, we must do what we can to keep ourselves safe. So, uncle, what do you think we should do to defeat the enemy?'

'Listen, nephew,' said Sthirajivi, 'aside from the five policies of accord, war, etc., that are mentioned in the Nitishastra, there is another one, which is often most effective—deception. Let me come up with a strategy, and I, alone, will go and deal with the owls. I'm certain that I'll be able to destroy them. It is said,

> People talented in duplicity
> and accomplished in chicanery
> manage to rob the wisest of all;
> like the crafty thieves who robbed
> the brahmin of his donkey.'

'What is this story, uncle?' Meghavarna asked, and Sthirajivi told him the tale.

THE TALE OF HOW THE BRAHMIN LOST HIS DONKEY TO THUGS

In a large village lived an Agnihotri brahmin called Mitrasharma. Once, during the month of Magha, when the chilly north wind blows, the sky is covered with a thin layer of clouds, and a slow and steady rain begins to fall, he decided to do a yajna on the day of Amavasya. To obtain an animal for sacrifice in the yajna, he went to the neighbouring village, hoping that some charitable, rich man would give him a goat in alms.

After knocking at the houses of a few wealthy men, he finally found one who was willing to give him a goat, and not just any goat but a plump, well-fed male goat, full of energy. Mitrasharma was grateful to receive him, but he was concerned that he would not be able to manage the animal on a tether. So, he decided to carry him on his shoulders.

On his way back to his village, the brahmin met three scoundrels. They were hungry and thirsty and ready to use whatever means necessary to obtain food. Seeing the brahmin carrying the fatted goat, one of them said, 'What luck to come upon this sight on this cold, wintry day. Let's treat ourselves to this goat. We'll steal it from this brahmin and cook ourselves a delicious meal.'

His companions agreed, and the three of them came up with a plan. They disguised themselves as common travellers and hurried along the path to meet with the brahmin up ahead. Soon, the brahmin saw a man coming towards him from the opposite direction. When he came up close, the man said to him, 'O ignorant Agnihotra, why are you doing this disdainful thing of carrying this impure animal—a dog—on your shoulders? Don't you know this will make you a subject of public ridicule, because the wise say,

> Touching a dog or a rooster
> is the same as touching an outcaste,
> and to touch an ass or a camel is worse.'

'Are you blind?' The Agnihotra said, wrathfully. 'Can't you see that it's not a dog that I'm carrying but a goat?'

The thug then said in a gentle tone, 'O respected brahmin. Please don't be upset. My apologies for interfering in your business. Please disregard what I said and go on your way and do what you please.'

After some time, the brahmin saw another man coming towards him. This man, too, looked at him with disdain, and said, 'Chhee chhee! This is a terrible thing you are doing. Even if you loved this dead calf, carrying his carcass on your shoulders does not behove a brahmin like you. The wise say,

> Not even cow's urine or a Chandrayana Vrata
> can cleanse the man who foolishly
> touches a dead animal or a human corpse.'

The brahmin replied, wrathfully. 'You must be a blind man, seeing a live yajna animal as a dead calf.'

This man, too, softened the tone of his voice and replied, 'Respected sir, why are you getting upset? It was my mistake to give you advice. Please forgive me. What you do is none of my business.'

After walking some distance, the brahmin saw a third man coming his way. 'Oho, what a terrible thing you are doing,' he said to the brahmin, 'carrying this ass on your shoulders. If I were you, I would throw him off this instant. The wise say,

> Whoever touches an ass knowingly or unknowingly,
> Must bathe in his clothes to cleanse himself pure.

That is why, I say, sir, you must throw down the ass before someone else sees you.'

By this time, Mitrasharma was quite perplexed. He wondered if, indeed, he had been duped and given an animal that was not a sacrificial goat. Or, perhaps, the animal was possessed by an evil spirit and was changing shapes. Whatever the case, the brahmin didn't want anything more to do with it. Flinging the goat on the ground, he fled from the place.

The three scoundrels came together, laughing at the success of their plan. Then they picked up the well-fed goat and, taking it home, enjoyed a sumptuous meal.

'Hence, I tell you,' Sthirajivi said to Meghavarna, 'when clever rascals work together, they can deceive even the wisest. Someone has rightly said,

> No man is wise enough not to be fooled
> by the diffidence of a new servant,
> by the tall tales of wanderers,
> by the weeping of beautiful women,
> and by the flowery words of thugs.

Besides, know that it is not wise to start a conflict with people in a group, even if they are weak and your victory is assured. It is said,

> Never conflict with an enemy
> that seems one but comprises many.
> It is hard to win against a multitude.
> Even a massive, hissing, venomous snake
> is killed from being bitten by a host of ants.'

'What is this story, uncle? Please tell me,' Meghavarna requested, and Sthirajivi told him the tale.

THE TALE OF HOW THE ANTS KILLED THE SNAKE

In a hole in the ground, in a forest, an enormous, black snake, called Atidarpana (deep reflections) used to live. One day, he decided to leave the hole though a passage he had never used before. However, the opening was narrower than he had expected, and as he tried to pass through it, his skin became badly scraped and bloody. The smell of blood brought out the ants, and, soon, hundreds and thousands of ants were on him, from all sides, sucking and biting him, driving him insane.

Atidarpana tried to dislodge as many of them as he could by thrashing his body this way and that, but, for the few hundred that fell off or died, thousands more climbed on him and clung to his lacerations. Soon, what started as scrapes on his body became deep wounds, and he died from the pain of it. In this way, that colossal snake, Atidarpana was killed by ants.

'That is why I advise you,' Sthirajivi said, 'never to take on a conflict with an enemy that consists of many, like the ants, otherwise you'll die the death of that serpent. Now, let me ask you something. After that, I want you to think very carefully and then do what you perceive as appropriate.'

'I'm yours to command, uncle. Please ask me, and I'll try to answer to the best of my ability.'

'Then, let me first tell you about the sixth method of deception that I've been discussing with you. This is how it can be employed in our current situation with the owls: declare me a traitor—a secret agent of the owls. After that, loudly denounce me, using disrespectful invective and lethal threats. Make sure that the enemy spies hear about all this, and they believe you. Then get blood from somewhere and smear it on me and throw me under this very bargad tree. After that, take your family to Rishyamuka Parvata and stay there. Here's what I'll do: I'll convince the enemy that I'm seeking vengeance against you, and that I'm willing to join forces with them. Once they take me inside their fortress, I'll monitor them, and, one opportune morning, when they are all blinded, I'll destroy them. This is the plan. I feel that this is the only way we can rid ourselves of them. There is no other way.'

'But how will you destroy all of them in one morning?' Meghavarna wanted to know.

'I know that the enemy fortress has only one gate for entry and exit. So, if they are inside, and the gate can't be opened, the fortress will become a death trap. Those who know statecraft say,

> A fortress is a true fortress
> if it has multiple means of escape.
> A fortress with only one gate
> is a prison; not a fortress.

Consider this scenario: if an enemy surrounds the single gate of the fortress, then everyone who is inside is caught, as though in a cage. That is why, a fortress must always have at least one other gate through which people can escape, when need be. And, as I said, I already know that the enemy's fortress has no other secret gates.'

'But, uncle, how can I let you face the enemy alone? What if something happens to you?'

'Don't worry about what will happen to me in the enemy camp, because,

> A king is advised to think of
> his loved and dear retainers
> only as pieces of dry wood
> to fuel the fire of battle.

So, don't think of me affectionately as your dear uncle; think of me cold-heartedly as only a necessary weapon in this battle. It is also said,

> A king protects his retainers with his life
> and cares for them as his own body, because
> one day, for him they will face the enemy.

That is why, O king, don't stop me from my mission. Besides, I have volunteered for it. Let me follow my plan. Two days from now, engage with me in an altercation that sounds like our differences are irrevocable and have me thrown out of the palace. Then, take your family and leave for Rishyamuka mountain and stay there for a few days.'

Two days later, Meghavarna and Sthirajivi began a mock fight, shouting at each other, making sounds with their wings, as though striking one another. These loud voices coming from the king's chamber, alarmed his attendants, and they rushed in. Sthirajivi then raised his voice even more and began making mutinous threats. The attendants pulled out their swords to cut him down.

'Leave him to me,' the king stated. 'I can handle this old bird, single-handedly. He's secretly working for the enemy, and I want to punish him myself. You can leave.' Then, dashing across, he landed on Sthirajivi's back and pretended to attack him with his beak. After the attendants left, he poured fake blood on him and helped him lie down on the floor, as though badly wounded. Then he called his attendants back and commanded them to throw the traitor out of the bargad. After that, he gathered his family and left for Rishyamuka mountain.

The falling out between Meghavarna and Sthirajivi did not go unnoticed by the owls. Krikalika, who was the owls' most proficient secret agent, saw it all and reported it to her husband. 'At this time, your enemy, Meghavarna, is fleeing; he's flying north with his family,' she told him.

As soon as the sun set, the owl king quickly gathered his soldiers to pursue Meghavarna. 'The wise say that luck is really in your favour if you can catch a fleeing enemy,' he told his soldiers,

> A fleeing enemy leaves himself open.
> Also, when he seeks shelter elsewhere,
> dealing with guards and king's men
> makes him anxious and vulnerable.'

Arriving at the bargad, Arimardana commanded his men to surround it and lay siege, even though they couldn't find a single crow in the tree or in its vicinity. Then, flying to the highest branch and perching on it with a self-congratulatory shake of his wings, he ordered his troops: 'Find out by which path these crows have left. We want to catch them while they are on the run—before they reach another fort and hide in it. It is said,

> A hiding enemy is hard to find
> even if it is in a bush of thorns.
> If he finds refuge in a well-stocked fort
> it gets that much harder to kill him.'

Lying bloodied at the base of the bargad, seeing that the owls seemed more interested in chasing a fleeing king than in questioning him, Sthirajivi thought, if they leave without noticing me, then all my effort and planning will come to naught. It is said,

> There's one sort of wisdom in not beginning a task.
> But to end a task already begun is another matter.

If I hadn't initiated this mission of destroying the enemy, it would have been fine, but now that I'm in the midst of it, how can I leave it unfinished? Therefore, let me try to attract their attention. Hence, Sthirajivi began to moan and groan as loudly as he could.

Hearing his constant 'caw, caw,' the owls descended on him, ready to kill him.

'Wait!' he called to them. 'I am Meghavarna's old minister, Sthirajivi. Meghavarna himself is responsible for my wretched state. Go, tell your king that I have many secrets to tell him.'

When the owls described Sthirajivi's condition to Arimardana and told him what he had said, Arimardana was delighted. He instantly flew to where Sthirajivi lay under the bargad tree. 'Why are you in this state?' he asked him. 'Tell me everything in detail.'

'Maharaj,' Sthirajivi began, 'last night, that wicked Meghavarna was very upset at seeing the carcasses of thousands of crows that you had killed. He wanted to find you and attack you. I stopped him. "Maharaj," I said to him, "it is not advised that you mount an attack on the owl king, because he is very powerful, and we are weak.

> A weak person wishing for his own well-being
> should not fight an enemy more powerful.
> While the enemy will hardly suffer a loss,
> he will be destroyed like a moth in a flame.

That is why, Maharaj, don't declare war on the owl king; instead, offer him a tribute and sign an accord with him. It is best to sign a peace treaty with a powerful enemy, because it is said,

> Wisdom is in surrendering one's all
> to an enemy known to be more powerful.
> If one's life is intact, wealth can be regained."

Meghavarna heard what I had to say, but he chose, instead, to believe his snitchers who said that I was a secret agent for the enemy, the owls. That is why I was beaten almost to death and flung out of the bargad tree, while Meghavarna left with all his crows. Now, I only seek refuge at your feet, Maharaj. What else can I say? I hate that wicked Meghavarna so much, and I'm so enraged at his unfair treatment that when I've recovered from my wounds and am able to fly again, I'll take you to his new residence so that you can destroy him and all the crows.'

After listening to Sthirajivi's account, Arimardana went to consult with his five ministers, who had served his father and grandfather. Their names were: Raktaksha (red eyes), Kruraksha (cruel eyes), Deeptaksha (light eyes), Vakranasa (curved nose), Prakarakarna (rampart ears). He first went to Raktaksha and asked him, 'What do you think we should do with the enemy minister we have captured?'

'What is there to think about, Maharaj,' Raktaksha said. 'Put him to death instantly, because it is said,

> As long as the enemy is weak,
> he can be killed with ease.
> If he regains strength and ability,
> he becomes difficult to defeat.

Besides, it is well known,

> If Lakshmi comes to you by herself
> and you don't accept the favour,
> Lakshmi will put a curse on you.

Also,

> If you are waiting for an opportune time,
> and a time does come that is opportune,
> if you fail to do what needs done in that time
> that opportunity will never come again.

It is also told,

> Look at your son's burning pyre,
> And look also at my bleeding hood,
> wounded by the strike of the club.
>
> A friendship once broken
> can never be repaired,
> no matter how much love
> is salved in the wound.'

'What is this story?' Arimardana asked, and Raktaksha began to narrate it.

THE TALE OF THE GOLD-GIVING SERPENT AND WHY HE KILLED THE FARMER'S SON

In a large village lived a brahmin named Haridatta. Every year, he tried to till his farm and grow crops, but he was never successful. One summer day, tired, and sweaty from ploughing the dry soil, he lay down in the shade of a tree to rest. When he turned his face, he saw an enormous, many-hooded, fear-instilling cobra coiled on the ground near a burrow. For a moment, the brahmin lay frozen in fright. Then he began to think, this is probably the guardian lord of this field. I have failed to offer him worship; that is why my field has never yielded a successful crop. I should pay my respects to this Naga deva.

Getting up quickly, the brahmin fetched a bowl of milk, but by the time he returned, the snake was gone. Placing the earthenware bowl near the burrow, he stood with folded hands and said, 'O guardian of the field, I did not know that you resided here; that is the reason I never offered you worship. Please forgive my transgression and accept this tiny offering of milk.' After that, Haridatta went home.

The following morning, the brahmin saw that the milk in the bowl was gone, but sitting in the bottom of it, glinting in the sun, was a gold mohur. From that day on, Haridatta began to offer the snake a bowl of milk every day and receive one gold mohur in return the following morning. Many months passed. One day, the brahmin had to go to another village for business. That morning, he brought his son to the field, showed him the serpent's burrow, and instructed him about what to do every day. 'Place the bowl of milk, right here,' he said, putting the bowl he had brought near the serpent's burrow. 'Then, bow and pray to the Naga deva like this,' and he bowed his head and thanked the serpent for his continued beneficence. 'Make sure that you do this every morning, while I am gone,' he reiterated. However, he did not say a word to his son about the gold mohurs.

The next morning when the son came to the field, carrying the bowl of milk, he saw that the bowl his father had placed there the day before had a gold mohur in it. 'Aha,' he said to himself, 'now I know why my father was so insistent that I do this every day. But why should we get the gold only piece by piece? There must be a large treasure of gold mohurs under this hole. I should kill the snake and just dig it up.' Hence, the next day, he came carrying not just the milk, but also a heavy club and a shovel. Placing the milk near the burrow, he stepped aside and waited, ready with his club. As soon as the snake glided out of the burrow and dipped his head into the bowl, the brahmin's son stepped forward and clubbed him. The wounded, writhing serpent reared its head and sank his venomous fangs into his foot, killing him almost instantly.

When the neighbours saw the son's body, clearly dead from snake poison, and they found the club on the ground beside him, they put two and two together. The neighbours and relatives then cremated the brahmin's son right there in the field.

When Haridatta returned, his relatives told him what happened and how his son had struck the serpent, and the serpent had retaliated by biting him.

'He got what he deserved,' Haridatta said.

> 'He who doesn't protect his old benefactors
> and gets involved with new refuge-seekers,
> ends up ruining all his prospects of benefaction,
> like the king who lost the gold hamsas of Padmavana.'

'What is this story?' the villagers asked, and he told them the tale.

THE TALE OF WHY THE GOLD HAMSAS LEFT PADMAVANA

There was once a king called Chitraratha (sun). He owned a beautiful garden, Padmavana, and in that garden was a large lotus lake called Padmasara. It was always guarded by thousands of soldiers, because the residents of that lake were gold hamsas, who, every six months, shed one gold feather, which the king took.

One day, a large gold bird of another species flew into the lake. The hamsas said to him, 'You can't live here with us. We have leased this lake from the king for one golden feather every six months.'

The new bird refused to leave, while the hamsas tried to push him out. Soon, the situation became quite heated. Finally, the new arrival went to the king to complain: 'Maharaj, those hamsa birds say they will not let any other birds live here in this lake, and when I told them that I was coming to you to complain about them, they replied, "What can the king do to us?" Now, Maharaj, you must do what you think is right.'

Taking umbrage at the haughtiness of the hamsas, the king sent his soldiers to the lake with the order: 'Kill them all!'

When the hamsas saw soldiers descending on the lake with sticks and staffs, they were terrified, certain that they would all be beaten to death. Then, an old hamsa advised his clan, 'We need to escape. Let's quickly leave this lake and find another place to live, or we'll all die.'

Agreeing with the senior member of their clan, the hamsas with gold-giving wings all flew away. Too late, the king realized what he had done. He had himself put an end to a fabulous income. And all this happened because he put the interest of his new sanctuary-seeker above the well-being of his old providers.

'That is why, I say,' said Haridatta to the villagers. 'If I don't protect my old benefactor, the snake, and abandon him for the grief I feel for my son, I'll lose my source of income. Therefore, even though the serpent is the one who bit my son and killed him, I'll continue to offer him milk every day.'

Thus, the following morning, Haridatta brought a bowl of milk and placing it near the serpent's lair, as usual, began to praise him in a very loud voice. The serpent listened to the brahmin for a while, and then spoke from inside his lair, 'O brahmin, your son is dead, but you seem to have forgotten that, and here you are praising me and bringing me milk because of your greed for gold. But now our friendship has been breached, and it can't be repaired. Your son, in the fervour of youth, struck me with his club, and I retaliated by biting him. How can I forget the beating I received, and how can you forget the grief of losing your son?

> Look at your son's burning pyre,
> and look also at my bleeding hood,
> wounded by the strike of his club.'

Saying this, the serpent suddenly emerged from his lair and gave the brahmin a valuable diamond. 'Here, take this as a parting gift,' he said. 'And don't come back to me.' Then he burrowed back into the ground, and the brahmin returned home with the diamond, cursing his son for his short-sightedness.

'That is why I say,' said Arimardana's minister, Raktaksha,

> A friendship once broken
> can never be repaired,
> no matter how much love
> is salved in the wound.

Hence, how can this crow become our friend. We have killed thousands of his clan. Therefore, Maharaj, my advice to you is to kill this Sthirajivi and safeguard your fort and your subjects.'

The king of owls then turned to his second minister, Kruraksha, and asked him, 'What is your opinion in this matter?'

'Maharaj, what my colleague has advised is very cold-hearted and ruthless, and it doesn't behove a king. How can you kill someone who is seeking sanctuary? One should never kill such a one. Let me tell you a story about this.

> If the refuge seeker is an enemy,
> he must still be protected and helped,
> even if one has to sacrifice one's life.
> A pigeon once fed his own flesh
> to an enemy who sought refuge.'

THE TALE OF THE CHATAKA BIRD WHO ROASTED HIS OWN FLESH FOR A FOWLER

In a dense forest, a wicked-minded, cruel fowler used to hunt birds, like Yama's messenger seeking victims. He didn't have any friends or relatives, because everyone had disowned him for his evil ways.

> This is the way it should be:
> people who are cruel and evil
> and hurt other living beings,
> living beings are afraid them.

And that hunter was such a man. Every day he would go into the forest, equipped with cages, nets, sticks, and nooses and kill whatever creature he could. One day, he caught a female chataka bird and trapped her in his cage. While he was still in the forest, the sky suddenly became overcast. Darkness spread, lightning flashed from one end of the sky to the other, and the roar of thunder echoed all around. Soon, the wind picked up, turning into a gale, and torrential rain, the kind predicted during pralaya, began to pour down.

Tossed around in the storm, thoroughly drenched, shivering with cold, that hunter began to search for some kind of shelter, and finally he just stood under a tree.

The storm passed as suddenly as it had come. The rain became no more than a light drizzle, and the sky cleared to reveal the first twinkling stars. However, by this time, the hunter was chilled to the bone and hungry and thirsty. Standing under the tree, he looked up at its branches and said, 'Whoever lives in this tree, I've come to you for refuge. I'm cold and hungry. Please help me.'

The chataka couple lived in that tree, and the male was up there in the branches. He had been searching for his wife, and, losing hope in the storm, had returned home. Perched in a thicket of leaves, he was lamenting for her: 'O dear one, the storm has passed, but why have you not come home to me? Without you, our home feels empty, and the forest seems frightening. If any husband has a wife as loving and caring as mine, he should consider himself lucky.'

> A house is not a home,
> it is the wife who makes it so.
> A house without a woman
> is no better than a wilderness
> full of pain and hardships.'

The chataka's wife was sitting trapped in the cage, which the bird-catcher had placed under the tree. Hearing her husband praise her and lament for her filled her heart with joy, and she said,

> 'The wife who cannot make her husband happy
> is a wife in name only.
> The wife whose husband is happy and content
> pleases even the gods.
> The wife whose husband isn't happy with her
> lives a futile life.
> Like a branch laden with flowers and sweet fruit
> that burns to ashes in a forest fire,
> her life should come to an end.
>
> A father supports his daughter.
> A brother supports his sister.
> A son supports his mother.
> A woman has many who provide
> her some wealth and happiness.
> But what a husband gives to his wife
> is unlimited wealth and unlimited joy.
> Such a husband is worthy of worship.'

Then the female chataka spoke to her mate from the cage, 'Dear husband, please listen to my words carefully, because they are in your best interest. Protect with your life the one who comes to you seeking asylum. Listen to this fowler, who has come to shelter under this tree, which is your residence. He is cold and hungry, and he is your guest. Take care of him with everything you have. I've heard it said,

> If you do not care for the guest
> who arrives in the evening
> with all your means and ability,
> that guest leaves you his sins
> and robs your merit of good deeds.

Also, dear husband, don't dwell, even for a moment, on the fact that he has captured your wife. I'm caught, not by this bird-catcher, but as a result of my own past karma. He is not to blame.

> All creatures' joys and sorrows
> are a direct result of their karma.
> Penury, disease, grief, and woe,
> also, hardship and imprisonment
> are fruits borne by our tree of sins.

I implore you to give up the anger and hostility that you feel toward him because of me and follow your dharma by caring for him with all you have and all your ability.'

Listening to his wife's advice about dharma, the male bird shed his fear and anger and called down to the fowler, 'Dear man, welcome! Thank you for gracing my home. It has given me pleasure. Please tell me, without hesitation, how I can help you. Don't harbour any feelings of chagrin in your heart, because this is your own home, and everything here is yours—to use for your own comfort and ease.'

The heartless man, the killer of birds, heard the chataka and, acknowledging his position of a guest, said to him without hesitation: 'I am chilled to the bone. Do something to alleviate the cold.'

The male bird flew to a nearby village and found a kitchen with a burning stove. Picking up a live ember in his beak, he brought it back to the forest and threw it on a pile of dry leaves. 'Please warm yourself at this fire,' he said to the bird-catcher. 'But I must apologize that I have no grain or food at home to appease your hunger.' Then he thought to himself,

> Some provide for thousands.
> Some provide for hundreds.
> Some take care of five or ten.
> But I am that unfortunate,
> miserable, small creature,
> who lacks enough to feed himself.
>
> If a man doesn't have the means
> to care for even one guest,
> who would want to stay in his house
> full of sorrows and discomforts?

Therefore, I should do something so meaningful with this tiny, insignificant body that never again will I have to say to a guest, 'I have nothing to give you.' Thus, castigating himself for his lack, the chataka said to the fowler, who was his wife's captor, 'Wait here for me, and I'll procure food for you.'

The dharma-following bird then circumambulated the fire and flew into it, as if it were his home.

Seeing the bird's body roast, the fowler became overcome with compassion, and he finally felt regret at what he had done. Grieving for the bird, he said,

> 'The man who does evil deeds
> loves not his very own soul,
> because the evil he does,
> results in suffering for the soul.

That is the kind of sinner I am—always engaged in evil deeds. I'll end up in naraka; there is no doubt about it. Look what this great soul, this chataka bird has done for a lowly, cruel sinner like me. By sacrificing himself, he has established a high ideal. Hence, from today, I, too, renounce all actions that are for the enjoyment and satisfaction of my sinner's body. Like the summer heat that dries up lakes and other waterbodies, I, too, will dry up my wants and desires. Suffering through cold, wind, and sweat, wearing humble clothing, fasting, and resolving, I will fulfil my highest dharma.' With this pronouncement, the hunter broke his staff, shredded his noose and net, and, setting the female bird free, smashed the cage.

Freed from the cage, the bird flew to the fire and, seeing her husband's burnt body on the ground amidst the flames, she wailed, 'O dear one, what need do I have of this life when I don't have you? I don't want to live without you. In any case, a widow's life is deplorable.

> Pride, ego, self-assurance,
> respect among relatives,
> servants at her beck and call—
> these privileges are taken away
> when a woman becomes a widow.'

Then, circumambulating the fire, she flew into it. As soon as her body burnt to ashes, she assumed divine form, adorned with silks and jewels. When she looked up at the sky, she saw her husband, who was also in divine form, coming to get her in an airborne chariot.

'Dear wife,' he said, 'you have done well by joining me in the fire.

> A human body has three and a half crore pores.
> The wife that becomes sati on a husband's pyre
> lives with him in heaven for that many years.'

The chataka couple began to live in heaven, enjoying ultimate happiness. People would sometimes see their flying chariot in the sky. The hunter, feeling true regret for his wicked deeds, renounced all violence and did rigorous penance. Following that, he went into the forest to live the life of a renunciate. One day, coming across a forest fire, he jumped into it and atoned for his sins. Then he, too, went to heaven and lived there in supreme joy.

After relating this story of the chataka birds, Kruraksha said to Arimardana, 'So you see, Maharaj, this is how one must treat those who come to seek sanctuary, even if they are enemies.'

Having heard what he had to say, Arimardana turned to his third minister, Deeptaksha and asked him, 'What is your opinion in this matter?'

'Maharaja, we should certainly not kill this Sthirajivi crow, because, as it is said,

> She who used to keep me at a distance
> is today taking me in her embraces.
> Priyakaraka, may you be blessed.
> Whatever I have is yours to steal.'

And the thief replied,

> You don't have anything I wish to steal.
> If you ever acquire something I want,
> or if your wife stops embracing you,
> be assured that I will be back.

'Who is this woman who didn't embrace her husband, and who is this thief? Please tell me in detail,' Arimardana said, and Deeptaksha told him the story.

THE TALE OF THE OLD MAN WHO THANKED THE THIEF IN HIS HOUSE

In a town lived an old moneylender by the name of Kamatura (fervently lustful). When his wife passed away, the old man, who had an insuppressible libido, paid a handsome sum to a poor moneylender in the village and married his young daughter. However, that young woman was repulsed by him and wouldn't so much as lift her eyes to look at him.

And it is right,

> The white hair one gains in old age
> is cause of rejection from young women.
> They stay away from a white-haired man
> just as the thirsty avoid a low caste's well
> whose parapet displays a white bone.

Also,

> With old age, a man's body and limbs shrink.
> His feet shuffle and his teeth fall out.
> His eyes become weak and his looks fade.
> He drools when he talks and his words slur.
> His relatives pay him no heed and his wife
> does not spare him a solitary glance.
> But the saddest of all consequences—
> his son slights him every chance he gets.

One day, Kamatura's wife was lying with him in bed, with her face turned away towards the door, when, suddenly, someone cracked open the door and slipped in. It was a thief with a ferocious face. Terrified at the sight, the wife, instinctively, turned around and, throwing her arms around her husband's neck, held him tightly.

For a moment, the old man lay completely still; then his whole body started trembling, filled with ecstasy. I wonder what has happened, he thought? What is the reason that my wife is holding me in her arms? When he looked around, he saw the thief hiding in a corner. 'Aha,' he said to himself. 'This is the reason she turned to me and caught me in an embrace.'

Then, loudly, he said to the thief, 'O thief, my young wife, who used to hate me and refused to even talk to me, has today, voluntarily, put her arms around me and is holding me in a tight embrace, all because of you. Therefore, O thief, you are my Priyakaraka, my beloved benefactor. You have brought me great happiness and I wish God's grace on you. Whatever you want from my house, feel free to steal it. I owe you this.'

Hearing the old man, the intelligent thief understood the situation and said, 'Sethji, at this time I don't see anything in your house worth stealing. But I'm warning you that if things change and you acquire anything worth stealing, I'll be back. And it'll only be worth stealing when your wife stops embracing you. That is when I'll certainly return.' Thus, subtly warning the wife, the thief left. Fearing that the frightening thief would make good his threat, the young woman not only began to show more affection to the old man, but she also started fulfilling his sexual needs. This is how the thief did the old man a favour and saved his unhappy marriage.

'So, Maharaj,' Deeptaksha said, 'If one can wish well upon a thief who did a small favour for an old man, then one who seeks sanctuary must surely be protected. That Sthirajivi has suffered at the hands of our enemies and has come to us for protection. Besides, consider this: he must have so much insight about the enemy. We can use him to get information. Therefore, I would advise you not to kill him.'

After listening to him, Arimardana turned to his fourth minister, Vakranasa, and asked him the same question: 'What do you think we should do?'

'Maharaj, I, too, think we should not kill him,' said Vakranasa. 'My reasoning is this: when the enemy fight among themselves, the benefit is reaped by others.

> Look here, when the thief saved his life,
> the rakshasa saved the pair of bulls.'

'What is this tale?' Arimardana asked, and Vakranasa told him the story.

THE TALE OF HOW THE BRAHMIN GOT RID OF THE THIEF AND THE RAKSHASA

In a village lived a poor brahmin called Drona. His livelihood was begging, which barely fulfilled his daily needs. He was so focused on just surviving that things of extravagance, such as silks, sandal, perfume, flower garlands, ornaments, paan, mithai, etc., did not even appear in his dreams. Because he identified so thoroughly with his penurious state, his appearance, too, had become unappealing: his hair was long and unkempt, turning into dreadlocks, his moustache had grown wild, and his nails were long and dirty. Also, suffering the vagaries of heat, cold, and rain, his body had become gaunt, and his skin was dry and wrinkled. In other words, he was the image of poverty.

One day, seeing his piteous state, a charitable person gave him a pair of male calves. The poor brahmin was thrilled but also apprehensive, because he had no means to feed them. Hence, he started begging for their fodder, along with his own food. Surprisingly, he received ample fodder every day, and soon, the two calves became big and strong bulls.

Once, a robber saw this pair of bulls who were in prime condition and became intent on stealing them. Therefore, one night, he set off for the brahmin's house, carrying a rope, thinking he might need it to tie around the bulls' necks. As he was hurrying along the way, he saw coming towards him was a terrifying being—a huge man with burning, red eyes, and sharp teeth with gaps between them. His skin was dry and cracked, and his veins protruded and pulsed. His limbs were long and the hair on his face and head was yellow, like a fire in an altar. Seeing this rakshasa, the robber's heart started to pound, and he was barely able to breathe. His mind a jumble of thoughts about escape, he, somehow, kept walking, and when the rakshasa came abreast, he asked him, as nonchalantly as he could, 'Who are you?'

'I am a Brahmarakshasa, and my name is Satyavana (one who speaks the truth). Who are you?'

'I am Krurakarma (cruel deeds), and I'm a thief. I'm on my way to a poor brahmin's house to steal his pair of bulls.'

'This is fortuitous,' said the rakshasa. 'I eat in the sixth pahar of the day, which is midnight. It is now time for my day's meal. Let's go together to the brahmin's house. I'll make him my food tonight.'

Hence, the two began walking together towards the brahmin's house, chit-chatting like old friends. When they arrived at the house, they found a hiding place and waited there for the right moment. As soon as the brahmin fell asleep, the rakshasa got up, intending to kill the man, but the thief stopped him. 'Not yet. Let me first steal the bulls. Then you can kill him and eat him.'

'No. No. That's not right. You wait till I've eaten him and then steal the bulls. What if the bulls get agitated when you are stealing them and begin to bellow? That'll wake up the brahmin.'

'And what if the brahmin starts screaming when you attack him. Then the whole neighbourhood will be here. How can I steal the bulls then? So, let me steal the bulls, and then you take the brahmin.'

'Absolutely not,' said the rakshasa. 'You wait for me.'

'No. You wait for me,' said the thief.

In this way, the rakshasa and the thief's argument about 'I, first,' 'I, first,' became so loud that it woke up the brahmin. 'Who's there?' he called, turning his head in the direction of the voices.

'O brahmin,' the thief called back, 'this rakshasa wants to eat you.'

'O brahmin,' the rakshasa called, 'this man is a thief, and he wants to steal your bulls.'

The brahmin got out of bed, fully alert to the dangers that lurked in his house. Purifying himself by washing his hands, feet, and mouth, he sat down to meditate, and with his mental power, he cast out the rakshasa. Then, squaring his shoulders, he picked up a staff to face the thief. Seeing his intent, the thief, too, quietly slunk away. This is how the brahmin saved both his life and his bulls

'That is why I said, Maharaj,' said, Vakranasa, 'when two enemies have a dispute, somebody else benefits from it. I'm certain, Sthirajivi's falling out with Meghavarna will prove profitable for us. Therefore, we should not kill him.'

Nodding to Vakranasa, Arimardana now turned to his fifth minister, Parkarakarna, and asked him the same question: 'What is your opinion? What should we do in this situation?'

'Maharaj, I, too, say we should not kill Sthirajivi. But my reasoning is this—if we tend to his wounds and save him and protect him, he'll think of us as his allies and will reveal to us secret information about the crows.

It is said,

> Those who cannot keep others' secrets
> are ruined like the two snakes—
> one in the stomach and one in the lair.'

'What is this story?' Arimardana asked, and Prakarakarna told him the tale.

THE TALE OF THE TWO SNAKES AND THEIR SECRETS

There was once a king called Devasharma. He had a son in whose stomach a snake had made his home. Consequently, day by day, the boy grew weaker in every limb. The king did everything he possibly could to cure his son: he hired the most well-known physicians; he bought the most expensive and scarce antidotes; and he tried every single remedy that the medical books prescribed. However, the prince's condition kept worsening, and, to make matters worse, the more his body deteriorated, the more frustrated and disheartened he became. Finally, the prince decided to leave home and spend the remainder of his days in a temple far away.

That land to which he moved had a king named Bali, and he had two grown-up daughters, who were both unmarried. Every morning, at daybreak, the two princesses would go to their father and bow at his feet to get his blessings. While bowing, the elder princess would say, 'Maharaj, victory to you! Because of your grace, we are able to live such a happy life.' But the younger princess would say, 'Maharaj, you'll reap the fruits of your karma.'

The king was pleased with what his elder daughter said to him every day, but the words of his younger daughter irked him. One day, he couldn't bear it any more, and he said to his ministers, 'I can't endure the harsh words that my daughter says to me every morning. Take her away and get her married to some poor foreigner. That'll teach her a lesson about reaping the rewards of her karma.'

Following the king's orders, the ministers found a poor stranger, who had just arrived in the city and was living in the big temple. They wed the princess to him and, giving her a dowry of one servant and a small sum of money, bid her farewell. The princess accepted her marriage to the beggar, who looked weak and pale.

The couple lived in the temple for some time and then decided to go and settle somewhere else. On the way, they came to a large city, which had a lake bordering it, and the couple decided to stay by the water's side for a while. Leaving her husband to watch over their possessions, the wife took her servant and went into the city to buy provisions, such as ghee, oil, salt, rice, dal, flour, etc. When she returned with her purchases, she saw that her husband was sleeping on the ground with his head resting near a snake hole. Also, to her utmost shock, she saw that a large snake's head with a flared hood was jutting out of her husband's mouth. As she watched in horror, another snake emerged from the snake hole. It was equally large and hooded, and it, too, just popped its head out, as though to take in air. When the two snakes came face to face, they both hissed, their eyes turned red, and their tongues flashed.

Then the snake from the ground said to the snake in the mouth, 'O evil-doer, why are you making this poor prince suffer so much? Stop leaching on him.'

'Are you any less of an evil-doer?' said the snake from the prince's belly. 'You are hoarding two pots of gold in your lair.'

Then the snake from the lair spoke again: 'You evil soul, no physician knows that the only way to kill you is to boil and ferment black mustard and have the prince drink that fermented water.'

'And nobody knows that to kill you, all one has to do is pour boiling water or oil down your hole,' said the other snake.

In this way, both the snakes gave away each other's secrets.

The princess, who was hiding behind a tree, heard these secrets. She quickly boiled water and poured it down the hole in the ground. Then she made the fermented drink from black mustard and fed it to her husband. In no time at all, her husband regained his health, and, together, they dug up the treasure, which the ground snake had been hoarding. Then the princess took her husband and her wealth to her father to show him the truth of her words. 'Look father,' she said, 'I have earned the rewards of my karma. Each person on this earth receives happiness and wealth in accordance with his or her past actions.'

Her parents and all the people in that land praised her for her wisdom, and she began to live there happily with her husband.

'So, you see, Maharaj,' Prakarakarna said to the owl king, 'those who can't keep each other's secrets get destroyed. In this situation, we can benefit from the secrets that old crow reveals; therefore, we shouldn't kill him.'

Thus, with four of the five ministers advising Arimardana to not kill Sthirajivi, he decided that the best course of action was to give him sanctuary.

When the first minister, Raktaksha, heard the king's decision, he could hardly believe his ears. 'What imbecilic advice are you giving to our king?' he scolded the other ministers. 'Your advice is contrary to the laws of statecraft, and by giving these erroneous opinions, you are ruining our king. It is said,

> Where people unworthy of worship are worshipped
> three consequences occur:
> famine, death, and civil disorder.

It is also said,

> Fools are they who believe false witnesses,
> even when the crime occurs before their eyes.
> Like the chariot-maker who saw his wife
> sleeping with her lover and yet took her
> and her lover riding through the village,
> all because she beguiled him with her lies.'

'What is this tale?' the ministers asked, and Raktaksha narrated the tale.

THE TALE OF THE MAN WHO WAS GRATEFUL TO BE CUCKOLDED

In a city lived a chariot-maker called Veeravara (brave bridegroom). He had a wife as beautiful as a lotus, and her name was Kamadamani (lotus jewel). She was a lustful and promiscuous woman, who was often the subject of gossip. Veeravara was aware of what people said about his wife, but he reluctant to believe it till he saw it with his own eyes, even though, he knew,

> If ever fire can be cool,
> or the moon can be hot,
> or the wicked can be allies,
> then women can be chaste.

What Veeravara wanted to know was the basis on which his wife had been labelled a wanton woman. It is aptly said,

> Some matters are not in the Vedas,
> they are not even in the shastras,
> and they are often unheard of,
> but if they exist in the universe,
> somehow people know about them.

Thus, one day, the chariot-maker said to his wife, 'Dear one, tomorrow I have to go to another town for business, and I'll be gone many days. Please make me some food to take for the journey.'

The wife was thrilled to hear that her husband was going out of town. She left all her other chores and got busy making for him the most delicious churma with plenty of ghee and sugar. Someone has aptly said,

> When the sky is dark with clouds,
> when the weather is miserable
> with heavy rain, fog, or snow,
> when outside is a wilderness,
> or roads are empty of people,
> and the husband is away travelling,
> a lascivious woman is ecstatic.

The following morning, the wife watched her husband leave the house at dawn. Filled with excitement and joy, she spent the whole afternoon beautifying herself with oils and perfumes and adorning herself with flower garlands and ornaments. When evening came, she went to make an assignation with her lover. 'My husband is away for many days,' she told him. 'Why don't you come to my house later tonight?'

Of course, the chariot-maker had not left town. He was using the subterfuge to test his wife. All day, he wandered around town, lurking in the shadows, and in the evening, he entered his home through the backdoor and, tiptoeing to the bedroom, hid under the bed. Sometime later, he heard the front door open and saw a man walk into the bedroom and sit down on the bed. The chariot-maker had a hard time controlling his fury. Should I just come out from under the bed and kill this rascal right now, he thought. Or should I wait till I see what my wicked wife does? Then I can kill both of them together. But then he thought, I should wait and see the evidence with my own eyes and listen to what is said with my own ears before I take any action. Hence, the chariot-maker remained hiding under the bed, waiting for his wife. He didn't have long to wait, because shortly thereafter the door to the room opened, and he saw his wife enter on soft feet and walk to their bed. She stopped there for a minute and then climbed onto the bed. As she was climbing, her foot accidently touched her husband. The contact was so slight that he did not feel it, but she did, and she realized what it meant. 'Aha!' she said to herself. 'So, my lying husband didn't actually leave town. He just said that to test me, and now he's hiding right here under this bed to catch me. Let me teach him something about women and how we can fool anyone.'

Just then, the woman's lover reached out his arms to embrace her.

'Wait right there, O guest,' the woman exclaimed loudly. 'Don't touch a hair on my body yet. I'm a chaste woman and a true wife. If you touch me, I'll burn you to ashes with my curse.'

Her lover pulled back in shock. 'If that is the case, then why did you invite me to your house?'

'Listen carefully to what I have to say,' she said to him. 'This morning I went to the temple of Devi Chandika. There, I heard a voice from heaven. It said to me, "Dear daughter, you are my greatest and truest devotee. But it is unfortunate that within six months you will lose your husband and become a widow." I was devastated to hear the Devi's prediction, so, with folded hands and bowed head, I begged her, "Devi, since you have foreknowledge of this tragedy that will strike me, surely you also know how I can prevent it. Please tell me if there is a remedy that can save my husband and ensure that he lives to be a hundred years old."

"Daughter, there is a remedy," the Devi said. "But it's not really a remedy. It is not something that I can help you with. It is something that only you can do. And, even for you, it is a difficult task."

"Devi, please tell me what it is. Even if I must sacrifice my life, I'm willing to do it for my husband," I said.

The Devi then said to me, "Here is what you must do: tonight, if you lie on your bed with a man who is not your husband and embrace him and engage with him in love play, your husband's untimely death will pass by him and grab the other man instead. Then your husband will live for a hundred years, but the other man will, one day, suddenly die an untimely death."

So, you see,' the wife said to her lover. 'I called you tonight to save my husband's life. Now you should do with me whatever you desire. I know that the Devi's words will never be false.'

The woman's lover understood the cryptic message she was conveying with her words and silently applauded her cleverness. Then, he took her in his embrace, and the two of them spent the night in carnal pleasure, while the husband, lying on the cold floor under the bed, happily bore it all, thinking about how much his wife loved him.

When day broke, and the wife and her lover finally stepped off the bed, the chariot-maker came out from under it and took his wife in his arms. 'You are blessed, my dear wife,' he said to her. 'And by being your husband, I, too, feel blessed. I'm so grateful to you for being my wife and to your parents and family for giving me such a true wife to grace my home and fulfil my life. Dearest, I was led astray by the wrongful accusations of the townsfolk. That's why I thought of testing you to determine for myself what is true and what is a lie. It is for that reason I had to lie to you about leaving town, when, in fact, my intention was to come here and lie under this bed to check on you. Can you ever forgive me for even thinking that you were at fault? But now I know the truth. People were vilifying you for no reason. They were lying about you. You are actually the best of all wives. Even while you were with another man, your focus was your dharma towards your husband. And you didn't hesitate to carry out such a difficult task to prolong my life and secure me a hundred years with the Devi's grace.'

In this way that fool of a chariot-maker praised his cheating wife and applauded her chaste character. Then, turning to the lover, who was standing nearby, watching the man make a fool of himself, he drew him into his embrace as well, and said, 'Thank you for helping prolong my life. I am favoured by luck because of you. You have done me a great service by being my wife's lover.' And, holding them both in his arms, he did a little jig of happiness. After that, that idiot rode around town in a chariot, with his wife and her lover sitting beside him, bragging to everyone about his wife's chastity.

'So, you see, Maharaj,' Raktaksha said to the owl king, 'how fools are convinced by false justifications, even if they witness something with their own eyes.' Then, turning to his colleagues, he admonished them, 'Your inane advice will wipe us out, because the wise have rightly said,

> Friends who overlook means of welfare
> and guide us towards paths of ruin
> are not friends; they are enemies.

Also,

> Bad advice from ministers who lack
> understanding of time and place
> can expel prosperity from a land
> like the dawn sun dispels darkness.'

However, Raktaksha's words of wisdom and warnings of ruin had little impact on the king and the other ministers. Ignoring him, they all began to carry Sthirajivi inside the fort so that they could tend to his wounds.

'O saviour,' Sthirajivi hailed the owl king in a fake, trembling voice that sounded weak with pain, 'My body is in such a condition that no matter how you care for it, it'll be futile. My wounds are too grave, and it seems that my death is near. What use can I be to you now? I think the best course for me in this last hour is to commit myself to the fire. Please, instead of taking me inside the fort, have a fire built for me.'

Hearing Sthirajivi say this, Raktaksha became even more suspicious. 'Why do you want to commit yourself to the fire and give up your life?' he asked him.

'That Meghavarna had me beaten, because he thought I was siding with the owls. I want to jump into the fire with the desire to become an owl in my next birth, and when I'm born as an owl, I'll avenge myself and teach that Meghavarna a lesson.'

The shrewd Raktaksha saw right through Sthirajivi's pronouncement. 'You are truly an excellent deceiver and very nimble in your lies,' he said to him. 'I know the likes of you. Even if, somehow, you manage to be born in the owl species, you'll have a crow's mind. You can never be a well-wisher of the owls. Let alone in this birth, in every subsequent birth, you will remain our enemy. Listen to this story that people tell about how one retains the predilection of one's own species, no matter how many births one takes,' he said to the other ministers.

> 'Rejecting the sun, clouds, wind, and mountain
> that Chuhiya chose the mouse as her spouse.

Partiality towards one's own kind is a hard habit to give up. Love for one's own kind can't be falsified so easily.'

'What is this story?' the ministers asked Raktaksha, and he told them the tale.

THE TALE OF CHUHIYA'S SELECTION OF A WORTHY HUSBAND

On the banks of the Ganga, where the water crashes on the high and low rocks, frightening the fish, whose acrobatics create rainbow-hued, boisterous waves is an ashram full of high-souled sadhus. They sit on the riverbank, meditating, chanting mantras, and doing all sorts of penance. Among them are also those highly evolved ascetics who survive only on a bit of water and roots, fruit, grass, and moss and wear only one piece of covering, no matter the weather. In that ashram there once lived the great Rishi Yajnavalkya.

One day, after his bath, as Yajnavalkya was taking a sip of water from his cupped palm to cleanse his mouth, a falcon flying in the sky above accidently dropped a mouse it was carrying in its beak, and she landed right in Yajnavalkya's palm. The rishi placed the little creature on a bargad leaf, and, leaving her safely on the bank, went to bathe again. When he returned, he cleansed his mouth and read a mantra that turned the mouse into a little girl. Bringing her to his ashram, he gave her to his wife. 'Here, dear one,' he said to her, 'you keep saying how sad you are that we have no children. See, I have brought you a child—a little girl. She is yours. Take care of her and bring her up with love and care.'

Yajnavalkya's wife joyfully accepted the baby girl and began rearing her with tender, loving care. In this way, twelve years passed, and the girl became of marriageable age.

'Dear husband,' Yajnavalkya's wife said to him one day, 'can't you see that the time of your daughter's marriage has arrived? You should find her a husband before any more time slips by.'

'You're right, dear one,' Yajnavalkya replied. 'I must find her a husband before she becomes pubescent. The spouse I find for her will be from my caste and someone who is worthy of her. It is said,

> A marriage alliance with a family
> of equivalent wealth and status
> is an alliance most likely to succeed.
> It is unwise to have an alliance with one
> wealthier than you or poorer than you.

Also,

> A father should seek these seven qualities
> in his daughter's husband to be:
> humility, affability, helpfulness,
> education, age, good looks,
> and his parents' good reputation.

If all seven can be found in someone, it is a good match. Therefore, in my estimation, Surya will make a perfect husband for our daughter. What do you think?'

'Yes. I agree with your choice,' his wife replied.

'Then, let me invite him,' Yajnavalkya said and chanted the mantras to call Surya. The sun god instantly appeared in the rishi's house. 'O great rishi, why have you called me?' he asked.

'Surya deva, my daughter has reached the age of marriage. I have invited you here so that she can meet you. If she is agreeable to the match, please accept her as your wife.'

Yajnavalkya then summoned his daughter and said to her, 'Dear daughter, do you want to marry Surya deva, who sheds light in the three worlds?'

'Father, he is bright and scorching. I wouldn't like to be married to him.'

Yajnavalkya apologized to Sun and asked him, 'O great one, is there anyone greater than you?'

'Yes. Cloud is greater than me. When he spreads across the sky, even I become invisible.'

And so, the rishi called Cloud and, summoning his daughter, asked her, 'Dear daughter, what do you think about Cloud? Will you accept him as your groom?'

'But Father, look at his dark and foreboding countenance. How can I live with someone who looks like that? Please find me somebody better than him.'

'Dear Cloud, my apologies,' Yajnavalkya said. 'But is there anyone greater than you?'

'Yes,' replied Cloud. 'Vayu is much greater. When the wind strikes me, I splinter into a thousand pieces.'

Therefore, the rishi called Vayu deva and asked his daughter, 'How about him? Is he a suitable husband for you?'

'No, not at all, Father. He is always moving. Look at him; he's never still. I wouldn't be able to live with him. Find me someone more stable.'

When Yajnavalkya asked Vayu if he knew of anyone more stable, he replied. 'Of course. Mountain. No matter how hard I push on him, he doesn't shift even one ratti. All my strength is useless before him.'

The rishi then called Mountain and presented him to his daughter. 'Dear one, should I marry you to this Mountain? Look how strong and stable he is.'

'He looks so stern and inflexible. And he is just rooted to one spot. I can't live my life with him. My husband has to be better than him.'

'Is there someone greater than you?' Yajnavalkya asked Mountain.

'He who is stronger and greater than me is Mouse. He can gnaw through my body and make me crumble.'

Rishi Yajnavalkya then called Mouse and summoned his daughter to meet him. 'Look daughter, this is the king of mice. Do you like him? Would you like to marry him?'

The young woman took one look at Mouse and fell in love. With shining eyes, she exclaimed to the rishi, 'O Father. He is exactly whom I want for my husband. But can you turn me into a chuhiya so that I can be of his kind and fulfil my dharma of being his wife?'

Yajnavalkya then used his ascetic merit to change the girl back into a mouse and married her to her chosen groom.

'That is why I say,' said Raktaksha, 'one never forgets one's own kind. Hence, this crow, though he professes to be hostile to his own kind, will never be our friend.'

However, despite his various arguments, Raktaksha could not dissuade Arimardana and the other ministers, and they carried Sthirajivi inside their fort. And the crafty, old crow, noting the way into the fort, enjoyed a good laugh in his mind, thinking how gullible and stupid the owls were. But he also acknowledged Raktaksha's sharpness. He is the only minister who knows the principles of statecraft and is intelligent, he thought. But, thankfully, no one is interested in what he has to say, which is to my benefit. If they had listened to this Raktaksha's advice and killed me, they would have saved themselves from the destruction that I will bring. Now, no one can save them. By not listening to their wise minister, they themselves have put their whole clan in jeopardy.

When Arimardana, the owl king, reached the gate of his fort, he said to his men, 'This Sthirajivi is our well-wisher, and we welcome him into our fort. Let him roam free and stay wherever he wishes.'

Sthirajivi was delighted by this extra privilege, but, he thought, I have to find a way to destroy these owls. If I live inside the fort, they'll soon find out about my comings and goings; therefore, it's best that I stay near the gate of the fort. Hence, he said to Arimardana, 'Maharaj, thank you for letting me choose where I will stay. However, please allow me to say this: I, too, know, a bit of jurisprudence. I am your natural enemy, although I have become your ardent supporter and greatest devotee. But, even then, it doesn't behove me to stay inside the fort. Please allow me to stay near the gate, outside the fort. I promise to come into your court every day to bow at your august feet and be at your service.'

Sthirajivi's flattering words made the owl king preen his feathers, and he commanded his ministers to have a comfortable place arranged for him near the gate. He also arranged for his own attendants to bring him his meals there, much of it consisting of nourishing meat. In this way, within just a few days, Sthirajivi became as plump and strong as a peacock.

Raktaksha was shocked at the lavish care that his king and fellow ministers were showering on Sthirajivi, and, one day, he couldn't help but say to the king and ministers, 'The way that you are looking after that enemy crow makes me think that you are bigger fools than I thought. This reminds me of that story:

> The number one fool is I.
> In second place is the fowler.
> The king and his ministers are next.
> In fact, this is all a nexus of fools.'

'What is this story?' the ministers asked him, and he narrated the tale.

THE TALE OF THE NEXUS OF FOOLS

In a mountainous region grew a magnificent tree on which lived a marvellous bird called Sindhuka (related to various men). He was a gold-giving bird: as soon as his droppings touched the ground, they turned into gold. One day, as a fowler was wandering around in the area, one of Sindhuka's droppings splattered at his feet, and the blob turned into pure gold. The fowler was astounded. He thought to himself, 'From childhood to now, I've been catching birds for eighty years, but never in my life have I seen a bird whose droppings become gold. What luck that I was able to see it happen today, before my very own eyes.' When he saw the bird flying towards a tree, he quickly spread his net on the branches. The foolish, unsuspecting Sindhuka alighted on it, without a thought, and was, instantly, trapped. Bringing the net down, the bird-catcher caged Sindhuka.

On his way home, the fowler began to think: if I keep this bird with me, I'll put my life in grave danger, because if anyone finds out that its droppings turn into gold, they will inform the king, and the king will summon me and punish me—perhaps even with the gallows. Therefore, it's not safe for me to keep this bird. Why don't I pre-empt the whole situation and just give him to the king myself?

Hence, the fowler went and gifted the bird to the king. The king was delighted to have such a bird and commanded his men, 'Soldiers, protect this bird with your life. Also, make sure he is fed the best of foods and given the sweetest and coolest water to quench his thirst.'

Hearing his orders, one of the ministers objected, 'Maharaj, it is not wise to believe this lowly, uncivilized fowler. Just because he says the bird's droppings turn into gold, doesn't mean it is so. I think it would be a waste of time and energy to cage this ordinary-looking bird and take care of it. It is very unlikely that he defecates gold.'

The king didn't want to appear like a fool in front of his men, so he had the bird released. Freed from the cage, the bird flew to the door, and, perching on the jamb, made a dropping that turned into gold as soon as it touched the floor.

Then, the bird spoke: 'The first fool was I who got trapped in the net; the second fool was the bird-catcher, who, even after he caught me, didn't keep me; after that, the king, too, is a fool, who listened to his minister and let me go. I would say that all the king's ministers are also fools, because they should have checked to see if the bird-catcher's words were true or not. So, this is really a nexus of fools. No one is wise here.'

Thus, declaring everyone a fool, the bird flew off into the sky to its desired destination.

'That is why I say, our owl king and his ministers are fools, because they themselves are empowering the enemy,' Raktaksha concluded.

Still, the king of owls and his ministers disregarded Raktaksha's advice and continued to feed the crow healthy food to aid his recovery.

Frustrated at the thick-headedness of the king and the ministers, Raktaksha called his relatives and close friends together, and said to them, 'I think our king's ability to protect us is in doubt. Also, I don't think that after today, our fort will be safe. As a royal minister, I gave the king advice about the dangers of harbouring an enemy. I also tried convincing him as much as I could, but he is just not willing to listen. Sadly, I have to tell you all that this may be the end of our king and our fort. Therefore, we should leave this place as soon as possible and find another, safer place. Each moment here is fraught with danger. It is said,

> He who carefully considers,
> before proceeding with action,
> enjoys success and happiness.
> He who acts without thought
> is left with nothing but regrets.
> I have grown old in this forest,
> and never have I heard the cave speak.'

'What is this story?' Raktaksha's friends and relatives asked, and he narrated the tale.

THE TALE OF THE SPEAKING CAVE

In a forest lived a lion called Kharankhara (sharp claws). Once, unable to find a single animal to prey on all day, he was distraught with hunger and thirst, when he found himself near a deep cave. Surely, surely, this cave belongs to a creature who will return at night to rest, he thought. Why don't I go inside and hide? As soon as that creature comes in, I'll kill him and eat him. And so the lion went into the cave and hid.

Later in the evening, the resident of the cave, a jackal called Dadhipuchh (curved tail), came home. Seeing lion footprints outside the cave, he became wary, especially when he noticed that while there were prints going towards the entrance, none were returning. 'Oh no! There is a lion in my cave,' he said to himself. 'How can I go inside?' But then he thought, how can I be sure that he is still inside. What if he left? I need to verify this. Thinking of a plan, he stood at a safe distance from the entrance of the cave and called loudly, 'O cave! O cave!' After a few moments of silence, he repeated, 'O cave! O cave!' When the silence remained unbroken, he said, 'O cave, have you forgotten our agreement—that every time I return, I'll call you before I enter, and you'll respond to me, so that I can enter? Now if you don't respond to my calls, I'll leave here and find another cave. I've been calling you, but you haven't responded even once.'

Hearing the jackal's words, the lion began to think: this cave seems to have made an agreement with the jackal, and it appears that every time the jackal returns, he calls the cave and the cave answers back. And today the cave is not responding because I've frightened it. Someone has rightly said,

> Hands and feet cease functioning,
> speech becomes a stutter,
> the body shivers in excess,
> when fear bewilders one's mind.

Therefore, since the cave is silent because of me, let me respond to the jackal. He'll think it is the cave, and that will satisfy him. Then he'll come inside, and I'll kill him. Thus, the lion called out to the jackal in his loudest voice. It was a roar so big that it not only filled the cave, but also it echoed in the farthest corners of the forest, making countless creatures quiver in fear. Hearing it, the jackal, took off into the forest saying,

> 'He who carefully considers
> before proceeding with action,
> enjoys success and happiness.
> He who acts without thought
> is left with nothing but regrets.
> I have grown old in this forest;
> never have I heard the cave speak.'

After telling this story, Raktaksha said to his friends and relatives, 'So you see, our fort, like that cave, has become dangerous, and every moment in it brings us closer to peril. It seems that the time of our king's doom has arrived. But we can save ourselves. Come with me; let's all go to a faraway land.' That night, many of Raktaksha's relatives left with him.

Sthirajivi was very pleased to learn about the departure of the astute Raktaksha. How fortuitous for us, he thought, that the only minister who was prescient and judicious in the owl court should decide to leave. All the other ministers are gullible fools. Now I can bring my plan to fruition without any opposition. It is said,

> The king who lacks ministers,
> farsighted and well-versed in polity
> will undoubtedly be soon destroyed.
> This fact is as definite as the polar star.

Also, the wise rightly say,

> Ministers who pursue a path
> contrary to what the shastras say
> are enemies disguised as well-wishers.

From then on, living in his nest outside the fort, Sthirajivi began to implement his plan. Every day, while the owls were confined to the fort, he gathered dry pieces of wood, and, one by one, piled them up near the gate. The owls noticed this stockpile of wood, but instead of questioning him about it, they just assumed that he was collecting twigs to expand his nest. Not for a moment did they think that it was to burn down the cave fortress in which they lived.

Someone has rightly said,

> When fate turns against you,
> even your mind stops thinking.

> You make enemies of your friends
> and treat friends like enemies.
> Then auspicious seems inauspicious,
> and evil action appears as good.
> Adversity brings this reversal of good sense.

When the wood pile reached the top of the fortress gate, Sthirajivi began to prepare for the final destruction. One morning, at daybreak, when all the owls were inside their cave blinded, the crow flew to his king, Meghavarna, and, updating him on his progress, said, 'Maharaj, I have stacked up a huge pile of dry wood at the gate of the enemy fort. Please gather our community and order each crow to bring a burning twig from a forest fire and throw it on the pile. I've stacked the wood so high that the blaze will be tremendous, leaving no escape route for even a single owl. They will all be incinerated inside the cave, as though suffering the tortures of Kumbhipaka.'

'Uncle, it is good to see you. How have you been?' Meghavarna started to say.

'This is no time for idle niceties,' Sthirajivi said, impatiently. 'What if some spy from the enemy camp has followed me here and has heard about our plan to burn down their cave. Even now he could be flying back to inform Arimardana. Then, everything I've accomplished so far will have been in vain, and we'll have to abort the plan. So, hurry up and give the order. There is no time to waste. It is said,

> A task needing immediate completion
> when delayed for some asinine reasons
> angers even the gods so much
> that they wreck it in its entirety.
> Hence, do what needs done right away.

Also, it is said,

> A task, especially result-oriented,
> not accomplished in good time,
> gives up the sweetness of its fruit
> to the consumption of Time.
> What results is a dried-up fruit,
> lacking the juicy joy of success.

Go and finish the task. After you have successfully destroyed your enemies, I'll sit with you, feeling relaxed, and tell you all about my time with the owls.'

Following Sthirajivi's directions, Meghavarna commanded all his crows to each collect one burning stick from a forest fire and fling it on the stack of dry wood at the gate of the owl fortress.

Soon the owl cave was aflame, and those owls, unable to escape through the blaze, bemoaning Sthirajivi's deception and cursing their own gullibility, turned to ashes inside their cave.

Freed from the threat of owls, Meghavarna returned to his ancestral home in the bargad tree, along with all the other crows. There, he held a great celebration to be re-crowned king of crows and to honour Sthirajivi. During the event, when everyone in the court was seated, he asked Sthirajivi, 'Please tell us how you spent your time among the enemy. I'm really curious about this, because I've heard that for noble and faithful servants of the king, spending even a moment in the company of the enemy is worse than being burnt alive in a fire. Consorting with the enemy is unbearable for them. Then how did you manage it?'

'Maharaj,' said Sthirajivi, 'when one has dedicated one's life to service of the king and is working towards a goal, then what is suffering in the line of duty? It is also said,

> When a person is faced with danger,
> he must think of an effective way out
> to save himself as painlessly as possible
> by using intelligence and decisiveness.

Remember,

> Arjuna, the holder of the Gandiva bow,
> whose fingers were deeply scarred
> from constantly pulling the bowstring,
> whose arms were muscled and rounded,
> like the powerful trunk of an elephant?
> Even he had to wear bangles on his wrists
> and dance and entertain as Brihannala
> to spend his days of hiding in Virata's palace.

> A wise person, though powerful he may be,
> in the quest of seeking an opportunity,
> should not hesitate to spend his time
> with the uncivilized, lowly, and of brash speech.
> Did not the most powerful Bhimasena

live in the kitchen of Matsya king, Virata,
wielding the ladle, face blackened with smoke?

Thus, when one finds oneself in hardship, one should be willing to do anything—good or bad—with eyes closed, waiting for the right moment.

> To achieve a desired objective,
> a wise person should conceal
> his pride and natural brilliance,
> his prowess, zeal, and talent
> and continue to work with patience,
> till destiny becomes favourable.
> Even the great dharmavira, Yudhishthira,
> whose brothers were brave and glorious,
> like the gods, Indra, Kubera, and Yamaraja,
> had to live in disguise as a poor ascetic,
> suffering many insults in King Virata's court.
>
> The handsome, noble, and very powerful
> sons of Kunti, Nakula, and Sahadeva,
> also spent their time of adversity
> working for a living as cowherds.
>
> Extraordinarily beauteous and youthful,
> replete with the best of qualities,
> born in the noble royal family of Panchala,
> radiant and graceful, like Lakshmi incarnate,
> Draupadi, the wife of the five Pandavas,
> also suffered the effects of fate's reversal.
>
> "Arrey, Saurandhri, do this; do that;
> grind sandal and make a paste for me—"
> such lowly orders she received as a servant.
> Didn't she suffer it all as fate's demand?'

Listening to Sthirajivi, Meghavarna stated, 'Uncle, staying with an enemy and then achieving your goal—this is as difficult a task as walking on the sharp edge of sword.'

'What you are saying is absolutely right, Maharaj,' Sthirajivi replied. 'Staying among the enemy is, indeed, as exacting as walking on the edge of a sword. But the group of complete idiots that I met in the enemy camp—

I've never seen the like before. I've also never met anyone with as acute an intelligence as their farsighted minister, Raktaksha. He was the only one among the ministers, who knew my truth, instantly. As soon as he saw me, he knew I was there to deceive the owls. But other than him, every owl I met was an imbecile. Or, perhaps, they were ministers in name only, serving the king only to fill their own bellies. But, overall, Arimardana's court was full of utter fools and ignoramuses, who didn't know the first thing about politics.

> An enemy servant who says
> he has deserted his master,
> or has had a fight with him,
> is evil and never to be trusted.
> With you he wishes to stay, but why?
> To serve as his master's spy?
> Beware a man such as this.
> Never employ a man who has
> lived in the house of the enemy.
> Never ever put your trust in him,
> no matter how carefully you live.
> Enemy spies wait and watch and
> strike where you least expect it—
> your seat, bed, food, vehicle, and
> your times of leisure, your means
> to acquire artha, dharma, and kama.
> The wise are they who protect
> themselves with utter vigilance.

Someone has rightly said,

> Anyone who eats and drinks for pleasure
> is careless and often invites sickness.
> A king whose ministers lack learning
> is likely to see errors in diplomacy.
> Who is not made arrogant with wealth?
> Who does not die at Death's hand?
> Who is not pained with lustful desires?
>
> A covetous man forfeits his good name.
> A bad karma forfeits many good works.
> A man in business forfeits his education.

> A miser forfeits his happiness for money.
> A king whose retainers are careless, unwise,
> short-sighted, and scatter-brained,
> forfeits his kingdom by retaining them.

O king, you're right when you said living among enemies was as hard as walking a sword's edge. I have experienced this with my own body. It is said,

> A wise person should pursue his desire
> even at the cost of pride, ideals, and respect,
> because it is foolish not to see a task through.
> The wise even carry an enemy on their shoulders,
> like that black serpent who carried frogs on his back
> to later have thousands of them for his consumption.'

'What is this story, uncle?' Meghavarna asked, and Sthirajivi told him the tale.

THE TALE OF WHY THE SERPENT BECAME THE VEHICLE OF FROGS

In Varunadri Mountains there was a region where an aged serpent called Mandavisha (mild venom) lived. One evening, he thought, what can I do that will ensure for me a regular livelihood and food supply but with the least amount of effort? After considering various options, he decided on a plan. Going to a large lake that was filled with frogs, he sat down by its side in a loose coil and put on an expression of sadness.

Swimming near that side, a frog, seeing the serpent looking sad and sluggish, asked, 'Uncle, why aren't you catching frogs today? Aren't you hungry?'

'Dear son, how can I? With my bad luck, I can't even attempt to hunt for food today. I'll tell you what happened to me last evening. I was wandering here and there looking for food, when I saw a frog. To catch him, I spread my hood, but even as I was about to catch him, he leapt into a group of brahmins who were chanting evening mantras, and disappeared. Searching for him among the bare feet of the brahmins, I mistook the toe of a brahmin boy as the mouth of the frog and bit it. That brahmin boy died instantly. His father was so angry and upset that he cursed me. "Wicked serpent," he said, "you bit my innocent boy for no reason at all. This is your punishment: from today you'll be a vehicle of frogs. And you will only eat what those frogs give you in charity." So, you see, son, today I'm not here to catch any of you for food; instead, I'm here to give you and your kin a ride. Consider me your vehicle.'

As soon as the frog heard this, he dived into the water, excitedly calling his friends and relatives to tell them what the serpent had told him. The other frogs were jubilant at finding out that he who used to hunt them and eat them would now be carrying them on his back and that they need not be afraid of him any more. The news of this spread rapidly through the frog community, and it also reached the ears of the king of frogs, Jalapada (walking in the water).

Jalapada summoned his ministers to share with them this incredible news. 'The serpent is now our vehicle,' he exclaimed. 'Let me be the first to climb on his back.' Then he swam to the side of the lake where Mandavisha was

was now lying uncoiled and, with a leap, jumped on to his back. The other frogs followed him, in order of their rank and status, and spread across the serpent's body, from his head to his tail, and those who couldn't find room on his back, ran behind him, as he glided away.

To show how committed he was to being the frogs' mount, Mandavisha made this first ride as fun-filled as he could, varying his pace from fast to slow, and his glide from side to side and undulating. The frogs were highly entertained. Jalapada, who was luxuriating in the feel of the serpent's soft, smooth skin under him, said to the snake, 'What a novel experience. Not on an elephant, not on a horse, not in a chariot, not on a boat, and not even on a human have I enjoyed myself as much as I am enjoying this ride on your back.'

The following morning, Mandavisha once again came to the lake to give the frogs a ride, but this time, when the king of frogs climbed on his back, he kept his movement slow and sluggish. 'Why are so slow this morning?' Jalapada asked.

'Maharaj, today, I don't have the energy to move. I haven't had a morsel of food in many days.'

'Oh, I see,' said Jalapada, and then added offhandedly. 'You have my permission to eat the frogs that are of the lowest rank.'

'Thank you, Maharaj,' the serpent replied in a deeply respectful tone. 'That is exactly the condition of the brahmin's curse. I can't even touch a frog without permission and can only eat what you give me. By giving me permission to eat, you've made me very happy. Now I'll be able to give you a jaunty ride.'

After that day, the serpent began to eat his way through the frog ranks, devouring delicious frog meat whenever he wished. He continued to provide rides to the king and high officials, laughing in his mind at the naiveté of the frogs, humming under his breath,

> 'Trapped in my net of deceit,
> these frogs of varying tastes
> and plentiful in number
> are my food for a long time.'

Once, Jalapada asked him the words to the song he was humming, but Mandavisha made up some false lyrics. In this way, the foolish frog king, delighting in his daily rides, continued to believe the wily serpent's manipulations, while he gobbled up dozens of frogs every day, without even having to hunt them.

One day, another huge serpent happened to come to that lake. Seeing one of his own kind carrying around frogs on his back, he was aghast. He waited till Mandavisha had dropped off his passengers and then asked, 'How is it that you are carrying frogs on your back; they are our food. Isn't this against accepted behaviours?'

'Friend, I know that I'm breaking conventional laws by carrying frogs on my back, but not for long. The truth is,

> I am waiting for the right moment,
> like that ghee-blinded brahmin,
> who kept waiting for opportunity.'

'What is this story?' the second serpent asked, and Mandavisha told him the tale.

THE TALE OF THE GHEE-BLINDED BRAHMIN

In a town lived a brahmin by the name of Yagyadatta, whose wife was carrying on a clandestine affair. Every day, she would make sweet dishes, like malpua and ghevar, with plenty of ghee and sugar, and sneak them out of the house to give to her lover.

Yagyadatta was ignorant of his wife's liaison, until one day when he saw his wife make the dishes and surreptitiously carry them out of the house. Becoming suspicious, he began to spy on her, and, finally, one morning, as she was preparing the treats, he confronted her: 'Who are you making all these ghee-soaked sweet dishes for, and where do you go every day? You better tell me the truth.'

The woman was very clever and quick thinking. 'Dear husband,' she replied. 'Nearby is a temple of Devi Bhagawati. Every day, I make these various sweet dishes as prasad and take them to the temple to offer worship to the devi.'

The brahmin pretended to accept her story and let her go, but as soon as she stepped out of the house, he began to follow her. The woman was too shrewd to be caught in that trap; therefore, that day, she headed straight for the devi temple. Leaving the food at the door to the shrine, she went to the river to bathe and stayed in the water long enough to ensure that her husband's suspicion had been allayed. However, her husband, too, was not so gullible. After his wife went to bathe, he hid behind the devi's idol.

Returning to the temple, the wife quickly completed her worship with flower garlands, incense, and puja, and then, standing before the devi idol with folded hands and bowed head, she said, 'Hey Devi Bhagawati, is there a way that my husband can become blind so that he can't interfere in my business?'

'Yes, child, there is,' replied her husband, imitating a female voice. 'If you feed your husband sweet dishes every day, like these made with ghee and sugar, he will soon go blind.'

The woman fell at Bhagavati's feet and thanked her for showing her a way. From that day on, she began to make delicious malpua and ghevar sweets soaked in ghee and sugar for her husband.

One day the brahmin said to his wife, 'Dear wife. I don't know what the matter is, but I can't see very well.'

The wife was thrilled to hear this and profusely thanked Devi Bhagawati in her mind. After that, she doubled the quantity of sweet dishes that she fed her husband. She also became more fearless and began meeting her lover again. Her lover, too, convinced that the brahmin was turning blind, began to visit the wife in her house.

On the other hand, the brahmin himself, eating such rich food every day, began to gain weight and became stronger and bulkier. Then, one day, when his wife's lover came into the house, he grabbed him by the hair and, forcefully, flung him to the floor. Then he kicked him and boxed him and beat him so much that he died on the spot. After that, he cut off his wife's nose and turned her out into the street.

'Just like that ghee-blinded brahmin, I'm waiting for the right moment,' Mandavisha said to the other serpent. 'Then, I'll finish off all the frogs.'

Satisfied with Mandavisha's reason for his unconventional behaviour, the other snake went on his way, and Mandavisha resumed his daily pursuit of giving rides to the higher echelon of frogs and eating the ones of low status. He also resumed his humming:

> Trapped in my net of deceit,
> these frogs of varying tastes
> and plentiful in number
> are my food for a long time.

Once, it so happened that, inadvertently, his voice became louder, and Jalapada heard the words of the song's first line. Agitated by what that could imply, he asked Mandavisha, 'What is that you just said about trapping us in your net of deceit? How can you say such thing?'

'No, no, Maharaj,' Mandavisha tried to pacify him. 'You heard wrong. That is not what I said. I can't even think of such a thing. As you know, there's a brahmin's curse on me, and I'm wholly dependent on your charity.'

Thus, Mandavisha was able to cajole Jalapada into trusting him again.

'What else can be said about this tale?' said Sthirajivi to Meghavarna.

'As you can imagine, Mandavisha, the serpent, kept the frogs lulled with his lies and enjoyable rides, while slowly devouring the whole clan, one frog at a time, till no frog remained in that lake. So, you see, Maharaj, if letting the enemy ride on your shoulders, as Mandavisha did, helps you achieve your goal of destroying the enemy, then you should not hesitate to do it, and, when the time is right, you should deliver the final death blow. Also, just like

Mandavisha emptied the lake of those frogs, I, too, was able to destroy the enemy in his cave. Somebody has rightly said,

> A forest fire turns to ashes
> all the trees in the forest,
> leaving every root intact.
> But when floodwaters come,
> they pull out even the roots.

Similarly, strategies to destroy the enemy can have the hotness of a blazing forest fire, or the coolness of floodwaters. While a hot strategy only kills the soldiers in battle, the cold strategy, like the flood, while appearing to be cool, uproots and thoroughly destroys the enemy.'

'Uncle,' said Meghavarna. 'I agree with what you're saying. I also know that great men, who are high-thinking and resolute, always follow through on tasks they take up, because it is said,

> The greatness of great men,
> experts in policy and diplomacy,
> is that whatever task they accept,
> they never leave it incomplete,
> no matter how toilsome it is.

On the other hand, as someone has said,

> The weak and lowly when given a task,
> daunted by the thought of its hurdles,
> do not even brave a beginning.
> A cut above them are they who begin,
> but no sooner do they face hurdles,
> lose heart and abandon the task.
> The best quality of men are they
> who, no matter the hindrance or pain,
> always finish the task they have started.

Like the latter kind of men, you destroyed my enemy, Uncle, and removed the thorn that was causing us pain. It is clear that you are an expert in policy and strategy. The wise say,

> He who never leaves
> the remainder of debt,
> the remainder of fire,

the remainder of the enemy,
the remainder of disease,
but destroys them utterly,
does not suffer sorrow or regret.'

'Maharaj, you are very fortunate,' Sthirajivi said, 'that your work is being accomplished so swiftly and with such ease. But do remember that tasks are not accomplished with just valour; sharp intelligence is the weapon that procures total success. It is said,

The enemy killed by weapons
is not truly dead.
Only intelligence can bring about
true destruction.

Weapons can only kill a warrior.
Intelligence can destroy his clan,
his fame, his fortune, his good name.
When both weapons and intelligence
are employed to accomplish tasks,
success comes without effort.

When advancement is destined,
a person's intellect feels inclined
to start new tasks of gain.
Memory becomes focused,
money becomes available,
and resources are easy to obtain.
None of his plans meet failure.
His thoughts are clear and true,
his mind is mature and progressive,
and he is interested in gainful tasks.

The charitable, valorous, and wise
are drawn to others of high qualities
and acquire those virtues themselves.
A virtuous man attracts riches and wealth.
And wealth begets fame, éclat, and glory.
Land follows the commands of glory.
And all these together court kingships.
This is how kingdoms are acquired.'

'I can see, Uncle, how fruitful it is to learn Nitishastra. It was because of your knowledge of policy that you were able to implement such a brilliant plan—becoming friends with the enemy and living with them, only to destroy them. I am grateful that you have rid my kingdom of the constant threat that those owls posed.'

'What I did by becoming friends with the enemy and destroying them was the right action. If a task that requires bloodshed can be accomplished by first trying peaceful means of friendship and trust, then that is what should be done.

> Before felling a tree in the forest,
> be it the highest and the best,
> one must honour it with puja,
> before the act of its cutting.

If a tree should be worshipped before it is cut down, what can one say about a king. That is why I propitiated Arimardana and served him, and then, when I got the opportunity, I did what I had to do. Also know,

> The plan that cannot be implemented,
> or whose implementation is difficult,
> is not a plan worthy of consideration.
> The best plans and strategies are
> easily availed and easily accomplished.
> An able minister of policy is he who
> can devise plans of achievable triumph.

Somebody has rightly said,

> Indecisive ministers who shirk work
> and express doubt at every step,
> or find a thousand faults in each plan,
> are often advisers of fruitless plans.
> Their advice only evokes mockery.
> Able, decisive, fearless, diligent ministers
> give advice that never fails to bring results.

Also,

> Even the smallest task must be undertaken
> with the best efforts and calculated plans.
> For each task, success or failure is at stake.'

'Maharaj,' continued Sthirajivi, 'I'm gratified that I was able to accomplish what I did. Hopefully, today our Maharaj will finally sleep peacefully, knowing the enemy is destroyed.

> How can one sleep a good night's sleep
> in a place where a snake has been sighted?
> But if the snake is caught, or is killed,
> how sweet the sleep in that safe place.

Also, it has been said,

> Big endeavours that need much planning
> and painstaking, relentless, hard work,
> endeavours for which one seeks blessings
> from teachers, elders, and well-wishers;
> endeavours which require keen policy
> and promise veritable benefits for many;
> endeavours one wishes oneself to undertake—
> unless these endeavours reach completion,
> how can the hearts of great men that are
> eager, valorous, assiduous, motivated,
> and filled with impatience to finish the work
> have room for the leisure of peace and content?

In truth, I, too, am experiencing a sense of peace. But, Maharaj, you should now start thinking about the welfare of the enemy land that has been evacuated by your enemies. With appropriate rituals of whisk, crown, and umbrella, take the throne as the new king, announce an heir to establish a stable government, and set up a system to care for the subjects of the land.

> The king who does not protect his people
> is as useless as a teat hanging from a ewe's neck.

> And the king devoted to virtue,
> who shuns drink, hunt, and women
> but welcomes meritorious ministers
> shines amidst the swishing of whisks
> and sparkles under the jewelled umbrella
> for a long, long time to come.

And, Maharaj, I also advise you not to become deluded with thoughts, such as, "I am the king; my enemies are all destroyed, and I have nothing to fear." Watch yourself. Don't let the intoxication of wealth make you arrogant, because,

> Sitting on a throne
> is like climbing a bamboo.
> While the climb is arduous,
> falling off is quick and easy.
> Royal glory is also capricious;
> like mercury, it is slippery.
> no matter how you hold it,
> it slips away every time.
> Like water on a lotus leaf,
> it does not attach to anyone.
> It is as quick-moving as wind.
> Just like with low-minded friends
> a relationship is never firm, and
> just like a snake is difficult to charm,
> so is royal wealth hard to serve.
>
> From the moment a king is enthroned,
> worries and hardships become his due,
> as though the urns of his ritual bath
> pour hardships on him along with water.

Hence, know that a king's throne comes with worry. But in this world, who is worry-free, or who can escape hardships?

> Knowing Shri Rama's fourteen-year exile;
> the powerful King Bali's confinement;
> the forest sojourn of the five Pandavas;
> the internecine destruction of the Yadavas;
> Raja Nala's expulsion from his kingdom;
> the heroic Arjuna dancing as a eunuch
> and teaching dance to royal princesses;
> the ruination of the powerful Ravana—
> this is what comes to mind: fate and time
> are the two in control of what happens.
> All men suffer hardships due to them.
> No one is yours; no one will protect you.
> Fate and Time make or break a man.

> Remember, Raja Dasharatha,
> invited to share Indra's heavenly throne?
> Raja Sagar, who measured the ocean?
> King Prithu churned from his father's right arm,
> who cleared the earth for cities and towns?
> Where are these great kings today?
> Winning victory over the three worlds,
> Raja Mandhata—where is he now?
> Nuhusha, who replaced Indra in heaven,
> and Manu, the son of Surya—where are they?
> Today, no one remembers they existed.
> It was Great Time that gave them fame
> and then erased all traces of their name.

We have to accept that:

> These great kings, these illustrious men,
> who used to be accompanied by crores of
> elephants, horses, chariots, and warriors,
> who Indra, himself, used to invite to heaven,
> were conjured up by the power of Time
> And Time it was who made them vanish.

> And along with them also vanished
> their wisest and ablest of ministers,
> their beautiful, intoxicating women,
> their bejewelled, magnificent palaces,
> their gardens, groves, and leisure lakes.
> All gone, stung by the serpent of Time.

O king, do not get caught up in the illusionary lustre of royal wealth and glory, which sways back and forth, like the ears of an intoxicated elephant. Hence, it will be your grave error if you let it go to your head. Enjoy it but don't lose sight of the path of truth and justice.'

Here ends Kakolukiyam, the third tantra of the *Panchatantra*. Its opening shloka was thus,

> Don't trust an enemy of yore,
> even if he comes as a friend.
> Heed! A cave full of owls,

all burnt alive in a fire
set aflame by the crows—
present friends but past foes.

FOURTH TANTRA
LABDHA PRANASHA
Loss of Acquired Gains

Let's start the fourth tantra, Labdha Pranasha, and here is the shloka to begin it:

> He who has acuity of mind when needful
> can escape even the inescapable,
> like the monkey stuck in waters vast,
> who escaped by dint of his intelligence.

There was once a mighty jamun tree, always laden with the sweetest of fruits, growing beside the ocean. On that tree lived a monkey called Raktamukha (ruddy face). One day, a crocodile named Karalamukha (big-toothed) came out of the water near that jamun tree and stretched out on the soft sand.

'Dear guest,' Raktamukha called down to him, 'welcome to my residence. Let me give you some sweet jamuns for your refreshment. It is said,

> Friend or foe, fool or pundit—
> a guest who comes
> at the time of a meal
> is the path to heaven.

I have heard that feeding this guest, opens the doors to heaven.

> A guest that arrives at your house
> at the conclusion of evening rituals,
> ask not his gotra, caste, or learning.
> Whoever he is, he is worship-worthy,
> an honoured guest who should be fed.
> This is what Manu says in Manusmriti.

> He who feeds and cares for a guest travelling long,
> wearied from the journey, arriving at your door
> for the evening meal, gains heaven after death.
> And the house from which a guest leaves unwelcomed,
> sighing, disappointed, hunger still burning in his belly,
> is shunned by both ancestors and gods alike.'

Saying these words, the monkey began to throw down sweet juicy fruits to the crocodile. Catching the jamuns in his mouth and relishing them, the crocodile, too, thoroughly appreciated the monkey's gesture. Thereafter, the two of them started talking and enjoyed each other's company until sundown. Then the crocodile, realizing how late it was, said goodbye to his new friend. The next day, the crocodile came again and lay down on the sand, under the cool shade of the tree, and he and the monkey spent another day talking and eating jamuns. In this way, Raktamukha, the monkey, and Karalamukha, the crocodile, became very good friends, spending every day together, telling stories, laughing, joking, while eating the sweet, juicy jamuns from the tree.

Every evening, when Karalamukha left, he would take with him the remainder of his share of jamuns and bring them to his wife. One morning, as he was getting ready to go and meet his friend, his wife asked him, 'From where do you get these delicious, sweet fruits every day?'

'Dear wife,' replied the crocodile, 'I have a very dear friend called Raktamukha. Due to the love and affection he bears me, he treats me to these fruits every day. He plucks these from the tree on which he lives.'

'Dear husband, I've been thinking that the creature who eats these sweet fruits regularly, how sweet and delicious his heart must be, like immortalizing amrita. If you love me and care for me, bring me his heart to eat. I'm certain that after eating that, old age and sickness will never come to me. Then, I can continue to enjoy many more of life's pleasures with you.'

'What are you saying, wife?' the crocodile was shocked. 'I can't take his heart. I've made him my oath-brother. Besides, doesn't he do enough of a favour to us by sharing his fruits every day? How can I even think of killing him? So, please stop thinking these thoughts and saying these things to me. It is said in the shastras,

> One brother is born from your mother's womb
> and another is made through spoken words.
> From these, the oath-brother is far more valued
> than a brother who shares your blood and mother.'

'Dearest, you have never before refused me anything,' Karalamukha's wife said to him with a pout. 'What is the matter today? Or, perhaps, that monkey you go to see every day is not a male but a female monkey. Maybe that's why you spend the whole day there. Now I see the truth, because,

> Neither do you speak sweet nothings to me.
> nor do you fulfil my heart's desires as before.
> At night you sigh deeply with breath as hot as fire,
> and your embraces are now cold and listless.
> Your kisses, too, have lost their forceful desire.
> It is clear from these signs that you love another.'

The crocodile could hardly believe what his wife was saying, but she was clearly upset, and he knew he had to appease her. Falling at her feet, he pleaded with folded hands and then gathered her onto his lap and cajoled her. 'Dearest, beloved wife, you know I am your servant, always ready to follow your command. If I have done anything wrong to displease you, please forgive me. Don't be angry with me. You know I love you.'

The crocodile's wife began to cry and big, fat tears rolled down her cheeks. 'You cheat,' she cried. 'Stop with these false professions of love. I can see that this other female, who is probably beautiful and charming, now lives in your heart, and you—caught in her romantic trap—are constantly making plans about how to fulfil your lascivious desires. When your heart is filled with that other woman, where is there room for me? Stop falling at my feet and embracing me and cajoling me, pretending you love me. Your heart and mind are stuck on this other female. And, if what you say is true and you're not attracted to her, then why aren't you agreeing to do what I asked? If this monkey is not a female, then tell me what sort of attachment do you have with him that you can refuse me—your wife? Who is he to you and why won't you kill him for me?'

'Dearest....' the crocodile began to say, to somehow explain his friendship with the monkey, but the wife would not let him speak.

'I don't want to hear or say anything more,' she stated emphatically. 'Except this—I vow that until I eat that monkey's heart, I will not put another morsel of food in my mouth, and you can watch me slowly die.'

'Oh no, my dearest wife, don't say that. Please take back your vow,' the crocodile begged, worry writ large on his face, wondering in his mind what he could do to make her change her mind. What should I do now? he asked himself. It seemed she had left him no choice. 'I'll have to kill that monkey,' he said to himself. 'But how can I do it? Somebody has rightly said,

> Glue, fool, woman, fish, and the colour blue—
> once they grab something, they don't let go.'

Thinking these thoughts, Karalamukha left his home and went to see Raktamukha. Sitting in his tree, watching the ocean, waiting for his friend, the monkey had been wondering what was keeping the crocodile, and when he arrived, but did not even call out a greeting, the monkey knew something was wrong. 'Dear friend,' he said. 'Why did you get so delayed today? And why are you not smiling and talking, or telling me which poem you'll read to me today? What is the matter?'

'Friend,' replied the crocodile, 'today your sister-in-law, my wife, was very upset with me. She said that I come here every day and enjoy your fruits and company, but I never pay it back. I never invite you to our home to show you our hospitality. She called me ungrateful and warned that the shastras enjoin strict penance for those who are not grateful. She is so angry with me that she has told me not to show her my face again, unless you are with me. This is what she said,

> "There is penance to atone for the sin of
> killing a brahmin, drinking alcohol,
> breaking a vow, and doing wicked acts,
> But for the ingrate, there is no penance."

Therefore, she has told me that today I must bring her brother-in-law—that is you—to our home, to return the favour, otherwise she'll give up her life. So, dear friend, I have come here at my wife's insistence, to invite you to our home. Please come with me. Your sister-in-law is making all kinds of preparations to welcome you. She's drawing auspicious rangoli in our courtyard and hanging flower garlands at the entrance. She herself is wearing new clothes and is adorned in ornaments to honour you. And she's eagerly awaiting your arrival, her eyes glued to the door.'

The monkey was delighted to hear the crocodile's invitation. 'Dear friend,' he said, 'my sister-in-law is right in sending you to me to with an invite, because it is said,

> Gives and takes,
> tells him secrets,
> asks his secrets,
> eats his food,
> invites him for food—
> these are the six signs of affection.

But, dear friend, I have a concern: I am a land dweller, and your home is in the water. How can I go there? Why don't you bring my sister-in-law here instead? That way I can bow at her feet and take her blessing.'

'Our house is not in the water,' the crocodile quickly explained. 'It's on the bank of a small, verdant island in the middle of the ocean. It is true that you have to cross an expanse of the water to get there, but I have a solution for that. If you climb on my back, I can take you there. All you have to do is sit comfortably on my back and enjoy the ride.'

'If that is so, then we shouldn't keep sister-in-law waiting. Let's go,' the monkey said, leaping from the tree onto the crocodile's back.

Losing no time, Karalamukha slipped into the water and began swimming as fast as he could towards his home. The waves of the ocean, moved by the wind and his rapid motion, rose around him and slapped against the monkey, making his perch on the crocodile's back quite precarious. 'Friend,' he called in a panicked voice, 'can you please go slowly? The ocean has such big waves, and I'm drenched. Also, your back is slick, and I'm afraid that I'll slip off and fall into the water and drown.'

The crocodile thought to himself, I should tell him my intention now. We're in the middle of the ocean. He can't make the slightest, sesame seed of a movement, or he'll fall. Even if I tell him, where will he go? I should tell him now so that he can at least spend his last moments thinking about his god. Hence, the crocodile said to the monkey, 'Friend, I have brought you here under false pretences. My wife made me do it. All that I said about my wife inviting you to our home as a guest is a lie. The fact is, I've brought you here to kill you. I'm telling you this so that you can offer your last prayers.'

The crocodile's words hit the monkey like a bolt of lightning. For a moment, he was speechless, then in a woeful voice he said, 'Brother. What wrong have I done to you or to your wife that you have orchestrated this plan to do me in?'

'My wife ate some of the amrita-sweet jamuns that I brought back with me, and now she wants to eat your heart, which she thinks must be as sweet as pure amrita, because you eat this fruit every day. Like a pregnant woman who has food cravings, she has suddenly developed this hankering. That is why I have to kill you, so that I can take your heart to her, and that is why I had to orchestrate this plan.'

The monkey was heartbroken that his friend was willing to kill him just to please his wife, but he had no time to dwell on his feelings. What he needed to do was to come up with an immediate plan of escape, and being the quick thinker that he was, he was able to do it. 'Oh, my friend,' he said to the crocodile, assuming a practical manner, 'why did you not tell me this back then when we were still at my tree? You see, I keep my heart hidden in a hole in the tree. If you had told me sister-in-law's desire, I would have brought my heart with me and presented it to her myself.'

'Really?' said the crocodile, relieved. 'Then let's go back and get your heart so that I can give it to my wicked wife, and she can eat it and stop all this nonsense about fasting to death. Hang on tight, and I'll take you back to your tree.' Speedily swimming back to the bank, Karalamukha brought Raktamukha directly under the jamun tree.

The monkey, who had been swearing oaths to all the gods, offering them different kinds of prasads if they got him home safely, now leapt to the highest branch of the jamun tree and released a deep breath of relief. 'Thank you, gods,' he said softly. 'I was caught in a dire situation. I thought I would surely die. It is only because of your grace that I have been able to escape with my life.' He felt like he had been given a new life. Someone has rightly said,

> Never trust a stranger,
> also never fully trust
> someone you know.
> Trust creates fear
> and situations of peril
> that end in utter destruction.

'O friend,' the crocodile called up to the monkey, 'Can you pass me down your heart now so that I can take it to my wife and pacify her?'

'You evil betrayer,' the monkey spat out the words, 'shame on you for breaking my trust.' Then, with a mocking laugh, he continued, 'You fool, can anyone be alive without a heart, or have two hearts? Which heart do you think I am hiding in the tree? Go away. Leave me and my tree alone, and never return. It is said,

> A person who agrees to be friends
> with a friend from a friendship soured
> invites death like the pregnant she-mule.'

The crocodile heard the monkey's reproach with chagrin. Oh no, he thought to himself, I shouldn't have revealed my intention. Now, what am I to do? Perhaps I can cajole him into trusting me again. Hence, he said to the monkey, feigning a playful laugh, 'Dear friend, this was all a joke. I wanted to test your friendship. How could you believe that my wife wants to eat your heart? That is not true at all. Actually, my wife has, indeed, invited you as a guest. Come on down and get on my back again, and I'll take you to my home. My wife is waiting.'

'Do you really believe that I'll go with you now? I told you to leave my bank right now. Haven't you heard,

What evil acts will a starving person not do?
Lowly, poor, and hungry become hard-hearted.
Go, dear lady, and tell the snake, Priyadarshana,
there is no way that Gangadatta, the frog,
will ever agree to return to this well again.'

'What is this story?' Karalamukha asked, and Raktamukha narrated the tale.

THE TALE OF HOW THE SNAKE LOST ALL SENSE OF MORALITY

In a village well lived the king of frogs, Gangadatta. One day, weary of the constant internecine fighting in his clan, he climbed up the pulley's chain of water buckets hanging down the well and came out with the intention of finding a way to ruin his enemies. It is said,

> Those who have harmed you during your hardship.
> Those you have mocked you when you were down.
> If you can harm these both and avenge yourself,
> consider yourself born again in a new life.

As Gangadatta was thinking thus, he saw an enormous black snake, called Priyadarshana (lovely to behold), burrow into a hole in the ground. 'That's the solution!' he exclaimed. 'What if I can take this snake to the well and have him destroy my enemies?' After all, the wise say,

> Have your powerful enemy
> clash with their powerful enemy.
> A sharp thorn is best suited to
> extract an embedded sharp thorn.
> A harmful enemy is destroyed
> by using him to fight another enemy.
> Thus, your purpose is fulfilled
> with little or no effort on your part.

Carefully scripting in his mind the words he would say to the snake to convince him, Gangadatta approached the hole and called, 'O Priyadarshana, can you please come out?'

The snake heard the frog and wondered who was calling him. It didn't sound like another snake's voice. What does someone, who is not from my clan, want from me? He thought: I should first find out what he wants before I go out. Brihaspati has said,

> Unless you know someone's
> character, family, and residence,
> it is best not to associate with him.

The way he is calling, he sounds like he is a snake charmer, chanting mantras to entice me. When I go out, will he nab me and put me in a basket? Or, maybe, it is someone who wants to employ me to bite his enemy. 'Who are you and why are you calling me?' the snake enquired.

'I am Gangadatta, the king of frogs, and I want a friendship with you.'

'Really?' Priyadarshana replied, 'But that sounds absurd. A friendship between us is as impossible as the friendship between hay and fire.

> A prey does not himself go
> to the one who preys upon him.

You want me to be your friend? How is this possible? Why are you wasting my time by saying such ridiculous things?'

'This is true, O snake,' Gangadatta replied. 'You are an enemy of my kind. But I am tired of the enemies in my own clan. I've come to you because I'm feeling defeated by their behaviour. It is said,

> When annihilation looms large,
> when peril threatens your life,
> respectfully bow to your enemy,
> and save your life and wealth.'

'O Gangadatta,' said the snake, 'Tell me who has defeated you.'

'My relatives, who are my partners.'

'Where do you live—in a tank, well, pond, or lake?'

'I live in a well that has a strong stone platform and parapet built around it.'

'Oh, that's too bad. We snakes have no feet. That's why it's impossible for us to climb into that kind of a well. And, if by some acrobatic feat, I am able do it, where will I live to carry out my plan of destroying your relatives? If all around is solid stone, I won't be able to burrow into it. So, I'm sorry, but I can't be of any help. And you should leave now, because the wise say,

> If you desire wellness, eat only those foods
> that you can digest and are nutritious.

And you look both digestible and nutritious to me.'

'Oh no. Please don't say this,' Gangadatta pleaded. 'I would really like you to help me. I promise I'll help you get into the well with great ease. Also, right beside the well is a soft mound over a hole that extends deep into the ground. You can use that as your residence while you implement your plan.'

After Gangadatta told him this, Priyadarshana began to ponder, I'm getting old, and it's becoming more and more difficult to catch mice. This offer promises a good meal of frogs. I should agree to it. So, he said to Gangadatta, 'All right. Let's try it out. Walk ahead of me and show the way to the well.'

'I'll take you there and show you the easiest way into the well. And I'll also show you the place where you can live. But first, please promise me that you will not harm me or those of my kin who are on my side. Devour only those relatives that I point out.'

'Sure,' said the snake. 'I'll devour only those frogs who you point out as your enemies. You are now my friend. Don't worry. I won't harm you or your friends.'

After all this had been sorted out, the snake emerged from his hole. For a moment the frog and the snake stood looking at each other, realizing the incongruity of the situation. Then, Priyadarshana reached forward and embraced Gangadatta. 'Lead the way,' he said.

Gangadatta took Priyadarshana to the high well and showed him how to descend into the water, using the water buckets on the pulley. After the snake and frog were both inside the well, Gangadatta pointed out his enemies to the snake, who wasted no time in making a quick meal of them. When all of Gangadatta's enemies were gone, the snake said to the frog, 'I have killed and eaten all your enemies, but now there is nothing for me to eat. I'm still hungry. Give me some more frogs. You are the one who brought me here; therefore, you are responsible for my food.'

'Friend,' said Gangadatta, 'you have fulfilled the role of a friend very well by destroying my enemies. Now, please return to your home by climbing out of this well, using the same method we used when I brought you here.'

'This is not right, O frog,' said the snake. 'I can't go back to my burrow now, because some other snake has probably taken it over. I must live right here. Bring me a couple of frogs every day as my food. I don't care if they are from your side or the other side. I just need my food. I'm warning you that if I'm not fed, I'll finish off all of you.'

The snake's words filled Gangadatta with dread. 'What have I done?' he asked himself. 'I shouldn't have brought this snake to our well. I've a done a terrible thing. Someone has rightly said,

> He who befriends an enemy,
> natural-born and strong,
> brings poison for himself
> in preparation for his own death.

What am I to do now? It seems I have no choice but to bring a couple of frogs to this wicked snake every day so that he doesn't eat all of us. It is said,

> If an enemy ready to rob your all,
> agrees to take just a small amount,
> the wise say to give him what he wants;
> just as the ocean appeases the Badv mare
> by feeding her small amounts of water.

As it is said,

> When all is in danger of being lost
> the wise give half and save half.
> Half is better than none at all.

Also,

> Do not harm many
> for the sake of a few.
> Better to lose a few
> and protect the many
> that is what prudence is.'

Thus, with a heavy heart, Gangadatta began to select two frogs every day and send them to their death. However, while Priyadarshana ate those two and seemed ostensibly satisfied for the day, he also began to devour a few more behind the frog king's back. Someone has rightly said,

> When clothes become soiled
> people sit here and there without care.
> One is careful about one's clothing
> only till it is white and clean,
> just as when one's virtue is lost
> one hardly bothers with good conduct.

In the same way, once Priyadarshana began his underhanded killing, he soon lost all sense of virtue and began to eat as many frogs as he liked. And then, one day, he killed and ate Gangadatta's son, Yamunadatta. When Gangadatta heard about this, he was beside himself with grief, regret, and self-loathing for having brought this calamity upon himself and his family and clan. Hearing him wail and lament incessantly, his wife said to him in disgust, 'You murderer of your own son and your own relatives, why are you crying now? With our clan destroyed, who will protect us? Besides, do you think that once the others are gone, he'll spare us? This wicked snake won't stop until all of us are gone. There's no point in crying. If you stay alive, find a way to either escape this well or to kill this snake.'

His wife's words helped quieten Gangadatta. However, no matter how hard he thought, he could not come up with a way to kill the snake, and every time he attempted to leave the well, he found the snake watching him. In the meantime, Priyadarshana continued to feed on the remaining frogs, and soon finished off every single frog in the well, except for Gangadatta.

'Hey Gangadatta, I'm starving,' he said to him, after he had eaten the last frog. 'There's not a single frog to be had here. You better arrange for some food for me from somewhere. After all, you're the one who brought me here.'

Priyadarshana's words triggered an idea in Gangadatta's head. 'Dear friend,' he said, 'you're right, there are no more frogs here in this well. Why don't I find you food from outside this well? I'll go to different wells and persuade other frogs to come to our well. That way you can be feeding on frogs as long I can convince them to come here.'

'You are truly an oath-brother, Gangadatta,' the snake replied. 'And it is for that reason I won't eat you. If you can bring other frogs from the surrounding wells and lakes, I'll think even more highly of you. I may even elevate you to the status of my father.'

Fervently thanking all the gods in his mind and promising to offer them many kinds of prasad in worship, Gangadatta made his way out of the well, using the chain of water buckets.

Priyadarshana waited for Gangadatta in the well for many days, anticipating the big frog meal that he would bring back. However, when much time had passed with no sign of Gangadatta, Priyadarshana went to the lizard who lived in a crack in the well. 'Dear lady,' he said to her. 'Can you do me a small favour? I'm asking you because you have known Gangadatta for a long time. Can you please go outside and find him and convey this message to him: "O Gangadatta, if you are not able to persuade other frogs to come into our well, it's all right. But you yourself should come back as soon as possible. I'm finding it hard to stay here in the well by myself. I miss you very much. And I promise you that I will not harm you in any way. I swear by dharma, who is my witness."'

'All right. I'll find Gangadatta and convey your message,' said the lizard and slithered out of the well. She soon found the frog swimming in a pond. 'Hey Gangadatta, 'she called out to him,' your friend, the snake, is eagerly awaiting your return. He said, you should come back to the well right away. And he also wants you to know that he is dharma-bound not to hurt you in any way. He has sworn by dharma and has made it his witness. So, don't be afraid and come on back.'

'Dear lady,' replied Gangadatta,

> 'A starving, impecunious person will stop at nothing.
> There is no sin on earth he will not commit,
> because in adversity people become devoid
> of all moral virtues of mercy and compassion.

So, dear lady, please go and say this to that snake Priyadarshana, "Having escaped your very hungry mouth, this Gangadatta will never return to the well under any circumstance. He can't believe in an iota of your oaths and swearing. So, pardon me, but we're done. As for me—I have reaped what I sowed."'

The lizard then returned to the well and informed the snake that the frog would never return to the well.

The monkey concluded the story and said to the crocodile, 'You wicked aquatic creature. Like that frog, Gangadatta, I, too, will never again go with you to your house.'

'Dear friend, please don't say that,' the crocodile begged. 'I made a mistake, and I want to make it up to you by bringing you to my house as a guest. If you don't come with me, I'll lie under your tree without food and water and fast unto death. And then, you'll be responsible for my death, and the sin of killing me will be yours.'

'You moron. Do you take me for a fool that despite knowing your evilness and trickery, I'll go to your house and myself offer you my life like that Lambakarna? This is what is said about him:

> He came, he suffered the lion's strike, he fled.
> Then the fool, void in heart and eyes and ears,
> returned to the very same spot to be killed.'

'Who was Lambakarna? What is this story? Please tell me,' said the crocodile, and the monkey told the tale.

THE TALE OF WHY THE DONKEY RETURNED TO THE LION TO BE KILLED

In a dense forest lived a lion called Karalakesara (saffron-toothed). He had a retainer—a jackal named Ghusaraka (dust-coloured), who followed him everywhere. Once, after fighting an elephant in rut, Karalakesara was so badly wounded that he became completely debilitated. Since the lion couldn't hunt, the jackal couldn't eat, and he began to starve. One day, he said to the lion, 'Maharaj, I'm feeling weak from hunger, and every step I take is an effort. Forgive me, but how can I attend to you in this state?'

'Ghusaraka, why don't you go into the forest and find an animal who is willing to come here. I may be in a weakened state, but I can still kill him and arrange for your food.'

Ghusaraka then went searching for an animal, and his search took him to a nearby village. There, beside a lake, he saw a donkey trying to eat the tiny, creeping doob grass that grows close to the ground, but he could barely graze it. The donkey's name was Lambakarna (long-eared). Approaching him, Ghusaraka bowed with respect and said, 'Namaste, uncle. I haven't seen you in a while. How are you and why have you grown so thin?'

'Nephew, what can I say. It's a sad story. My owner, the washerman, is cruel and heartless. He works me to the bone, making me carry heavy loads, but he doesn't feed me even a fistful of grass. I have to make do by grazing on this barely grown doob grass. That's why I have become so thin. How can one feel content with an empty stomach?'

'In that case, uncle, you should come with me. I'll take you to this beautiful spot beside a river that is covered with soft grass as green as emerald. There, you and I can sit and enjoy some poetry together. You can get plenty to eat every day, and I can enjoy your company.'

'That is very kind of you, nephew, but you know that I'm an urban creature, happier in a village than in the wilderness. Besides, the wild is full of predators, like lions, tigers, and other such animals. If I go with you, I'll certainly be eaten by one of them. So, that beautiful place beside the river with soft green grass is not for me.'

'Don't say that, uncle. I, myself, protect that place like a warrior. That's why no other wild animals even venture into that spot. Besides, just a few days ago, I took three female donkeys there. They, too, were relentlessly worked and overburdened by their washermen. But now they live in that place, carefree and happy, eating the grass, becoming plump and attractive, and enjoying youthful pleasures. They also don't have a mate. One day, they requested me: "Uncle, if we are truly your nieces, then go and search for a healthy, good-looking mate for us." That is the reason I made that proposition to you.'

The jackal's description of the young jennies made Lambakarna drool with desire. 'If that is the case,' he said to Ghusaraka, 'take me there.' It is rightfully said,

> There is no greater amrita,
> nor is there greater poison
> than a woman beautiful and young,
> because being with her is life
> and separation from her is death.

As someone has said,

> They whose very name evokes desire,
> imagine if one were to meet them in person
> and be the target of their flirtatious innuendoes.
> Not being stirred by them—that's inconceivable.

Hence, the jackal led the donkey to where the lion was waiting. As soon as the donkey drew near, the lion made a great effort and pounced on him, but his wounds made his movements slow, and the donkey was able to scamper away. All the lion could do was let out a big, ferocious roar.

'What was that lame attack, my lord,' the jackal admonished. 'Have you grown so weak that even a donkey is able to escape from you? If you can't kill a standing donkey, how will you tackle elephants? Sorry to say, but your prowess today leaves much to be desired.'

'Oh, what a miss,' the lion said with an embarrassed laugh. 'Actually, you came so suddenly with the donkey that I didn't get a chance to strategize my attack. Otherwise, what is a donkey, even an elephant can't survive the blow of my mighty paw.'

'Fine. I'll bring him to you one more time. But, this time, be prepared with your strategy.'

'Dear fellow, I don't think you can bring him back. He has seen me here, why would he return? Let that donkey be and find another animal.'

'Why are you worried whether the donkey will return or not? Leave that to me. You just be prepared. Watch how quickly I bring him back.'

While the lion sat down to concentrate on his right paw and the manoeuvre he would use to smack the donkey, the jackal went in pursuit of Lambakarna. He found him in the same spot—in the village, by the lake, trying to graze on the barely visible doob grass.

When the donkey saw the jackal, he said in affront: 'Well, dear nephew, you adeptly took me to the mouth of death. I would have been killed if it hadn't been for a stroke of good luck. But do tell me, nephew, who was this creature, whose lightning-sharp, fearful, and weighty blow I was able to escape?'

'Uncle,' the jackal said with a laugh. 'That was one of the jennies. She saw you and wanted to take you in her arms. And because she couldn't control her desire, she extended her arms to draw you close. But you proved to be a coward—afraid even of an embrace. She has sent me back to you with the message that she can't live without you. So, come back with me, uncle. She's waiting for you. And she says that unless you come, she'll not eat a morsel. She told me, "If this Lambakarna doesn't become my husband, I'll jump into the fire and kill myself. I'd rather die than live separated from him." Needless to say, dear uncle, Lambakarna, I'm here to take you back. Please come with me, otherwise you'll suffer the sin of having killed a female and Kamadeva will be angry at you. It is said,

> Kamadeva's writ is like a feminine force,
> bestowing all happiness and wealth.
> Those dimwits who oppose this writ
> and go into the forest to be sanyasis,
> becoming celibate, renouncing women,
> are severely punished by his deva of desire:
> some stripped naked, others shaved bald,
> some given dreadlocks, others even worse—
> beaten and bloodied or made a Kapalika.'

The donkey let the jackal persuade him, mostly because the thought of the jenny pining for him was too irresistible. Hence, once again he followed Ghusaraka into the forest, where Karalakesara the lion was waiting. Someone has rightly said,

> People who well know right and wrong
> still engage in acts that accrue bad karma,

being so induced by an invisible force.
Otherwise, who willingly commits bad acts?

This time, when Lambakarna arrived, Karalakesara was fully prepared, and it only took one strike of his paw to kill the donkey.

Karalakesara then asked the jackal to watch over the meat, while he went to bathe and cleanse himself. Ghusaraka watched the dead donkey for a few minutes; then his greed overpowered him, and he reached with his mouth for the donkey's long ears. After that, he slowly inched forward and ate his juicy, delicious heart.

In the meantime, Karalakesara, having finished his bath and worship to the gods and ancestors, came back to his kill. Seeing the donkey's ears gone and a bloody hole in his body where his heart used to be, he was livid. With eyes as red as his saffron-coloured teeth, he glared at Ghusaraka and roared, 'How dare you put your mouth to my meat before me?'

'Maharaj,' said the jackal in a gentle tone, 'please don't blame me. I didn't eat any portion of him. This donkey did not have ears and a heart to begin with. That is why he returned to you a second time, even though he saw you that first time and heard you roar. If he had a heart and ears, would he have come back with me, knowing his death was certain? He would have thought about it and refused to come. Therefore, this donkey was obviously void in his heart, eyes, and ears.'

The jackal's words made sense to the lion. Calming down, he started his meal and invited the jackal to join him.

'You see, Lambakarna was a crest jewel among fools,' the monkey said to the crocodile. 'But I'm not Lambakarna that I will return with you. In fact, you are the fool. Your scheme was top notch, but, like that potter, Yudhishthira, who couldn't keep from revealing the truth; you ruined your own plan by making a show of telling me the truth. Someone has rightly said,

> He who touts his selfish design
> by bragging about the truth,
> ruins his own chances of success,
> like that potter, Yudhishthira.'

'What is this story?' the crocodile asked, and the monkey narrated it to him.

THE TALE OF THE POTTER WHO RUINED HIS OWN CHANCES

In a town lived a potter called Yudhishthira. One day, carelessly running around in his house, he fell on some sharp pieces of broken pots, and a shard of clay pierced his forehead. Although the wound was deep, he did not take care of it. Also, because he did not have the energy to cook, he only ate unwholesome food for many days following the injury. Consequently, the cut on his forehead became infected. Eventually, with proper unguents, medicines, and rest, the wound healed, but it left a deep scar on his forehead.

Once, the land was hit by famine, and the potter, starving to death, joined a troop of royal guards and went to another land, where he was accepted into employment by the king. The king had taken one look at the impressive scar on his forehead and had hired him instantly, thinking he must have received it in some great, valorous battle. For this reason, the king treated Yudhishthira with utmost respect and was always more favourable toward him. Consequently, the king's other men resented the potter and were jealous of him, but they were too afraid to say anything to the king.

Many years passed. Then, that kingdom went to war with another, and, just before the first battle, as the elephants were being adorned, horses' saddles were being tightened, and soldiers were gathering, the king took the potter aside and asked him, 'O honoured soldier, what is your name and what is your caste? In which battle did you get such a deep wound on your forehead?'

'Maharaj, this wound is not from a weapon,' said the potter with pride. 'It is a mark of my profession. I am a potter by caste. My name is Yudhishthira. In my house, broken pieces of clay are often just lying around. One day, in an intoxicated state, I was running around my house, carelessly, and I fell on a sharp piece of clay that cut my forehead. Further carelessness on my part worsened the wound, and it got infected. That is why the scar it left is so prominent. But this is not a wound I received in a battle.'

The king was shocked and embarrassed to hear the potter's explanation. Calling his guards, he said 'I feel cheated that that soldier's emblazoning scar is not a battle injury. Throw him out. I don't want to see him within my boundary walls.'

Following the king's orders, the guards took the potter in a headlock and were about to drag him out when he began to plead with the king, 'Maharaj, please don't throw me out. At least wait to the see my prowess in battle.'

'Arrey,' said the king, 'you may have all the best qualities, but I don't want you here. I say to you,

> Child, you may be valorous in war,
> you may be a scholar of shastras,
> you may be the most handsome,
> but in the clan that you are born,
> hunting elephants is not a practice.'

'What is this story, Maharaj?' the potter asked, and the king narrated it to him.

THE TALE OF THE JACKAL
WHO THOUGHT HE WAS A LION

In a certain land there lived a lion couple. After the lioness gave birth to two cubs, the lion hunted deer every day and brought the meat back to his wife. One day, the lion couldn't find any prey, although he searched from dawn till dusk. As he was returning to his cave, he came upon a jackal pup. Carefully grabbing the tiny creature with his teeth, the lion brought him home to his wife—alive.

'Dear husband, what is this?' she asked. 'And have you brought us some other food, as well, other than this tiny creature?'

'Today, I could only find this jackal pup. I couldn't catch anything else. I also couldn't kill him, because he's just a baby, and, like us, he is from the clan of meat-eaters. So I brought him here alive. It is said,

> Woman, child, brahmin, or sanyasi
> should never be struck by you,
> even if your own life is at stake
> and especially if they trust you.

But, if you please, you can eat this pup and satisfy your hunger. Tomorrow, I'll go into the forest again and, hopefully, have better luck.'

'Since you couldn't kill this little baby, how can I kill him and eat him? It is said,

> Refrain from unrightful acts
> even if it means your death.
> Always say yes to rightful acts
> even if it means your death.
> This is the Sanatana dharma.

That is why I won't kill this jackal pup. Instead, I'll rear him, along with our children. He'll be my third son.' Hence, the lioness adopted the jackal pup and gave him her teat, and he began to feed at her breast like her own two cubs. In this way, the three little ones, who had no idea about caste or clan, began growing up together, sharing their mother's milk, and the food their father caught. They also sported together, learned together, and enjoyed together a life of a carefree childhood.

One day, the three young ones were playing in the forest, when a wild elephant suddenly appeared. Seeing him, the two lion cubs growled and then pounced on him, but the jackal pup exclaimed, 'That's an elephant—our natural enemy. We shouldn't even go near him, or he'll kill us.' Then he sprinted home. Seeing their elder brother flee, the two lion cubs also lost their confidence. Someone has rightly said,

> Just one brave soldier in the battlefield
> fills the whole army with will and hope.
> Just one cowardly soldier fleeing from battle
> breaks the will and hope of the whole army,
> planting the thought of flight in everyone's mind.

As someone has said,

> A king should always fill his army
> with strong, brave, and inspiring men,
> not the cowardly, weak, and fearful.

Thus, the two lion cubs backed away from the elephant and followed the jackal home. There, they mimicked their elder brother's fright before their parents with much mockery and playfulness, demonstrating how just the sight of the elephant sent him fleeing home.

The jackal was upset at being ridiculed by his brothers. With trembling lips and reddened eyes, he told his brothers to stop and called them all kinds of names. The lioness then took the jackal aside and said to him, 'Son, don't be so angry. These two are your younger brothers. You should not get upset with them.'

'But mother,' the jackal exclaimed, getting even more worked up, 'am I any less brave, smart, good looking, studious than them that they are laughing at me? I'm going to kill them for making fun of me.'

The lioness smiled to herself and then said to him, 'Dear son, you are brave, good at your studies, and handsome. But the clan in which you were born does not kill elephants. That is your only lack. Listen to me carefully, son. You are the son of a jackal. Your father found you when you were a baby, and I took pity on you and let you feed at my breast with my two cubs. My babies haven't seen you as anything other than their brother until now, but before they understand what happened today, you should leave and find your own kind. I fear that when they realize that you are a jackal, they will kill you.'

When the jackal heard this, he was dumbfounded. Then, with a pounding heart, he backed away from the lioness and ran out of the cave. Eventually, he found a pack of jackals and joined it.

'O potter, in the same way that the cubs didn't know the jackal, my soldiers don't know that you are not a warrior. Before they find out that you are a potter, my advice to you is to run away as quickly as you can. Otherwise, I fear, my warriors will not let you live.'

The potter did not wait another moment, and quickly left that land.

After narrating this tale, the monkey said to the crocodile, 'O vile water creature, that's why I say that those who tell the truth for selfish reasons, ruin their own plans. But you are a bigger fool than even that; you agreed to betray a friend to fulfil a woman's wishes. One should never trust a woman. It is said,

> She for whom I left my family,
> she to whom I gave half my life—
> that wife of mine has left me,
> saying she loves me no more.
> Which intelligent man is there
> who will put his trust in women?'

'What is this story?' the crocodile asked, and the monkey narrated it.

THE TALE OF THE BRAHMIN WHO LOVED HIS WIFE WHO LOVED A CRIPPLE

In a town lived a brahmin who loved his wife more than his own life. This wife was a quarrelsome woman. Every day, she would pick a fight with someone in the family and then bicker for hours. The brahmin was aggrieved at the discord his wife created, but, because he loved her very much, he did not admonish her. Instead, he decided to leave the family and go elsewhere with his wife.

On their way, as they were crossing a dense forest, the brahmin's wife felt thirsty and requested him to search for water. Seating her in a safe spot and asking her to remain there, the brahmin went looking for water. He found a stream and filled a cup, but when he returned with it to his wife, he found her lying dead on the ground. The brahmin was beside himself with grief. Lamenting loudly, he sat down beside the corpse and wailed to the gods about this injustice and begged them to return her to him. Suddenly, a celestial voice spoke to him from the sky: 'O brahmin, if you love this woman that much, then give her half your life. Swear on it, and she will be restored to life.'

Quickly wiping his tears, the brahmin rushed to the stream to purify himself by washing his hands and feet and cleansing his mouth. Then, returning to his wife's body, he took water in the cup of his hand and swore three times that half his life would now be his wife's. As soon as the vow was sealed by the triple oath, the wife came alive. She had no idea what had transpired and thought she had just woken up from a nap, and that is what the brahmin let her believe.

The two of them then drank some water, ate whatever fruits they could find, and continued their journey. Finally, they arrived at the outskirts of a city that had a beautiful flower garden near the boundary wall, and that's where they decided to rest and make further plans. 'Dear one, stay here for a while,' the brahmin said to his wife. 'I'll go into the city and get us some food.'

Left alone in the garden, the wife wandered around and came upon a cripple who was drawing water from the well. After he had had a drink, he sat down and started to sing. He had such a beautiful singing voice that every taan he took struck the woman like an arrow of desire from Kamadeva's bow. Approaching the musician, the women said to him, 'I've fallen in love with you and want you to be my lover. If you don't satisfy my desire right now, I'll give up my life, and you'll have to suffer the sin of killing a woman.'

'My dear woman, as you can see, I'm a cripple,' the man said. 'Why would you want to have any physical intimacy with me?'

'I just do. And I mean what I say. If you don't take me in your arms and fulfil my desire, I'll kill myself.'

The man acquiesced and wrapped his arms around her.

When the brahmin returned from the city with food and sat down with his wife to eat it, she said to him, 'See that cripple near the well. He seems hungry. Why don't you share some of our food with him?'

Thinking what a generous heart his wife had, the brahmin brought the cripple some food on a platter. Later, when they were ready to leave the garden, the wife said to her husband, 'Why don't we take the cripple with us. You need a helper, and I need someone to talk to, especially when you leave me to get food, and all. I hate being alone.'

'Bringing him along will be more of a burden than a help, dear wife. I get exhausted just carrying our belongings; imagine how tired I'll feel if I have to carry the cripple as well.'

'Please!' the wife pleaded. 'You don't have to carry him. I will. I'll pack him in my trunk and carry him on my head.'

The brahmin loved his wife too much to refuse her anything, so he agreed. The woman then helped the cripple into the trunk and, thereafter, she carried him on her head wherever they went.

After days of journeying, they stopped at a well to rest. As he did at every stop, the brahmin went into the nearest city to bring food, and the three of them ate it. Thereafter, the brahmin lay down on the wide parapet of the well and, lulled by its coolness, soon fell asleep. Suddenly, the wife got up and pushed her husband into the well. Then, helping the cripple back into the trunk, she lifted that on her head and began to walking towards the city.

That day, the city was teeming with soldiers; they were posted everywhere. The police chief had received a tip-off about some thieves from another place who had come here to sell their stolen goods. Therefore, when the woman entered the city gates, the soldiers thought she was part of the gang and was carrying stolen goods in her trunk. Apprehending her, they took her and her trunk to the king's court. When the king had the trunk opened, he saw the cripple in it.

'What is this?' the king asked the woman.

'Maharaj, this cripple is my husband,' the woman replied. 'He has been crippled because of disease. When we were living with his family, his relatives constantly abused him and tried to snatch his share of the property from him. I love my husband very much and couldn't bear to see him suffer like that, so I put him in a trunk and carried him to this city, to keep him safe.'

The king was very impressed by the woman's dedication to her crippled husband. 'From today you are my sworn sister,' he said to the brahmin's wife. 'And I gift you two villages. Live there happily with your husband without worrying about anything.'

Hence, the woman began living with her cripple lover in one of the two villages that she had been gifted.

Back at the well, a forest-dwelling sadhu heard the brahmin's calls for help and rescued him from the well. Recovering from his ordeal, the brahmin walked for many days, looking for his wife, and then, by coincidence, came to the village where she lived with the cripple. One day, the woman saw him walking down the street. Rushing to the king, she told him that she had seen one of her husband's abusive relatives and that he had, most likely, come here to kill them. The king ordered his soldiers to catch the man and hang him, but, before the sentence was carried out, he wanted to question him in court.

When the brahmin was presented in the court, he was shocked to see his wife there and to learn that she was responsible for his death sentence. He also learned about the story that she had concocted about herself and her cripple lover. 'Maharaj,' he said to the king. 'This woman has something of mine. You've already announced my death sentence, so please consider this my last wish. If you are a follower of dharma, then please have her return that which is mine.'

'Dear sister,' the king said to the woman, 'if you have something belonging to this man, then please return it.'

'But I haven't taken anything from this man,' she exclaimed.

'Yes, you have. I gave you half my life. I ask for that back. Swear three times that you return it.'

The brahmin's wife had no idea what her husband was talking about, but she wanted to get rid of him as soon as possible to prevent him from revealing any more truths about her. Therefore, she hurriedly said three times: 'I return to him half of his life that he gave me.' As soon as she spoke the oath the third time, she fell down dead.

The king was dismayed. 'What is the meaning of this?' he asked the brahmin, and the man told him the whole story of how his wife had died, how he had given her half his life, and how she had taken the cripple as lover and had tried to kill him by pushing him into the well.

'So, you see how women dupe men,' the monkey said to the crocodile. 'Here's another story about how men cater to the whims of women.

> Where those who are not horses, neigh,
> in that place, I, too, have shaved my head.'

THE TALE OF HOW FAR MEN WILL GO TO PLEASE WOMEN

In the olden days, in this our land Bharata, there used to be a city called Patliputra. It was ruled by Raja Nanda, who was known for his courage and strength. He was such an illustrious king that his footstool used to shine with the brilliance of rays coming from the hundreds of crowns that bowed at his feet. Yet, his glory was as gentle and radiant as the moon's rays after the winter season. That Nanda Raja had a prime minister called Vararuchi, who was not only well-versed in all the shastras, but he was also a very wise man.

Once Vararuchi had a lover's dispute with his wife, and she was very upset at him. Vararuchi was deeply in love with his wife, and he tried various ways to appease her, but she rejected him every time. Then, Vararuchi said to her, 'Dear one, tell me what will make you happy? No matter what it is, just say it, and I'll do it.'

To test his devotion to her, Vararuchi's wife said to him, 'Are you sure you'll do what I ask? Are you sure you'll not change your mind after I tell you what I want?'

'Of course. Just say the word.'

'Then shave your head and come and bow at my feet. That'll please me.'

One night, Vararuchi actually shaved his head and placed it on his wife's feet, just to see her smile.

Another time, Nanda Raja's wife, too, was peeved at something her husband had said and was not willing to be placated. Nanda Raja also said to his wife, as husbands who love their wives tend to say, 'Dearest beloved, you know I can't live without you even for a moment. Therefore, I'm rubbing my nose in the dirt at your feet, begging you to spit out your peeve. Tell me what I can do to make you happy.'

'Are you sure you want to know?' she asked. 'Will you do it?'

'Of course. Just say the word and consider it done.'

'Okay, then. I want you to come to me wearing a horse's bridle. I want to hold the reins and race you like a horse, and as you're galloping, I want you to also neigh like a horse. If you do this, I'll be happy.'

So, one night, poor Raja Nanda came to his wife, bridled as horse, and she raced him all night while he neighed like a horse. Coincidentally, it was on this very night that Vararuchi shaved his head.

The following morning, when the court assembled and Raja Nanda saw his prime minister's shaved head, he became curious to know the reason. 'Dear Vararuchi for what holy festival have you shaved your head?' he asked.

'What does a man not do at the entreaty of a wife, Maharaj?' Vararuchi replied. 'In the festival where men neigh like horses, I, too, have shaved my head.'

You see, Vararuchi had received a boon from Devi Saraswati—simply by mediating on her, he would instantly be privy to anyone's life, at any given time. That is why he was able to know about the king's equestrian pursuits and neighing of the night before.

'Evil crocodile, you, too, are being controlled by your wife, like Vararuchi and Nanda Raja. To appease your wife, you schemed to kill me, but, by mistake, you spilled the beans and revealed your scheme. Someone has rightly said,

> Those who speak too much
> are caught and caged
> like the tota and myna birds;
> whereas, the silent crane,
> curbing its speech, roams free.

Also,

> A carefully kept secret was
> the donkey in a tiger's hide.
> He was killed because he brayed.

'Tell me that story,' the crocodile asked, the monkey related the tale.

THE TALE OF HOW THE DONKEY GAVE HIMSELF AWAY

In a town lived a washerman called Shudhapatta (pure, ritual cloth). He had a donkey who had grown feeble, because the washerman had no money to feed him. One day, as the man was walking through the forest, he saw a dead tiger, and an idea came to him: why don't I take this tiger's hide and put it on my donkey and let him loose in the fields of grain? No one will dare drive him out, or even approach him, because they'll think it's a tiger and will be too afraid. And so, the washerman skinned the tiger and took his hide home. That evening, he covered his donkey with the tiger skin and let him loose in the barley fields. The donkey, too, was thrilled to have so much lush grain at his disposal. He ate a bellyful and then some. When morning arrived, the washerman quickly drove his donkey home before anyone saw him.

Many days passed. Every morning, the watchmen of the fields would notice their barley eaten, and every night they would see a tiger in their fields; but, neither could they comprehend what the tiger was doing in a field of barley, nor could they drive him away. As for the donkey—he soon became plump and healthy from grazing on nutritious barley every night. He also began to gain strength and became so powerful and wayward, that the washerman had to struggle to pull him out of the field every morning.

Then, one evening, as the donkey was happily grazing, he heard a female donkey somewhere in the distance. He got so excited by that sound that he raised his head and began to bray. The crop watchers, who had been observing the tiger, exclaimed, 'Oh, it's a donkey! He's just wearing a tiger's skin. How he had us fooled.' And, shouting and throwing sticks and stones, they drove him out of the fields.

As the crocodile was listening to the monkey's stories, some water creature came swimming up to the bank and informed him, 'O crocodile, your wife waited and waited for you. Since you didn't return, she thought you had broken your word to her and gave up her life.'

The crocodile burst into loud sobs. 'O what is this tragedy?' he wailed. 'Why has fate dealt me this blow? It is said,

> A man without a loving mother,
> or a wife who speaks in sweet words
> should leave home and go to the forest,
> because his home is no better than a forest.'

'Dear friend,' he said to monkey, tears rolling down his scaly face, 'Forgive me for everything I've done to hurt you, and all the sins I have committed against you. I'll go and enter the flames with my wife now. My life has no meaning without her.'

'I knew it,' the monkey exclaimed with a triumphant laugh. 'I knew you were controlled by your wife. She had you completely wrapped around her little finger, so to speak. What you just said has convinced me of this. That is why, instead of celebrating your freedom, you are grieving. Haven't you heard what people say,

> A woman cruel and quarrelsome
> Is not a woman but a disease?

And it is also true that:

> Women are often quarrelsome and cruel.
> For self-preservation it is best to avoid them.

> What is in a woman's heart
> is never on her tongue.
> And what is on her tongue
> is never what she reveals.
> What she reveals to all
> is never what a woman does.
> Strange are the ways of women.

> Like moths attracted to a flame
> plummet into it and burn to death,
> men enticed by a woman's beauty
> that is radiant on the outside,
> get trapped in it and are destroyed.

> Women are by nature poisonous,
> but their appearance is alluring,
> like the eye-catching gunjaphal.

> They who are by nature dry and cruel,
> how can one seek in them the dew of love?
>
> They who are by nature of harsh hearts,
> how can one seek in them soft warmth?
> They who are by nature arid and sparse,
> only fools and fledglings seek in them nectar.
> The wise and intelligent never trust women.'

'What you say is true,' the crocodile said to the monkey. 'But I've been struck by a double tragedy. First, my home is ruined because my wife is dead, and second, I've lost a wise and generous friend like you. That's why I'm grieving so much. These kinds of terrible tragedies only strike as a consequence of fate. Who else can be blamed? After all, it is said,

> I was clever, but you thought you were cleverer,
> yet you have lost both your lover and husband.
> Now, you shameless slut, what else will you do,
> sitting here in the nude, embarrassed, penniless?'

'What is this about?' the monkey asked, and the crocodile told him the tale.

THE TALE OF THE NAKED WOMAN AND HOW SHE LOST BOTH HER HUSBAND AND LOVER

In a village lived a rich farmer and his wife. The farmer was old and decrepit, whereas, his wife was still quite young and energetic; therefore, she was always seeking the company of younger men. It so happened that once a thug noticed her, and after observing her for some time, seeing how she was always looking for younger men and how she lavishly spent money on them, he approached her. 'Beautiful lady,' he said in a silky voice, 'my wife has passed away, and I live alone. As soon as I saw you, I fell in love with you. Please have mercy on me and come into my embrace.'

'Really?' the woman was excited to learn that this handsome young man was not only single but also interested in being her lover. 'That is a persuasive offer. My husband is old and can hardly move around. So, it will not be hard for me to come and live with you, but do you have any means to support me?'

'No,' said the thug. 'I don't. But what I have is a heart that desires you and a young and strong body. And I can tell you that if you come to me, we'll enjoy many pleasures together.'

The woman smiled. 'You are, indeed, a handsome man. That's why I'll take care of the expenses. Don't worry. I'll just steal the money from my husband's safe and bring it with me, and we can leave this place and go and live happily somewhere else.'

'That sounds like a great plan, beautiful lady,' said the thug. 'Tomorrow morning, at dawn, come to this same place with the money, and you and I will leave this village and find a suitable city to live in, where we can spend our lives, enjoying the pleasures of life.'

'Oh, yes,' replied the woman. 'I promise I'll be here tomorrow,' and, giggling with excitement, went home. That night, after her husband fell asleep, she got up quietly, opened the safe, took all the money and jewels from it and tied them into a bundle, and then sat down to wait till dawn. When the first rays of the sun spread across the sky, she sneaked out of the house, carrying her bundle, and ran to the assigned spot. The thug was already waiting there, and, as soon as the woman arrived, he took her hand and began walking south.

After they had walked about two yojanas, they came to a river. As the thug stood on the riverbank considering the best way to cross the river, he began to think, what am I doing with this old, adulterous hag? Besides, what if her husband sends out a search party and they catch up with us? It'll put me in a real difficult situation. This is where I should take her money and cut her loose. Hence, turning to the woman, he said to her with a charming smile, 'Dear one, we have to cross the river now. But the water is deep. You won't be able to cross it by yourself. Give me your heavy bundle, and I'll take it across, and then I'll come back and put you on my back and help you cross. You can just enjoy the ride. You don't need to get your pretty feet wet.'

'Okay,' the woman said and handed him the bundle of money and jewels.

'Dearest, I just thought of something else,' the thug said. 'Take off your sari and shawl, and all the other clothes you are wearing, and I'll take those across as well. That way they won't get wet, and you'll have dry clothes waiting on the other side.'

The woman took off all her clothes and handed them to the thug, as well.

Carrying the bundle of money and clothing, the thug swam across the river as quickly as he could and, reaching the other bank, disappeared into the nearby jungle.

As the woman sat in the sand, a bit confused, quite a bit embarrassed at her nudity, covering her breasts with her arms, waiting for her lover to return, a vixen arrived on the bank, carrying a piece of meat in her mouth. Suddenly she saw a big fish lying dead in the sand. Dropping the meat from her mouth, she ran to grab the fish. Just then a hawk descended and grabbed the meat that the vixen had dropped and flew off. In the meantime, the fish, with a sudden flurry, jumped back into the water. Hence, left with no fish and no meat, the vixen turned her head to first look at the sky and then at the river.

Watching her, the woman burst into laughter. 'Clever vixen!' she said mockingly. 'The hawk took your meat, and the river took your fish. So, you lost both. Now what are you looking at?'

Turning to look at the woman, the vixen also laughed. 'Naked woman, if I am clever, then you are cleverer. Neither did you get your lover, nor your husband, and you've lost all your money. Now, sitting here naked, what are you looking at?'

As the crocodile was telling this tale, some other water creatures swam up to the bank to inform him that his house had been seized by another, larger crocodile. 'Oh, what travesty of fate this is,' he cried. 'What bad times I'm experiencing. My dear friend became my enemy, my beloved wife died, and now I'm robbed of my house. What other calamity is going to hit me? Someone has rightly said,

> Hurt upon hurt is often the case.
> Having no food intensifies hunger.
> Calamities always breed enmities.
> These are symptoms of bad days.

Now what should I do? Should I go and fight that other crocodile? Or should I try to reason with him that he leave my house? Maybe I should pay him off, or, perhaps, I could create dissension in his life to get my revenge?' Caught in the tangle of the situation, the crocodile was struck by a thought: why not ask the monkey for advice? It is said,

> He who uses his elders' advice
> in the undertaking of any task
> prevents obstacles in the path
> and works towards success.

Thinking this, the crocodile inched closer to the jamun tree and called up to the monkey, 'Look at my ill-fate. As though my situation wasn't bad enough, now, a larger, much stronger crocodile has claimed ownership of my house. I want to ask you for advice. Please tell me what measure I should use to reclaim my house: request him, pay him, fight him, or create discord in his life?'

'You ingrate, why do you keep bothering me, even though I've told you numerous times to leave me alone. I don't want to waste my breath advising fools like you.'

'I agree that I committed a grave sin against you. But can you put that aside for a moment and remember our past friendship? I beg you, for the sake of what we meant to each other in the past, please counsel me as you used to in the past.'

'I don't even want to think about our past relationship, you evil crocodile. You ruined what we had by listening to your wife and luring me into the water to kill me. It is easy for you to say, "Forget that," but how can I? You're not the one who was almost killed. It may be true that all men love their wives, some more than others, but how many take their best friends to the middle of the sea at their wives' behest and try to drown them? You are a complete fool, and because of your utter lack of intelligence, I actually foresaw your ruin.'

'Dear friend,' said the crocodile. 'I'm an ingrate and a transgressor. I violated your friendship. Even then, please help me. It is said,

> One who is good to those
> who have done a good turn
> is deserving of praise, indeed,
> but one who is good to those
> who have done them harm
> is a true saint. So say the wise.

'Fine,' said the monkey. 'Here is my advice: go home and fight that other crocodile. What he has done to you by robbing you of your home deserves a battle. And know this,

> If you die in battle you will go to heaven.
> If you win you will get your home and fame.
> Battle in a situation like this is a win-win.

Besides, here is what the wise say:

> To the ones stronger than you, bow.
> With valiant ones, divide and rule.
> The lesser ones, appease with charity.
> And the ones who are your equal—
> battle them to achieve what you desire.'

'What is this story?' the crocodile asked, and the monkey related it.

THE TALE OF THE CLEVER WOLF WHO KNEW CHANAKYA NITI

In a forest lived a wolf called Mahachatura (very clever). Once he came upon a dead elephant and was elated to have an enormous amount of meat to eat. However, no matter where he tried to dig his teeth into the elephant's body, he couldn't bite through the tough skin. Searching for a soft spot, he was circling the elephant, when a lion came that way. Seeing him, the wolf touched his forehead to the ground and said in an obeisant voice, 'I am your servant, Maharaj—your soldier. I was just watching over this elephant for you. But now that you are here, please enjoy yourself.'

'Arrey, I don't even touch prey that has been killed by another,' the lion declared, disdainfully. 'Don't you know,

> The lion will eat only meat
> of deer he himself has killed.
> If no prey comes his way
> he will starve but not eat grass.

People of principle, like me, never give up the rightful path, no matter what hardship comes their way. Therefore, I gift you this elephant. Enjoy him.'

The wolf was relieved to hear the lion say this. 'Maharaj, your lordship is exemplary,' he said ingratiatingly. 'All lords and masters should demonstrate such generosity toward their servants. It is said,

> The noble maintain their nobility,
> even in times of adversity, because
> they are born into virtuous families.
> Nobleness in them is ingrained.
> See, even when the conch is burnt
> flames blacken its whiteness, but
> it remains as white and pure as ever.'

The lion nodded, accepting the praise as his due and went on his way, leaving the wolf alone to eat the whole elephant. Once again, as the wolf stood contemplating where to make the first cut, a tiger came that way. 'Oh, no. I just kissed the ground to convince one wicked predator to leave, and now, here is another,' the wolf said to himself, annoyed. 'I'll have to get rid of him, as well. I know this one to be quite a warrior; therefore, the best strategy to use on him would be to cause discord between him and the lion.'

> Even a well-rounded man with good qualities
> can be defeated with the fear of division.
> Just like the pearl is perfect and lustrous
> yet with a hole in its heart, it can be strung.

In the same way, a wealthy, truthful, innocent person can be threatened by the fear of division. Thus, adopting a haughty stance, with his neck stiff and his nose in the air, the wolf said to the tiger, 'Uncle, have you come here to face death? This elephant is the lion's kill. He has stationed me to watch it while he bathes in the river. And, before he left, he specifically commanded me that if any tiger comes here, I must inform him immediately, so that he can annihilate him. The reason for his hostility is that once before when he had gone to bathe after killing an elephant, a tiger had come and eaten his kill. "I'm very incensed at tigers," he said to me. "I'll kill any tiger I see."'

The wolf's words put the fear of death in the tiger's heart, and his limbs began to shake. 'Nephew, please, I beg you. Spare my life. Please don't mention anything about me to the lion. I'm leaving this instance.' And the tiger fled.

But even as the wolf turned to the elephant again, a young cheetah arrived at the spot. Oh no, thought the wolf. Now I'll have to deal with this one, too. And he began to think what strategy to use this time. Then the thought came to him that the cheetah's teeth and nails are adamantine, and he could use them to his benefit. So, he said to cheetah, 'Dear nephew, I'm seeing you after a long time. How are you? Are you well? It looks like you're starving. How fortuitous for you that the lion has left me here with this elephant that he killed, while he takes a bath. Today, you're my guest. Feel free to eat as much of this elephant meat as you wish, and then leave before the lion arrives.'

'Uncle, thank you for the invitation, but if this elephant is the lion's kill, I shouldn't eat it, because it is said,

> As long as a man remains alive
> he will enjoy many moments of joy.

If I dare to eat this elephant's meat, the lion will surely take my life, and that will end all the moments I may still experience. So, keep your hospitality to yourself, uncle. Besides, it is said,

> If one wishes for one's own well-being,
> one should eat only what can be eaten,
> what can be digested without a problem,
> and once digested, does the body good.

Eating this elephant's meat and provoking the lion's anger will be like eating food that can't be digested. I think it's best that I leave this instant.'

'Arrey, you coward! Why are you so afraid? Eat fearlessly. I'll stand watch, and, as soon as I see the lion coming, I'll give you a signal.'

The cheetah thought for a moment and then decided to take the wolf up on his offer. The wolf pretending to watch the path to the river, moved to stand at a distance, from where he kept an eye on the cheetah who sank his sharp teeth into the elephant's flank and tore at it. But even as he made the first cut, the wolf suddenly cried, 'Oh nephew, run! Quickly! The lion—he's headed this way and will be here in no time.'

Not even able to get one mouthful of meat, the cheetah fled from the place. But, fortunately, for the wolf, the tear he had made in the elephant's flank was enough for him to dig in. However, no sooner had he taken his first bite, when another wolf suddenly appeared on the scene. He seemed to be in a rage, as he came snarling and baring his teeth to stand squarely before his rival. Knowing him to be of equal strength, the first wolf spoke the following shloka:

> To the ones stronger than you, bow.
> With the valiant ones, divide and rule.
> The lesser ones, appease with charity.
> And the ones who are your equal—
> battle them to achieve what you desire.

Then he charged at the new arrival and, with a violent attack of teeth and nails, shredded him to pieces. Destroying him, sacrificing him to the elements, and then shaking himself free of battle frenzy, he finally sat down to enjoy a delicious meal of elephant meat.

'You see,' said the monkey to the crocodile, 'just like this wolf, you, too, should know what niti to apply in which situation. In my estimation, it is time for danda niti—the strategy of punishment. Go and fight that enemy, because he is from your clan and is your equal. Destroy him, or, at least, defeat him and throw him out of your house; otherwise, he'll put down roots and settle in, and then you'll never be able to oust him. In fact, he may then kill you, because it is said,

> Wealth from cows is possible.
> Austerity in a brahmin is possible.
> Fickleness in women is possible.
> And also possible is fear from kin.

And this:

> There is food aplenty in a foreign land,
> and woman are lax and easy-going.
> But the problem in a foreign land is this:
> Clansmen there are so full of animosity,
> animosity becomes the meaning of clan.

'What is this story?' the crocodile asked, and the monkey told the tale.

THE TALE OF THE DOG IN A FOREIGN LAND

In a certain town lived a dog called Chitranga (picturesque body). For years, that town had been suffering famine, and there was no food or grain left. Hence, the dogs and cats and other domestic animals were dying of starvation. Those that could, fled to other lands. Chitranga, too, feeble with thirst and hunger, made his way to another town. There, he was lucky enough to find a house where the wife was careless about where she stored the food. Thus, Chitranga was able to easily find food in that house, and he began sneaking in every day. The only problem was that every time he exited the house, he was accosted by other street dogs, who were bigger than him and vicious. They would surround him and bite him till he bled.

One day, he was in so much pain from the encounter with the dogs that he couldn't help asking himself: 'Why did I ever leave my town? I was happy there. There was famine, admittedly, but at least, I lived in peace and free from pain. No one accosted me every day and bit me till I bled. I think it is best that I return home.' And, making that wise decision, Chitranga returned home.

When he returned, his relatives asked him, 'How is the foreign land? Tell us everything about it. How are the people? How do they live? What do they eat?'

'Oh, what to say about the foreign land,' Chitranga replied. 'It is such a glorious place. There are all sorts of foods and comforts there. And women are more engaged in enjoying life than protecting their cooking. That's why it's easy for dogs to find food. There's only one problem: your own clan is your enemy.'

'I see what you're saying,' the crocodile said to the monkey. 'Thank you for the advice.' Then, determining to fight his enemy, even if he perished, he said goodbye to the monkey.

By the time the crocodile reached home, he was filled with such passionate resolve that as soon as he saw the squatter, he struck him with a powerful blow of his tail. After that, it took only a brief battle to defeat and kill the enemy. Then, reclaiming his home, Karalamukha lived there in peace for many years. It is rightly said,

> Wealth gotten by luck
> may be worth enjoying,

> but it gives no pleasure.
> Even an old bull can live
> on grass he finds by chance.
> Only wealth well earned
> and gained with good intentions
> brings true happiness in life.
> Advancement in life results from
> ability and hard work, not fate.

With this ends Labdha Pranasha, the fourth tantra of the *Panchatantra*. Its opening shloka was as follows:

> He who has acuity of mind when needful
> can escape even the inescapable,
> like the monkey stuck in waters vast,
> who escaped by dint of his intelligence.

FIFTH TANTRA
APARIKSHITA KARAKAM
Impetuous Actions

Here is the first shloka of the fifth tantra, titled Aparikshita Karakam:

> One should not act upon anything
> without first distinctly seeing it,
> without fully understanding it,
> without thoroughly examining it,
> just as the foolhardy barber did.

This is the story that is told by elders:

In the southern region is a city called Patliputra. In this city used to live a rich businessman, whose name was Manibhadra (excellent jewel). He had invested much of his money in trade, but he still spent large sums on charitable acts. Yet, despite all this expenditure, he was able to spend lavishly on food, celebrations, and yajnas. Once, in a twist of fate, he lost all his money. When he became destitute, people began to treat him with disrespect. This treatment hurt him even more than losing his wealth. One night, lying awake in bed, he said to himself, 'Ah! poverty is a terrible thing. Someone has rightly said,

> A man may have many qualities:
> modesty, cleanliness, tolerance.
> He may be clever, skilled, eloquent.
> But none of these are lauded
> if he lacks the virtue of wealth.

> When a man loses wealth,
> he also loses his good traits:
> esteem, self-respect, pride,
> skilfulness, clarity, and wisdom.

> Just like springtime's soft breezes
> lessen every day the power of winter,
> a wise man's mind is daily lessened
> by worries of how to care for family.

> The worry of not having enough money
> for household needs of daily use like
> ghee, salt, oil, rice, clothes, and wood,
> can destroy the minds of the wisest.

> A moneyless man's house,
> beautiful though it may be,
> is terrifying, empty, and sad,

like the sky without stars,
like a lake without water,
or, like a cremation ground.

Just like bubbles in water
form and vanish in water,
a poor man, though existing,
is rendered invisible to all.

Unlike a poor man, who is
noble, able, and gracious,
but never loved by anyone,
a rich man, lacking these virtues,
is loved like a wishing tree by all.

When the affluent behave improperly,
no one in the world calls them out,
Just as no one criticizes the roaring
but water-rich ocean and clouds.'

Thus, Manibhadra decided that it was worthless living in poverty and that he would give up his life. While he was thinking these thoughts, he fell asleep and had a dream: a treasure called Padma was standing before him in physical form, wearing the clothes of a Buddhist monk. 'Do not be sad,' he said to Manibhadra. 'I'm Padmanidhi. Your ancestors realized me, and when I manifested before them, they buried me in the ground to keep me safe until I was needed by you or someone in your family. Tomorrow morning, I will appear before you as a bhikshu. As soon as you see me, you should hit me on the head with a staff. I will then become a pile of gold and live in your house forever. After that your wealth will never diminish.' Saying this, Padmanidhi vanished.

When the businessman woke up in the morning, he wondered if his dream was true. 'It's probably not,' he said to himself, resignedly. 'I'm always thinking about money, day and night; this was probably a result of that. Someone has rightly said,

The dreams dreamt by people who are
sick, grieving, worried, lustful, and drunk
are always meaningless and nonsensical.

Then, one day, as Manibhadra was sitting in his courtyard, talking to his wife, who had called a barber home to get a manicure, he suddenly saw the bhikshu he had seen in his dream, standing there before him. He could hardly believe his eyes, but he joyfully picked up a staff and hit the monk on the head with it. Instantly, the man became a pile of gold. Manibhadra quickly gathered all the gold and took it inside the house and hid it safely. Then, he gave the barber, who had seen the whole incident, a set of new clothes and some money and said to him, 'Brother, please don't tell anyone about what you have seen here.'

The barber was flabbergasted at what he had seen. On his way home, he began to think: that man whom the businessman hit was a Buddhist monk. It seems that these bhikshus turn into gold when they are hit on the head with a staff. Why don't I invite a few monks to my house and hit each one on the head? That way I'll have many piles of gold.

The barber spent a restless night, trying to work out a plan and, as soon as it was morning, he found a big wooden staff which he put in corner where he could easily reach it. Then he went to the Buddhist monastery, and, circumambulating the idol of Lord Buddha, sat down crossed-legged, with his face respectfully covered in a shawl, while reciting the following shlokas:

> Victory to those Jina, masters of knowledge,
> whose mind field is infertile to the seeds of karma
> from the time they are born into this world.
>
> Praise be to that tongue
> that sings the glory of the Jina.
> Praise be to the mind
> that is devoted to the Jina.
> Praise be to the hands
> that offer worship to the Jina.

After that, he bowed obeisantly to the chief of the sangha.

'May you always follow the path of dharma,' the bhikshu said, blessing him and giving him a sacred thread to wear around his neck.

'Swami,' the barber said, touching his head to the floor at the bhikshu's feet. 'I have come to invite you and the other bhikshus to my house. Please come with me and eat at my house.'

'O devotee, knowing the practices of our dharma, how you can say this? We are not like brahmins, whom you can invite to your house for meals. We beg for our food from house to house, and the true devotees of our faith give us food in alms. And, even though they press us repeatedly to take more, we only eat a handful of food, just so our bodies can subsist. Go now, and don't ever say again what you just said.'

'Swami, I know very well the precepts of your faith. And I also know that there are many households that are ever ready to give you food; therefore, I fear my turn may never come. That is why I request you to grace my house. Another reason why I make the request is that I've collected various expensive fabrics that you can use to wrap your holy books. I want to give those to you along with the money I have put aside for the sangha to get more books scribed. Swami, I have followed my dharma by making the request; now you must do what you think is right.'

After that, the barber returned home and made sure that the staff of khair wood he had put in the corner was still there, within easy reach, and the locks on the doors worked. At one-and-a-half pahar of the day, he went back to the monastery and sat down at its gate to wait. Soon, the gate opened, and the monks came out in single file, ready to disperse around the neighbourhoods to make their daily begging rounds. The barber fell at the chief bhikshu's feet and begged him once again to bring all the bhikshus to his house to receive food and take the fabrics and money that he had earlier promised.

He did not have to plead for long; the idea of the fabrics and money had already enticed the chief bhikshu. 'O devotee, lead the way to your house,' he said to the barber.

Someone has rightly said,

> What a wonder it is:
> living alone, renouncing family,
> surviving on alms, clad in the sky,
> ascetic in every way,
> but still lured by desire.

> In old age, hair turns grey,
> teeth loosen and fall,
> eyes and ears weaken.
> But desire—like rising youth—
> never stops growing.

In this way, the barber lured the bhikshus into his house, and once they were all inside, he shut the doors and secured the locks. Then, grabbing the staff, he began striking each bhikshu on the head. Many of the monks died on the spot, others fell unconscious, and some, who were still conscious, began screaming for help.

Their loud cries were heard in the police station, and the chief of police ordered his men to investigate what was going on. Following the sound of the cries, the soldiers arrived at the barber's house and banged at the door, and when no one opened, they broke it down. What they saw inside was mayhem: many monks on the floor, either dead or bleeding to death and wailing and groaning in pain, while many others ran around in a panic, screaming, trying to save themselves from the barber who was relentlessly wielding his staff, raining blows on their heads.

The soldiers grabbed the barber and, putting him in ropes, brought him and the few monks who were still able to walk, to court.

'What is the reason for this unconscionable act?' the judges asked the barber.

'What can I tell you, noble sirs. I did exactly what I saw Manibhadra do. I saw him hit a monk on the head with a staff; the monk vanished, but in his stead, there was a pile of gold on the floor.'

The judges then summoned Manibhadra to court and asked him, 'Did you hit any ascetic on the head?'

Manibhadra told the judges the whole story about his dream and Padmanidhi's instructions, and how the barber had witnessed him strike the ascetic, who was just a personified form of the treasure.

'So, without knowing or examining the matter, you killed a number of monks, simply on an assumption,' the chief judge said to the barber. 'For this heinous crime, I sentence you to death.'

Thus the barber was hanged to death, and the judges all said this,

> One should not act upon anything
> without first distinctly seeing it,
> without fully understanding it,
> without thoroughly examining it,
> or one will suffer the fate of the barber.

The judges also said,

> One should not do anything
> unless one has investigated
> and clearly thought it through,
> otherwise, regret is what one feels
> as did the brahmin woman who
> thoughtlessly killed the mongoose.

'What is that story, noble sirs?' Manibhadra asked the judges, and they narrated the tale.

THE TALE OF THE WOMAN WHO KILLED HER MONGOOSE SON

In a town lived a brahmin called Devasharma. The day that his wife gave birth to a son, a mongoose, too, birthed a pup. Sadly, the mongoose mother died while delivering her baby; hence, the brahmin mother took the mongoose pup in and began to take care of him, along with her son, to the extent of letting him suckle at her breast. However, despite providing him a mother's nurturing, she never truly trusted the mongoose. 'I hope he doesn't act according to his natural instincts and hurt my son,' she would often say.

It is rightly said,

> One's son may be worthless.
> He may be unlearned, ugly,
> and foolish and cruel too.
> But he is one's own and dear.
> People say, sandal is cooling,
> but the touch of a son's body
> is more cooling and pleasurable.

One day, needing to fetch water from the river, she laid her infant son on the bed and, picking up the water pot, said to her husband, 'I'm going to the river. Please take care of our son while I'm gone, and, also, don't forget to take care of the mongoose.'

The brahmin nodded in distraction; and, after some time, he, too, stepped out with his begging bowl, leaving the boy and the pup by themselves in the house. As it happened, a big, black snake found its way into the house. Seeing him, the mongoose pup pounced on him, as mongooses do when they see their natural enemy, but for this pup, it was more than just natural instinct; he wanted to protect his brother. There was a fierce battle between the two, but the mongoose finally prevailed. He subdued the snake and tore it to pieces.

When the brahmin woman came back, the mongoose pup gleefully went to door to greet her. But, seeing his mouth and body covered with blood, the woman screamed, 'Oh no! He has killed my son.' And in a fit of grief and rage, she flung the water-filled pot at him, killing him instantly.

Sobbing and wailing, the woman ran indoors only to see her son playing happily on the bed, with not a scratch on him. Then, when she saw a mangled dead snake beside the bed, she realized the mistake she had made. Falling to the floor, she beat her breasts and lamented, 'What have I done?'

She was still sobbing, when the brahmin returned. 'You greedy, uncaring man,' she screamed at him. 'Look, what your greed has done. I told you to take care our sons, but you couldn't resist the temptation. Now our son is gone. Suffer! Someone has rightly said,

> A man not able to abjure all greed,
> should make all effort to curtail it.
> The man with uncontrolled greed
> has a wheel revolving in his head.'

'What is this tale?' the brahmin asked his wife, and she related it to him.

THE TALE OF THE WHEEL OF GREED

In a city lived four poor brahmin youths, who were great friends. One day, discussing how they never had any money, they all exclaimed, 'This poverty be damned!' Then they shared their views about what has rightly been said,

> Better to live in a forest full of wild creatures.
> Better to sleep on bare ground and leaves.
> Better to have for clothing the bark of trees.
> But to live among kith and kin in poverty
> is the most deplorable situation of all.
>
> A poor man may serve with all sincerity,
> but his employer will suspect his service.
> Penury makes his best qualities fade away.
> A poor man is abandoned by kith and kin.
> Even his sons do not want to bother with him.
> Every day brings new calamities on the poor.
> What else can be said about his misfortunes,
> except to say that even his wife leaves him,
> and his friends want nothing to do with him.
> Hence, without money, a man's life is worthless.
>
> In this world a man may be brave, handsome,
> fortunate, learned in shastras, and eloquent,
> but if he has no wealth, he receives no respect.

See this wonder of the world:

> Men have the same five senses,
> Some, the same sharp intelligence,
> and the same manner of speech.
> But as soon as a man loses his money,
> he falls in people's estimation.

So, friends, let's go and make some money.

Agreeing upon this resolve, the friends bid their families farewell, left their homes, left their city, and started on a journey to acquire wealth. Someone has rightly said,

> Fraught with worry about money,
> one is likely to disregard truth,
> abandon friends and relatives,
> leave parents and homeland,
> and go to troubled foreign lands—
> all in the pursuit of money.

After many days of travelling by foot, the four brahmin youths reached the city of Ujjain. Cleansing themselves in the Sipra River, they went to worship at Mahakala temple. As they were leaving the temple, they met a tantric yogi named Bhairavananda, who invited them to come and stay with him in the monastery.

After the evening meal, as they were all sitting and relaxing, the tantric asked the four young men, 'Where have you come from, and where are you going? What is the objective of your travel?'

'We've left home to acquire wealth,' they told Bhairavananda. 'We'll go wherever we have to in the pursuit of wealth. We're determined that either we procure money, or we give up our lives. Someone has said,

> A daring man has the will
> to acquire anything he wants—
> an arduous divine power,
> or his intended wealth,
> even if it costs him his life.

Also, we believe,

> Hard work is no less powerful than luck.
> See, rain is a matter of chance in farming,
> but by digging a canal, water is still attainable.
>
> All of one's desires are fulfilled
> by living a good life and doing hard work.
> Luck, as people say, is just a part of life.
>
> Two kinds of people are most surprising:
> those with zeal, who can stake their lives
> if need be; and those with such big hearts
> that they are ever ready to give their all.

> One cannot attain happiness
> without working hard for it.
> Even Vishnu had to churn the ocean
> to attain his beloved Lakshmi.

So, we're ready to do whatever is necessary to acquire wealth. Please advise us about what to do, whether it is going down a mouse hole all the way to the netherworld, or it is through the tantric path of ghosts and spirits, or obeisance to Dakini-Shakini. Whether it is by living in the cremation ground or by selling our own flesh, we're ready to do it. We know that you are a realized and famed tantric, but we, too, have courage and zeal. Somebody has rightly said,

> Only great men can help others in great tasks.
> It is only the ocean that can bear a volcano.'

Bhairavananda agreed to help the young men achieve their desire and made for each of them a talismanic ball of string. Then he instructed them, 'Go north towards Himalaya, and wherever this ball falls from your hand, start digging in that spot. Whatever you unearth from that hole, take it, and return home.'

Receiving the balls from the tantric, the four young brahmins set out on the journey northwards, crossing many forests and hills. As they were climbing up the side of a mountain, one of them felt the ball slipping out of his hand. Squatting right there, the brahmin youth began digging in the exact spot where it had fallen, as the tantric had advised, and soon came upon a copper mine. 'Brothers,' he called to his friends in excitement, 'come! Take as much copper as you want from this pile.'

'You fool,' the others admonished. 'What'll we do with copper? No matter how much of it we take, we can never become rich with it. So, leave the copper and come with us. Let's press on.'

'You go, if you want,' the young man who had found copper replied. 'I'm satisfied with this treasure.' And, gathering as many of the copper nuggets as he could carry, he returned to his home.

The remaining three brahmins continued up the mountain, and, after some time, another one's ball fell to the ground. When he dug at that spot, he discovered a silver mine. 'Arrey,' he called to the others in elation. 'I found silver. Come. Take as much as you want. We don't need to go any further.'

'No brother,' the other two replied. 'Back there was copper, and here there is silver, which means that further up, there'll be a gold mine. Why should we be satisfied with silver when we can get gold. We should keep going.'

'You go on, if you like. I'm satisfied with this silver,' the second brahmin youth said, and, gathering as much silver as he could, he returned home.

A little bit further up, the third young man's ball fell to the ground, and when he dug in the spot, he discovered a gold mine. 'Look! Gold!' he said to his friend. 'Let's take as much as we can and return home. What can be better than gold?'

'Use your intelligence,' the other brahmin said. 'First copper, then silver, and then gold. I'm certain that the next mine will be precious gems. All one needs to become rich is one truly perfect gem. Instead of carrying a load of gold, let's find that gem.'

'I don't want to go any further,' replied the young man who had found gold. 'I'll just sit here and wait for you to return. You go on. I'm satisfied with gold.'

The fourth young man kept climbing and climbing. But then, the terrain became rough and untrodden, and the sun's rays began to scorch. Before long, suffering from exhaustion and thirst, he became disoriented. As he wandered in the mountain, he came upon a man, whose clothes were soaked with blood that was pouring from a deep, open gash in his head, where a wheel was constantly spinning.

'Who are you?' the brahmin asked the man. 'And why is there a spinning wheel in your head? By the way, I'm looking for water. Have you seen a lake or a pond somewhere close by?'

As soon as the brahmin asked these questions, the wheel flew out of the man's head and lodged itself in the brahmin's head, still spinning.

'Oh! What just happened?' the brahmin cried in pain. 'How did the wheel leave your head and get stuck in mine? How can I get rid of it?'

'When someone else like you, carrying a talisman and seeking wealth, comes to you on this mountain and talks to you, the wheel will leave you and get attached to him,' said the man.

'How long will that be?'

'I've lost count of time. Who is currently the ruler of earth?'

'Vatsaraja Udayana,' said the brahmin.

'When I came to this mountain, the ruler on earth was Shri Rama of Ayodhya, so you, yourself, can estimate how much time has passed. I was poverty-stricken, and, I came this way, seeking wealth. That's when I saw another man here who had this wheel in his head. As soon as I talked to him, the wheel flew from his head and started revolving in my head. It's been there ever since.'

'But where did you find food and water on this mountain? How did you eat?'

'Lord Kubera's treasures are buried in this mountain. To prevent people from stealing them, he has created this wheel; that is why no one ventures here. But if some greedy person does come this way, this wheel of greed gets stuck in his head, and all other needs—hunger, thirst, sleep, etc., are forgotten. Now, I'll take your leave,' said the man. 'Finally freed from this wheel, I want to leave this mountain as soon as I can.' Saying this, he quickly descended the mountain.

In the meantime, the brahmin who had stopped by the gold mine came searching for his friend by tracing his footprints. Seeing the rotating wheel in his friend's head and his blood-soaked clothes, he was shocked. 'What happened to you?' he asked his friend with concern.

'This is god's will and a consequence of my own fate.'

'Tell me what happened,' the friend asked, and the wheel-bearing brahmin told him the whole story of how he met the previous wheel-bearer and how the wheel transferred from his head to his own.

'I told you not to go any further. I tried to stop you, but you didn't want to listen. You're such a learned man, and you come from such a noble family, but you lack intelligence. Someone has rightly said,

> Intelligence is superior to erudition.
> See, despite having the knowledge,
> but lacking common intelligence,
> those lion-reviving scholars lost their lives.'

'What is this story?' the wheel-bearing brahmin asked, and his friend told him the tale.

THE TALE OF THE INTELLIGENT YOUNG MEN WHO REVIVED A LION

In a city lived four brahmins who were fast friends. Three of them were scholars of learning, but they had no common sense. The fourth, whose name was Subudhi (good intellect), had no formal learning, but he was highly intelligent. However, no matter their level of intelligence, they all believed that the learning which could not be used to impress kings and procure wealth was of no use. Therefore, one day, they decided to head east to seek wealth.

After they had gone a short distance, the eldest among them said, 'Friends, I've been thinking: this fourth among us has no learning. All he has is intelligence, but one can't impress kings with just intelligence; and so, his intelligence will be of no use to us in gaining wealth. Therefore, I say that when we gain wealth by using our learning, he shouldn't receive a share of it. In fact, I think it is better that he go back right now.'

The second man also agreed, 'Hey, intelligent one, go home,' he said to the fourth man. 'You have no real knowledge of anything.'

'That's not right,' the third friend said. 'We've all grown up together and done everything together since we were children. Let this poor man accompany us. We'll give him a small share of the money we generate. It is said,

> "This is mine;" "this is yours" are thoughts
> that people of meagre minds have.
> For the magnanimous, all the people
> on earth are like one large family.'

Talking in this manner among themselves, they came upon a pile of bones.

'Brothers,' said one of them, 'this is the perfect opportunity to demonstrate what learning can do. Look at these bones. Using our learning, let's try to put life back into this animal. Let me first arrange these bones in the shape of a body.' And using his knowledge of anatomy, he began matching the bones, as in a puzzle, and laid them out to form a skeleton. It was a lion's. Then, the second brahmin also used his knowledge and created flesh and skin and blood around the bones. Just as the third friend was about to use his learning to breathe life into the flesh and blood and bones, Subudhi, the fourth friend who had no learning but keen intelligence, stopped him. 'What are you doing?' he said. 'You're reviving a lion. Once he comes alive, he'll devour us.'

'You are an uneducated and unlearned oaf. Why should I listen to you?' said the third brahmin. 'I'm not going to let my knowledge go untested just because you say so. The others have demonstrated their knowledge; now it's my turn.'

'Fine,' said Subudhi. 'Do as you please, but wait just a few moments. Let me climb up on this tree before you demonstrate your knowledge.' Subudhi then quickly climbed up a tree, and the third brahmin used his knowledge to instil life into the corpse. As soon as the lion came alive, he leapt on the three brahmins and killed them. Subudhi waited him to disappear into the forest before descending from the tree and returning home.

'That is why I say,' said the gold-receiving brahmin, 'common sense is greater than book-learning.'

'I don't completely agree with you,' said the wheel-bearer,

> 'The most intelligent are sometimes
> destroyed by the adverse effect of fate.
> Whereas, those of little intelligence
> live happily because fate is favourable.

Someone has rightly said,

> The unprotected live protected,
> if they are protected by fate.
> And the protected can be destroyed
> when fate withdraws its favour.
> Orphaned and unsheltered, a being
> can survive unharmed in a forest.
> But a person safe and secure at home
> can be destroyed if fate so wills.

> Look dear,
> that Shatabudhi is lying dead on the fisherman's head,
> Sahastrabudhi is hanging lifeless from his shoulder,
> while I, Ekabudhi, am living happily in this lake.'

'What is this tale?' the gold-receiving brahmin asked, and his friend, narrated the tale.

THE TALE OF HOW THE OVERCONFIDENT FISH BROUGHT ABOUT THEIR OWN DEMISE

In a lake lived two fish by the names of Shatabudhi (he who has the intelligence of a hundred) and Sahastrabudhi (he who has the intelligence of a thousand). They had a frog friend, whose name was Ekabudhi (he who has the intelligence of one). The three spent all their time together, swimming and frolicking in the water. One evening, as they were enjoying a leisurely swim along the lake's side, they saw many fishermen headed home, carrying big baskets full of fish on their heads and large nets over the shoulders. As they walked along the lakeside, they said to each other, 'It seems that this lake is full of fish, and the water level is low. That means it'll be easy to cast our nets. Why don't we come here tomorrow to catch fish?'

Hearing what the fishermen intended, the frog was very perturbed. 'This is terrible news,' he said. 'What are we to do? Dear friend, Shatabudhi, what do you think we should do now? Should we flee from this place or stay here?'

'Don't be afraid, dear friend,' Sahastrabudhi said with a laugh. 'One shouldn't become fearful just by hearing something that someone has said. People say,

> If the desires of the wicked and cruel
> and of robbers and thugs and snakes
> were all fulfilled all the time,
> this world would have long ceased to be.

More than likely, what we heard was just talk, and the fishermen will not return here. And if, by chance, they do return, I'll save you by using my superior intelligence that equals a thousand intelligences. I can find numerous ways to escape from this lake.'

'You're very right,' Shatabudhi agreed with Sahastrabudhi. 'You truly do have the intelligence of a thousand. Someone has rightly said,

> There is nothing that intelligent people cannot accomplish.
> See, how the erudite brahmin, Chanakya,
> unaided and singlehanded, using just intelligence,
> destroyed the vast army of the Nanda empire.

> The intellect can reach even those places
> untouched by the wind and the sun's rays.

That is why I agree with Sahastrabudhi. We can't just leave this lake where our fathers and grandfathers lived, just because we heard some idle talk among fishermen. It is said,

> Heaven may be adorned with celestials, apsaras, and the like.
> But it is no match to the ordinary sight of one's homeland.

That's why, Ekabudhi, you should not leave this lake.'

'Dear friend, you have multiple intelligences. I have only one. And my single intelligence is telling me to run. I think I'm going to take my wife and move somewhere that feels safe.' And that very night, Ekabudhi, the frog, took his wife to another lake nearby.

The following morning, the fishermen came to the lake and cast their nets, catching many of the fish, turtles, crabs, and other creatures. Shatabudhi and Sahastrabudhi, along with their wives and children, tried their best to hide, or to somehow escape from the lake but ultimately they were caught, and they died soon after.

That evening, when the fishermen, satisfied with the day's catch, started on their way home, they put some of the fish in a basket to carry on their heads, and the rest, they strung together with a rope and threw on their shoulders. That is how Shatabudhi ended up in a basket and Sahastrabudhi on a shoulder. And that is also why, watching the fishermen from his safe haven, Ekabudhi the frog, said to his wife,

> Look, dear,
> that Shatabudhi is lying dead on the fisherman's head,
> Sahastrabudhi is hanging lifeless from his shoulder,
> while I, Ekabudhi, the frog, am living happily in this lake.

'Therefore, as I was telling you,' said the wheel-bearing brahmin, 'intelligence is not the only thing that can get you through.'

'Okay, fine,' said his friend. 'But to ignore the advice of friends is also not right. I told you numerous times to rein in your desires and stop coveting. But your mind was so clouded with greed and the arrogance of your learning that you didn't listen to me. Now you are suffering the result of that. Somebody has rightly said,

Well done, dear uncle. I told you,
"Stop singing!" But you didn't listen.
Now enjoy your reward—a millstone,
like a jewel, tied around your neck.'

'What is this story?' the wheel-bearer asked, and his friend narrated the tale.

THE TALE OF THE DONKEY
WHO LOVED TO SING

In a town lived a donkey called Uddhat (insolent). All day, he carried loads on his back for his owner, who was a washerman and dyer, and all night he wandered around wherever he pleased. But, as soon the sun dawned, he himself returned to the washerman's house to begin the day's work, and because the washerman trusted his donkey to show up every morning, he did not tie him up at night.

Once, during his nightly rove in a cucumber field, the donkey met a jackal and became friends with him. From then on, the two of them together began to raid cucumber fields. The donkey was strong, and he would break the fence to enter a field, and then the two of them would eat cucumbers to their heart's content all night.

One night the carefree donkey said to the jackal, 'Look nephew, what a clear, beautiful, starry night it is. Such a night is for singing. Tell me what raga shall I sing?'

'Uncle,' said the jackal. 'What is this urge? Please don't do this disastrous thing. As it is, we have broken into the field like thieves. Thieves don't declare themselves. They keep themselves hidden. It is said,

> If you cough all the time
> stop being a thief.
> If you fall sleep at night
> stop visiting prostitutes.
> If you are ill but want to live
> stop pleasuring your tongue.

And, to top it off, you don't even have a singing voice. In, fact, you sound as tuneless as a conch shell. Besides, the sound of a voice carries far. If the men guarding this field hear you, they'll come and beat us up or they'll tether you and beat me. So, enjoy the sweet juicy cucumbers, and forget the singing.'

'Arrey, you are a creature of the wild. How would you know the joy of a good song? That's why you are preventing me from singing. This is what people say about music:

> When the darkness is dispelled by
> the moonlight of a winter's night,
> then, sitting with your beloved,
> if you hear sweet strains of music,
> how lucky you are; how blessed.'

'I hear what you're saying,' the jackal replied, 'but you don't even know how to sing. All you can do is bray. Please, I beg you, stay quiet and do what you've come here to do, or we'll both get caught. Then, our nightly feeding in lush fields of cucumbers will cease. I'm telling you, don't sing—for your own sake.'

'Fool! Shame on you for saying that I don't know how to sing. Listen, I'll tell you all the elements of music:

> Seven notes, three octaves weaving
> with twenty-one melodies to form
> forty-nine different types of taanas.
> Three beats, five measures, three tempos,
> three resting notes and three starting points
> bound together in patterns of three kinds.
> Forty principles and nine rasas expressing
> ragas and raginis that number thirty-six.
> Bharata Muni totals these musical elements
> as one hundred and eighty-five.
>
> Nothing is dearer to the gods than music.
> It was by playing ragas on a veena stringed
> with his own dried-up sinews that Ravana
> pleased the Great Lord Shiva Mahadeva.

See, how much I know about music? How can you say I don't know the art of singing?'

'Uncle, if your desire to sing is so strong, then let me go and stand by the gate to watch for the owner of the field. Then you can sing to your heart's content.'

Hence, the jackal left the field, the donkey began to sing, and the inevitable happened. Hearing the donkey's loud braying, the owner of the field picked up a stick and ran towards him, gnashing his teeth. He beat the donkey so hard that the animal fell to the ground in a faint. Then the man tied a millstone around his neck and went back to sleep.

After some time, when the pains in the donkey's body had lessened, as it naturally happens with animals, such as dogs, horses, and especially, donkeys, he got up and ran towards the fence, ramming it with the millstone that was tied around his neck, and managed to escape.

Watching him from a distance, the jackal said with a laugh,

> 'Well done, dear uncle. I told you,
> "Stop singing!" But you didn't listen.
> Now enjoy your reward—a millstone,
> like a jewel, tied around your neck.'

'Dear friend, just like this foolhardy donkey, you didn't listen to me, and now look at the pain you're in,' said the brahmin, who was satisfied with gold, to his friend, who had the wheel of greed spinning in his forehead.

'You're right,' the wheel-bearer replied.

> 'He who has no common sense of his own,
> and does not listen to the advice of friends,
> summons his own death, like Mantharaka the weaver.'

'What is this story?' the gold-receiving brahmin asked, and his friend told the tale.

THE TALE OF THE WEAVER WHO WISHED FOR TWO HEADS AND FOUR HANDS

In a village lived a weaver named Mantharaka (slow). Over the years, he had used his weaving equipment so much that its wooden beams had begun to crack. One day, deciding to make new beams, he took his axe and went into the forest. On the ocean's shore he saw a sheesham tree. 'How fortunate,' he said to himself. 'This is a such a big tree that I can get all the wood I need from it.'

In that tree lived a ghost. He said to the weaver, 'Arrey, don't cut this tree. I live here. This is my home. I love living here on the ocean's shore where I can enjoy the cool breeze.'

'Brother, what should I do? Without my equipment, I have no livelihood, and my children have no food. Why don't you leave this tree and find another home? I'm going to cut this one down.'

'I'll give you a boon. Whatever you want, ask for it, and it'll be fulfilled. But promise me that you won't cut this tree.'

'You'll really grant me a boon?' said the weaver. 'Let me go home and consult with my wife and friends about what boon to ask.'

'That's fine. Go and ask.'

The weaver rushed home in excitement. Just outside the village, he met his friend, a barber, and told him about his encounter with the ghost. 'So, tell me what boon should I ask for?' he said to his friend.

'Ask him for a kingdom,' the friend suggested. 'When you become king, I can be your prime minister. That way, both of us will spend a kingly life, which will also guarantee us a good afterlife, because, as they say,

> A charitable king not only gains glory in this life
> but also enjoys the company of gods in the afterlife.

'I like the idea of being a king,' said the weaver. 'But let me also ask my wife her opinion.'

'No, you shouldn't do that,' said his friend. 'Asking for a woman's advice is against the shastras, because the intelligence of women is meagre. It is said,

> With delicious food,
> fine clothes, jewellery, and

embraces in the cold season
keep your woman happy,
but never ask her for advice.

A home ruled by a woman, gambler, or child
quickly meets its ruin, says Muni Bhargava.

As long as a man is heedless to a woman's words,
he is happy; he is devoted to parents and teachers.
As soon as he heeds a woman's words, his happiness,
peace, love for parents and teachers, all disappear.

Women are selfish creatures.
They only care about themselves.
A husband, a son—they don't matter.

'You're right in everything you say,' the weaver said. 'But I must still ask my wife. I never do anything without asking her. My wife is very devoted to me.'

Hence, the weaver went home and told his wife, 'Today I met a ghost who has become obligated to me. He wants to give me a boon—anything that I desire. So, dearest, what should I ask for? I met my barber friend on the way here, and he says I should ask for a kingdom.'

'Dearest, the barber hardly has any intelligence. That is why people say,

Never seek advice from children,
and bards, beggars, and barbers.

Ruling a kingdom is fraught with worry:
attack, war, alliance, fortification, and
decisions about which kings to seek for help.
Ruling a kingdom is to invite unhappiness.
Hardships begin from the time of one's anointing,
as though the pitchers full of sacred water
pour hardships on one's head along with the water.

So, dearest, in my opinion, a wise man should never hope to acquire a kingdom.

Kingdoms make enemies of brothers, sons, and kinsfolk,
who always seek an opportune moment to kill the king.'

'You're absolutely right, dearest,' the weaver said to his wife. 'I should certainly not ask for a kingdom. Then tell me what I should ask for.'

'You weave one piece of fabric every day, and that gives us enough money to manage our household. Why don't you ask the ghost to give you two more hands and another head? That way you can weave two pieces of fabric every day. The money you earn from one will be for the household expenses, and the money from the other can be for special things. That way, you will not only become happier, but you'll also gain respect in your tribe.'

'What a brilliant idea, my ever-loving wife. This is exactly what I will ask for.'

Hence, going back to the sheesham, the weaver said to the ghost, 'This is the boon I want: give me two more hands and another head.'

'Be it so,' the ghost declared, and instantly the weaver's body sprouted two more hands and another head.

Very pleased with his extra limbs and head, as he was walking jauntily back to his village, the weaver met a group of people. As soon as they saw him, they began to scream, thinking he was a rakshasa. Then they beat him with sticks and stones till he died.

'Like this weaver, I should have listened to you, my friend,' said the wheel-bearer. 'But, you see, I was trapped in false hope. It is said,

> He who worries needlessly
> for what hasn't even happened
> becomes pale even in his sleep,
> Like Somanatha Sharma's father.'

'What is this story?' the gold-receiving brahmin asked his friend, the wheel-bearer, who told him the tale.

THE TALE OF SOMANATHA SHARMA'S DAYDREAMING FATHER

In a town lived a brahmin called Svabhava Kripana (miserly by nature). Every day, he received a few handfuls of sattu (a mixture of ground barley and pulses), in alms, from which he drank half and saved the other half. Soon, he had saved a potful of sattu. Hanging the pot from the ceiling, he put his cot under it so that he could watch it all the time. One day, lying in bed, his eyes trained on the pot, he began to think: what if there is a famine? Then my big pot of sattu will sell for no less than a hundred silver coins. With that money, I'll buy two goats. In six to twelve months, they'll have kids that'll grow up, and before you know it, I'll have a whole flock of goats. I will then sell the goats and buy cows, and after that, buffaloes, and from their sale, horses and mares. When the mares foal, I'll have a whole stable of horses. From the sale of those horses, I'll build a big, four-storeyed house, and some brahmin will marry his beautiful young daughter to me. When she gives birth to a son, I'll name the boy Somanatha Sharma. When he is old enough to crawl, I'll take him to watch the horses, and if he crawls too close to them, I'll chide my wife for not watching him. But she'll be busy with her chores and pay me no heed. Then, upset at her disregard, I'll kick her like this. Thinking this, he kicked hard. His foot hit the sattu pot and broke it, and yellow sattu poured down on him, turning his whole body pale.

'That's why, a man should not build castles in the air,' said the wheel-bearer with a heavy sigh.

'Don't blame yourself so much,' his friend consoled him. 'The greatest of men are known to have been trapped by greed. It is said,

> A person who acts, influenced by greed
> with not a thought to the consequences,
> ends up suffering like that King Chandra.

'What is this story?' the wheel-bearing brahmin asked, and his friend narrated it.

THE TALE OF HOW THE KING'S RASH DECISION LED TO THE MONKEY'S REVENGE

A city was ruled by a king by the name of Chandra. He had many sons, and they loved monkeys. They would play with the animals all day long and feed them all kinds of delicious foods and mithai.

The chief of that troop of monkeys was very learned and well-versed in all niti ideals expounded in law books such as Shukra Niti, Brihaspati Niti, and Chanakya Niti. He also lived his life according to these ideals and taught his monkeys the same.

In the king's palace was a flock of sheep who were also the princes' playmates. The boys would climb on their backs and ride around, as they ran here and there, bleating. One of the sheep had developed the habit of sneaking into the kitchen to eat whatever it could find, and every time it did that, the servants would chase it out, trying to hit it with whatever they could lay their hands on—pots and pans made of copper, bronze, wood, or clay.

The chief of the monkeys watched this tableau play out every morning—the sheep entering the kitchen, foraging for food, and the kitchen staff chasing him out. He had a feeling that this daily contention would end up hurting the monkeys. He reasoned with himself: this sheep has acquired the taste of grain, and the people who work in the kitchen are getting angrier by the day, chasing him out with whatever they can lay their hands on. Right now, they're grabbing pots and pans to hit him. Tomorrow, they may even grab a burning log of wood from the stove. If they touch that sheep with it, he'll instantly catch fire, because he hasn't been shorn, and his wool is long and combustible. The sheep will then run out, bleating in pain, and make for the stable to roll in the hay. But the hay in the stable is dry, and it'll burst into flames, instantly. Soon, the whole stable will be aflame, and the king's best horses will get burned. The divine physician of horses, Shalihotra, has said that fat from a monkey's body is the best salve to alleviate the pain of a horse's burn wounds. Therefore, I foresee us monkeys meeting a quick demise, if such an eventuality occurs.

Thus, the monkey chief called his troop and apprised them of what was happening in the kitchen every day and how it could imperil them. He said to them,

> The house with needless conflict
> is not a suitable place to live.
> Anyone who values his life
> should leave it as soon as possible,

Also,

> Strife destroys homes.
> Bitter words destroy friendships.
> A cruel king destroys the kingdom.
> Bad action destroys a good name.

So, my friends, we should leave this place and go to the forest before we are killed because of some silly conflict between the kitchen staff and that food-loving sheep.'

Some of the younger monkeys laughed at the old chief's warning. 'It appears that old age has affected your intelligence,' they said to him. 'It is said,

> The mouths of infants and aged
> are toothless and drooling,
> So also is their intelligence.

Are you telling us to leave the luxuries of the palace and all the delicious mithai that the princes feed us and go off into the forest, where we'll have to eat tart, bitter and dried up fruits from the trees? How can we do that?'

The old monkey's eyes filled with tears. 'You young fools, you don't know,

> Luxuries can yield results
> as harmful as poison,
> just like a kuchla fruit is
> sweet but deadening.

Obviously, you don't want to heed my warning. But I can't stay here and see the destruction of my clan with my own eyes; therefore, I'm leaving for the forest. It is said,

> Those people are blessed who don't have to see
> friends in adversity, enemies ruling their land,
> their clan's ruin, and dissolution of their country.'

Hence, the old monkey chief left for the forest, and the very next morning, as he had foreseen, when the sheep got into the kitchen, the cook, not finding anything else within reach, took a burning log and hit him with it.

The sheep's wool immediately caught fire, and he ran out, bleating in pain, heading straight for the hay in the stable. The dry hay lit into a blaze, and the whole stable was engulfed in flames. Many of the horses burned to death, others became blinded, and still others broke their tethers and began to run helter-skelter, squealing and neighing.

The men who took care of the stable were thrown into confusion, not knowing whether to put out the fire or to rescue the horses. When the king got news of the injuries his royal horses had received in the fire, he immediately called the veterinarians and commanded them to prepare an ointment to relieve the pain of his horses. The physicians consulted their books and said to the king, 'Maharaj, Lord Shalihotraji himself has said,

> Monkeys' fat can alleviate the pain
> of horses suffering from burns,
> as quickly as the sun dispels darkness.

Hence, you should acquire monkeys' fat as soon as you can, or the horses will expire from their burns.'

Consequently, the king ordered all the monkeys in the kingdom to be put to death.

'What else, can I tell you?' said the wheel-bearer. 'The king's soldiers set out with arrows, sticks, stones, and other weapons and soon killed every single monkey in that city. When that old chief monkey heard about how his sons, nephews, brothers, and friends were slaughtered, he was deeply grieved. For days, he wandered in the forest, despondent, not eating or drinking. Then he began to think about revenge.

It is said,

> Be it through greed or fear,
> but those who can bear to see
> their clan being harmed by enemies
> are detestable and dastardly.

One day, that old monkey, looking for water to quench his thirst by chance came upon a lake adorned with lotuses. Approaching it, he carefully looked around and noticed that while there were plenty of footprints, of both animals and people going to the lake, there were none returning. Thus, he knew that this lake was inhabited by a crocodile or some other feral creature, who pulled anyone that touched the water into the lake. Therefore, to avoid direct contact with the water, the monkey broke off a lotus stalk and, dipping it in the lake, sucked the water through it.

As he took a long draught of cool water, a ferocious rakshasa, wearing a brilliant necklace of jewels, rose out of the lake.

'O monkey,' the rakshasa thundered. 'This is my lake. Anyone who immerses even a toe into it becomes my food. I eat him up. But you are more intelligent than anyone I have seen. I'm very impressed by the way you are drinking without letting even a tip of your toe touch the water. I'm very pleased with your intelligent mind. Ask me for a boon—anything you desire.'

'How much can you eat?' the monkey asked the rakshasa.

'If a hundred, or a thousand, or ten thousand, or even a lakh creatures come into my lake, I can devour all of them. But outside this lake, even a tiny fox can scare me. I have no power outside the water.'

'I have a great enemy—a king. If you can lend me your jewelled necklace, I can entice him to come here to this lake, along with his family.'

The rakshasa did not even pause to think. Removing his necklace, he handed it to the monkey. 'Friend, here it is. Go and do what you have to.'

The monkey put the necklace around his neck and went to pay a visit to the king's neighbourhood. There, swinging from tree to tree, walking in plain sight on the roofs of buildings, he made sure he was seen by several people. They asked him, 'O monkey chief, where have you been all these days? And where did you get such a beautiful necklace that outshines even the sun?'

'In the forest, in a certain spot, there is a big lake that Lord Kubera has built. Whoever bathes in that lake on Ravivaar (Sunday) at exactly the time when the sun is half risen, he will emerge from the lake with just such a necklace around his neck.'

As the monkey had hoped, his words soon reached the king, and he ordered his men to bring the monkey to him. 'O chief of monkeys, is there really such a lake in the forest where you can receive such a jewelled necklace simply by bathing in it?' he asked. 'Is this true?'

'Maharaj, see this necklace around my neck. Is this not proof of what I say? If you, too, desire such a necklace, then send someone with me, and I'll show him where the lake is.'

'If that is the case, I, myself, will come with you, along with all my servants and my family, and all of us will take a dip. That way each of us can receive such a necklace.'

On the night before the sun rose on Ravivaar, the king ordered his carriages and, carrying the monkey on his lap, he rode all night with his whole family and entourage of servants, to arrive at the lake just as dawn was breaking.

Someone has rightly said,

> She who subjugates even the richest,
> making them wander from place to place
> and do evil acts of injustice grave—
> propitiations to that Devi of Craving.
>
> He who has a hundred, craves for a thousand.
> He who has a thousand, craves for a lakh.
> An owner of a lakh, craves a kingdom.
> And one who rules a kingdom, craves for gold.
> All are enslaved by craving; no one is content.
>
> In old age, hair turns grey,
> teeth and nails fall out,
> ears, eyes, all other senses dull.
> But craving remains forever youthful.

As the sun began to peek over the horizon, the monkey reminded the king, 'To achieve the boon of the necklace, you have to take a dip in the lake at exactly the time when the sun is half risen. Therefore, please advise your men and family members to jump in exactly at that time. I, myself, will wait here with you and, after that, I'll take you to a special spot in the lake where there are numerous such jewelled necklaces.'

At the king's order at mid-sunrise, everyone jumped into the lake. And, as soon as they did, the rakshasa devoured them. The king watched the water for a long time, waiting for them to emerge, and when not a single one reappeared, he turned to the monkey and asked him, 'Why isn't anyone coming out? Why is it taking them so long?'

The monkey didn't respond. Instead, he leapt on a tree and climbed to a high branch, and from there he spoke: 'O evil king, your relatives and attendants have all been eaten by the rakshasa who lives in the lake. I have taken my revenge. Just be thankful that I spared you. It is said,

> Do to others what they do to you.
> Harm him who harms you.
> Be cruel to him who is cruel to you.
> You will not be faulted for this.

You killed my clan, O king, and I have killed yours.'

People say that that king was so devastated that he refused the carriages and walked all the way home. After he had left, the rakshasa emerged from the water and said to the monkey, 'By drinking water with a lotus stalk you not only managed to get your revenge, but you also won my friendship. And you brought the jewelled necklace back intact as well. Your intelligence is truly applaudable.'

'That is why I said to you,' said the gold-receiving brahmin to the wheel-bearer, 'extreme greed combined with rash decisions can cause you a lot of suffering, as it did King Chandra. Now friend, give me permission to leave. I wish to go home.'

'Dear friend, one gathers wealth and makes friends for times of adversity. Please don't leave me in my time of need. It is said,

> The cold-hearted person who leaves his friends
> struggling in times of their hardships,
> commits a sin that condemns him to hell.'

'You're right, my friend. If I had any control over this situation, I wouldn't ever think about leaving you, but this is divine ground. No one has the power to free you from this. Also, I can see the extreme pain that the spinning wheel in your head is causing you. That is another reason why I must leave right away. I fear that if I stay here any longer, I, too, may get trapped in some equally difficult situation. It is said,

> O monkey, from the way your face is shadowed,
> it seems that you, too, are caught by Vikala.
> At this time, whoever runs away, keeps his life.'

'What is this story?' the wheel-bearer asked, and his friend related it to him.

THE TALE OF THE FEARFUL RAKSHASA VIKALA

In a city lived a king called Bhadrasena. He had a beautiful daughter replete with all good qualities. But a rakshasa had fallen in love with her and wanted to abduct her. Therefore, the king had protected his daughter with mantras and tantras so powerful that the rakshasa could not breach them. However, he used to visit her every night and just sit in one corner, watching her with lovelorn eyes. No one could see him, but his very presence made the princess tremble so uncontrollably, it was as though she were caught in a fever, and that is how her friends and attendants knew that the rakshasa was nearby. The rakshasa, however, did not know that his proximity affected the princess, or that she was aware of his presence in any way.

One day when the rakshasa came to the princess's room at midnight and sat down in a corner near her bed, the princess, feeling his presence, said to her attendant, 'That vikala rakshasa is here again. He comes every night and bothers me. I wish there was away to get rid of him!'

The rakshasa heard the princess and thought that this 'Vikala' that she was referring to was another rakshasa who also visited her every night and was probably also prevented from touching her by the wall of mantras that protected her. 'I should see what this other rakshasa looks like,' he said to himself. 'Let me assume the form of a horse. That way he won't know who I am, and I'll be able to see him and assess his strength as a contender.'

And so the rakshasa changed himself into a horse and joined the other horses in the royal stable. It so happened that that night a thief had also come into the stable to steal a horse. He looked at all the horses and chose the most handsome of them, which, of course, was the rakshasa in disguise. Saddling him quickly, the horse thief swung on to his back and rode away.

'This must be Vikala,' the rakshasa said to himself while he was being ridden strenuously, . 'He has recognized me and probably wants to kill me. What should I do?' Just then, the thief whipped the horse, urging it to go faster, and the rakshasa's fear was confirmed.

After they had gone quite a distance, the thief pulled on the reins to stop the horse, but the rakshasa kept galloping as fast as he could, trying to flee Vikala. The thief tried many times to halt the horse, but it seemed that the more he pulled on the reins, the faster the horse sped. 'This is not an ordinary horse,' the thief said to himself. 'Which horse does not stop when his reins are pulled? Is this a rakshasa in a horse's form?' Just the thought of that made him shudder in fright, and he began to look for a sandy bank where he could land safely when he jumped off the horse. He was certain that if he remained on this rakshasa's back much longer, he would surely be killed—either he would fall off the speeding horse-rakshasa and break his neck, or the rakshasa would eat him when he stopped.

Then, to his relief, the thief saw a big bargad tree in the distance, and, as soon as the horse galloped under it, he grabbed a branch and climbed up into the tree.

Thus, both the rakshasa and thief, freed from each other, thanked the gods for their escape, feeling like they had received a new life.

On that bargad tree lived a monkey who was great friends with the rakshasa. Seeing his friend speeding away in the form of a horse, he called after him, 'O friend, why are you running away in such fear? This is a man whom you had on your back. He's your food. Why don't you just eat him?'

Hearing the monkey's words, the rakshasa stopped in his tracks, and changing himself back to this original form, retraced his steps.

When the thief heard the monkey call the rakshasa back, and he saw the rakshasa returning to the tree, he was so angry at the monkey that he took his long tail between his teeth and bit down hard on it. The monkey wanted to scream in pain, but he thought that this man was more dangerous than a rakshasa, so he restrained himself. However, his face displayed such an expression of pain that when the rakshasa saw it, he couldn't help but exclaim, 'O monkey, the expression on your face clearly tells me that like me, you, too, have been grabbed by the rakshasa, Vikala. Therefore, I think the best course for me is to leave as quickly as possible.' And so the rakshasa ran away.

'You see, dear friend,' said the gold-receiving brahmin to the wheel-bearer, 'sometimes it's best to just run away. I wish you forbearance, as you suffer the fruits of the tree of greed.'

'This has nothing to do with greed,' said the wheel-bearer. 'It is a matter of fate. People suffer the consequences of good and bad fate. Look,

> He whose fort was Trikutagiri,
> whose moat was the ocean,
> whose guards were rakshasas,

> whose coffers held Kubera's wealth,
> whose guidance was Shukra's Nitishastra—
> this powerful Ravana was also destroyed
> by none other than unpropitious fate.

Besides,

> Andhaka, Kubjaka, and princess Tristani,
> despite following a wrongful path
> achieved ends that were rightful,
> simply because they were favoured by fate.'

'What is this story?' the gold-receiver asked, and the wheel-bearer narrated the tale.

THE TALE OF THE BLIND MAN, HUNCHBACK, AND THE THREE-BREASTED WOMAN

In the northerly direction, there is a town called Madhupura that was ruled by a king called Madhusena, whose every action was oriented by dharma. However, despite the king's dharma-abiding ways, the queen gave birth to a daughter who had three breasts.

When the king received this news, he said to his trusted minister, 'Take this tristani (three-breasted) to the forest and leave her somewhere for the wild animals. And don't say a word to anyone.'

'Maharaj,' the minister suggested, 'everyone knows that a three-breasted daughter is inauspicious. But still, you should take the advice of brahmins to ensure that your actions don't earn you reproach in this birth and suffering in the next. I say this because,

> He who always takes the advice of elders,
> gives his intelligence a means to bloom
> like a lotus flower in the rays of the sun.

Also,

> Even though one might know everything,
> one should always ascertain by questioning,
> like the brahmin who escaped the rakshasa,
> simply because he asked a question.'

'What is this story?' the king asked, and his minister told him the tale.

THE TALE OF HOW THE BRAHMIN ESCAPED THE RAKSHASA BY ASKING A QUESTION

In a forest lived a rakshasa called Chandakarma (violent acts). One day, he captured a brahmin and, climbing onto his shoulders, said to him, 'Arrey, brahmin, I want to ride you. Move!'

The brahmin was so terrified that, without uttering a word, he began to walk with the rakshasa on his shoulders. After some time, when the brahmin lost some of his fear and began to relax, he noticed that the rakshasa's feet were as soft and tender as lotus petals, and he wondered how this terrifying, ugly creature had such delicate feet. He thought about asking him but then worried that it would offend him. However, he was so curious that he couldn't help asking. 'O, rakshasa, why are your feet so soft and tender?'

'I never put my bare feet on the ground, and especially not when my feet are wet,' the rakshasa replied. 'This is my oath to myself. That is why my feet are soft and tender.'

Soon, the two of them came to a lake. Ordering the brahmin to walk up to the water's edge, the rakshasa got off his shoulders, saying, 'I'm going to bathe now and do my puja to Lord Shiva. I'll return soon. Don't go anywhere. Stay right here.'

When the rakshasa was in the water, the brahmin began to think: I'm his food. He'll probably eat me right after he has bathed and done his puja. I should leave. This is the perfect time for me to get away. But then he thought, what if he chases me? He's a rakshasa; he'll catch up with me in just one stride. That is when he remembered what the rakshasa had said in response to his question about his feet—that he had taken an oath to never put his bare feet on the ground, and especially not when his feet were wet. 'Aha!' said the brahmin to himself. 'When the rakshasa comes out of the water, he won't be able to chase me, because his feet will be wet.'

As soon as he realized that, the brahmin ran away. The rakshasa saw him leave, but he could not follow him, because he had revealed his secret oath to him, simply because he had asked a question.

'That is how the brahmin escaped the rakshasa, simply by asking a question,' said the minister.

Taking his minister's advice, the king called his brahmins, and after duly honouring them, said to them, 'My wife has given birth to a girl who has three breasts. Is there any way to be rid of this inauspiciousness?'

'Maharaja,' said the brahmins, 'a daughter who lacks limbs or has an additional body part is calamitous for her husband and damaging to her own wifely dharma. Moreover, if the father of this three-breasted girl sees her face, he will soon die. Therefore, we advise you to marry her as soon as you can; that is, if you can find a groom who is willing to accept her. Send her away without a thought to her happiness and comfort. That is how you will not face any condemnation in this life, and you will not have to suffer in the afterlife.'

Tristani was kept in the palace, hidden away in a remote corner, where her father would never look upon her face. As soon as she became old enough to be wed, the king sent a kettledrum town crier to announce to the populace that whoever agreed to marry this tristani would receive one lakh gold mohurs from the king, with the condition that he would take his wife and immediately leave this land.

In this town, there was a blind man, called Andhaka (blind), whose friend Kubjaka (hunchback), used to lead him around by holding his walking stick. These two also heard the town crier, and the blind man decided that he would touch the kettledrum. 'If I marry the princess, we will get a lot of money, which will bring an end to this pathetic poverty,' he reasoned with his friend. 'And if I happen to die because of her inauspiciousness, then so be it. We're hardly alive anyway—I, suffering from this blindness, and you, from this bodily disfigurement.'

Hence, the blind man, led by the hunchback, touched the kettledrum and exclaimed, 'I'm ready to marry this tristani, if the king is willing to accept me.'

When the king was informed, his response was, 'Blind, dead, leper, low caste—it doesn't matter. I'm ready to give him my daughter and the one lakh gold mohurs I promised, provided he leaves my kingdom immediately after the wedding.'

The king's ministers took tristani and the blind man to a secluded beach and performed a wedding ceremony. Then, handing the groom one lakh gold mohurs, they put the newlyweds and the hunchback in a boat and ordered the boatman, 'Take these three far away to a remote land and leave them in some town or village.'

Exiled by the king, the three arrived in a faraway land, and here they purchased a house and began to live quite happily. Every day, while Andhaka sat on the bed, Kubjaka helped Tristani with all the chores. After many months of working together, the princess and the hunchback began a secret love affair. Someone has rightly said,

> A faithful wife is as impossible as
> coolness in flames and heat in the moon,
> or sweetness in the waters of the sea.

One day, Tristani said to the hunchback, 'O, my handsome beloved, if this blind man dies, our lives will be so much happier. Why don't you bring me some poison, and I will give it to him?'

It so happened that, by chance, on his way home that day, the hunchback found a dead black snake on the road. Picking it up, he brought it to Tristani. 'Look beautiful. I found this black snake,' he said. 'Cut it up and mix it with fish and dress up the meat with all kinds of spices and gravy. I know Andhaka loves gravy dishes. Feed him that while I'm gone.'

Tristani cut the snake into pieces, and, adding spices and water to the meat, she put it on the stove and went to summon Andhaka. 'Dear husband, I know how much you love fish. You've been asking me to make it for many days. So, I ordered fish today. It's on the stove. Will you do me a favour please? While I am busy with other chores, can you just stir the meat from time to time?'

Licking his lips in anticipation of the fish curry, the blind man went into the kitchen and began to stir the pot. When the snake meat started to boil, poisonous fumes arose from the pot and wafted towards him, seeping into his eyes. Slowly, the blue-coloured membrane of blindness that covered his eyeballs began to dissolve and, before long, the blind man was able to see. Wondering what fumes could have caused such a miracle, he lifted the lid to look inside the pot and saw pieces of black snake in gravy. 'What is this?' he said, shocked. 'She told me she was cooking fish, but this is a black snake. Is this some kind of plot? Is this Tristani's attempt to kill me? Or is it to kill the hunchback? Or, maybe, it's to kill someone else.' Deciding to wait and see, Andhaka continued to stir the pot.

After some time, the hunchback returned home. Making himself comfortable on the bed, he called Tristani to him. Still standing by the stove, Andhaka heard their laughter and giggles, and came out of the kitchen to see what they were up to. When he saw them locked in each other's arms, a fiery shaft of wrath shot through his body, and he looked around frantically for some weapon—a sword, a knife, or even a piece of wood. Not finding a thing, he grabbed the hunchback by his feet, lifted him off the bed, swung him around, and then flung him back on the bed, smack into Tristani's chest. The impact was so great that Tristani's third breast was pushed inside her body, and the hunchback's spine straightened up.

'So, you see, friend,' said the wheel-bearer, 'fate is a powerful thing. If it is favourable, it even rewards those who are hardly good, like the blind man, hunchback, and the three-breasted woman.'

'Fine. I agree with you that all happiness and wealth is subject to fate's dictates. But people should still listen to elders and good men. He who doesn't listen, becomes miserable, like you. Also,

> Men who do not work with each other
> are destroyed like the bherunda bird,
> who had one stomach and two heads
> that were always at cross-purposes.'

'How does this story go?' asked the wheel-bearer, and the gold-receiving brahmin narrated the tale.

THE TALE OF THE TWO-HEADED BHERUNDA BIRD

In a lake near the sea lived a bherunda bird. He had one stomach but two heads. One day, wandering near the water's edge, he found a fruit that had drifted ashore, and it was as sweet as amrita. One of his beaks picked up the fruit and started eating it. 'I've never had such a sweet fruit,' the head that was eating the fruit said. 'Is this fruit from Kalapataru, the desire-fulfilling tree from heaven? Or is it a fruit of the heavenly sandalwood? Or is it amrita itself in the form of the fruit that has been bestowed on me?'

Hearing these enticing words, the other head said, 'Dear brother, can you give me a little of that fruit, so that I, too, can taste its sweetness?'

'Arrey, we have one stomach. So just one of us needs to eat it for our stomach to receive it. There's no point in both of us eating it. Besides, I want to share this with my beloved.' And he gave the remainder of the fruit to his bherundi. She was very pleased to receive the fruit and began showering love on the head that had given her the fruit.

From that day on, the other head, feeling rejected and unhappy, waited for his turn. One day, this other head found a poison flower. Picking it up with his beak, he said to the first head, 'You ungrateful wretch, you selfish bird, look what I just found—a poison flower. I'm going to pay you back for your insult by eating it all by myself.'

'Stop, you fool!' cried the first head. 'Don't eat this, or we'll both die.'

But the other head did not listen and ate the poison flower. And that is how the bherunda bird with two heads died.

'That's why I said men should learn to work together and listen to each other,' the gold-receiving brahmin said.

'You're right,' his wheel-bearing friend replied. 'I should have listened to you. Now, dear friend, go home. But I advise you not to go alone. It is said,

> Never eat a sweet dish by yourself.
> Never stay awake if everyone is asleep.
> Never travel without a companion.
> Never cogitate serious issues by yourself.

Also,

> Even if your travelling companion
> is weak, cowardly, and useless,
> trust him to be of some use. Look!
> The crab saved the brahmin's life.'

'What is this story?' the gold-receiver asked, and the wheel-bearer narrated it.

THE TALE OF HOW A CRAB SAVED THE BRAHMIN

In a village lived a brahmin named Brahmadatta. One day, as he was getting ready to go to another village on some business, his mother said to him, 'Why are you going by yourself? Find someone who will go with you.'

'Don't be afraid, mother,' he said. 'The road I'm taking is very safe. I have some business to take care of, and I'll be fine by myself.'

His mother then caught a crab from the nearby pond and brought it to her son. 'If you must go, then I won't stop you. But take this crab with you. He'll give you company. You must not go alone.'

'Fine, mother, if it makes you happy,' the brahmin said and, taking the crab from her, put it in a can of camphor, which he stuck into his bundle of things before he set off.

After he had walked some distance in the summer heat, the brahmin felt tired, so he sat down in the shade of a tree and fell asleep. A snake lived in a hollow in that tree. Sensing a human body, he emerged from his lair and glided towards the brahmin. However, captivated by the smell of camphor, he changed course, and, instead of going to the brahmin, he slithered into the bundle lying beside him. When he pushed open the camphor can with his hood, the crab crawled out of it. He caught the snake's head between his pincers and wrenched it right off.

Sometime later, when the brahmin woke up and saw a snake's tail hanging out of his bundle, he quickly opened it. Inside, he found the dead snake and the open can of camphor. Realizing that it was the crab that had killed the snake and saved his life, he said,

> 'A man should not go to a foreign land all alone.
> He should always take someone with him.
> I listened to my mother like an obedient son,
> and look how the crab saved me from the snake.

Someone has rightly said,

> Mantra, pilgrimage, or brahmin,
> any god, astrologer, cure, or guru—

whatever faith one puts in them
is the amount of reward one reaps.'

'So, dear friend,' said the wheel-bearer, 'go and find someone to accompany you on your journey and keep your faith in him.'

Assuring his friend that he would find a travelling companion, the gold-receiver started on his way back home.

Here ends the fifth tantra, Aparikshita Karakam, whose opening shloka was this:

One should not act upon anything
without first distinctly seeing it,
without fully understanding it,
without thoroughly examining it,
just as the foolhardy barber did.

And with this ends the *Panchatantra*, the Nitishastra that Vishnusharma composed to teach prudence and polity to the king's sons. May it also enlighten others in worldly wisdom by reflecting the light of numerous shastras.

NOTES AND REFERENCES

DEDICATION

vii   **as well as the other scholars of niti**: Customary and social laws, especially about conduct, that facilitate a happy life.

INTRODUCTION

xiii   **And that is how Burzoe's story and the secret of the elixir was revealed to the world**: Esin Atil, *Kalila wa Dimna: Fables from a Fourteenth-Century Arabic Manuscript*, Washington DC: Smithsonian Institution Press, 1981, pp. 12–16.

xiv   **Underpinning these laws are the ethical principles of purushartha**: Purushartha is a key concept in Hinduism, comprising four goals of life—dharma, artha (wealth), kama (desire, including sexual desire), and moksha. The first three principles of dharma, artha, and kama are considered life-affirming, and the fourth, moksha, is life-negating.

xiv   **'extracting the summary of all popular nitishastras of statecraft and polity'**: From the Kathamukha.

xiv   **Many Indian scholars believe that Vishnusharma**: Guru Prasad Shastri, 'Kathasara', *Śri Vis‚n‚u Śarmàs Pañcatantram*, Varanasi: Chaukhamba Surbharti Prakashan, 2018.

xv   Hence the 'delightful, edifying Panchatantra' began to be hailed for its 'beneficence [to] humanity': Kathamukha.

xv   **Within this structure, numerous tales are 'emboxed'**: 'Emboxment' describes the story within a story structure, with a frame story serving as an outer box containing another story within it, which, in turn, serves as another box containing another story, and so on.

xvi   **even translates this word as klugheitsfall**: McComas Taylor, *The Fall of the Indigo Jackal: The Discourse of Division and Purnabhadra's Pancatantra*, New York: SUNY Press, 2007, p. 31.

xvi   **However, its most significant meaning is 'warp', as in a loom**: 'Tantra', M. Monier-Williams, *A Sanskrit English Dictionary*. New Delhi: Motilal Banarsidass, 2005, p. 436.

xvi   **to make complex narrative prose more fluid and to give verse a narrative progression**: Tirthanand Mishra, चम्पूकाव्यम् Champukayam, *International Journal of Applied Research*, 2019, Vol. 5, No. 6, pp. 434–35.

xvi   **Later scholars added more meaning to Dandin's simple definition by describing champu style**: Ibid.

xvi   **Monier-Williams definition adds more clarity**: 'Champu', M. Monier-Williams. *A Sanskrit English Dictionary*, New Delhi: Motilal Banarsidass, 2005, p. 389.

xvii	When the writer's key purpose is elucidation rather than beauty and elegance, then the use of champu makes learning easier: Mishra, चम्पूकाव्यम् (Champukavyam), pp. 434–35.
xviii	And the narrative itself generates an answer: Christine Ivanovic, 'Talking Animals and Politics of World Literature', *Comparative Literature Studies*, Vol. 54, No. 4, 2017, pp. 702–30.
xviii	A trickster character, as a Jungian archetype: Mary Jo Meadow, 'Archetypes and Patriarchy: Eliade and Jung', *Journal of Religion and Health*, Vol. 31, No. 3, Fall 1992, pp. 187–95.
xix	They are 'the bifurcation of one single synthetic character': T. V. Danylova, 'Overcoming the Anomalies of Human Existence: Ontology of Trickster', *Anthropological Measurements of Philosophical Research*, pp. 17–23.
xxi	The methods Kautilya prescribes are 'peace (sandhi), war (vigraha), observance of neutrality (āsana), marching (yāna), alliance (samsraya), and making peace with one and waging war with another': Kautilya, *The Arthashastra*, Lexington: Eternal Sun Books, 2016, p. 193.
xxiii	However, the nineteenth-century Sanskrit scholar, M. R. Kale, referencing H. H. Wilson, a renowned orientalist and first professor of Sanskrit at Oxford University: M. R. Kale's *Pañcatantra* was the prevalent Indian version contemporaneous to the critical editions of Western scholars Johannes Hertel and Franklin Edgerton.
xxiv	And Vishnusharma himself, satisfied at having accomplished what he set out to do, hopes that the *Panchatantra* will serve to enlighten other people, as well: M. R. Kale, 'Notes', *Pañcatantra of Viṣṇuśarman*, Delhi: Motilal Banarsidass, 2018, (first edition, 1912).
xxiv	In his *Phaedo* (fourth century BCE), Plato talks about how Socrates, while awaiting his death sentence: Plato, *Phaedo*, in Twelve Volumes, Vol. 1 translated by Harold North Fowler; Introduction by W. R. M. Lamb, Cambridge, MA: Harvard University Press; London: William Heinemann Ltd, 1966.
xxiv	How interesting it is that the great philosopher who gave to the world the Socratic method of argumentation would, in his last hours, gain a sense of peace from the simplicity of animal stories: Nicholas Howe, 'Fabling Beasts: Traces in Memory', *Social Research*, Vol. 62, No. 3, 1995, p. 645.
xxiv	For instance, in Mesopotamian myths, there is evidence of embedded animal fables dating to the old Babylonian period (seventh century BCE): Ronald J. Williams, 'The Literary History of a Mesopotamian Fable', *Phoenix*, Vol. 10, No. 2, Summer 1956, Vol. 10, No. 2 (Summer, 1956), pp. 70–77.
xxv	Ever united, named alike: Translation by Som Raj Gupta, *The Word Speaks to the Faustian Man*, Vol. 2, New Delhi: Motilal Banarsidass, 1995.
xxv	Chandra Ranjan, a Sanskrit scholar and a translator of the *Panchatantra*, believes that the 'animal characters are really people wearing animal masks. The use of masks is a distancing device that is more effective in conveying comments and criticism': Chandra Ranjan, 'Introduction', *The Pañcatantra*, New Delhi: Penguin Books, 1993, p. 8.

xxvi   'the world of parallel animal society built according to the same principles of government and political science as the human': Patrick Olivelle, 'Introduction', *The Pañcatantra: The Book of India's Folk Wisdom*, Oxford: Oxford University Press, 2009, p. xvii.

xxvii   But, because in 'the spirit of the apologue, the dramatis personae are moved by the same man-like traits which they acquired in the earliest examples of the fable': V. M. Pérez Perozo, Fables and Fable-Writers, *Books Abroad*, Vol. 20, No. 4, Autumn 1946, pp. 363–67.

xxvii   Patrick Olivelle, a scholar of Sanskrit literature, citing Hertel, states: Olivelle, 'Introduction', p. xxxii.

xxvii   Thus, 'it is the truth value of the parables themselves that is put into focus, as well as how we deal with them': Christine Ivanovic, 'Talking Animals and Politics of World Literature', *Comparative Literature Studies*, Vol. 54, No. 4, 2017, p. 719.

xxvii   At last count, there were at least 200 versions of the texts in more than fifty languages: Franklin Edgerton quoted in Olivelle, 'Introduction', 2009, p. ix.

xxvii   rediscovered in 1870 in a monastery in Mardin, Turkey: Olivelle, 'Introduction', p. xvii.

xxviii   '[it] was of central importance to the spread of the *Pañcatantra*, because it was the source, directly or indirectly, of all further translations into the languages of the Middle East and Europe': Taylor, *The Fall of the Indigo Jackal*, p. 3.

xxviii   The latter, titled *Buch der Beispiele der alten Weisen* or *Book of examples of the old ways*, was one of the first books to be published: Ibid.

xxviii   'was found in translation from Iceland to Bali, and from Mongolia to Ethiopia': Johannes Hertel quoted in Taylor, *The Fall of the Indigo Jackal*, p. 3.

xxviii   In other words, the Panchatantra is, perhaps, one of the most widely known works of literature': Franklin Edgerton quoted in Olivelle, 'Introduction', p. ix.

xxix   However, Franklin Edgerton, the pioneer American linguist, who in 1924 reconstructed the 'lost' Southern recension, believed that it contains seventy-five percent of the original prose: Ibid., p. xlii.

xxix   'the only version which contain[ed] the unabbreviated and no intentionally altered language of the author': Franklin Edgerton quoted in Taylor, *The Fall of the Indigo Jackal*, p. 20.

xxix   In India, the Panchatantra tradition has passed through 'roughly 90 to 96 human generations': Nilanjana S. Roy, 'The Panchatantra: The ancient "viral memes" still with us', Culture: Stories that Shaped the World, BBC, 17 June 2018.

AUTHOR'S NOTE

xxxii   Rajan herself admits in her introduction that neither of these names 'convey what the Sanskrit names express so well': Chandra Rajan, 'Introduction', *The Pañcatantra*, New Delhi: Penguin Books, 1993, p. xiii.

'FIRST TANTRA: MITRA BHEDA'

17 **For instance, you must have heard of Amir kingdom, where the valuable Chandrakanta gem sells for just three cowries**: Cowrie shells were used as currency in many countries in the ancient world, including India.

34 **the nature of the world: ruled by the social laws of sama, dana, danda, bheda (persuasion, pay-off, punishment, and discord)**: According to social law books, these are four methods of diplomacy to arrive at a solution. This policy is mentioned in the *Arthashastra* and is often referred to as Chanakya Niti.

37 **Ashadhabhuti went to see Devasharma at the monastery, and, chanting the Shivaya mantra greeting, bowed to him by laying his head at his feet**: A basic mantra dedicated to Lord Shiva, chanted to receive his blessings.

37 **And, if one is a Brahmin, Kshatriya, or any of the twice born**: Dvija—twice born; the first three varnas of the caste system—Brahmins, Kshatriyas, Vaishyas; their ritual initiation is considered a second birth.

38 His village was celebrating Shiva's grand festival, and they wanted him to come and perform the **sanctification rituals** to successfully conclude the festival: This is a twelve-month festival that concludes in the month of Shravana. At its conclusion, the image of Shiva is garlanded with sacred silk threads to ensure forgiveness for whatever errors may have occurred during its execution.

44 **and horrific poison of Halahala burns in their heart**: The poison that oozed out of the ocean floor during the Churning of the Ocean.

45 **like the scarlet ratti pea that looks pretty**: Gunja seeds that are bright red in colour with a black eye. They were used as a measurement of mass in ancient India. One gram = 5.49 ratti.

48 **because combined with either destiny's design or divine plan, intelligence can bring about desired outcomes**: The word used here is Ghunakshara Nyaya. It comes from the craft of wood. Sometimes, when craftsmen are working with wood, they find pictures or images etched in it, naturally formed, as though drawn by magic. It is used as a metaphor for those coincidences that just happen by themselves.

78 **like Kalakuta poison that was lodged in Shri Mahadev's throat and earned him the title of Neelakantha**: Also known as Halahala; deadly poison that oozed out of the ocean floor during Samudra Manthan. Shiva drank this poison to save the world.

99 **to win victory over rain clouds**: The zodiacal Libra is in September and October, right after the monsoon and just before winter. Hence the sun in these months is able to shine through the rain clouds. The scales of Libra also connote balance—risk = reward.

113 **summons his own death like the mule mare does**: Mules cannot reproduce.

129 **made of iron, weighing one thousand pala**: Unit of capacity in ancient India; 1 pala equals about 27.2 grams.

135 **One day, as the four of them were crossing through a settlement of Kiratas**: A community of forest-dwelling tribal Bhils; currently there are Bhil communities in Nepal and the Northeastern region of India.

SECOND TANTRA: MITRA SAMPRAPTI

143 **shone as pure white as the nirgundi flower**: Five-leaved flower used in Ayurvedic medicine to cure many illnesses.

145 **like Shankha Nidhi which brings wealth**: According to Amarakosha, there are nine nidhis (wealth) or treasures of Kubera. Shankha (conch nidhi) is the third. This wealth when acquired is aplenty, but the person who acquires it cannot spend a paisa of it. And when it is lost, it takes with it other wealth.

151 **like the female mule who dies**: Mules are infertile.

152 **and Jaimini, the author of Mimansa**: Treatise on Sanskrit prosody; third to second century BCE.

152 **Chhandashastra**: Treatise on Sanskrit prosody; third to second century BCE.

157 **even by the sixteen divine arts of Krishna**: Krishna is a purna avatara (complete avatara) because he is proficient in all the sixteen divine arts or attributes, which include, compassion, detachment, intrinsic beauty, etc.

162 **Once upon a time, during the Chaturmasya Vrata**: This is a four-month fast beginning on Sayana Ekadasi in June–July and ending on Uthana Ekadasi in October–November. Hindus believe that Vishnu goes to sleep on his serpent bed in the cosmic ocean on Sayana Ekadashi (sleep on the eleventh day of the lunar phase) and awakens on Uthana Ekadasi (waking up on the eleventh day of the lunar phase). In these four holy months, Hindus performs many rituals, clean their homes and temples, and abstain from certain foods.

162 **Today is Dakshinayana Sankranti**: The sun begins its journey south on this day—between the summer and winter solstices.

176 **Then, taking her right hand in his right hand**: In a Hindu ceremony the right hand of the bride is placed in the groom's right hand.

177 **that brahmins test the colours of homa fire**: Homa agni prashna is a way of posing questions to the ritual fire to predict the auspiciousness or inauspiciousness of something. The predictions are assessed from the form and colour of the flames.

179 **it doesn't walk with you even five steps**: Reference to the custom of walking a short distance, accompanying loved ones, to see them off.

186 **Indra himself pours water in its beak**: It is believed that the chataka bird drinks only raindrops. Also, it only drinks the first few drops that fall.

200 **is a mitra—a two-syllable word**: 'Mi' means fixed or erected, and 'tra' means protection.

THIRD TANTRA: KAKOLUKIYAM

208 **Dug a mountain, found a mouse**: Hindi proverb; khoda pahar, mili chuhiya.

211 **in the Kartika or Chaitra months**: Kartika in the Hindu calendar falls between October and November, and Chaitra falls between March and April.

220 **a mirror to prevent manglik Vaastu dosh**: Malefic effect of Mars in Vastu astrology.

220 **Gorochana placed nearby, and singing minstrels and bards**: Term used for Bezoar stone—found in either the urine or the head of a cow; a yellow pigment used as a cosmetic and also as an antidote for poison.

221	**is annihilating during pralaya**: The Puranas state that at the end of time, seven suns will rise and scorch the three worlds.
222	**and it was being fed by Patala Ganga**: According to Puranas, Ganga has three streams, Swargaganga (heavenly Ganga—Mandakini), Bhooganga (earth Ganga, Bhagirathi), and Patalaganga (Ganga of the underworld—Bhagavati). Aside from myth, in the backwaters of River Krishna is a deep gorge that is called Patala Ganga. It is a holy spot and mentioned in many ancient Hindu texts.
234	**Agnihotri brahmin**: Brahmins who maintained the sacred fire during ritual ceremonies.
34	**yajna on the day of Amavasya**: Day of the new moon.
4	**carrying this impure animal—a dog—on your shoulders**: In Hinduism, dogs are considered unclean because they are scavengers by nature.
235	**Not even cow's urine or a Chandrayana Vrata**: An ancient ritual fast that is observed for a whole month. It entails gradually reducing food till the full moon, and then gradually increasing it after the new moon.
251	**whose parapet displays a white bone**: In the olden days of caste segregation, water wells for the low caste were distinguished by a bone that was hung from the parapet.
253	I am a **Brahmarakshasa**: Fierce, highly evolved rakshasa
253	I eat in the sixth **pahar** of the day: Unit of time in ancient India. Each pahar is about three hours, and there are eight pahars in a day.
264	**In this way, twelve years passed, and the girl became marriageable**: In ancient India, girls were married just before puberty.
266	No matter how hard I push on him, he doesn't shift even one **ratti**: An ancient Indian unit of measurement for mass.
272	**They will all be incinerated inside the cave, as though suffering the tortures of Kumbhipaka**: According to Hindu tradition, as described in a number of Puranas, such as *Bhagavata* and *Garuda*, Kumbhipaka is one of the twenty-eight hells. The word means 'cooked in a pot'; thus, a person condemned to this hell is cooked in a pot of boiling oil. Ironically, the evil deed that condemns a person to this hell is 'cooking' or burning alive of animals or birds.

FOURTH TANTRA: LABDHA PRANASHA

300	**just as the ocean appeases the Badv mare**: Badv fire is a submarine fire in the form of a mare, and it is believed to be banked in the ocean floor. If the ocean does not feed it with water in small amounts, it will devour the whole ocean. According to myth, this fire is a controlled form of Shiva's rage and sexual energy, which Brahma confined in the shape of a mare so that it could be kept banked in the ocean. It will be released at the time of pralaya.
305	**beaten and bloodied or made a Kapalika**: Skull-carrying tantric order; adherents are called Kapalikas.
309	**This is the Sanatana dharma**: Eternal truths and ideals of Hinduism.
312	**He had such a beautiful singing voice that every taan**: An improvised, fast-paced melodic pattern of Hindustani classical music.

319 **Like the eye-catching gunjaphal**: Crab eye or rosary eye; the seeds are bright red and attractive but are poisonous. They are used in Ayurveda.
323 **Please tell me what measure I should use to reclaim my house: request him, pay him, fight him, or create disunity in his life**: Sama, Dama, Danda, Bheda. This is a common phrase mentioned in Kautilya's *Arthashastra*. It is called Chanakya Niti, and it encompasses the four prescribed ways to deal with an enemy.

FIFTH TANTRA: APRIKSHITA KARAKAM

334 **Victory to those Jina**: Epithet of Buddha; however, the way the word is used in these shlokas gives it the meaning of 'Great Teachers' of Jainism. Perhaps, this is a deliberate linking of the two faiths heretical to Brahmanism, or it may be a statement on the barber, who doesn't know the difference between the two.
35 **At one-and-a-half pahar of the day, he went back to the monastery and sat down at its gate to wait**: Unit of time in India. The day has eight pahar; each pahar is three hours; the first pahar begins at sunrise.
341 **or obeisance to Dakini-Shakini**: Minor nature goddesses in Tanta associated with the yogic chakras in the body.
342 **When I came to this mountain, the ruler on earth was Shri Rama of Ayodhya**: According to the Yuga theory of Hindu mythology, cosmic time is divided into four yugas, Krita, Treta, Dwapara, and Kaliyuga. Rama is supposed to have ruled Ayodhya in Treta Yuga, which spans 1,296,000 mortal years; Dwapara Yuga, that follows, is 864,000 years. Vatsaraja was a king of Vatsa in the last yuga—Kaliyuga; (historically, that began in fifth–sixth century BCE). Also, at the time of the *Panchatantra*'s composition, about four thousand years of Kaliyuga had passed. Hence, the man with the wheel had been roaming in the mountain for about 2,063,000 years.
356 **The divine physician of horses, Shalihotra**: Shalihotra Samhita is a third-century treatise on veterinary medicine.
362 **That vikala rakshasa is here again**: Untimely, disfigured, distorted.
367 **These two also heard the town crier, and the blind man decided that he would touch the kettledrum**: According to custom, touching the kettledrum was indication of accepting the offer.

BIBLIOGRAPHY

The Arthashastra by Kautilya. (Translated) Lexington: Eternal Sun Books, 2016.

Atil, Esin. *Kalila wa Dimna: Fables from a Fourteenth-Century Arabic Manuscript.* Washington DC, Smithsonian Institution Press, 1981.

Chandogya Upanishad. Translation by Som Raj Gupta. *The Word Speaks to the Faustian Man*, Vol. IV. New Delhi, Motilal Banarsidass Publishers, 1995.

Danylova, Tatiana. 'Overcoming the Anomalies of Human Existence: Ontology of Trickster.' Антропологічні виміри філософських досліджень, [Anthropological Measurements of Philosophical Research], 2014, issue 6, 17–20. https://www.academia.edu/12780175/Overcoming_the_Antinomies_of_Human_Existence_Ontology_of_Trickster. Accessed May 1, 2022.

Edgerton, Franklin as quoted in Patrick Olivelle. 'Introduction,' *The Pañcatantra: The Book of India's Folk Wisdom.* Oxford, Oxford University Press, 2009.

———. as quoted in McComas Taylor. *The Fall of the Indigo Jackal. The Discourse of Division and Purnabhadra's Pancatantra.* State University of New York Press, 2007. ProQuest Ebook Central, http://ebookcentral.proquest.com/lib/nvcc/detail.action?docID=3407370;.

Hertel, Johannes, as quoted in McComas Taylor. *The Fall of the Indigo Jackal: The Discourse of Division and Purnabhadra's Pancatantra.* New York: SUNY Press, 2007, ProQuest Ebook Central.

———. *The Panchatantra-Text of Purnabhadra* (Critical Introduction and List of Variants by Johannes Hertel). Forgotten Books, 2012.

Howe, Nicholas. 'Fabling Beasts: Traces in Memory.' *Social Research*, Vol. 6, No. 3, 641–659, 1995.

Ivanovic, Christine. 'Talking Animals and Politics of World Literature.' *Comparative Literature Studies*, Vol. 54, No. 4, 702–730, 2017, https://muse.jhu.edu/article/680886. Accessed May 20, 2022.

Kale, M. R. 'Notes.' *Pañcatantra of Viṣṇuśarman.* Delhi, Motilal Banarsidass, 2018 (first edition, 1912).

The Panchatantra a Collection of Ancient Hindu Tales in the Recension, called Panchakhyanaka, and dated 1199 A.D., of the Jaina Monk, Purnabhadra. Critically Edited in the Original Sanskrit by Dr. Johannes Hertel. *Harvard Oriental Series*, Vol XI., 1908. https://ia902608.us.archive.org/16/items/panchatantracoll00purnuoft/panchatantra-coll00purnuoft.pdf. Accessed, April 30, 2022.

Meadow, Mary Jo. 'Archetypes and Patriarchy: Eliade and Jung.' *Journal of Religion and Health,* Fall, 1992, Vol. 31, No. 3, 187–195. https://www.jstor.org/stable/27510694. Accessed June 25, 2022.

Mishra, Tirthanand. चम्पूकाव्यम् [Champukavyam]. *International Journal of Applied Research*, 2019; 5(6), www.allresearchjournal.com. Accessed May 27, 2022.

Monier-Williams, M. 'Tantra.' *A Sanskrit English Dictionary*. New Delhi, Motilal Banarsidass, 2005.

Mundaka Upansishad. Translation by Som Raj Gupta, *The Word Speaks to the Faustian Man*, Vol. II. New Delhi, Motilal Banarsidass Publishers, 1995.

Olivelle, Patrick. 'Introduction.' *The Pañcatantra: The Book of India's Folk Wisdom*. Oxford: Oxford University Press, 2009.

Perozo, V. M. P. 'Fables and Fable-Writers.' *Books Abroad*, Vol. 20, No. 4, 1946, 363–367. https://doi.org/10.2307/40088489. Accessed July 2, 2022.

Plato, *Phaedo*. Vol. 1 translated by Harold North Fowler. Cambridge, MA, London, William Heinemann Ltd. 1966. Perseus Digital Library. https://www.perseus.tufts.edu/hopper/. Accessed July 1, 2022.

Rajan, Chandra. 'Introduction.' *The Pañcatantra*. New Delhi: Penguin Books, Ltd. 1993.

Roy, Nilanjana S. 'The Panchatantra: The ancient "viral memes" still with us.' *Culture: Stories that Shaped the World*, BBC, 17 June, 2018. https://www.bbc.com/culture/article/20180517-the-panchatantra-the-ancient-viral-memes-still-with-us. Accessed, June 18, 2022.

Shastri, Guru Prasad and Sitaram Shastri. 'Kathasara.' श्री विष्णुशर्मविरचितम पच्चतन्त्रम् [*Śri Viṣṇu Śarma"s Composition Pañcatantram*]. Varanasi, Chaukhamba Surbharti Prakashan, 2018.

Taylor, McComas. *The Fall of the Indigo Jackal: The Discourse of Division and Purnabhadra's Pancatantra*. New York, SUNY Press, 2007, ProQuest Ebook Central.

Williams, Ronald J. 'The Literary History of a Mesopotamian Fable.' *Phoenix*, Summer, 1956, Vol. 10, No. 2, 70–77. https://www.jstor.org/stable/1086441. Accessed April 2, 2022.